Villa for Rent on St Barts
By Kiki Astor

Table of Contents

Chapter 1

The tiny plane crested the hill and abruptly shot up, making Brooke glad for her lap belt. Thermal updraft, she reasoned, trying to focus more on the sundry white sailboats scattered on the sapphire sea beyond the runway, rather than on the white crosses dotting the rocky hill. She held her breath, swallowing to equalize the pressure in her ears. This was when she noticed that the plane's engines were oddly quiet. Yes. Against all logic, they were turned off. *What the hell?*

She pivoted her head, to see whether any of the other passengers had noticed anything. Elizabeth, a skinny platinum blonde with oversized round blue eyes who was one of Brooke and Hunter's houseguests for the week, seemed blissfully unaware. This was on brand, for her. Brooke's husband of ten years, Hunter, was staring furiously out the window, his usually handsome face contorted into a grimace. The cool blonde sitting in the back of the plane, who had been on their flight from New York, too, looked bored. At least Elizabeth's husband Quentin, a bespectacled New England preppy type with slicked back salt and pepper hair, had the sense to return Brooke's worried glance. Brooke's throat constricted, and her eyes must have widened in panic as she caught the young pilot's eye in the mirror set in the instrument panel, ready to say something, because the pilot started to laugh.

"Oh. Sorry. This is our new technique. We find it's much smoother to cut the engines and coast in."

That might have been something good to know before it happened, Brooke thought. And honestly, knowing she wasn't plummeting to certain death scarcely made her feel better. Her heart had been aching, nausea threatening, ever since they had left New York. To be honest, she'd been feeling that way for weeks now. She couldn't put her finger on it, but Hunter had been acting off. Not like they'd been lovey-dovey in a while, but they had at least been cohabitating comfortably. The butterflies and romance had long ago flitted away, but it wasn't like there was anyone else she'd rather be with. And she had assumed Hunter felt the same. They had a good life, with the right balance of social engagements, the right level of success, and a regular schedule of vacations. They were good friends. Good friends who were still reasonably attracted to each other, in fact. Well, it had been a while since they'd been intimate, but compared to a lot of people they knew, who were either worn down by childcare or fighting like cats and dogs, or in some phase of a messy divorce or another, they had it good. And she'd been looking forward to this vacation for a long time. Saint Bart's was their happy place. Maybe they would find each other again, fix the things that had been broken. It wasn't too late, was it?

As the plane engines turned back on, Brooke looked towards Hunter, hoping to exchange a friendly smile with him, something that would communicate her hopefulness. But he was still staring out the window, as he'd been doing ever since they boarded the plane, his body posture screaming that he was acutely uncomfortable. *Weird.* On the flight to Saint Martin, he'd been mostly busy with his phone, which was his default, though he'd been looking annoyed, which she also had to admit was his go-to expression lately. Maybe it was too late to fix this thing, after all.

The plane's wheels hit the runway and Brooke turned around, intending to smile reassuringly at Elizabeth and Quentin. But Quentin now had his eyes closed and was massaging the bridge of his nose, and Elizabeth was trying to talk to the blonde in the back of the plane. It was just as well. Brooke had tried to dissuade Hunter from inviting people this year, but Quentin was apparently working on some super important business deal with him, so that was that. Hunter had said it would be nice for Brooke to "have a friend" while they talked shop, but Brooke and Elizabeth were hardly friends. Elizabeth was familiar to Brooke from the charity circuit. They had both worked on the ballet event this year, and she had found Elizabeth to be a busybody who annoyingly wore single designers head to toe.

Now, a whole week in Saint Barth with these people loomed ahead of Brooke just as the mountains had, moments ago. At least, after this week, Brooke and Hunter would be on their own, for better or for worse. Hunter had had the good sense not to invite his sister, her Golden Retriever of a husband, and their hyperactive progeny this year. The one positive side effect of their disastrous stay the year before had been that Brooke had found herself at peace with the fact that, after two years of trying, she and Hunter didn't have any children yet. Considering how things were headed, she realized that it might never happen.

The plane came to a stop on the tarmac. Brooke couldn't help but register the little burst of joy that snuck into her heart. Maybe this trip would be good for them. Maybe being back on their beloved beaches, the ones they'd been coming to each year of their marriage, maybe being back in her adored island house, maybe the romantic sound of the tree frogs at night, would take them back to happier times? Brooke remembered what it had been like when they had first started coming, even before they had the house. Always alone, so they could enjoy each other. They would spend late nights wrapped up in each other, the spinning palm frond fan teasing their sweat from the sheets. Mornings were for lazily deciding which beach they would visit next, which ones were private enough so that they could skinny dip- and whatever went with that- in peace.

But then, little by little, the friends started trickling in, first as a distraction, and then as an obligation. It was incredible how things could change so radically in 10 short years. In just 10 years, Brooke felt that she had lost all her real friends and had gained social appendages in their stead. Was it Hunter's fault that she felt so dissatisfied in their marriage? Maybe not completely. She had, after all, agreed to play in this charade.

"Here we are," Brooke said brightly.

Elizabeth finally decided to tear her attention from the blonde and started cooing.

"I'm so excited. Last time, we were here we were with the Van der Lindermeiers. You know they've got that great villa up on the mountain, with a saltwater pool and that great shower. Remember the shower, Quentin?"

Elizabeth winked theatrically at her husband. Since the beginning of this journey with Elizabeth and Quentin as a couple, less than eight hours ago, Brooke had already counted about ten allusions to their very active sex life. Brooke had started off mildly envious, then bemused, then annoyed, then frankly a little grossed out. Now, at the tail end of this leg of travel, she had decided to just view it as an abstract thing that was so far removed from her reality that it didn't concern her.

"I can't wait to see your house," Elizabeth was saying. "Tell me, Hunter, is it really as beautiful as Brooke says? She's always boasting about it, you know?"

Hunter had finally unstuck his gaze from the window and now gave Brooke a brief side eye, his pewter gaze chilly. Years ago, it would have been a look of shared amusement, both mocking Elizabeth for her petty jealousy, but now, Brooke felt as if the look was accusatory, like she'd done something wrong, and Hunter was judging her for it. At least, Hunter started focusing intently on wiping the lenses of his sunglasses without responding to Elizabeth. Brooke gave Elizabeth a tight smile, not bothering with a response either.

They stepped off the plane, and into the thick, heavy heat of a Saint Barth afternoon. It hit Brooke like a wet embrace, instantly gluing her city clothing to her body. It was good to feel warm. It had been cold in New York that whole autumn, and the holiday season had been particularly frigid.

Just a few short years ago, back when Brooke's parents were still alive, they used to alternate between her parents' house and Hunter's family home. Then, they had each lost both parents. At first, that was something that they had bonded over. But then, when Brooke realized that she had built Sea Grapes with the entirety of her inheritance, while Hunter had hidden all his assets in a blind trust, the balance between them had been destroyed. She had started feeling like he was keeping secrets from her. And now, everything was, for some reason, feeling like it had come to a head.

They waited on the tarmac, broiling in the hot sun until an airport employee came to fetch them. Their luggage was placed on a rolling cart, and Elizabeth tried to retrieve her giant suitcase, only to be rebuffed by a porter.

"You'll pick it up in the airport," the airport employee said, his Creole lilt music to Brooke's ears.

Brooke and Hunter did not have luggage beyond the carry-ons they had put in the back of the main cabin.

"She got her suitcase," said Elizabeth, pointing to the blonde woman, who was standing apart from the group, playing with her phone, just as Hunter was. Nobody commented on Elizabeth's complaint.

"So, what are we going to do next?" asked Elizabeth, as they finally started following a woman with an official looking clipboard and a uniform consisting of navy shorts and a matching shirt with white piping towards the small airport.

"We'll pick up your luggage, and then the driver should be there to drive us to the villa. We can decide whether we want to have dinner out, or whether we want to have dinner at home," Brooke said. "I'm sure Nathalie stocked the fridge for us."

At least she hoped Nathalie had stocked the fridge. She realized that she'd been too busy all week to check in with her friend and island factotum.

"We're going out," said Hunter, looking up from his phone just long enough to deliver this edict in the annoying categorical tone he had begun to adopt of late. "Quentin and I wanted to go to Nikki Beach."

"Oh, yay! That sounds fun," Elizabeth cooed.

Brooke tried to keep from rolling her eyes. Elizabeth was definitely one of those "pick me" girls in high school and college, she decided.

As they waited for Elizabeth and Quentin's matching monogrammed Goyard luggage to come around the conveyor belt, Hunter jabbing at his phone a few steps away, Brooke looked at all the people in the airport. There were couples and families arriving around the same time as them, and others leaving, looking regretful or relieved. Two teens, siblings, she decided, with massive sunburns, a group of girlfriends looking forward to a week on the island, from what she overheard. Two frat boy types looking exhausted. Probably hung over. Most newcomers looked delighted to be there. Which drove home the strange, insidious despair that had wormed its way deep into Brooke's heart.

A familiar figure strode into the airport's main room.

"Hey look, it's Pierre," Hunter said, finally putting on an authentic smile. "Pierre, my man. Good to see you. How have things been?"

"Great," said Pierre, shaking hands with Hunter and Brooke. "We weathered the hurricanes this summer. Don't worry, your house is looking great. It's a great month to be here. Nathalie filled the fridge. The cars are all charged and gassed up for you."

Hunter smiled. They had two cars on the island. Brooke's pink Mini Moke, and the light aqua Land Rover Defender, which was Hunter's pride and joy. He'd had it imported specially and had had to jump through many hoops, since St. Barth mostly only allowed electric cars on the island.

At last, Quentin and Elizabeth retrieved their suitcases and joined the group. Quentin shook hands with Pierre as they were introduced, while Elizabeth reserved her most fake greeting for the wiry Frenchman, the one she reserved for underlings. Little did she know, Pierre wasn't some lackey. Well educated, from an intellectual family, he had chosen to come to Saint Barth for the simple life and was doing photography and writing novels in his spare time. He was a frequent contributor for the glossy magazines produced on the island that were a thinly disguised luxury watch and yacht advertising vehicle, but entertaining and well-produced, nonetheless. There was nothing inferior about Pierre. He did his job well. He had pride in what he did, and he was living his best life with his partner, a retired model agent, in a charmingly run-down cottage on one of the windward bluffs.

As Brooke waited on the sidewalk for her guests to pile into the Land Rover, something caught her eye. It was a van, bright turquoise, with bright coral colored block letters on its side spelling out the words *Meat* and *Fish*. Oh, that would be useful. Brooke had attended the Cordon Bleu in Paris and had always enjoyed flexing her cooking skills with local ingredients when on the island. In the past few years, she had been reading about some of the family farms cropping up, making the quality of the ingredients better than ever. But then, she forgot all about cooking. Her attention was captured by the man standing in front of the van, partially blocking the words. Not just a man, but a particularly good looking one. All right, more than good looking. He was objectively hot, even if he wasn't exactly Brooke's type. She didn't usually go for bronzed beach boys with rumpled gold locks and scruffy facial hair that perfectly framed their lips, not like there were many on offer in New York City. As if on cue, the man lifted his hand and ran it through his mane, revealing a sliver of tanned stomach and the elastic waistband of his boxer shorts, peeking out from sun-bleached linen shorts. Brooke tore her eyes away from where they wanted to go from there, and she found herself looking straight into the man's eyes. Eyes that were a perfect Caribbean water blue. *Of course.* She felt a jolt as the man gave her a smile, revealing perfect white teeth. *Conceited. Obviously.*

Then, the man seemed to see the person he must have been there to pick up, coming from the airport, behind Brooke, because his eyes moved away from hers and focused beyond her. She wouldn't turn around. She willed herself not to. Who cared who he was picking up? As the man stepped away from the van, to greet whoever this person was, Brooke realized that she had misread the words on the van. It wasn't Meat and Fish. It was Meat my Fish. What a dumb name. OK, she had to give this guy his due. He might be conceited, but if he had come up with that name himself, maybe he didn't take himself too seriously, after all.

Brooke got into the Land Rover. She had the second row to herself; Quentin and Elizabeth having tucked themselves into the back and Hunter being up front with Pierre.

As they pulled away, Brooke smiled. Not just because of the ridiculous business name. Not because at least, *someone* was having fun with life. But because it had been such a long time since she'd felt that jolt of attraction to someone. She'd started to worry that that part of her had been irretrievably lost. And now she knew it wasn't. If anything, it made her more motivated than ever to figure out this thing with Hunter. Before it was too late.

Chapter 2

They pulled off the main airport road and started heading up the hill towards the peninsula that the villa sat on. Up in the front seat, Hunter was still peppering Pierre with questions about what had been happening on the island.

"What about our favorite billionaire?" Hunter asked.

Brooke and Hunter's next-door neighbor, or at least the owner of the only other house on the tip of their peninsula, was Carlos White, an elusive but storied financial tech tycoon. Brooke had only once seen Carlos in person. He had never accepted their invitations to dinner, nor had he extended any of his own, but he had once sent over a bottle of champagne to them at Nikki Beach, so they felt they were on good terms. There were plenty of fawning articles in the press and paparazzi shots of him on board his yacht, accompanied by his girlfriend du jour, so Brooke felt an artificial sense of familiarity with him.

"Nothing new," said Pierre. "Rumor has it he's planning on developing some more properties on the island. He's been lying low this season, but I'm sure he'll pop up."

"Which billionaire is he talking about?" Elizabeth stage whispered.

"Oh, you know," said Brooke, enjoying the frustrated look on Elizabeth's face. Elizabeth hated it when people withheld gossip from her.

"Carlos White," Quentin said, his tone reverential.

Not surprising. Carlos White was the hero of finance and tech bros everywhere. His real name was no doubt Charles, and Carlos was probably just what that one nanny had called him, and then his

9

frat brothers had sealed the deal because it helped him to pick up chicks.

The Land Rover made its way up the steep and narrow road, Mini Mokes and Mini Coopers buzzing by impossibly fast. It always took Brooke a few days to adjust to island driving. It was a bit terrifying, especially when your vehicle was so large compared to the road. She focused on the jewel toned sea in the distance, and on the greenery of the hills. She'd missed seeing green. The gray canyons of New York made her completely depressed all through the winter. This was her well-deserved reprieve.

At last, they arrived at a polished wooden gate. Brooke read the discreet sign, even though she knew what it said: Sea Grapes. She smiled to herself. This was truly her happy place. The gate slid open, and the Land Rover edged its way up the driveway. The mid-afternoon light made the house glow. Brooke had insisted on a special plaster with marble mixed into it, so that the walls were almost reflective. But it was a warm sheen, not a cold one. Hunter had complained that the effect would be blinding, but it was exactly right. There were enough warm wooden details throughout the home to break up all the white expanses. The whole place felt both ancient and modern, reminiscent of a finca in Ibiza. It was exactly what Brooke had wanted.

"It's so good to be back," she breathed, to no one in particular. Quentin was on his phone, probably trying to check the strength of the Wi-Fi, Elizabeth had a look of concentration that told Brooke she was busy measuring the square footage in her head, and Hunter didn't seem to care about how Brooke felt at any given moment these days. They all hopped out of the Land Rover and walked up the path to the house. The door, tall, broad, the same polished wood as the gate, pivoted open, operated by a petite, curvy brunette, disconcertingly pale, with a spray of freckles on her exposed face and arms that were the only sign of her island life. Nathalie. Brooke's face broke into a broad smile at last. She adored Nathalie. Nathalie was more than just a housekeeper. She was a confidante. A friend. She was the consummate professional, but also possessed a warmth that Brooke had seldom encountered anywhere else, which was what had started to make them close, and not just in a boss/employee sense. Nathalie's adorable son went to school just down the street, and it always made Brooke smile when she drove by and caught a glimpse of him on the playground. Ziggy was always laughing. Always sporting a big toothy smile, his eyes sparkling with the sort of joie de vivre that Brooke could only hope to regain one day. Ziggy's father was a Jamaican musician who had long since departed for other shores. But Nathalie made single mom life look easy, thanks to her organizational skills and positivity.

"We have a lot to catch up on," Nathalie whispered to Brooke as they all walked in. There was something off about her energy, but Brooke chalked it up to Hunter not approving of their close friendship, which meant that they tried to be discreet about it. Brooke noticed that music was playing softly from the speakers installed in the corners of each room. Her favorite playlist, of course.

"I've made you all a welcome drink," Nathalie said. She hustled over to the kitchen and came back, wielding a rattan tray laden with glasses full of colorful fruit punch. Brooke knew from experience that this punch would be much more deadly than one might imagine. Nathalie's Breton father, who had lived on the island his whole life, made his own rum at home, and it was deceptively strong. Brooke took a little sip and smiled to herself as she noticed Elizabeth and Quentin downing the liquid as if it was an innocent fruit juice.

"Let me show you the different bedrooms you can choose from," Brooke said.

"I'm going to go check the office," Hunter mumbled.

Brooke led Quentin and Elizabeth down the hall.

"Here's the first room," she said, opening the door. This was the room she called the Garden Room. It was the most private room, with less of a view, but with its own private garden, complete with an outdoor shower and a tub.

"I can just imagine taking a naughty bath with you in there, Quentin," said Elizabeth. Brooke noticed that she was trying to give him a saucy look, but at least he had the common decency to seem a little bit embarrassed.

"Can we reserve our right to choose until we've seen all the rooms?" Elizabeth asked.

"Of course," said Brooke.

She expected nothing less. They walked further down the hall, passing the office, where she noticed that Hunter was going through a stack of envelopes, all of them with identical writing on them, as far as Brooke could tell. She wondered what was going on. As they walked past, Hunter shoved the envelopes into a drawer, looking flustered. This might be something Brooke would need to investigate, later.

She opened another door.

"This is the pool bedroom. If you want to just get right up and dive into the pool, this is the one you'll want to choose."

"Are we allowed to skinny dip?" Elizabeth asked.

"Let your modesty be your guide," said Brooke. "The final bedrooms are up here," she told the couple, leading them up the rough-hewn limestone stairs.

"This one is lovely," said Brooke, walking into the back bedroom. Though it had good views, this room had always had the least personality, and was seldom used. Elizabeth nodded, unimpressed.

"This one has the best view, but no outdoor space," said Brooke as she gestured around the next room.

Please let them not want this one, she thought. Most guests tended to avoid this bedroom, which Brooke had originally designed as a nursery, in favor of the downstairs rooms, because even though this one had the best view, being closest to the master bedroom, it lacked privacy. Then again, she sensed an exhibitionist bent in Elizabeth, and feared the worst.

"Is that the master bedroom, there?" Elizabeth asked, venturing back into the hallway, gesturing to an open door, beyond which Nathalie could be seen unpacking Hunter's carry-on. Brooke unpacked her own stuff.

"You might hear us, if we're being naughty at night," Elizabeth added.

God, she was being relentless, Brooke thought. Brooke had observed Elizabeth being competitive in various ways before, but this was the first time she'd noticed this bawdiness. There was a good chance that Elizabeth had noticed the cold front between her hosts, Brooke decided, and now she was trying to find a sensitive sore spot she could exploit. Realizing this made her feel marginally better. They re-entered the nursery and Elizabeth gasped as she took in the vista that lay beyond the French doors. Just past a short expanse of green shrubs, one hundred eighty degrees of Caribbean Sea lay before them, in undulating shades of teal, navy, and turquoise.

"Duh, of course we'll take this one," said Elizabeth. "We don't get a view like this in New York. I mean, we do get something similar in our Hamptons house..."

Of course, she had to talk about the Hamptons house. Anytime anyone referred to the Saint Barth house in front of her, Elizabeth had to jump in and describe the Hamptons house in excruciating detail. Brooke and Hunter, and now that she thought about it, no one they knew, had ever been invited, not that she would have wanted to go.

Chapter 3

After getting Elizabeth and Quentin settled in, Brooke headed towards her own bedroom suite, the one she had shared with Hunter all these years, with dread in the pit of her stomach. Was he still in the office? What were those papers he had been so intent on hiding as she walked by? She had a bad feeling. This home had always been her happy place, but now, it felt like her life was teetering on the brink of some precipice, about to change irremediably, probably for the worse. How had it come to this? Brooke realized she'd been like the proverbial frog, happily sitting in water that was gradually approaching a boil. Everything had been wonderful. Until it hadn't been, but it had happened so slowly that she hadn't noticed until she'd had irrefutable proof that her marriage was broken beyond repair. Hunter didn't even know that she had that proof. The knowledge was like a bomb, waiting to detonate. When would be the best time to bring it out in the open? Having Elizabeth and Quentin there was hardly ideal. But she couldn't imagine spending an entire week with Hunter being this way.

She slowly made her way into her room. Nathalie had finished putting Hunter's things away and Brooke noticed that her own bag had been placed on an upholstered bench, ready to be unpacked. It made Brooke happy to see that the beautiful fabrics and finishes she had so carefully selected for the space still looked just as perfect as ever. She admired the way that the canopy bed was bathed in afternoon light. Took in the view of the ocean and of the swimming pool below. It couldn't be more perfect. She stepped into her elegant bathroom, where mosaic tiles in shades of sand, cream, and morning sky glistened like mother-of-pearl. Hunter had expressed concern that the material was more suited to a swimming pool, but it made Brooke feel like she was on the inside of a seashell. This bathroom was her haven. After she'd freshened up a bit, she headed towards her closet. Lined in warm tropical wood, the closet held her collection of resort wear. It was a luxury being able to travel with nothing more than a carry-on bag. Every time she came back here, it felt like a surprise or a gift to find those old favorites again. The garments ranged from pieces she'd had custom made by her favorite local seamstress, to the vintage caftans that her glamorous Tunisian mother had worn during her own teenage years in the Bahamas, where Brooke's grandfather had served as Ambassador for several years. Being in the Caribbean was in Brooke's blood, on both sides. There was significant French ancestry on her father's maternal side, through which she was descended from the same Norman and Breton sailors who had originally populated St. Barth. In fact, she'd gone to the cemetery and had found some familiar family names, and it gave her comfort to know that she belonged in this place. Going back to New York was always like being torn from a womb. But she had to face facts. New York was her real life, where her responsibilities lay. Not that those responsibilities felt very meaningful anymore. Not after she had figured out what Hunter was up to.

As she was trying to decide and pick between a beaded tunic and a pink silk frock, she heard the door of the bedroom open. She froze. Was it Nathalie coming in for a little gossip?

"Everything OK?" she called out, from inside the closet.

"Yeah. I was just looking through paperwork."

No such luck, it was her husband.

"How much paperwork could we possibly have?"

"Well, Brooke, if you would pay attention to what's going on around here, maybe I wouldn't have to do that when we get here. Maybe I could just enjoy myself and go for a swim," he said.

That's rich, thought Brooke.

She didn't have any financial autonomy, and it felt like it was lessening every day. At the beginning of their marriage, they had shared everything, from bank accounts to credit cards. But now, Brooke only had access to the one account stateside, which she felt Hunter was only dropping a small portion of his income into. Not that she complained, because it was always enough to cover household expenses, but, now that she thought of it, she hadn't really spoiled herself in a long time, hadn't gone shopping or gone to the spa, like most of her friends did. Brooke was certain that Hunter purposely kept financial details away from her eyes as his way of gaining more control. Yet he blamed her for it all the time. She didn't know what he had to complain about. Other wives in their social circle spent their days spending their husband's money, while Brooke, without even noticing, had gradually stopped. She'd been much more preoccupied, she realized, with trying to figure out how to give her life purpose. But all the online classes and volunteer board positions in the world wouldn't fill the void.

"Which bedroom did Elizabeth and Quentin choose?" Hunter asked.

Brooke sighed, giving Hunter a wry smile as she emerged from the closet.

"I'll give you a hint. Get your earbuds ready. Apparently, there will be a lot of moaning and banging in the middle of the night. Must be nice."

She noticed Hunter stiffening, his body language registering his displeasure.

"What's that supposed to mean?"

"It's OK," Brooke said. "I was just kidding. I'm looking forward to going to Nikki Beach," she said. "There's always such great music. I wonder if the same DJ from last year is still there."

"Probably not," said Hunter. "Nobody lasts very long on this Godforsaken Island."

"Godforsaken? Most people think this is paradise," Brooke responded. "Anyway, turquoise tunic or pink mini dress?"

"Whichever is fine," Hunter responded, completely disinterested.

Years ago, he would have weighed in. He would have campaigned for the one he wanted to see her in, or something that he couldn't wait to take off her, something that would be easy access, in case he managed to catch her by surprise in a private corner. She remembered how it used to be, dinners spent sitting at a small table across from each other, he leaning forward, as if he were hanging onto her every word, which he was, but he also had his hand up her skirt, between her legs, teasing her, amused by her efforts to pretend everything was innocent and normal. But now, Hunter couldn't care less. And even though Brooke truthfully didn't care that much either, it still stung.

"Well, I'm going to take a shower," she said.

That too, would have been taken as an invitation he couldn't refuse, back in the day. She happened to know that the water pressure from the handheld shower hit just right, especially when Hunter was wielding it as she crouched in front of him, pleasuring him, using her tongue in that way she knew made him go wild. Correction. *Used* to make him go wild. She had retired that trick a while back.

"I'm going to take a quick swim," Hunter said. "Let's leave here at six."

He left the room without further preamble.

Quentin and Elizabeth were probably having wild sex by now, Brooke thought bitterly. *Whatever.* She stripped off her travel clothes, dumped them in the hamper, and stepped into the shower enclosure. She'd insisted on having a rainwater collection system installed on the roof, so she didn't feel as guilty about using the scant resources available on the island. Once the water had reached the ideal temperature, she stepped under the shower-head, soaped up, and imagined the suds carrying away all her negative feelings. She focused on thinking of any possible activity that would be enjoyable in the coming weeks. Swimming in the sea here always made her happy. It was magical. Hopefully, she would get a chance to gossip with Nathalie, and try out some new recipes with the ingredients one could only get here. Other than that, she was really dreading this so-called vacation. She felt that she had been robbed. This used to be her happy place, and now, it had been poisoned. When would she bring up what she knew to Hunter?

She stepped out of the shower and got dressed. She was almost ready when she heard a knock at the door. It was Elizabeth, of course.

"Do you have a hair dryer?" Elizabeth asked.

Brooke looked at her blankly. A hair dryer? In the tropics? Whenever Brooke came to the Caribbean, she relished the shortcut of just putting coconut oil in her hair and letting it dry naturally, allowing her natural curls to come out to play. When she was in New York, she was so buttoned up, so perfectly groomed. It was her little secret that she had curls in her hair. Brooke's French-Tunisian heritage meant she had darker coloring than most of her social circle, many of whom were ice-cold blondes. People always asked her where she was from, even though she was from the same place as them. Yes, her mother had had that peripatetic upbringing, but her parents had met in their New England boarding school, and Brooke had mostly grown up in Darien, Connecticut. Absolutely nothing exotic about that.

"I think I may have one somewhere," Brooke said, retreating to the bathroom. She fished a hair dryer out from under her sink. "You can keep it for the duration," she said. "I never blow dry my hair when I'm here."

"You're so brave. I didn't know your hair was curly," said Elizabeth, a mocking smile on her lips, as if curly hair was something to be ashamed of.

"Well, now you know," said Brooke. "We'll be leaving at 6."

She checked her watch, her precious gold Cartier Tank Française, which her parents had gifted her for her college graduation, and which she rarely took off. Maybe she could catch Nathalie before she left. She finished getting ready quickly. Considering her reflection, she added some of the pearl jewelry she'd collected over the years, and which she kept here in Saint Barth. The freshwater pearls, organic shapes strung on leather cords, made her feel like she was something from the sea. She completed the look with some sparkly flat sandals, and lipstick in a bright shade of coral she would never use in New York. As she hurried downstairs, she noticed that Nathalie looked to be almost out the door. She paused as she noticed Brooke. Oddly, her smile looked more sad than conspiratorial.

"Leaving already?" Brooke asked, disappointed. "When are we having our catch-up drink together?"

"I don't know," said Nathalie, shaking her head, her lips pinched together. "Hunter wants to reduce my hours. I can't afford to..."

"Well, that's not his decision," said Brooke.

Nathalie looked uncertain.

"What?" asked Brooke.

"Come on. When were you going to tell me?" Nathalie asked, a bitter expression on her face.

"Tell you what?" Panic pinballed around in Brooke's brain.

"That you guys are thinking of selling this place," said Nathalie.

Shock made Brooke's mouth fall open, a painful pang in her heart. So, she'd been correct in feeling that there was something worrisome about Hunter's behavior of late, something beyond simple infidelity. But she doubled down. This was a mere misunderstanding. It had to be.

"What are you talking about? This place is mine. We would never sell it. And you and Ziggy always have a home here, as long as you need it."

"OK," said Nathalie, looking unsure. "We are ...outgrowing the apartment...but...are you sure, Brooke? You haven't talked about selling?"

"Absolutely not. What made you think that?"

"Rumor has it your neighbor might be very interested in this place."

Brooke thought of the stack of envelopes in the study. Was that what those were? Requests to purchase the house? Hunter had never mentioned anything. A headache started to make its way behind her eyes. They were going to have to talk about this, sooner rather than later.

"So, what do you have planned for this week?" Nathalie asked. "Mr. Hunter mentioned something about a meal at the house, with the neighbors?"

"Ugh. This week?"

Brooke was in no mood to cook for a group this week. But now, she thought she remembered that there was some link between Quentin and one of their two sets of neighbors, couples who owned villas just down the street, at the base of the peninsula, on the other side of Carlos White's place.

"That's what he said."

Since when was Hunter making decisions without consulting her? Since...well, for a while now, she realized.

"I guess we'll just call Mr. Vincent, and he can prepare something for us," said Brooke. Mr. Vincent was a sweet older gentleman who was originally from Haiti, but who had done quite well for himself on St Barth and Saint Martin. He was famous for his cod fritters, *accras de morue*.

"Mr. Vincent passed away," said Nathalie, shaking her head sadly.

"Oh! I'm so sorry," said Brooke, but selfishly, she immediately started worrying about where she was supposed to get her seafood now. Her thoughts went to the van she had seen at the airport. And the man. Was she about to find the perfect excuse to meet Mr. Meat my Fish?

"There's a guy in town," said Nathalie. "He's opened a newer business. Meat my Fish."

Brooke got a little thrill when Nathalie said the name.

"Oh, thank goodness. And he's a good fishmonger?"

"He's much more than that," said Nathalie. "If I find his card, I'll leave it on the kitchen counter. Otherwise, I'll have him swing by."

Brooke started to blush at the thought of the bronzed god she had seen at the airport coming over to her house. *Stop it,* she thought. Chances are, he was just one of the employees, and the one who would come by was some old fart.

"I need to go," said Nathalie. "Ziggy."

"Got it," said Brooke, noting that Nathalie hadn't offered a time or place for their catch-up.

Nathalie frowned for a second.

"Are you OK, Brooke?"

"I'm fine. We'll talk, whenever you have time." said Brooke.

When Nathalie was gone, Brooke went to the kitchen and poured herself a glass of cold white wine from the refrigerator. Sancerre. Her favorite. She stood there at the French doors leading to the veranda, sipping her wine, and drinking in the view. She would never tire of it. The changing colors of the ocean and of the sky. The muffled sound of the waves in the distance. They were medicine for her soul. Some people came to Saint Barth just for the yachts and for the glittering scene. And some people really understood what it was truly about. This rock in the middle of the Caribbean Sea, it had a history. It had people that loved it and felt at home there, and other people who didn't understand it at all, but thought that they could make it their place. She took another sip of wine, and groaned inwardly as she heard a commotion behind her. The rest of the crew had come downstairs.

"Ready to go?" Hunter asked. "Why did you open the wine when you knew we were about to leave?"

Brooke ignored the rhetorical question.

"I'm so ready to check out Nikki Beach," chirped Elizabeth.

Quentin looked a little tired, whether from the journey or from Elizabeth, Brooke couldn't tell. Whatever. It was none of her business. They headed down the path to the parking area, and Hunter got behind the wheel of the Land Rover.

"You take the front seat," Brooke said to Quentin.

She hopped into the back with Elizabeth, whose head was still swiveling as if on a greased stick.

"It's so cute here. You're so lucky. What did you do to get this house? You must have given a lot of blowjobs," she said.

Brooke blinked twice, a trick she'd had to learn to prevent herself from rolling her eyes. She had emptied her entire inheritance account to build this house, after receiving the OK from her parents to access her trust early to buy the once-in-a-lifetime property. It had nothing to do with blowjobs. Not that she had a problem with giving a good one, but... She felt offended that that was the perception. She checked briefly to see if Hunter was listening or if he was busy with his own conversation with Quentin.

"Actually, I paid for this house with my own money," said Brooke quietly.

"Really," said Elizabeth loudly, as if she wanted Hunter to hear and as if this would help her to catch Brooke in a lie. Brooke shuddered. She knew that Hunter wanted people to assume that he funded their entire lifestyle.

"What are you in the mood to eat?" Brooke asked, changing the subject.

"Is it the same Nikki beach as Dubai and Miami?" Elizabeth asked, happy to show off that she was well traveled and in the know. Brooke remembered Elizabeth boasting to a girl at one of their charity meetings how much she adored the Nikki Beach in Dubai.

"Oh, don't worry, it's not as tacky as those," said Brooke. "It's just good fun. A good DJ, decent food. A fabulous view. It's a good first night spot... and then we can go to some more authentic places."

"There are lots of hot chicks there," Hunter added.

"Quentin loves to look at hot chicks," said Elizabeth. "He gets all horny, but then he comes home to me. It's like a threesome, without the emotional mess."

God, thought Brooke, *don't let me throw up in my mouth*.

Chapter 4

They pulled up to Nikki Beach and handed the car keys to a young man in a white valet parking uniform. They proceeded into the beach club. The sound of bass music hit them just before the spectacular sight of clear water rendered in pastel tones in the waning light of day flooded their eyeballs. Nikki Beach hadn't changed one bit. It was a good standby. Always dependable for a fun time. Brooke's eyes swept the room to see if she recognized anyone from their previous trips. There were a few groups that looked vaguely familiar. These were people who rented yachts or houses at the same time of year. There were very few people who were homeowners. Those usually didn't mix with tourists, or they were enjoying a meal at home. Very few homeowners spent the whole year on the island, most of them preferring to commute from New York or Europe to Saint Barth.

The group ordered their drinks and some Asian rolls and entertained themselves by looking at the people walking past them. There were gorgeous young girls trying way harder than they needed to. Old guys whose bellies and obvious air of wealth preceded them, accompanied by a trophy wife or girlfriend or two. The DJ was doing a great job keeping the mood festive.

"This is great music," Elizabeth yelled over the noise. "Makes me want to dance on the tables." Of course. Elizabeth was ever the exhibitionist.

"A little early for that," said Quentin.

"Come on," Elizabeth begged Brooke, "let's go dance."

"Fine," said Brooke, pushing her chair back, mostly because she knew that it would embarrass Hunter. They cleared a little space around themselves, and a few other women joined in. As they gyrated to the music, Brooke let go of some of the tension that had been threatening to subsume her all day. She had always liked to dance. She was good at it, too. She had been a night club maven during her one year of being single in New York. Now, she could sense several men's eyes on her. It gave her a modicum of satisfaction. She wasn't dead after all. She liked to feel that some men appreciated her, even if her own husband did not always seem to. If she'd been feeling a bit cheekier, she would have returned their gaze, but she didn't. After all, she was still hoping to fix the situation with Hunter, no matter how dire it seemed.

"Looks like a few of these guys are drooling over you," Elizabeth hissed into her ear. Elizabeth was always quick to compare, to analyze, to be envious. If only she knew how miserable Brooke's life was right now.

"You're so lucky that you get to stay here for a whole month," said Elizabeth. "I would come here every other night."

"Yeah, I'm blessed," said Brooke, wishing she could believe that it was so.

The evening went along smoothly enough. Brooke drank more than she should have. But then again, she reasoned with herself, it was necessary. They made it home, had a nightcap, and went off to their rooms.

Once they had brushed their teeth and were finally in bed, Hunter's hands started running over Brooke's body. In the dark, she knew it was easy for him to pretend she was just about anyone, whether it was the last girl he'd noticed walking across the dance floor, his hot coworker, or the neighbors' nanny. Even though Brooke had been desperate for Hunter's attention for a while, now, the thought of the neighbor's nanny shut her down. She didn't know why she was fixating on that girl. The text exchanges she had seen, when Hunter had gone to the restroom during a dinner party, were from an unattributed number, and she hadn't been able to get access to his phone since then to do a reverse lookup; she had no proof that the nanny and Hunter were actually a thing, but a few times, when Hunter had been running late to a dinner or event, and Brooke had used Find my Phone to figure out when he might arrive, she had noticed that he was at the neighbors' place. They had never been that terribly friendly with Tim and Allegra, who had a gaggle of kids and not much in common with them, so what was Hunter doing there, if not the nanny?

Hunter became more insistent. Even though Brooke had her back turned to him, she could feel the heat starting to radiate off him. He put his hands on her hips and pulled her close, so she could feel his erection nestled between her butt cheeks. He started rubbing himself against her, lifting her upper body up so he could wrap his arms around and cup her breasts with his hands. When he pinched her nipples, she groaned. She had been left wanting for so long. Two could play this game. Brooke squeezed her eyes shut and imagined that Hunter was anyone, anyone but himself. How about that guy she'd seen as they had arrived at the airport? Meat my Fish, indeed. Cheeky. She would like to have *his* meat right now. She replayed the image of him that was stuck in her mind. The darkly tanned skin. The light eyes. The muscular calves. The sliver of tanned abs she'd spotted when his shirt had lifted up. The bulge she had noticed in his shorts- even though she'd been trying not to look. She imagined it was this man's strong, probably calloused hands rubbing her, instead of Hunter's pale, overly soft, manicured ones. What would it feel like to have this island man undressing her? Before she knew it, she was feeling that tingling and throbbing between her legs, that yearning to be filled, that want, which made her open her thighs enough to let Hunter slip in. As he entered her, she thought of tanned skin. Light eyes. Wiry muscles. The smell of the sea. She arched her back and angled her hips to allow Hunter to thrust more deeply inside of her. She bit her lip to stop herself from crying out. She hadn't been this wet for him in months. But it wasn't really for Hunter, was it? She felt teeth on her neck, and it sent shock waves of surprise and pleasure through her body. Whoever he was pretending she was, he was a lot more rough, less careful, with her. But that was what Brooke needed right now. She shoved Hunter away, and before he could protest, pushed him onto his back. She closed her eyes to bring the illusion back. *There.* She could see the bronze skin in her mind's eye. The hard muscles. She was hungry for him, needed him back inside of her. She straddled him and lowered herself onto his shaft, moaning as he filled her. It was enough to send shock waves of pleasure through her as she came, whimpering as she ground against him, riding him for the duration of her orgasm, which shook her entire body. She knew Hunter well, knew that feeling her come was usually all he needed. He was bucking under her now, wanting to fuck her harder before he finished, but she took his hands from her hips and held them down on the bed.

"Slow down," she growled. "You owe me another orgasm. It's been a long time."

She learned over, her breasts hovering over his mouth. He hungrily sucked on her nipples, teasing them with his teeth. She squeezed her eyes shut harder, imagining the stranger underneath her, doing these things to her, instead of the husband who she was so sure had betrayed her. For years, she hadn't been able to imagine what it would be like to be with somebody else, but now, she could. All too vividly. She clearly saw the mystery man's face in her mind's eye now and ground herself harder against Hunter's pubic bone. After ten years, she knew how to angle herself just right, so that his hard shaft rubbed that spot that always magically got her off. She climaxed again, sending shudders of pleasure coursing through her body. She hadn't come this hard in recent memory. Feeling her body contracting around his cock, Hunter came now, too. He moaned and squeezed her buttocks hard as he shoved into her, and she felt him throb, heat and more wetness shooting deep into her.

When it was done, they disengaged from each other and lay there in silence. They knew each other well enough to know that this time had been different. He didn't know who she had been imagining, and she didn't know who he had been imagining, but at this point it was crystal clear that it almost didn't matter anymore. When were they going to talk about it? As they lay there in silence, neither one wanting to speak about anything that might cause a fight and ruin this rare moment, they heard the headboard in the next room banging rhythmically against the wall, Elizabeth's exaggerated cries ringing out into the Caribbean night, competing with the cries of the tree frogs. Competitive to the end.

It broke the spell. Brooke got up to use the bathroom, freshen up, and wipe away any trace of Hunter. When she got back to bed, he was already asleep.

Chapter 5

T he next morning when Brooke woke up, Hunter was already up
and out. *Thank goodness,* she thought. She didn't want to have
to make awkward conversation. If this was like every other year,
Nathalie would have prepared a beautiful breakfast for them. Brooke
took a quick shower, threw on her beach wear, and padded
downstairs in her bare feet. Sure enough, there was a coffee pot, some
beautifully sliced fruit, and some fresh pastries on the counter.
Nathalie's voice rang out behind her.

"Good morning. Did you sleep well?"

"I slept OK," said Brooke. "How are you? How's Ziggy?"

"Great. He has a field trip today. Would you like some eggs?"

"I would love some," said Brooke. "Thank you."

"Miss Elizabeth and Mr. Quentin got up already and went for a
hike," said Nathalie.

"Of course, they did," said Brooke. "She's addicted to exercise."

"She looks like it," said Nathalie.

"Well, in any case, I'm looking forward to a beach day. I don't
know where they want to eat."

"Oh," said Nathalie. "Mr. Hunter said that you have lunch on
somebody's yacht today."

Brooke straightened. "We do?"

She didn't know anyone who was renting a yacht at that
moment. She hoped they weren't going to have to make small talk
with strangers thanks to Quentin's mysterious project.

"That's what he said," said Nathalie.

Strange. Brooke would have to ask Hunter about it. He hadn't mentioned anything. Nor had he mentioned the dinner she was meant to be organizing for the neighbors.

"Oh, do you have the fish guy's card for me?" Brooke asked.

Before moving to New York, before she met Hunter, Brooke had gone to cooking school at the Cordon Bleu, in France, and had learned how to make sophisticated French dishes, and things that were deceptively simple but tasted beautiful. She was looking forward to playing around with the Caribbean ingredients again. Each year, the selection and quality of what was available on St Bart had been improving.

"Oh, yes," said Nathalie. "Thank you for reminding me."

She went into her purse and deposited a card on the kitchen counter, after which she went about making an omelet for Brooke. Sipping on her coffee, Brooke went to pick up the card. On the back was a logo featuring a cow and an eel, with the words *Meat my Fish* underneath in italics. She blushed violently. Was she going to have a run-in with the same man who'd been in her bed in her imagination, the night before? Well, she would see what he could do for her. In terms of food, of course.

Chapter 6

"Is that what you're planning on wearing?" Hunter asked as he walked into the kitchen. Brooke was just finishing her breakfast, and still had on her beach outfit, until further notice. It was simple but elegant- a one-piece black swimsuit that perfectly highlighted her figure, a linen kaftan in lavender ikat trimmed with hot pink cord, and her simple flat sandals she had gotten at Rondini in Saint Tropez the year before. She was keeping her makeup minimal, just counting on sunscreen and a coat of waterproof mascara. After all, on their first day, they liked to go to a beach club, such as the Gypsea or the Nao. These spots were glamorous, but on the casual side. Only tourists got dolled up to go there.

"I thought we might go to Gypsea," she said.

"Change of plans," said Hunter. "We got invited to lunch. On a yacht."

"Which one?" asked Brooke.

They knew a handful of people who tended to rent yachts. They didn't circulate with the uber-wealthy crowd that actually owned them. Those would be oligarchs. Tech billionaires. Most people in their social circle found it tacky to waste that much on a depreciating asset.

"Quentin knows a guy who has a yacht. He wants to introduce us- we might be able to do some business together."

"Oh," said Brooke.

She knew better than to weigh in on this. Nothing good would come of doing business with someone who owned a yacht. Making that kind of money often smacked of illegality. But oh well, she could always have fun at lunch. There would be a lot to look at, and probably some great gossip.

"OK, so what do you *want* me to wear?" Brooke asked.

"I think you could make a little bit more of an effort," Hunter said. "Apparently these are billionaires with some major trophy wives and girlfriends."

Probably some hired girlfriends too, thought Brooke, but she kept that to herself.

"Got it," she said. She'd been with Hunter for long enough to know how to translate his dress code requirements.

She headed upstairs and into her closet, and changed into a swimsuit that was lower cut and exposed more of her bust. She swapped the linen caftan for a dressier chiffon one with bejeweled details. The flat sandals were replaced with some platform espadrilles made of raw silk. They were wildly impractical, and absolutely not meant for the beach, despite their styling. As a finishing touch, she selected a pair of chunky gold hoop earrings. *There.* That should do. She took one last look in the mirror and headed downstairs. Hunter did not like to wait. Quentin and Elizabeth were already there, in the foyer. Elizabeth had gone over the top as always, but Brooke had to admit that she did look stunning with her platinum hair blown out just so, a large pair of turquoise earrings, and a matching pendant nestled between her surgically enhanced assets. Elizabeth had on a similar caftan to Brooke's. People in their circle tended to go shopping in the same places, and one of their mutual friends had a caftan business. Everyone knew the garments were wildly overpriced, but it was a social opportunity, and competitive buying ensued whenever these trunk shows took place at one of their contemporaries' elegant Upper East Side apartments. Not buying something at one of these was akin to social suicide, and no one was willing to take the risk of looking like a cheap-ass.

As they headed outside, Elizabeth rushed towards the Land Rover, eager to have a spot in the front seat for once.

"Actually," said Hunter, "let's take the Moke. Parking in Gustavia is a nightmare."

Brooke loved the Mini Moke. She'd gotten it a few years ago and had had it painted in a vivid shade of pink. It was her little toy, her 30th birthday gift to herself. Too bad Hunter seemed to act like it belonged to him. But she knew the truth.

With the press of a button, Hunter opened the door to the garage, revealing the charming vehicle. This one was electric- Brooke had insisted on it.

"So cute!" Elizabeth shrieked.

Brooke tried not to flinch at the tone of her voice. This week was going to be a very long one. As they all got into the car, Hunter's phone pinged. Brooke discreetly looked at him out of the corner of her eye and saw a frown playing on his lips. Better than the surreptitious smile she'd noticed before when he was presumably texting the neighbors' nanny. He quickly fired off a reply, put the phone back in his shirt pocket, and then gave Brooke a side glance, which she could have sworn was slightly guilty.

They made their way down the hill, towards Gustavia.

"I just can't believe how gorgeous it is," Elizabeth trilled. "Quentin, we should really get a house here, don't you think?"

Quentin nodded stupidly at first, but then seemed to wake up and had the good sense to set Elizabeth straight.

"When are we ever going to spend time here? You'd have to give up one of the places. So, which one is it going to be? Hamptons or Wellington?"

Elizabeth pouted petulantly but winked at Brooke, as if to say, *I'll get what I want, you'll see.*

There was a snarl of traffic in downtown Gustavia, people pouring in for lunchtime. The sparkling yachts were lined up in the harbor as usual. There were a few empty spots compared to last year. Apparently, the oligarchs were not parked here out of fear of getting their boats seized by the American government. And of course, yacht design trends were tending towards massive super yachts that couldn't even fit in the harbor. What was the point?

They found a parking spot on a side street not too far from the waterfront and tumbled out of the Mini Moke. Some shops were closing for the midday period. This was good news, considering that Elizabeth had announced that she was feeling like some retail therapy, and Brooke was feeling petty, and glad to see her frustrated in this small way. They made their way to the string of yachts docked at the harbor.

"I think it's this one over here," said Quentin.

He gestured to a big red yacht which stood out like a sore thumb compared to all the white and navy-blue ones, which Brooke found more tasteful, and the nouveau riche matte black ones she hoped would stop being a thing sooner rather than later.

They were greeted by the gangplank by a handsome crew member in a white polo shirt with red embroidery spelling out the name of the ship. "I'd like to welcome you aboard," he said. "Mr. Holmes is wrapping up a meeting. Can I offer you something to drink as I take you on a brief tour?"

"I'll have a glass of Chardonnay," Elizabeth trilled.

"Scotch on the rocks," said Quentin.

Hunter simply made a gesture that indicated he would have the same.

"I'll have some Sancerre, if you have some," said Brooke. "Otherwise, rosé is fine."

They admired the view from the deck as their drinks were prepared. The young man came back with the drinks on a tray. They all helped themselves.

"I'm Patrick, by the way. So, shall I show you around? This the main deck. We'll be having lunch here." He gestured at a well-set table. Brooke nodded approvingly. Somebody on this boat had taste. Other than the color of the hull, of course. But the red and white touches on the Hermes porcelain were a tasteful nod to the color scheme.

"This is the salon," said Patrick, as he walked them through the yacht's main room. He gestured at a large piece of digital art. An image of a Damian Hirst gold mammoth skeleton. "That's the actual NFT," he said. "This doubles as a TV, which is pretty cool."

"We have one of those at home," said Elizabeth. Quentin gave her a look. "I mean, we don't have an NFT on ours."

Patrick showed them the wet bar, a foredeck with a hot tub and loungers, a sitting room, and a few cabins upstairs.

"Below deck is Mr. Holmes's stateroom and office," said Patrick. "Excuse me. I see that Mr. Holmes' other lunch guests are arriving now," he said.

He left the group behind to look around some more and admire their surroundings. It was a beautiful day, as always. They could see people sunbathing on the decks of their yachts.

If I had a yacht, thought Brooke, *I would take it to one of the beautiful little bays around the island to sunbathe in private.* It felt a bit exhibitionistic to do so at the harbor. But different strokes for different folks she supposed. She peered over to see what the other guests looked like. It was a couple. The woman was a tall icy blonde. Possibly once a model, but she had aged out from the peak of her career. The man was balding and rotund. The sunlight glinted off his gold Rolex Submariner watch. Brooke knew the type. He probably had a place in Miami, a place in the Hamptons, and vacationed here. Lunch was going to be boring with these two, Brooke imagined. She would make the best of it, though. It was certainly better than having to face Elizabeth, Quentin, and Hunter with no other distractions.

They made their way back to the part of the deck where the new couple had alighted and were now drinking glasses of rosé.

"Hi," said Quentin, shaking the man's hand. "It's been a while." He introduced the others in the group.

"Nice to meet you all," said the man. He had a distinctly Russian accent. "I'm Boris. This is my wife, Natasha."

"Are you serious?" Brooke laughed. She couldn't help herself. She ignored Hunter's scowl.

"Yes, I know," said Boris, "We never saw the cartoon, but we've been told that it's funny. And now we collect Boris and Natasha things."

"*He* collects them. His favorite is the hideous bobble heads," Natasha said, sighing but smiling at her husband indulgently.

Now, Brooke had a slightly more positive opinion of the couple. Seeing Natasha more closely, she realized that she was significantly older than she had first assumed, the illusion of youth carefully crafted through strategic artifice, abnegation, and sheer force of will. Russian women were truly formidable creatures. She also realized they had met before. But where?

"You look familiar, Natasha," said Brooke.

"Yes! We attended a lunch together once," said Natasha. "It was for that charity for baby clothes for Haiti."

"That was the one!" said Brooke. "I can't believe you remembered."

"Well, first of all, there was that scuffle with those women who thought the baby clothes needed to be designer. And you told me something very interesting about a podcast you'd been listening to about La Castiglione," said Natasha. "I never forget a face once I've spoken to somebody interesting."

That was more than Brooke could say for many of her peers in New York, for whom pretending not to remember somebody was social currency and the ultimate mindfuck. Maybe this lunch was going to be better than she'd imagined. The men and Elizabeth were chatting happily with Boris. Suddenly, Brooke noticed a hush coming from their group. She turned her head. A figure was coming up the stairs from below deck. Mr. Holmes, she assumed. The men snapped to attention. Brooke wished she'd paid more attention to who this Mr. Holmes was, but now it was too late.

"How do you know this Holmes guy?" she whispered to Natasha.

"I assume he's done business with Boris," said Natasha, shrugging.

Soon, the Mr. Holmes in question was introducing himself to the group. He was a powerful man with still-dark hair, a thick neck, meaty forearms, sinewy hands, and of course the obligatory collector's watch from Hublot. He was the sort of man you wouldn't want to cross in a dark alley, and probably not in a boardroom either, but he also had something sad about him. They had started making small talk when they were distracted again by another figure coming up the stairs. This one was a spectacular brunette younger than anyone on board, including Patrick, who looked like he was on a gap year from college.

"Ah, this is my friend, Olga," said Mr. Holmes.

Olga elbowed him in the ribs.

"Girlfriend," she corrected.

Interesting, Mr. Holmes did not seem like a Russian, but he had Russian friends and a Russian girlfriend. Olga peeled off towards the bar. She seemed bored already. This was awkward.

"I'm sorry, Mr. Holmes, I didn't catch your first name," said Natacha. Brooke gave her a grateful look. She had been scared to ask.

"Peter."

"Well, nice to meet you, Peter," said Natasha.

She seemed like the kind of woman who would never be intimidated by anyone, no matter how big their yacht or how foreboding their appearance.

They continued making small talk. The four men put themselves in a corner and started discussing something in a low voice- probably business. So now Brooke was stuck with Elizabeth, Olga, and Natasha. They spent a few minutes talking about which new shops had opened on Saint Barth, and which new restaurants were worth going to. It wasn't scintillating conversation, but at least it would pass the time. Eventually, they were called to the table. The conversation flowed easily enough, though most of it was grandstanding and competitive comparisons, and talking about where one spent vacation. But then, Boris said something that caught Brooke's attention and made her freeze.

"So, are you guys considering Carlos' offer?"

He was looking Hunter straight in the eye as he said it.

"Which offer?" asked Brooke.

"We haven't decided," said Hunter, and then he made sure to change the subject swiftly to the merits of Gstaad versus Megève.

As they were wrapping up and saying their goodbyes, Brooke briefly took Natasha aside.

"Do you know what Boris was talking about, Carlos' offer?"

"I didn't realize it was your house," said Natasha. "There's a rumor all over the island that Carlos wants to buy your house to use as a guest house. He thinks it's got a better view than his or something. But I almost feel like he's just wanting it because it's a challenge."

"I would never sell my house," said Brooke.

"Funny, that's not what your husband seemed to tell mine," said Natasha, "but I don't want to talk out of school."

"No, that's fine. I'm sure it's a misunderstanding," said Brooke.

"OK," said Natasha. She didn't look convinced but was being polite, and Brooke was afraid to push it further, as she probably didn't want to know the truth. Still, she was going to have to go into the office and look at those envelopes that Hunter had so carefully hidden away from her. How long had Carlos been trying to buy their property? Surely Hunter would never. The house was hers. But who knew what he was thinking these days? She would have to confront him. When the time was right, as if the time was ever right.

When they got off the yacht, it was evident that most of the boutiques had reopened. Of course, Elizabeth forced them all to make an appearance at Prada, Louis Vuitton, Chanel, and Hermès. Brooke knew that most of this was second rate stuff. The resort wear would be there, but nothing of note would be on offer, unless you paid a premium for it. But she didn't say anything. At least it was passing the time- it was too late to go to the beach, too early to think about dinner, and she didn't relish the thought of going home and being alone with Hunter.

Elizabeth was busy trying on a last-season Chanel jacket and Brooke was lost in her own thoughts when her phone pinged. It was Nathalie.

I know you've got that dinner at the house tomorrow night, so I took the liberty of setting up a meeting with the fish guy. Is it OK if he comes to the house today at 5:00 to talk to you about your needs?

That's fine, Brooke typed back absently. She checked her watch. They would be home by then. She would have to ask Hunter what he had in mind menu-wise before she met this person.

At last, they headed back to the Mini Moke. Quentin was bogged down with an armful of shopping bags. How Elizabeth was going to bring all this stuff back home, Brooke could not imagine, but it was not her problem. Elizabeth had teased Hunter and asked him why he wouldn't buy Brooke anything, hinting that she might be tempted to leave him for a better provider. Hunter had simply rolled his eyes.

Chapter 7

They got back to the house and Brooke breathed a sigh of relief. She didn't know what their dinner plans were, but maybe she could beg off and hang out in the pool, swimming by herself and reading a nice book. It would be preferable to having to endure these people for any more time, but in the meantime, she had to think about her meeting.

"Hey Hunter, can I talk to you?" she said as he parked the car. He raised his eyebrows, looking panicked for a moment.

"I want to talk about our dinner plan for tomorrow. You wanted me to cook, right?"

Relief flooded Hunter's face before he controlled himself and put back on his neutral mask.

"Great. Yeah, I was thinking of inviting the neighbors. They're arriving tonight."

"Which neighbors? Judy and Rick?" asked Brooke.

Those were her favorite neighbors, in any case.

"No. Margot and Gus," said Hunter.

"If we're doing a dinner, shouldn't we invite the others as well? Might as well kill two birds with one stone."

"Fine," said Hunter.

"So, I was thinking of doing some kind of local seafood, and starting off with a salad…"

"Great."

"Well … I'm meeting the meat and fish guy in half an hour. Can you get me a final number?"

"Yeah, I'll go call them."

Hunter headed off towards his office. Brooke went up to the master bedroom and played with her hair in the vanity mirror, thinking how much easier it would be if she chopped it all off.

Ten minutes later, there was a knock on the door.

"Come in," said Brooke.

"So, they're all in," Hunter said, as he opened the door. "That makes eight of us for dinner. Try to make it spectacular. I need Gus to invest in this project Quentin and I have in mind."

"OK," Brooke said. Another mysterious project. "Well, while I'm at it, I should maybe order some more stuff that I can freeze, right? Since we're here for the whole month. How many other people do we have coming?"

"About that," said Hunter.

Something in the tone of his voice made Brooke spin around from her seat at the vanity and actually pay attention to him. She searched his face with her eyes. *Oh oh.* There was something very wrong. She had the instinctual feeling that this was one of those moments where one's whole life might change, and not necessarily in a good way. She thought about the water glass Elizabeth had tipped over at lunch. It had rolled to the edge of the table and had miraculously stopped; and just as everyone was laughing in relief and congratulating themselves on the fact that it hadn't been worse, that it was just water, and not even that much of it, the glass had rolled off and shattered on the ground.

"I decided to cut our trip short," said Hunter.

"You decided?" Brooke stared at him in horror.

"I hope you don't mind, but this deal that Quentin and I have... If it works out, I'm better off in New York and London."

"So, wait- you're talking about cutting our trip short... From a month to...what, exactly?"

"A week?" said Hunter, his tone muffled, far from that aggressive, confident one he'd been putting on for the others.

Brooke gaped at her husband, shock running through her body.

A week?

She'd been looking forward to spending a quiet month here. Not that she'd wanted to spend it with Hunter if they turned out not being able to resolve their issues. But the prospect of being in New York and having to put on airs and keep the façade, as she'd started to suspect that there was something very wrong, that Hunter was cheating on her, was exhausting. She'd been thrilled to beg off from the list of social events she'd been invited to over the month. And now, Hunter thought she'd be fine with going back? What would she do? Hide out in her apartment? Or crawl back and say that she could make those events after all? It was horrible to go to these things, but the fear of missing out was real if she was in the city and decided to skip out on principle. Either option was too terrible to contemplate.

"What if I stayed behind?" asked Brooke. She wasn't even sure if she meant it, or if she was simply testing her husband.

"Well, if you want to stay behind, I guess you can," said Hunter.

He said it too quickly. Like that's what he would prefer. *Maybe that would be a good thing*, Brooke thought to herself. What was she afraid of? It's not like he was going to cheat on her any more or less depending on whether she was in town or not. And maybe his missing her would help their relationship.

"Yeah, I'll think about it," said Brooke. But now, she realized it- of course she would stay. She could read, and maybe get massages, and swim. She didn't want to give Hunter the satisfaction of knowing that she'd made up her mind just yet. She still wanted to see how this would play out.

"I'll let you know what I decide. I mean, I am probably needed in New York. The ladies on the zoo board make stupid decisions when I'm not there. You should see what they thought was appropriate as a theme last time. But I could stay here and just get massages and..."

"About that," said Hunter. "We need to talk. About a budget."

A budget? Brooke stared at him, her mouth falling open. She had been closing her eyes as he screwed around, just so she wouldn't rock the boat, and he probably knew that she knew by now, and now he wanted to talk budgets?

"Later," she said, checking her watch. "The fish guy is due any minute."

She checked herself in the mirror to make sure that she was still fit to be seen. Just in case it was hot airport guy, and not some crusty old dude.

"We can talk now," said Hunter. "This is important, and you know how they are in the Caribbean- he'll probably be on island time."

But as if on cue, the doorbell rang.

Brooke gave Hunter a final glare and hustled downstairs just in time to see Nathalie hurrying to open the door.

"You don't have to open the door for me, Nathalie. Come on. I'm right here," said Brooke, smiling.

"Well, if I don't look busy, Mr. Hunter will ask why I'm here at all," said Nathalie.

Fair enough.

The door swung open. And there he stood, the guy from the airport, in all his glory. The name of his company might have been silly, but he was a seriously fine specimen. There was something about him that made Brooke's body respond instantly. It was odd how she could be married to someone objectively extremely handsome, like Hunter; someone elegant, who knew how to dress and how to present himself, who did his hair just so, who knew what set off his eye color, who tailored his suits to highlight his perfect athletic build ...Yet here was this fishmonger, on a tiny island, who had just jumped out of a delivery van wearing ratty espadrilles, of all things, and he blew Hunter straight out of the water. There was a magnetism about him that made Brooke want to throw caution to the wind and launch herself at him. She shook her head, squeezed her eyes shut and opened them again. She was being ridiculous. What was wrong with her? Did she have sunstroke?

"Hi," she stammered. "You're the fish guy."

"I guess I am that," he laughed.

"I'm Brooke Thompson," she said, rather formally, she realized. "Pleased to meet you."

"Antoine de Fontenay," the man replied with a slight bow.

Fancy name for a fishmonger, thought Brooke.

"I think I knew some Fontenays in New York, a few years back. Two older guys who used to go to the Eurotrash nightclubs."

"Yes, we're related," Antoine said, and squeezed his lips together in a way that communicated that he was not in the mood to discuss the matter further. "I think I saw you at the airport," he said.

Brooke was about to nod, but she decided to play coy.

"Oh? Maybe." As if she hadn't been fantasizing about him ever since.

"So, what can I do for you? What do you need?"

Well, Brooke needed a lot of things. Not many of which she wanted to admit to Antoine. Oh, he meant what kind of *food* did she need.

"What do you have? What's in season, what's fabulous?" she asked.

Antoine smiled.

"Fabulous? The bar is set high, I see."

He proceeded to outline what he had available.

"And you know," he said, "I also have things from the family farms on the island. I'm the one stop shop. Do you need eggs, vegetables, fruits?"

"Oh, that's amazing. I had no idea," said Brooke. "You don't sell wine though, do you?"

"No, well...but." He seemed to hesitate, then corrected course. "A friend of mine does. I'll give you the contact information," said Antoine.

"Here, come have a seat, while I get my list together. Want something to drink?" Brooke gestured at the dining room table. The patio doors were open, and a lovely breeze was wafting through.

"A glass of water would be great," he said.

Nathalie went to fetch a glass of water, and Brooke blushed, not wanting this man, of all people, to see how spoiled she was, and how she wasn't even capable of getting a glass of water for a visitor.

"Merci, Nathalie," Antoine said. "We're old friends," he told Brooke.

"Even if he's technically a Metro," Nathalie laughed.

Brooke wasn't sure what a *metro* was, but she wasn't about to ask and look stupid. They sat down and elaborated a menu for eight people.

"Wow, this all sounds delicious," said Antoine. "I wish I could be there. Where did you learn to cook?"

"I went to chef school," said Brooke.

"You did?"

"Le Cordon Bleu."

Antoine's eyes widened.

"I didn't think a fancy girl like you would do something like that," he said.

"I was a rebel," said Brooke.

"Really," said Antoine. He gave her a look that she almost felt physically. She wasn't going to act on it, but it felt good to get that kind of attention from a man. It had been so long since Hunter had looked at her that way. Most of the time, when they had sex, it felt like it was an obligation thing, and the other day didn't count- she could tell he was pretending she was someone else. That was fair enough. She had been pretending Hunter was someone else too, and in fact, that someone else was the very man sitting at her dining room table. She blushed again.

"Alright, so I'll deliver everything tomorrow- is mid-morning good for you?"

"Perfect," said Brooke. "Anyway, Nathalie will be there if I'm not."

She hoped that she *would* be there. There was something about this guy that made her feel alive, and she craved his presence now, even after having just been in it for a few minutes.

"All right, well, it was nice meeting you," Antoine said.

That's when Brooke noticed his exact eye color. Turquoise blue, her favorite shade, the one she had chosen for the Land Rover. Set into a tanned face, framed with dark golden hair, and a beard a shade darker. He was quite an arresting image. She usually leaned towards clean cut, serious looking men with dark hair, like Hunter, but would be willing to make an exception for Antoine. In her fantasies, at least.

"Well, I'll see you tomorrow morning," he said, rising from his chair.

"Great," she said.

Just as the door closed behind Antoine, Hunter burst into the room.

"Was that the fish guy? Did he leave already?"

"Yeah, why?" asked Brooke.

"I just wanted to make sure he wasn't going to screw us on the price."

Brooke froze. *Shit.* She realized she hadn't even talked about cost.

"How much did he say it was?"

"He's going to send me an invoice," Brooke lied. Well, it wasn't her fault they hadn't discussed that. Maybe he was just as distracted as she was. But that was wishful thinking.

"Sorry, I need to go to the bathroom," she told Hunter.

She hurried back to her room, grabbed her handbag, and found the card that Nathalie had given her on the first day. She entered the number into her phone and sent a text message.

Oops! We forgot to talk about how much this was going to cost, and how I can pay you, she typed. The response came quickly.

Sorry- you distracted me.

Brooke smiled to herself. The second part of the message came through.

I have a new customer special. How's €250?

Brooke did a quick calculation in her head, thinking back to all the things she had ordered.

250? Are you sure?

She knew that food on an island was expensive.

Positive.

Thank you so much, she wrote back. *I'll see you tomorrow.*

Chapter 8

B rooke headed back downstairs, planning to report the good news to Hunter, but as she made her way past the office, she noticed that he was not in it. This was her opportunity. She slid into the room, closing the door behind her. There was no lock on the door, unfortunately, because if there had been she would have probably engaged it, not that it wouldn't be suspicious to him, but at least it would delay his coming in and surprising her *in flagrante*, rifling through his papers. Then again, they were a married couple. Didn't she have the right to look through *their* papers and *their* mail? Some of it could be for her. She went to the drawer she had seen Hunter putting the envelopes into. Sure enough, a stack of envelopes, all of them opened, lay inside. She'd been right, they were all from the same person. She felt a pang in her heart as she confirmed that they were all from the office of Carlos White. She chose an envelope at random and started taking the paper out of it, her hands shaking. Before she could unfold the paper, she noticed the sound of the door opening.

"What the hell are you doing?" Hunter exclaimed. "You're snooping in my papers?"

"I was just going through the mail," said Brooke, more calmly than she felt. "I was wondering if there was something for me."

"From the moment I put something in my drawer," said Hunter, "doesn't that mean it's private?"

"We're married," said Brooke. "Aren't we supposed to share everything?"

Hunter had the gall to scoff at this.

"Well, there's nothing for you here. Put it back," he said.

Brooke waved the papers in her hand, indignant. He was acting like she hadn't seen what the letters were about.

"Put it back? This has something to do with me, I would say. How long were you planning on hiding this from me? Why didn't you talk to me about this?"

"You've been busy," said Hunter.

"Busy?" Brooke felt her right eye start to twitch. Was she in the Twilight Zone? Talk about gaslighting.

"Yeah. With your charity stuff..." Hunter began, but Brooke interrupted him, livid.

"I would say that you've been a lot busier, Hunter. I'm not the one who's been fucking around."

"What do you mean?" asked Hunter, his eyes narrowing.

"Oh, come on, I know about the neighbor's nanny. I'm not stupid- and she's probably not the only one."

Hunter froze. Brooke could see the gears grinding in his head. See him debating whether to break down and admit to the truth, or to keep lying.

"I think you're pathetic to be jealous of that poor young girl. I'm just helping her with her résumé," he said.

Oh wow, so he'd chosen lies. That was new. Usually, Hunter didn't hesitate to obfuscate, to smudge crucial details; he would lie by omission, but he didn't out and out lie.

"Her résumé for what?" Brooke hissed. "I think that she's done quite well for herself as a sugar baby already, wouldn't you say?"

"Don't say that about her," said Hunter. "I am not cheating on you with her."

Brooke froze as she heard the exact words coming out of Hunter's mouth.

"Not cheating on me with *her*, huh? I believe you- but then who are you cheating with? I know there's someone!"

"It's already over, as if you care. I don't think there's anything left for us left to talk about," said Hunter. "Why don't you just get dressed for dinner?"

"Oh, I think we have quite a lot to talk about," said Brooke. "Let me explain something to you. I will never sell this house, so I don't know what you're trying to work out with this Carlos character, but it's not going to happen."

"We need the money," said Hunter.

Brooke burst into bitter laughter.

"We need the money? You spend money hand over fist. You hide all of it in your blind trust, and you're trying to tell me that you need *more* money? You give me a paltry allowance to try to keep up appearances on. How in the world can we not have money?"

"My business deals haven't been going well," Hunter said in a low voice.

"Well then stop spending money on other women, and maybe you can save more," Brooke started.

"The saving money ship has sailed," said Hunter. "I'm in big trouble."

Brooke glared at him.

"You know that if I divorce your ass and I take half of everything, you're going to be even worse off," she said, with a bravado she wasn't really feeling.

"Half of zero is still zero," said Hunter.

Brooke froze. *Shit.* She had finally forced him to express the hideous truth he'd been hiding for however long. She almost laughed at her own stupidity. This whole time, she'd been feeling sick to her stomach, worrying about Hunter cheating on her, as if that was the worst thing that could happen, and it turned out that it was just the tip of the iceberg.

"So, there's seriously nothing left?" she asked, defeated.

"How was I supposed to know my stupid parents would let my trust fund dwindle so much before they kicked the bucket?"

Brooke shuddered. She'd never liked Hunter's parents. Her in-laws had never been welcoming to her, she had never had a warm and fuzzy relationship with them. They acted like she was less than because her parents didn't act like the typical WASPs. As if her parents hadn't been a thousand times more worldly, polite, and elegant than either one of them. But at the same time, she knew that they had spoiled Hunter rotten until their deaths, and nobody deserved for their own son to talk about them that way.

"If you'd been focusing as hard on your wallet as you were on your dick, maybe you wouldn't be in this predicament," said Brooke.

"Don't speak that way. You're being vulgar," said Hunter.

"You've been *acting* vulgar."

"Fair enough," said Hunter, "but now, here we are. So, what are we going to do?"

"There's no we here," said Brooke, clarity suddenly flooding her mind.

She wasn't going to go home. Not this month, not next month, not ever. There was no home to go back to.

"What about the apartment? We still own that, right?"

"I refinanced. And took out another mortgage..." Hunter admitted. "There's almost no equity."

Brooke now felt like she was in free-fall, on the big drop on the roller-coaster, and not quite sure when it would finally level out.

"Then it looks to me like we're both on our own," Brooke finally said, once she had composed herself. "I hope you're good for the €250 I promised to the fish and meat guy because this supper is going to be our last hurrah."

"Yeah. But after I leave on Saturday," said Hunter quietly, "what are you planning to do? Also ... God, Nathalie needs to get paid. You need to tell her... Never mind. I'll tell her. It's my fault."

It was almost funny how, now that everything was out in the open, Brooke wasn't as hurt as she thought she would be. And she wasn't feeling as helpless as she thought she might. And now, they were almost acting as a team. They were almost civilized. It was ironic and really, really sad.

"I think I'm going to stay here," Brooke said. "You didn't do anything with this house, did you? It's all still in my name, right? You promise?"

"It is," said Hunter. "But I thought you understood- we literally have almost nothing to our names. That's why it's so important that I impress Quentin, and Gus, and Mr. Holmes."

"I don't really have a dog in this race anymore," said Brooke. "But I'll do you this favor, which you don't deserve. I won't say anything. But if you get a deal, you'd better be fair."

"Thanks," said Hunter. "And there's one more thing. I need you to not say anything about this to anyone until we figure it out."

"Why? Why can't I say anything?"

Hunter rubbed the space between his eyebrows.

"Honestly? I might have mentioned that Sea Grapes was collateral. For some of the deals. I didn't have any cash to put up."

Brooke stared at her husband.

"You said what? Hunter, you would put this house in danger? For another failed business deal?"

"This one had better succeed. But don't worry. I'm not crazy. I simply intimated it. I swear to you I never signed any official documents."

"Hunter, we need to divorce before anything gets worse."

"Just a couple more weeks. Please. I promise you won't regret it. Right now, you wouldn't get anything from me. If this deal works out, I'll give you your due. I promise. I know I messed up. Sea Grapes is yours. Unequivocally. Listen, I've got to go see what the others want to do tonight. We need to keep up the pretense."

"Fine. I'll go get ready."

Brooke slowly went up the stairs, deep in thought, feeling drained. She liked this version of Hunter a bit more. The apologetic, soft spoken Hunter. But, she reasoned, that version of Hunter barely ever existed, other than in her wishful thinking. Even now, she couldn't be sure that he wasn't speaking out of his delusion that everything would work out. He obviously couldn't be trusted to do what was best, or they wouldn't have ended up in this situation. And he was leaving her high and dry. How could he have let it get this bad without bringing it up with her? He had never considered her as an equal. She looked around the house. Her beautiful house. What was she going to do, with this house and no money, no job, and no desire to leave this island for the time being? Well, she would have to figure it out. There was no alternative. She couldn't very well go back to New York with Hunter. At least this way, she didn't need to see all the same people who would be judging her, watching her downfall, her tumble from her lofty perch.

A few moments later, Brooke was staring into the mirror on her vanity, half-heartedly trying to decide between two pairs of earrings, when Hunter entered the room.

"They want to go to town. Quentin chose the spot, so he says it's his treat."

Brooke stared at Hunter's reflection in the mirror.

"So that's how bad you let it get- we're down to our last dollars?"

Hunter looked at her. She waited. He didn't say anything. That was enough of an answer for her. She sighed deeply.

"Please present my regrets to them. You go and have a good time. I need to stay behind and gather my thoughts. Tell them I'm planning the dinner."

"Got it," said Hunter. He walked out of the room.

Chapter 9

B rooke stayed in the bedroom until she heard the Land Rover depart. *Stupid*, she thought. *Stop wasting gas.* She was going to need to figure out how to make some quick cash. That was the most immediate problem, but could she really do this thing? Could she really stay on this island? Where she knew almost no one? Administratively, it was possible, she supposed. She had French citizenship, through her mother's complex family history. When she was young, she didn't really care about it, but her mother had insisted on it. Brooke had resented the time spent waiting at the consulate, but now, she realized what a gift it was. The world was her oyster. Also, she remembered that St. Barth didn't have any income or property taxes, which would always come in handy, even though the cost of living was nearly triple that of any surrounding island. There had to be a way. This was an island that lived off near constant tourism, with tourists with deep pockets, to boot. Surely, she could tap into that. The terrifying thing was that, despite her busy volunteer life, she felt that she had no work skills to speak of. Her last work experience was for Sotheby's art auction department, over ten years earlier. It was too late for regrets, though. She wasn't the only woman in this situation. She took out a notebook from the nightstand. She had sworn to write her dreams in it, before realizing that each night here, she fell into a deep slumber that was as thick as soup, blissfully dreamless save for vague images drifting across her consciousness. She opened the notebook and wrote down all the challenges in her life. She needed a plan. She paused to think about this. She knew how to make a beautiful home, that was for sure. She had some computer skills. She could be charming. She knew how to cook. That was pretty much it. Maybe she was being hard on herself, but honestly, this was not the proudest point in her life. Her mind was racing. What could she do with her beautiful home, her limited skills, and her lack of resources? She was going to have to sell something- that was evident. She hurried down to the office and pawed through the safe. Inside were slim pickings. A few pieces of jewelry that would probably be sold for their weight in gold, which sadly wasn't really what one thought of when one said something was worth its weight in gold. She peered at her wrist. Yes, there was the gold watch her parents had given her, and the Cartier Love bracelet Hunter had given her when they'd first gotten together. How funny that she couldn't take off this shackle until she got access to a special screwdriver. She had the diamond studs she wore in her ears. She wasn't even sure if those were real anymore. And her mother had always told her: don't sell the jewelry. Was this really her lowest point? She proceeded to go around the house, assessing every object in it. Were there other things she could sell? Could she do some kind of a tag sale? Was that even done on Saint Barth? She'd never seen one, but maybe on parts of the island that had more locals living in them...though her decor was hardly something that locals would buy. There were a few interior design places. Maybe they would be willing to purchase some of the designer furniture, but then her home would be less stunning. All that furniture had been chosen expressly for it. She was getting palpitations. She realized that there was nothing more she could do at this juncture. Her thoughts just needed to percolate, and usually what helped with that was swimming.

She walked through the house and over to the pool, and stripped off all her clothing, not bothering with a bathing suit. That was the advantage of having your own pool. She dove in, breaking the water smoothly, with nary a splash. She swam back and forth, as fast as possible, underwater, screaming a few times for effect. But the bubbles were surprisingly soundless, powerless, just like her plan.

She whipped her limbs through the water, trying to exhaust herself physically, hoping that that would lead to her mind slowing down. What was she going to do about her life in New York? Was she just going to leave it behind without saying anything to anyone? But when she really thought about it, she had very few real friends. Just the superficial women who were on the charity circuit with her. She didn't have the true bonding that came with raising children together, or from doing something you loved just for the hell of it, or from going through any kind of authentic struggles with anyone. No one she knew had been sick or in need. She realized what a bubble she lived in. She dove back underwater and screamed again. Well, this swim certainly wasn't making her feel that much better, was it? She was debating on whether to get out of the pool or not, when she heard the door of the Land Rover slam shut. *Damn it.* The group had returned already- ridiculously early- and here she was, naked in the pool. She heard gravel crunching as Hunter and the other two approached the house. Elizabeth was obviously drunk. She was giggling, saying stupid things in that high pitched babyish voice that set Brooke's teeth on edge. Quentin had a great honking laugh, as well. She didn't hear anything from Hunter, knowing him, following their discussion, he had probably been quiet all evening. He had probably bored the hell out of them, which was why they had not lingered. Now, Brooke's immediate issue was getting out of the pool without them all seeing her naked. Not that she cared anymore. She felt that everything was about to be laid bare, anyway. This was the least of her problems. She saw the lights inside the foyer come on as the group entered the house. The French doors to the pool were open; they would notice soon enough that she was out there. As expected, they all spilled out into the night, and Elizabeth's stupid voice rang out.

"Oh my God. Are you skinny dipping?"

"Nope, I'm swimming," said Brooke. "Skinny dipping is something stupid people do for a thrill. This is my pool. I do what I want."

"Wow, someone's in a bad mood," said Elizabeth. "You should have come out with us. We had such a great time. We're definitely going to get a place here, right, Quentin?"

Quentin was silent. It was becoming rather obvious that their so-called perfect relationship wasn't exactly what Elizabeth wanted to portray it as.

"We're going to bed," Elizabeth giggled. "Not to sleep, but you know. So, you can get out of the pool- we won't peek."

Brooke let them retreat to the house without comment. Hunter stayed behind.

"I brought you a doggy bag," he said, his eyes downcast.

"I'm not hungry," said Brooke.

How could she even think about food at a time like this? It was amazing that Hunter was able to disconnect so easily and transition from the conversation they'd had to an allegedly fun evening out.

"Well, I'll put it in the fridge in case you change your mind."

Brooke watched him go, simmering. After a moment, Hunter came back with a towel and a bathrobe. This was the first time he'd been so considerate in a long time. The irony of it struck her, and a bitter laugh escaped her lips.

"What?" He asked.

"Nothing. Thank you."

"OK. No problem. See you in a minute."

"I would like you to go sleep in the guest room," said Brooke quietly.

"I understand," said Hunter.

Well at least there was that. She'd been worried about having an explosive fight, full of drama and hysterics, both on her part and on his, and somehow, they were doing what some lifestyle gurus would call conscious uncoupling. She almost laughed again at how ridiculous that was.

Once Hunter was gone, Brooke got out of the pool at last and made her way up to the bedroom.

She brushed her teeth and went to bed. As she lay there, her mind still spinning, she realized this was the first time she'd ever been in this bed alone. And then, of course, she heard Quentin and Elizabeth starting to go at it again. How did Quentin maintain an erection with that voice in his ear? She wondered. As Elizabeth's moans got louder and Quentin started grunting, Brooke put her pillow over her ears to try to drown it out. She allowed herself to think of Antoine the fishmonger. How would it be to have him in this bed with her? Would it be weird? She hadn't been with anyone other than Hunter in ten years. She couldn't believe that time had gone by so quickly. There had to be something to show for it. Some kind of life skills, some kind of experience. Her mind still spun. What did she know? What might she do? What were her skills? She ran through her list again; she'd done the charity circuit. She knew how to be welcoming. She'd created a beautiful house. And she knew how to cook. Then it came to her. What if she rented out the house and acted as house manager and chef, all in one? There was the issue of where to live while she was doing this. She wouldn't kick Nathalie and Ziggy out of the downstairs apartment. Would she even be able to afford Nathalie? Might she be able to use the office as a bedroom? She would have to figure it out. But yes, this was her best option. Being in a service position would be a hard pill to swallow. But she could get back on her feet. Relieved that she had found a potential plan, she finally sank into oblivion, much needed sleep.

Chapter 10

The next morning, Brooke woke up with a pounding headache. Funny, she hadn't even had anything to drink, and she remembered that she had newfound clarity. Would she really be able to do this? Before she could worry about that, though, she needed to organize this famous last supper. She checked her watch- she only had a few minutes until Antoine was scheduled to deliver all the food. She splashed her face with water, tousled her hair, and threw on a casual outfit of shorts and a tank top and flat sandals. Depending on what the plan was for lunch, she would primp later, if she decided to go with the group. The doorbell rang just as she was coming downstairs. Where was Nathalie? She checked her phone to find a message from her.

Ziggy is not feeling well, Nathalie had written. *We're at my mother's house.*

Take your time, Brooke typed back.

Sorry. I mean, we moved to my mother's house. I wasn't planning on coming back. Hunter told me there's no money left.

Brooke felt a stabbing in her heart. Why hadn't Nathalie told her she was planning to move out? She remembered her saying something about growing out of the apartment, but this was a step beyond. So that was it? She had no help anymore? It was all happening faster than she had thought it would. But at the same time, there was relief. Brooke could stay in the downstairs apartment now.

She heard a buzzing at the intercom near the door. It must be Antoine. She pushed the button to open the gate, and spent a few seconds composing herself, taking deep breaths and fighting to keep the tears back until the doorbell rang.

She opened the door and found herself looking right into that gorgeous pair of aqua eyes.

"Hi," she said shyly.

"Hi back," Antoine retorted. "I have everything in the truck- where do you want me to put it all?"

"You can just bring it to the kitchen," Brooke responded. "Did you get it all?"

"Yes, and a few bonus things. Here- here's a bottle of local rum. A welcome gift."

Brooke took the bottle.

"Oh! Thank you! That's so kind."

"It's tradition on the island. Did you need to order anything else for the rest of your stay?"

There was no use beating around the bush.

"Well...yes and no. Everyone else is going back at the end of the week, but I'm staying on."

Antoine's eyebrows shot up. He looked at her quizzically.

"You and your husband, you mean?"

"Alone."

"But...why?"

Brooke thought for a moment. She didn't want to spill the beans about her separation, just as Hunter had requested, but she also needed to get the word out about her money-making attempts. She had no idea how this house rental thing might work, but it was too late for pride- and for overthinking; she needed to get the word out.

"I'm going to be trying to do cooking events...and maybe retreats...and maybe renting the house out."

"Oh." Antoine looked surprised. "Where will you stay?"

"Nathalie just vacated the downstairs apartment, so I can stay there. So... I'll be working with you more often, I imagine."

Antoine was still looking puzzled.

"What does your husband think of all this?"

"He's OK with it," Brooke said, vaguely. She peered at Antoine, whose expression was still surprised.

"Why do you look so shocked?" she asked. "I'm sure I'm not the only person you've ever met who decided to stay longer in paradise. Have you ever spent a winter in New York?"

"No, it's not that...it's a funny coincidence. A friend of mine just started a high-end rental agency. She asked me to mention it to anyone who might be interested. Since it's so new, the onboarding process is simple, apparently. Apparently, they have clients still looking for houses this late in the season."

Brooke stared at him.

"Really? That's amazing news! Simple sounds great to me. I'm a little overwhelmed, to say the least."

Antoine looked down at his phone.

"I'll forward it to you now."

"You have my number?"

Antoine nodded.

"You texted me, remember?"

Brooke's phone pinged.

"Got it. Thanks."

She looked up and into Antoine's eyes. She gulped. He had her number, and she had his. She wasn't that kind of girl, but if she was, she would be sorely tempted to make a booty call. Antoine was looking into her eyes, too, and she felt that if one of them didn't look away soon, something untoward might happen. Antoine broke the spell first.

"Well, let me bring everything in before it cooks in the truck."

He headed out to the van, and she watched him as he walked away. He had a cute muscular ass, beautiful shoulders, and a slim waist. She wondered what it would be like to run her fingers through that dark gold hair. She forced herself to take her eyes off him and headed to the kitchen. Once Antoine had dropped all the food on the kitchen island, he held up his phone.

"I have your digital receipt for €250 here. Text or email?"

"Oh, I don't need a receipt," said Brooke absently.

She had the cash ready for him. Hunter had slid the bills under the bedroom door with an apologetic note earlier that morning. That €250 had seemed like such a deal just the day before, but now, she realized how much €250 actually was. How much did they have left? She didn't even want to know, she realized.

"Listen, if you're going to be making a business of this, you're going to want to keep your receipts," Antoine admonished.

Brooke peered at him. *Crap.* He was right. She was so poorly equipped to run a business. Was she being crazy?

"By the way, how are you going to stay here longer than 90 days? Did you get a visa?"

"Oh, I have French citizenship, through my mom. I applied when we decided to buy on the island- We thought it would make things easier."

"Oh. Good," said Antoine.

He gathered up his cooler bags and started to make his way to the door.

Brooke followed him out, her mind racing.

How was she going to survive on this island, where everything cost so much more, without any guaranteed income? She wasn't 100% sure whether Hunter was telling the truth about having no money left at all or not, but right now, it was a moot point. She knew that everything was hidden away in a blind trust no matter what. So even if he had the money, she doubted she would see any of it. Which was why it was so important for her to be nice to Hunter, and to hold on to this house.

As if he was reading her mind, Antoine turned back to face her.

"So, you're really staying, not just getting ready to sell this place?" he asked.

Brooke froze.

"What do you mean? What did you hear?"

"I mean. I'm not a gossip," said Antoine. "But the whole island is saying that Carlos White is buying your house. I thought it was a done deal."

"Absolutely not," said Brooke.

"Well, I must have heard wrong- just be careful..." Antoine stopped himself mid-sentence.

Brooke froze.

"Careful of what?"

"Gossip like that is the equivalent of blood in the water for sharks...," said Antoine.

A chill ran down Brooke's back. She momentarily forgot her attraction to Antoine.

"What do you mean?"

"Oh, it's nothing as sinister as I made it sound. And besides, technically, that whole blood thing isn't technically correct. They like chum," Antoine said. "There are maybe some people you should watch out for on the island. I would tell you...maybe in exchange for one of your meals..."

"I'm gonna hold you to that," said Brooke. "As soon as everyone is gone, I'll make you dinner, and you can tell me everything."

"As soon as your husband leaves, you're inviting me over? That's a little bit scandalous," Antoine winked. But Brooke thought she could also detect distaste in his expression. *Great*. Now he probably thought she was one of these women whose morals flew out the window the minute they went on vacation.

"As friends," said Brooke, more firmly than she felt.

"Ah. In that case, gladly. This is an island where you need friends."

Did she imagine it, or was his tone a little odd? Antoine headed back to his van, and Brooke forced herself to close the door without watching him go.

She had a Last Supper to prepare.

Chapter 11

B rooke stood in the kitchen contemplating all the ingredients Antoine had brought to the house. This was the first time since she'd been coming to the island that there was such a variety of produce available. She admired the shiny red tomatoes and the bright green leaves of salad. She knew she'd had a plan before the delivery, but seeing these fresh ingredients, she decided to showcase them more by keeping the meal simple and allowing each element to shine. She was going to outdo herself. Just because her life was falling apart didn't mean that she should let everything else go by the wayside, too. She wasn't going to just sleepwalk through this meal. She used to have so much fun cooking. She needed to recapture that for herself. What was she going to do? Now that Hunter had told her the truth about their finances, how would she proceed? Was she really going to stay here in Saint Barth forever? Was this going to be her life? Would she really manage to make a living? She thought about the neighbors and friends who were going to come for dinner. It had usually been a treat to see them when they used to visit every year, but now, it wouldn't be the same. It would be hard to listen to Margot and Gus boasting about their vacation plans, and about the new apartment they were going to buy because their daughter was going to school in Miami. Judy and Rick were a lot of fun before, but now, Judy's perfectly put together ensembles full of the latest fashions might be a little bit triggering for Brooke. Not that she really cared that much, but she had been playing the keeping up with the Joneses game. And look where it had gotten her: nowhere. She thought about the designer things she had sitting in her closet in New York. What would she do about those? Would Hunter send them to her if she stayed here? Could she maybe sell some? She regretted now that she hadn't bought that Birkin Elizabeth had been trying to push her to obtain last year. It would have kept its value and provided her with some liquidity. She would get Hunter to trade in her plane ticket for credit and make sure it was in her name, she thought. And then, when she had gotten back on her feet, she would go back to New York, to settle her affairs.

She kept busy around the kitchen, remembering past years, when Nathalie would have been helping her as sous-chef, the two of them enjoying a glass or two of wine as they gossiped. But this time, Nathalie had been busy in other parts of the house, cleaning up and setting the table. What was Brooke going to do about Nathalie? She wished she could have been the one to tell her about their change in circumstance. Nathalie had deserved to know about it earlier, as soon as Hunter began to suspect they were having problems. She would have had more time to find another job. Would this affect their friendship? Yes, it probably would. But now they would be on more equal footing, wouldn't they?

Brooke had finished assembling most of the dishes when she checked the time and realized that their guests were coming soon. She hadn't seen Hunter all afternoon. He and Quentin had probably gone into town for a drink at one of the bars frequented by the yacht people. She hoped that Hunter hadn't gotten drunk and bought another watch. That was what he usually did, and now, Brooke knew that that was not a good idea. She needed to get ready quickly. If they were still keeping up appearances, she would make an extra effort. Looking good was half the battle, wasn't it? She hurried upstairs, jumped into the shower, lathered herself up, and rinsed off with cool water. She would keep her hair wet and slicked back into a braid. It was too hot to think about styling it any other way. She was looking forward to the trade winds that usually came through in the evening, cooling off the island. It was getting later, and she could hear the first of the tree frogs starting to chirp. Night always fell so early in the winter in the Caribbean. It was incongruous, because you expected it to be like summer, when the days were long. But that wasn't the case here. Brooke chose a yellow silk one-shouldered dress that set off her olive skin. Hunter had never liked it. He didn't like anything asymmetrical; he had told her once that he found it destabilizing. *Too bad for him.* She smiled, knowing that she was going to be looking good, but all the while subtly annoying her soon to be ex-husband. Hunter's taste was super conventional. His mother would never have worn anything odd or artistic. She had always been so buttoned up and proper in her Chanel suits and her St John ensembles. Hunter's family had never come to their house in the Caribbean, Brooke realized. She wondered if it was because it was technically her house. As she put on a little bit of makeup to highlight her dark eyes, she suddenly froze. The house was completely in her name, wasn't it? How was Hunter even thinking that he would have a chance to sell it? She needed to have lawyer look at the papers as soon as possible. Hunter would do the honorable thing, right? He would never try to sell the house from out from under her, would he? Yet all signs pointed to the fact that Hunter was not in his right mind right now. Brooke swiped on a bit of coral colored lip gloss. She slid a few silver and gold bangles onto her arm and considered her left hand. When should she take off her wedding ring? It was funny that she was being so calm about this. She considered that, if she didn't take it off soon, she would end up with a tan and a telltale white ring mark. It might be time. *Yes.* She took the ring off and put it in her drawer. She would remember to put it somewhere safer a little later. In its place, she put a chunky gold and silver ring that coordinated nicely with the bracelets. She hoped that Hunter or Elizabeth wouldn't say anything about it in front of the others. She didn't want to have to explain herself at this juncture. She hurried downstairs as Nathalie was leaving.

"I'm sorry- I have to go pick up my boy. You'll be OK, right?" Nathalie asked, a look of concern in her eye. It was as if she had sensed that something had changed.

"I'll be fine. I do need to talk to you," said Brooke. Nathalie's eyes narrowed as she considered her friend.

"Tomorrow morning?" asked Brooke.

"All right," said Nathalie. "Tomorrow morning."

Brooke stood there as she heard Nathalie's little car drive away. Nathalie would leave the gate open so that their guests could enter without having to be buzzed in. Security wasn't such a huge concern on the island but ever since St. Martin had been getting progressively more consumed by drug culture, things had been changing a little bit. One couldn't be too careful. Still, there were all of four houses on their peninsula. Their neighbors were at the base of the point, and of course, there was Carlos next door. If someone came all the way here, they had a reason for it. It was funny that they'd never invited Carlos over for lunch or dinner- was it just because he was a billionaire? He was still a neighbor, wasn't he? But it had never happened, whether because Hunter felt intimidated, or because Carlos couldn't be bothered.

Brooke headed to the kitchen and pulled her appetizer dish out of the refrigerator to make sure the presentation was perfect. She had created a crudo of local Hamachi, with various ultra-thin slices of citrus, and in another dish, she had done paper thin slices of beets marinated in a citrus glaze and dotted with edible flowers and herbs. It would be delicious, she decided. Next, a salad of little gems with local tomatoes. This was the first time she had bought high quality tomatoes on the island. According to Antoine, these were grown here by a charming family on the other side of the island. The main dish was to be miso glazed local cod, prepared on the grill, and accompanied by local sweet potatoes dotted with yogurt sauce and herbs. She added pomegranate seeds for brightness. Dessert was a chocolate mousse accompanied by tropical fruits. It was a simple but beautiful meal, and she hoped that everyone would enjoy it. She checked to make sure that the champagne and wine were perfectly chilled, which they were. Nathalie had already put a few bottles in an ice bucket, and had set the table, showcasing some of Brooke's favorite China, along with some stunning ceramics she had collected in the past few years from a local artist. Nathalie had artfully arranged cut leaves from the garden in each ceramic bud vase. The overall effect was spectacular. They would have cocktails by the pool, along with the traditional island dish of salted cod fritters, which Nathalie had made, and which Brooke was keeping warm in the oven. What would she do without Nathalie's help, she wondered. It was going to be weird.

Elizabeth tromped down the stairs in dizzyingly high heels. She wore a bejeweled body-con dress that looked more appropriate for a nightclub than for a private dinner party. Clearly, Elizabeth hadn't gotten the memo on how to dress.

"Can I get you anything?" Brooke asked her politely.

"I'd love some champagne," said Elizabeth, leaning against the kitchen island in mock exhaustion. "Oh my God, Quentin's been an animal since we've been here. He won't leave me alone. We definitely need to get a house in the tropics. He's so horny. I'll bet that Hunter doesn't keep his hands off you, either. How do you even get anything done when you're here?"

Brooke turned her back to Elizabeth so she could roll her eyes in peace. She picked up a champagne flute and opened a bottle with a festive pop. Surely Elizabeth had noticed that things between Brooke and Hunter were not exactly cozy. She thought it was rather rude of her to be rubbing it in.

"So, what are we doing tomorrow?" asked Elizabeth.

"I think we'll go to the Gypsea Beach Club. You'll love it," said Brooke.

Brooke loved the Gypsea. It was a little bit more casual, yet more elegant than Nikki Beach. The people who frequented the Gypsea tended to be more European, and less of the yacht rental crowd. It made a real difference to the atmosphere.

"So, tell me a little bit about the people who are coming to dinner," said Elizabeth.

Elizabeth always wanted to know everything about everyone. It helped her to know whether she needed to make an effort, or not.

"Well, there's Judy and Rick. You'll love them. They're from Boston. They have a house here that they visit, usually around the same time we're here, and maybe a little bit longer. Which I would too if I lived in Boston," said Brooke. "Judy is the head of a charity board, and Rick is a financial whiz. Judy dresses beautifully, and she's quite funny, if you give her the chance," said Brooke. "And then Margot and Gus. They're lovely. They tend to vacation quite a bit. They're young, retired, but Gus still likes to make deals whenever possible. It does create a little bit of a disconnect, though, I have to say. We're not at the same phase in life, you know what I mean?"

"I would love to be retired," said Elizabeth. "That would be so much fun. I could just golf, do yoga, and have boozy lunches every day."

"I wouldn't know what to do with myself," said Brooke.

"What are you talking about?" Elizabeth laughed. "I was joking, before. We're both stay-at-home wives with no kids. It's like we're retired already. What I described *is* my life."

Ouch. That hurt. And the fact that it hurt was probably proof that Brooke really did need to start doing something more with her life.

The two men came into the room, both wearing some variation on the New York Man in the Tropics Vacation Ensemble. Light trousers, suede driving moccasins, and a linen shirt. They both looked handsome, with their wet hair brushed back.

"They'll be here any minute," Hunter remarked. "I see you already have Champagne, Elizabeth. Quentin, can I get you anything? We can go by the pool- we'll hear them arrive from there."

Hunter poured Champagne for everyone, and they all adjourned to the pool, which was lit up, so it shone in that bright turquoise color that Brooke loved so much. Beyond that, very few lights could be seen- just a sailboat here and there, and the distant lights of Saint Martin. Some people preferred to live above Gustavia so they could see the twinkling lights of town and of the yachts. Brooke supposed that that had its appeal. But she loved the feeling of being all alone out here, on their peninsula. Never mind the billionaire next door, who apparently was hoping to be truly all alone on his peninsula. She would never let that happen. Regardless of what he wanted; Carlos was probably somebody who wasn't used to having people refuse him. But Brooke would certainly show him that that's what happened in the real world.

Soon both couples of guests had arrived. As expected, Judy was looking glamorous, in a jeweled kaftan and Hermes sandals. She wore stunning gemstones in her ears and on her fingers. Brooke recognized the work of a famous French jeweler. Judy was probably wearing 5 million on her person. It boggled the mind. Margot was more restrained, always cool and elegant with her long swan-like neck and her all-white uniform. Her jewelry was less extravagant looking, but probably no less expensive. Brooke recognized the Bulgari diamond snake necklace winkling around her neck. She had long admired Margot's alternative sense of style. It was refreshing. They settled into an easy pattern of conversation. The two other couples spoke excitedly about their plans to go sailing, and to host dinners in their respective homes. Brooke noticed that Hunter was being a little quiet, no doubt because he had not told them yet that he wasn't planning on staying.

"Will you come sailing with us?" Judy asked. "We're chartering a yacht to go to Saint John. I've been dying to go snorkeling in Caneel Bay."

Hunter set his lips in a straight line. Brooke piped up.

"Let us know the dates, but I'm not sure it's going to work. We have a lot of things going on this year."

"Oh?" asked Margot, her tone begging for further explanation.

Brooke was going to leave that to Hunter.

"Yeah, there's a lot going on. With the business," said Hunter.

"A lot of exciting stuff," said Quentin, rubbing his hands together gleefully. Brooke was starting to understand that Quentin didn't seem to have the slightest grasp of which businesses would work out and which would not. She was starting to realize that much of Quentin's success came from strong-arming people into investing in his harebrained schemes. She was also realizing that Hunter, as a trust fund baby who hadn't really started anything of his own, was at a distinct disadvantage when it came to the world of business. He could get his foot in the door thanks to his breeding. But then his lack of work ethic and realism made things fall apart. It was sad that the scales were falling from Brooke's eyes only now when it was much too late.

"I'm sorry- what were you saying?" said Brooke to Judy. "Those tree frogs could drown out a foghorn."

"Oh, I was asking, have you planned on inviting your neighbor?"

There was a sparkle in Judy's eye as she asked it. Judy had admitted to Brooke that she had a crush on Carlos, and Brooke had found that completely not understandable at all. She personally found Carlos off-putting, not that she had spent much time with him, or even any time with him, to be fair. Judy insisted that Carlos had that small man's energy that made him try harder, be funnier, and have a bolder personality. Brooke would have to take her word for it.

After cocktails, the group was seated. They all oohed and aahed over the table setting and over each dish.

"You've really outdone yourself, Brooke. It's amazing. You should have a restaurant," said Margot.

That's an idea, Brooke mused. But she knew that the best way to make a small fortune in restaurants was to start with a large fortune. It seemed too risky. However, she was pleased that her talent in cooking did not go unnoticed.

"So, I heard a rumor," said Margot.

Everyone swiveled their heads to look at her. People loved gossip. Even if you *said* you didn't love gossip, you loved gossip. On an island like St. Barth, gossip ran like wildfire, even more quickly than in New York, where the avenues flowed with gossip, dense and deep like arterial blood.

"Do tell," said Elizabeth, clapping her hands and kicking her feet excitedly, like a child.

Margot shot Brooke a discreet smile, as if to signal that she found Elizabeth as off-putting as Brooke did.

"Well, I heard that our neighborhood billionaire wants to buy a certain house on a certain peninsula. Have you guys been entertaining it? I would never sell this place," said Margot. "And besides, your other neighbors are awesome."

"It's just a rumor," said Brooke. "There's no truth to it."

"I don't know, I might entertain it if it was a great offer," Judy ventured.

"It definitely bears thinking about," Hunter started.

Brooke's mouth fell open.

"Are you kidding me, Hunter? I thought we agreed that that's not even a possibility. If you think we need to discuss this again, we'll do it later, in private, but this is my house, and it will always be a resounding *no*."

Hunter clamped his mouth shut, looking to the others as though he were a beaten husband. That was one of the things he did that drove Brooke crazy. He would employ others as witnesses to prove that he was the sweet browbeaten husband, innocent in the face of Brooke's shrieking harpy-ness. It drove Brooke crazy. And Brooke could tell, that, while Hunter was pretending to be confounded, he was livid that she had mentioned that the house was hers.

"I wonder why Carlos would even care about this place," said Brooke. "He's already got over a quarter of the peninsula. Our property is smaller than his."

"He's a billionaire, and he wants it. And he can afford it. That's reason enough," said Judy's husband Rick. Judy definitely had a type. Brooke had never been a huge fan of Rick.

"Well, he's going to have to look for another *raison d'être*, because he can't have this," said Brooke.

"I've heard some rather unsavory rumors about his behavior," Margot continued. "When he doesn't get his way, he can be pretty nasty."

Brooke froze. What did she mean? After Antoine's warning, this was coming off as positively sinister.

"Oh, come on, Margot, you can't believe everything you hear," said Judy, defending her crush. "It's not like he goes around with a bunch of goons breaking kneecaps..."

"Maybe not kneecaps, but... Maybe Hunter should go talk to him while you guys are here," Margot suggested.

"I might have to go to New York next week," Hunter mumbled.

Brooke looked at him, shocked. She thought they had agreed they weren't going to tell anyone, so that they didn't ruin the dinner.

"What? You're going back already?" Rick asked, looking sullen. "I thought we had plans. What the Hell's going on?"

"None of your business," said Hunter.

That was it. The atmosphere sank like a lead balloon. Quentin tried to make a few jokes and get the guys to talk more business with Gus, but no one was much in the mood. Brooke sat there, feeling very alone in the world. Soon, she would be the subject of Judy and Margot's gossip, if she wasn't already. She shuddered at the thought that Carlos would not play fair if she went against his wishes. Well, too bad. She was capable of not playing fair either, she decided.

After dessert, the two other couples politely thanked their hosts and made excuses about being tired and having an early start the next day.

"Early start on vacation?" Hunter groused to Brooke once everyone was gone and he was helping her with the dishes.

"I think they could just feel that it was a tense atmosphere," said Brooke. "This whole thing isn't making us very popular; you know. The sooner we make it clear and right, the better, I think. Nobody likes a nebulous situation."

"Well, I can't afford to make it clear right now," said Hunter. "You've got to trust me."

"Ha! That ship has sailed."

"I'll do whatever you need me to do, but can we please not mention divorce? Until I've straightened some financial things out?"

Brooke shot him a look.

"You'd better not fuck me over Hunter," she said.

She saw him wince. He hated it when she swore, but these were desperate times.

"I would never," he responded.

Yeah right, Brooke thought bitterly. He would never...Just like he would never cheat on her with the neighbors' nanny, just like he would never lose all their money, just like he would never do a million of the other things that he had done to them during their marriage. She chose not to pick on that fact. What would that even change? It's not like they were going to fix anything. She just didn't want anything to break further than it already was.

"Quentin and Elizabeth went to bed mighty quickly," said Hunter, trying to change the subject.

"They're as frisky as two teenagers," Brooke noted.

"Elizabeth probably just didn't want to help with the dishes," Hunter said unkindly. "Sorry, but it's true. There's no way anybody has that much sex with their spouse, after over 10 years of marriage, give me a break. Who are they trying to fool?"

With their spouse being the operative phrase, Brooke thought. It was crazy how things had gone from seemingly fine to irretrievably broken in such a short time.

It was true that, seen from the outside, they'd had everything. The stylish New York apartment, their looks, their health. A beautiful place in the Caribbean. An easy lifestyle, which allowed Brooke to study the things that interested her and to volunteer. Lots of friends. But none of it meant anything.

"Well," said Brooke once they'd finished putting the dishes away. "I'm going to go to bed."

"Can I join you?" asked Hunter.

"I'd really rather you didn't," said Brooke.

Hunter looked down, chastened.

"You took off your wedding ring already," he observed.

"What's the use of pretending anymore?"

"Why don't we enjoy the rest of this week," said Hunter. "And we can discuss it when we're back in New York?"

"No, I'm staying here," said Brooke. "I decided. I'll come back to collect my stuff when I'm settled in, and when I figure things out."

"But people are going to..."

"Hunter, people are going to do whatever they're going to do. Now it's time for me to start acting for me. We don't need to discuss anything. The lawyers will figure it out."

"Please don't bring any lawyers into this," Hunter begged. "I'll do what's right. But I need some time. Don't tell anyone, for now."

"We'll see," said Brooke.

She trudged up the stairs and closed the door to her bedroom behind her. It wasn't until she sank gratefully into her pillow-topped bed that she heard the headboard in Quentin and Elizabeth's room start to slam against the wall. *Right on cue*, she thought. *Don't tell me that they're not doing this for our so-called benefit.*

Chapter 12

B rooke stood by the car in front of the airport, watching the plane take off over the water. When it had disappeared, she took a deep breath and got behind the wheel of the Land Rover.

This was it.

Hunter was gone. The last remains of her previous life were over. She didn't fully trust that Hunter would send any of her things to her, as he had promised. Maybe she knew him better than he knew himself, something she'd told him relatively often, at least in the last years of their marriage. She had to admit to herself that it must have been infuriating to him, her telling him that. What to do now? She wondered. As she pulled out of the airport, she noticed a familiar van pulling in. The Meat my Fish guy was making another stop at the airport. It seemed like he had a lot of people coming in and out. She noticed a pretty blonde girl sitting in the passenger side. The girl looked familiar, but Brooke couldn't place her. Probably his girlfriend. That settled it. Brooke needed to stop thinking about Antoine. It was way smarter to follow through with her albeit insincere pledge of friendship. She would need him in the future, whether her plans to be a chef or have a cooking school panned out, or whether she ended up renting out the house. At this point, she was firing on all cylinders and not ruling out any options. She and Hunter hadn't had another money talk, but she couldn't justify staying for long without earning something. Her first step was to ascertain what she needed to do to get the house rental ready. She'd filled in all the information for the rental agency whose contact Antoine had given her, and she had a phone call scheduled with an old school friend who owned another rental agency, an international one with a branch in St Barth, at noon. She hoped that she could start getting people in as quickly as possible. Driving along the familiar bumpy potholed road, she felt herself growing carsick, even though she was the one driving. Or was it just nervousness in the pit of her stomach? She'd never really been on her own. She and Hunter had met so early in her life, not long after she'd finished the program at the Cordon Bleu, right after she'd gotten back from Paris and was half-heartedly working for the Sotheby's auction house in New York, and she felt like she had gone directly from her parents' house to his apartment. He'd been a few years older, and she'd felt like he had his shit together. He'd taken care of everything without question. And now, here she was, expected to do everything on her own. It felt exhilarating, but it also felt terrifying.

She pulled up to her gate, noticing something strange on its wooden surface. Something reddish glinting in the midday sun. What the hell? She thought to herself. She got out of the car and approached to take a closer look. The smell hit her first, and then she noticed the flies buzzing around. She couldn't be sure, but it looked like blood. What was that supposed to mean? It couldn't be anything but intentional. She looked around to see if there were any wounded animals around, not that there was anything on the island big enough to bleed that much if it was hit by a car, unless it was a goat or a large dog. But the blood looked like it had been poured from above. She checked the trees around for a bird of prey, and, seeing nothing else, shook her head and retreated to the car. She would have to wash this off later today. She hadn't yet had the difficult conversation with Nathalie about what lay in their future. They were going to have to figure that out together. But right now, she didn't feel like she could ask her to help with this distasteful task. She pulled up to the front of the house, parked, and opened the front door, stepping into the coolness of her island home.

It was strange to be in here alone, she realized. This was her new normal, wasn't it? She grabbed a notebook from the junk drawer in the kitchen, and walked from room to room, taking notes on what needed to be done. She should purchase inexpensive matching plates, and plastic cups that could be used outside. She noticed the BBQ grill was missing its tools. Somebody must have misplaced them or accidentally thrown them away. She would have to get some more of those. She checked each guest room. Ideally, she would have bought new sheets specifically for the rentals. But that might be time consuming and expensive, and she decided that any vacationers would be thrilled with the high thread count sheets she had carefully selected for herself and for her guests. She counted towels, deciding that she needed to buy a few more. She surveyed the situation around the pool, deciding that it was as good as it was going to get.

Armed with a small shopping list, she headed back out. As she opened the gate, she cursed herself for having forgotten to bring something to wash off whatever it was that was splashed on it. By now, she'd decided that it was the doing of some bird of prey, even though panic still pinged like an alarm in her mind. She would have to do it when she got back. It was getting hotter out, and she was hoping she might be able to go to the beach in the afternoon, after her phone call.

She rushed down to the convenience store and purchased a few overpriced items that were strictly necessary. She decided that her own plates would be good enough, and that she would wait for some of the other items. After all, she didn't know how dire the financial situation actually was, but she kept expecting the rug to come out from under her, and for Hunter to call her and tell her to stop trying to draw money from their accounts. She hustled back home and spent the remaining minutes before her phone call repurposing the description of the house she had composed for the other site, hoping that it would attract renters.

*Stunning architect designed villa with a sparkling infinity edge
pool and expansive water views. Five comfortable guest suites. Main
bedroom suite with walk in closets and spa bath. Gourmet kitchen
with classically trained chef available. Yoga by the pool? Excursions?
Everything is possible,* she had written.

She hadn't been down to the staff quarters they had built as
an afterthought in years, she realized. She'd never had a reason to,
and, up until recently, Nathalie had been living down there. But she
decided that she should go check it out, because this would be her
new home as she rented the house out. It would be a lot to get
used to, but she didn't have a choice. She headed down the veranda
stairs and around the side of the house and opened the door to the
basement. The light, bright, spacious rooms were replaced by a more
cramped space, which at least opened out onto its own small terrace.
Brooke looked around. It hadn't been decorated at all, but she could
make it homey, couldn't she? She should consider herself lucky to
have that option at all. She came back upstairs. Checking her watch
and seeing that she still had 15 minutes before her phone call, she
wandered around the house picking and choosing decorations that
would make the downstairs space more comfortable and personal,
without taking away from the main space. She selected an aqua
colored throw blanket, a few beautiful pillows, some art that she had
never taken the time to put up. Two silver picture frames containing
photos of her parents. After her parents' death, she had really
depended on Hunter as her sole family, and now she felt a renewed
sense of loss. She squeezed her eyes shut and took a deep breath. She
checked her watch again and hustled upstairs, where she knew the
reception was better for her phone call. The phone rang a minute
before noon, startling her.

"Ford!" she exclaimed as she answered, trying to make her voice
cheerful. "Thanks for getting back to me."

"Brooke. It's been far too long."

Ford's voice was deep, suave... hardly the nasal whine Brooke remembered from boarding school, but Ford had been a late bloomer, and when he'd finally grown up, he'd developed a sense of style that had set him apart from the rest. Many people had ignored him in school, deeming him uninteresting, but Brooke had appreciated how, whenever there had been an issue or a dispute, Ford had always been a precious source of advice. He had always looked at things quite magnanimously and fairly. Brooke had always thought that he would end up being a doctor or a therapist. But here he was, organizing high end rentals throughout the world. He owned a few family properties, and had accumulated more of his own, and had branched out from there. He currently split his time between Palm Springs and Palm Beach.

Anywhere they have palm trees, really, he had quipped once. Once they had briefly caught up, and Brooke had learned that Ford's new husband was hoping to have children, while Ford wasn't so sure how he felt about it, they started talking business.

"But I thought you loved spending as much time as possible at the Saint Barth house," Ford told Brooke, his tone puzzled. "Don't you want to keep it open for impromptu trips?"

"My circumstances have changed," said Brooke.

"Tell me more," said Ford.

Brooke took a deep breath. She was going to honor Hunter's wishes and not say anything about a divorce, or financial difficulties, but it wasn't easy to explain it otherwise.

"We made the decision not to have kids," said Brooke, "and, well, I guess that opens me up to new possibilities. Doing charity work is not filling my cup anymore."

"I'm shocked," said Ford. "You always wanted kids..."

"Things change. In any case, I wanted to see if renting the house out makes sense."

"Are you sure you want to do that?" Ford asked. "It just sounds like a really weird situation for you..."

"I'm not saying it's not going to be weird," said Brooke, losing patience. "But let's see how it goes. How much do you think I can get per week?

"How many did you say it sleeps again?"

"We've got 5 bedrooms in all," said Brooke. She didn't mention the downstairs suite. "Each one of them has either an *en suite* or a Jack and Jill. And of course, there's the pool and a living room, dining room, outdoor dining. Private yoga garden, outdoor bathroom."

"It sounds dreamy," said Ford.

"Remember that I invited you to come. And you never did," Brooke accused.

"I know. Maybe I'll rent it," Ford laughed. "Can you send me some pictures?"

"Sure," said Brooke. "And I also have descriptions written up."

"Wow, look at you, you're a pro," said Ford. "OK, you send me all of that, and I'll try to come back to you with some kind of pricing. And what are you gonna do if it rents? Check yourself into the Eden Roc, knowing you?"

"Ha," said Brooke.

"Anyway, don't worry," said Ford. "Most people have already locked in their rentals for the season. There's a good chance you won't have to worry about where to go."

Brooke was silent. It was almost sad that Ford viewed renting the house out as something that Brooke didn't actually *need* to do.

"I don't think you understand," said Brooke. "This is something I really want to do."

"OK, I'll do my best," said Ford. "You never know. Some people like to do things at the last minute. Hell, I just rented out a house in Anguilla for next week."

Brooke's heart was hammering in her chest. She was literally having palpitations. She didn't want Ford to hear how desperate she was.

"All right, I'll get the stuff to you as soon as possible," she said. "Sorry, I'd better go. I have a yoga class," she lied. In reality, she'd felt the tears threatening, and knew she couldn't keep it together for a moment more.

They hung up, and once she'd had a nice, panicked cry, Brooke spent the next couple hours taking photos of the house and polishing her description. She sent everything off to Ford via email, saying a silent prayer as she hit the *send* button. She had earned a trip to the beach, she decided. Which beach would she go to? She didn't want to be seen at Nikki Beach, for fear of bumping into her neighbors. So, she made the decision to go down the street to their neighborhood beach. In the past, she had not tended to go there, even though it was a lovely one, because it was frequented by more locals, and she found that a bit intimidating. Also, Carlos owned some beach frontage there, and she would hate to bump into him. Though Carlos had a yacht and a pool, so what would he be doing going to the beach?

Brooke was almost ready to go when she remembered that she hadn't washed off the gate.

Chapter 13

S he grabbed a bucket and filled it with soapy water, tossed a sponge into it, and headed down the driveway, cringing in advance as she thought of the unpleasant task of washing whatever gore was on the gate off it. But when she arrived at the gate, clicking it open, and then closed, to stand on the street side, where the blood had been, she stood there baffled. There was nothing on the gate. She came in closer to peer at it and saw a few tiny traces of what had been on it, but it was generally clean. Well, since she was here, she took the sponge, and gave it another good scrubbing, even though most of the work had been done already. *How strange.* Maybe Nathalie had been by. But Nathalie hadn't been by since the dinner the other night, skipping the conversation she had planned, and not responding to her messages. Brooke needed to call Nathalie later and broach the difficult subject of whether she was still working for her, and whether they were still friends, if they ever had been.

She dumped the water in the bushes and hurried back to the house, where she cleaned herself up and changed into a beach outfit. Since she was just heading to the neighborhood beach, she didn't make too much of an effort. After all, she was going for a swim, not for a see and be seen adventure. She put on her one-piece suit, which was a fetching shade of cocoa, selected some terry cloth shorts, a tank top, and some sandals, loaded a towel and some sunscreen into her straw beach bag that she had gotten at the market in Saint Tropez, and headed back to the car. Should she take the Mini Moke? Why not? It would be more fun than trying to navigate the big Land Rover in the narrow parking lot at the beach.

Brooke opened the garage door and smiled when she saw her little festively colored vehicle sitting there waiting for her. She got behind the wheel and headed down to the beach. As she passed the imposing metal gates at the entrance to Carlos' property, she shuddered. She noticed a big sign on the gate. She squinted at it, slowing down enough to read it. It was a building permit. What was he going to build now? She wondered. Probably some kind of super villain detail like a helipad or something. As long as he didn't have people flying in and out constantly, what did she care? She decided not to be nosey.

When she arrived at the beach lot, she was pleased to notice that there were very few cars there, and just a few scooters. Finding the closest spot to the beach, she parked, grabbed her market bag, and wandered down to the sand through a strand of sea grapes. As usual, there was a group of young, hip French people sitting in a group to the left of the path. These were the typical French kids who came to work on the island for six months at a time. Most of them were smoking cigarettes and drinking beer. She veered to the right, found a relatively secluded spot, and spread out her towel. It would feel good to lie in the sun a little bit and enjoy her book for a moment before going for a swim. As she sat on the towel, rummaging through her beach bag to find her book, she noticed a familiar figure walking from the direction of the parking lot. She took in the light chestnut hair glinting gold in the sun, and the sleek muscles beneath tanned skin as the man strode with a naturally athletic gait. He noticed her at the same time that she noticed him. She noticed that his expression was strangely intense for someone planning on taking a waterfront stroll. He had looked worried. Maybe even annoyed.

"Brooke!"

"Antoine. Hi. I didn't expect to see you at the beach in the middle of a workday."

"And I would have thought this beach was too local for you," he responded, smiling, and winking at her.

"Well, it is my neighborhood beach," Brooke retorted. She noticed that Antoine's eyes were now roaming over her body. She hoped he liked what he saw. But suddenly, his whole demeanor changed.

"How was the food the other night? Did it all work out?" he asked.

"It did," said Brooke. "Thank you so much. You really outdid yourself picking the best ingredients."

"So, where's your husband today?" asked Antoine, looking around.

"I told you- he went back to New York. I'm here on my own."

Had he not listened at all to what she'd said the other day?

"Oh. Honestly, I thought you would change your mind. I've heard people say that sort of thing before, that they want to stay, and then..." he made a dismissive waving gesture.

"I guess I'm different."

"Aren't you going to get bored?"

Brooke was growing annoyed, now.

"Um, hello? I told you I wanted to rent the house out and manage it, remember? You gave me the website?"

"Oh," said Antoine. "I would think you would just want to enjoy the island, not be working while you're here."

"OK..." Now Brooke was officially done with this bullshit. He might be hot, but it wasn't worth it if this was how he was going to be.

"I'm so sorry," said Antoine, shaking his head. "I'm being indiscreet. Not to mention being a jerk. It's none of my business. So...were you also serious about dinner, then? As friends?"

"As long as you stop assuming I'm a spoiled princess who is going to go running back to New York at any moment and is afraid of getting her hands dirty," said Brooke, even though she pretty much was exactly that.

She would have hoped that Antoine would have at least looked more pleased about this, but his eyes shifted towards where Carlos's house was, up on the hill.

"Cool," he said. "It was nice seeing you."

"Oh. I thought you were here for a swim."

"Yeah, I forgot I needed to do something before day's end. I'll reach out to you about that dinner."

"Great."

Brooke watched him leave, disappointed. And why the hell was she disappointed? She thought. Antoine was nothing more than a stranger to her, albeit a gorgeous one. And what was up with the whole hot and cold thing? Once he had gone out of sight, Brooke decided to go swimming. Diving into the cool turquoise water was exactly what she had needed. She felt much of the stress slide away as she glided under the surface. She should have brought her snorkeling mask, to see all the beautiful tropical fish, but she'd been preoccupied. She would remember to pack the mask next time. She swam out a bit further, relishing the feel of the water against her legs as she kicked them. It really was the perfect temperature. She had made the right decision, deciding to stay here, hadn't she? She hadn't gotten it figured all out yet, but hopefully she would manage to make a living, and manage to keep her house.

Having lost her family, and now her marriage, keeping the house felt like the only real purpose she had left. She turned and looked back towards land. Noticing how Carlos's house was perched above them. Her house, Sea Grapes, was just around the point of the peninsula, invisible from where she was, but if she swam out a bit further, she'd be able to see it. Now, though, she felt the current pulling her further out into the sea. That was too far, she decided, especially with no one watching from shore to make sure she was

OK. She kicked powerfully, struggling a little bit and panicking, as she wondered whether she would be carried out by the riptide. She forced herself to calm down and swam parallel to shore, and soon enough, noticed that the current was no longer tugging her out to sea. She breathed a sigh of relief. By the time she made it back to the beach, she was a bit out of breath, her heart beating double time. But she felt alive. She stumbled back to her towel, noticing the appreciative looks from a few of the young men from the group she'd noticed when she'd first arrived. Yes, she knew she looked OK. She made sure to maintain her figure as much as possible, to compete with the New York socialites. But she was older than any of these kids on the beach. Certainly not that much to look at, after she'd nearly drowned. Maybe it was her darker coloring that intrigued them. Most of the girls who came to work on Saint Barth seemed to be cut from the same mold. Northern French types with big blue eyes. Once she had dried off a bit, she felt herself getting antsy. She didn't have the desire to sit and read her book, as it felt like she had other fish to fry. Maybe she would go to the market, in fact, or pick up vegetables from one of the local stands. She would cook herself something nice, maybe experiment with a new recipe that she could use on her future guests. Also, she wanted to check her email to see if Ford or the other rental company had gotten back to her.

She made her way to the parking lot. As she approached her Mini Moke, something seemed off. She couldn't quite put her finger on it. And then, she noticed what it was: one of the tires was flat. Good thing she had an emergency tire hidden in the back of the vehicle. Her father had always taught her to be prepared. Since cell phone reception was not ideal all over the island, she'd often thought that having a flat tire without a replacement could mean a big setback, and a lot of time wasted. As she retrieved her tire changing kit and squatted down by the wheel, she noticed that the tire hadn't just deflated due to a screw or a nail. It looked like the it had been slashed intentionally. Who would do such a thing? Ice started to form in her veins as she realized that this was the second bizarre occurrence of the day. The blood on the gate and now the slashed tire- it was very threatening. Was somebody trying to scare her? Her mind leapt to Carlos and to his supposed goons. But she had no proof, of course. She made quick work of changing the tire, and threw the damaged one in the back, her heart beating. She just wanted to get home and have a quiet evening, and hopefully tomorrow would be a better day. She drove up the hill from the beach, and as she was about to pass Carlos's gates, she noticed a van coming down the driveway towards the street. Meat my Fish. *What a coincidence,* she thought. She had been wanting to get some fish for dinner. Maybe she could intercept him and see if Antoine had anything good for her in the van. She pulled the car up, blocking the van in.

"Hey," she said. "Surprised to see you here."

"Yeah, I needed to make a delivery," he said.

"Well, it works out well for me- Do you happen to have anything really fresh and wonderful- a single portion?" Brooke asked. "I was going to go visit your shop, but since you're here, I thought that maybe I would just ask you directly."

"It seems a shame to be cooking for one," Antoine said.

"Well, that's just my new reality," she responded. "So do you have anything?"

"I believe I have some really delicious tuna at the shop," he responded. "But it's two portions. I could bring it to you around... I don't know- 6:00 o'clock or so?"

"I suppose that's OK," Brooke said, hoping it wouldn't be too expensive, and deciding that she could freeze a portion or cook it and eat it the next day.

"Is that too late? I know it's around dinner time," Antoine said, giving her a grin. He was back to being flirtatious.

"Are you trying to invite yourself over for dinner?" Brooke asked.

"Was I being that unsubtle? What can I bring, other than the fish?"

"Throw in some wine, and you've got a deal," Brooke responded, smiling at her own boldness. "I'll make some side dishes."

"Sounds great," said Antoine. "And I know where you live. I'll see you at 6:00."

"It's a date," said Brooke, cringing internally after she said it. "I mean, it's not a date, it's a friend thing... you know what I mean," she said.

"Absolutely," said Antoine, smiling.

Chapter 14

B rooke went about the rest of her day, smiling a bit more. It was fun to have something to look forward to, even if inviting the local fish merchant was hardly a big social plan. Still, there was something about the way he carried himself with such confidence. And he was so damn good looking. It was a shame to just be friends. It wouldn't hurt to use him as a fling, to get her over the bad taste in her mouth left from Hunter. What could it hurt? She remembered that gossip was rife on the island, but who cared? Her reputation was her own. She could ruin it if she wanted to. Once she had ruined her reputation, she would have the freedom to do whatever she wanted, she reasoned. Nothing wrong with that. The worst that could happen would be that she would not get the best cuts of meat or the first choice of the fish. But that would be worth it. She didn't know why she was assuming that the fling wouldn't go well. Maybe they would get along wonderfully and would have a good time together for a month or two. And then that would be that and things would end naturally with no drama. *God, Brooke, stop thinking that way, you weirdo*, she admonished herself. She scored some lovely endive and cheese at the market. Some tomatoes that she would stuff with rice and herbs to accompany the fish. Nothing fancy, but it would be delicious.

She took a quick shower and spent more time than usual picking out her outfit. She settled for a two-piece navy-blue silk set that was casual but elegant, paired with hot pink Moroccan slippers that added a touch of color. She found some earrings in the same tones that completed the outfit. She kept checking her watch until 6:00 rolled around.

When she and Hunter had met, at some charity event or another, she couldn't be bothered to remember which one, she had been barely working at Sotheby's, in the European Art department, naturally, even though her training had been at the Cordon Bleu in Paris. Mummy had decided that she would never meet a man working in such a barbarian environment as a kitchen, surrounded by convicts and drug addicts. So off to Sotheby's she went. She had of course been vastly underpaid, but at least she had felt that she was contributing some sort of value to the world. But ever since she and Hunter had gotten together, she had been expected to become the perfect trophy wife. Hunter gave her an allowance, and she didn't have to worry about anything run-of-the-mill like grocery shopping or maintaining the house, so she spent her days shopping for the next designer outfit with which to adorn herself, for an endless string of social obligations on their calendar. Occasionally, sitting in the hairdresser's chair or in the esthetician's care, she would be still for long enough to wonder: when would she find a purpose in life again? She was ashamed that, even though her lifestyle had grown less lavish over the years, as the allowance had dwindled, it had always been enough for her to go on as before, not looking for anything more. Maybe she was somehow deficient.

The buzzer went off, alerting her that Antoine was at the gate. She pressed the button and waited for him at the door.

"Hey," said Brooke, opening the door. She looked Antoine up and down. He looked freshly showered, his wet hair curling around his ears. She could smell the aftershave on him, a mix of basil and mandarin that she found even more delicious mixed with his male musk.

"Where's the van?" she asked, looking out into the driveway.

"I thought I would spare you," he said, smiling. "I took the scooter."

Brooke waved Antoine inside the house.

"I made us a cocktail. Fresh citrus, and some fruits from my garden."

She handed him a glass.

"I like that you assumed I would be on time," said Antoine.

"Well, I noticed last time that you weren't on Caribbean time like everyone else," Brooke laughed.

She clinked her glass against his. He took a sip.

"You really do have a knack for this stuff," he said looking at her, surprised.

"I don't know what part of Cordon Bleu you didn't understand?" Brooke said, laughing. "Speaking of food stuff, what in the world made you decide to become a meat and fish dealer, on this island of all things? And what in the world possessed you to call it what you did?"

"Oh, you should have seen what I was going to have as a tag line," said Antoine.

"Don't tell me," said Brooke.

"You can't beat my meat," they both said at the same time. A laugh escaped Brooke's lips.

"I can't believe I said that out loud, but then again, so did you."

"True," he said. "Honestly, that just boils down to pure stubbornness. When I was starting my company, everybody laughed at me and said I couldn't possibly... So of course, that meant I had to."

"All right, fair enough. But rewind...why meat and fish purveyor?"

"Well, I started off working in wine in France. With family. So, this seemed like the next logical step," he said evasively.

"Yeah, super logical," said Brooke.

"Actually, I have a family history here," said Antoine.

"You do?" Brooke exclaimed. "So do I!"

"Really?" asked Antoine, considering her. "Not to generalize, but you don't look like the typical Breton sailor girl..."

"I know," said Brooke. "I'm Tunisian on my mother's side, but my dad's side has French ancestry. There are some graves in the cemetery that have our family names on them."

"Me, too," said Antoine. "I wonder if we're related."

God, I hope not, thought Brooke. Then she mentally rebuked herself. She was silly. What did it matter? It wasn't like she was going to marry this guy. And if they were related at all, it was surely distantly enough to make no difference for an affair.

"So maybe you are a local after all," said Antoine.

"OK, back to the meat and fish." Brooke could be tenacious, especially when she sensed that someone was being evasive.

"I was looking for what I could do to really be part of the fabric of this island. And well, I went to work for someone who taught me a lot."

"Mr. Vincent?" "You knew Mr. Vincent?"

"Best cod fritters ever," said Brooke, nodding.

"Exactly," said Antoine. "So, he expected me to be his successor, and then I thought I would, you know, improve on it, add my own twist. So, I expanded into meats as well, and well, I got an investor."

"And that's how you bought your fancy van and opened the shop?"

"Pretty much," said Antoine, shrugging.

"Well, are you happy?" Brooke asked. It was a bit of a non-sequitur, sure, but she was curious. There was something about Antoine. Something more complex.

"Sometimes," Antoine admitted. "Sometimes I wonder why I made this decision to be on this godforsaken island. It's a rock in the middle of nowhere."

"You're funny. Most people would call it paradise."

"Well, paradise has a funny way of turning to into hell, if the wrong people are there," said Antoine.

"Fair enough," Brooke responded. She'd decided not to pry, after all. "So, what's it like, having relationships and friendships on this island?"

It was as if a thundercloud had passed over Antoine's handsome face, but he soon returned to a pleasant expression.

"Friendships are interesting. People tend not to stay for so long, and you learn not to get too attached. As for romantic relationships, well, I guess you could say there's a lot of distraction. Some of the guys make it a sport to bed as many tourists as possible. I find it gets old."

"How about long-term relationships- amongst locals?"

"Well, personally, I haven't really had a serious relationship since I left France," said Antoine.

"Have you ever been married?" Brooke hoped he wouldn't mind that she was peppering him with questions.

"Almost," said Antoine, "but she ended up leaving me after... she ended up leaving me. And I can't blame her. We're still friendly enough. She's got kids now. They call me Uncle Antoine when I go back to visit, which I find weird. But anyway, that's the closest I ever came."

"Ah," said Brooke.

"Am I allowed to ask you questions now?" asked Antoine.

"I guess it's only fair," said Brooke. She steeled herself, bracing for the inevitable questions about the nature of her relationship with Hunter...

"So...you're... happily married?" asked Antoine, right out of the gate.

Brooke considered him. Surely, something she said to the fish and meat purveyor on Saint Barth was not going to get back to Hunter's investors' ears. But you never did know.

"Well, things aren't that great, in case you couldn't guess..." said Brooke carefully. "I guess you would say we are taking a break."

"Really," said Antoine, eyeing her suspiciously, she thought. Brooke shrugged. She didn't owe him any explanations, did she?

"So, you don't know how long you'll stay?" asked Antoine.

"I'm planning on staying here for the long run, I think. How about you?" she asked.

"Well, I'm kind of all in now," said Antoine. "So, I don't have much of a choice in the matter. I guess I'll make the best of it. I keep feeling that maybe there's something more, though. You know what I mean?"

"Yes, I do know what you mean," said Brooke. She was silent for a moment. She knew what he meant. But she didn't know what to do about it.

"Look, the sun is setting," said Antoine.

They stepped outside, looking towards a spectacular sunset.

"You do have a glorious view here," said Antoine. "It's quite a luxury to have a home like this one. Your husband must be very wealthy. Sorry- I know that's an indiscreet thing to say, but then again, everyone here is wealthy."

"Well, it's a long and complicated story, but actually, the house is mine," said Brooke. Too bad for Hunter. She had spent all the money from her parents on it and now that she was in a position where she was forced to stand on her own 2 feet, and that the house was everything she had, she would definitely claim it.

"This house is everything I have," she said. "So don't go thinking I'm some kind of spoiled rich girl, because I'm not...at least not right now."

"Uh," said Antoine. "Nathalie said."

"Nathalie said what?" asked Brooke. She was shocked that Nathalie would talk behind her back like that.

"She mentioned that you'd have a hard time paying, and I just want you to know that..."

"I'll tell you if I can't afford something," Brooke snapped.

"No, it's not that," said Antoine. "I was going to say, I can give you an advance if necessary- whatever you need. You're a local. We help each other."

"I hope it won't come to that," said Brooke. She hated the idea of needing favors. She looked at him, then. He looked back, and they had another one of those awkward moments where he looked into her eyes, and she couldn't look away. Finally, she looked away first, breaking the spell before she did something silly. The sun had just disappeared below the horizon line.

"Why don't we go in, and you can watch me cook?"

"I would love that," said Antoine.

He placed his hand on the small of her back as they walked towards the house. She shivered, and he quickly took his hand away. That whole friendship thing was of course the right thing to do, but... What wouldn't she give for that hand of his to wander just a little bit? She thought again of the fantasy she'd had the first night on the island. What could it hurt? Well, maybe everything, was the answer to *that* question.

"Let me go get the fish. I've got it in a cooler on the scooter," said Antoine.

He headed back outside while Brooke chopped vegetables into a julienne.

"Here are the tuna steaks," said Antoine. "They're fresh, and I made sure to keep them at the right temperature."

"You angel," said Brooke. "Here, I made you some baba ghanoush* with crostini."

"Delicious," said Antoine. "Not as oily as the ones I've had before. You made it? I thought that was the sort of thing one just buys in a store."

"I have secret shortcut. Maybe if you're good, I'll tell you sometime," Brooke teased.

She tried not to focus on the fact that Antoine was watching her intently as she created an aromatic miso glaze* and rubbed it into the tuna steaks.

"I would grill these outside, but I think it'll be tastier if we sauté them in a pan," said Brooke. "With a bit of sesame oil."

"Sounds amazing," said Antoine, watching her as she kept chopping vegetables. "You've got some impressive knife skills, there."

"Best in my class," said Brooke.

"I'm impressed," said Antoine. "So, what do you like to prepare most?"

"I don't know. It depends on the day. I just like using ingredients in surprising ways. Some of the vegetables that you brought me the other day were so fresh, so delicious, that it really inspired me. Look, I picked up some endive from the market. What do you think?"

"Those look excellent," said Antoine. "Local?"

"Yes," said Brooke. "Here, taste."

She slipped a piece of endive with Roquefort cheese and a walnut on it into his mouth, and immediately blushed at the intimacy of the gesture.

"Sorry, I'm just so used to feeding people, including my friends... it's a weird trait of mine."

"I liked it," said Antoine, giving her that look again. The one that friends did not give each other.

In fact, this friendship thing really was going to be a challenge, Brooke decided. She focused on finishing her preparations as Antoine watched, peppering her with questions about food, which was easier than answering questions about her relationship. This was nice. It was easy. It felt good. She hoped that this wouldn't be the last dinner with Antoine, but she also realized that she needed to make some more friends, especially if she planned on ruining this friendship with a fling. Would she dare? She wondered. They sat down to dinner at the table outside, the tree frogs belting out their chorus, and Antoine progressively grew more serious.

"You asked if I plan on staying here," he said. "I mean, I really do love this island. I feel like I do belong here, but again...there's something, you know, something more... there's a lot of inequality here. The expenses..."

"Yes, I definitely noticed that everything is so expensive," Brooke agreed. "I wish... I don't know... I wish that there was something to support locals."

"Yes, that's what I was thinking too," said Antoine. "By the way, has there been any progress on your plan to cook or to rent the house out? I know it's only been a couple days but..."

"Funny you should ask. I just checked, and that website you gave me- it actually yielded a bite. I think I might have rented the house out for a week, just a few days from now. I can't believe it. I have so much to do."

"You did?" asked Antoine. "Who are the renters?"

"I don't know, some Argentines," said Brooke. "I hope they'll be nice."

"Yes, well, hopefully you'll blow them away with your cooking as well, right? Who's going to be managing the house while they're here?"

"I will be," said Brooke. "I'm going to be staying downstairs in Nathalie's old suite."

"Oh," said Antoine, looking surprised. "I would have thought you would have stayed in some more glamorous spot."

"As I said, I want to stand on my own two feet," said Brooke.

As she said it, she worried that she wouldn't be able to cut it, and again felt like a jerk for finding it normal that Nathalie would have been fine with that life, if she was not.

"Well," said Antoine, after a while. "I suppose I need to go. I have an early morning."

"All right," said Brooke regretfully. "I'll walk you to the door."

"Do you want me to help you with the dishes?" asked Antoine.

"It's just two of us," said Brooke. "It'll take me seconds. It's actually kind of a meditation for me, cleaning up after dinner."

"Well, thank you so much. I hope we'll do this again," said Antoine. "And don't forget to ping me if you need anything."

"Thank you. I will," said Brooke, standing by the door awkwardly.

Was he going to give her a hug? A peck on the cheek? Antoine leaned in and... it was the peck on the cheek. Well, a bit more than a peck. He did linger. But not nearly long enough.

Brooke went back to her empty kitchen, dejected, and started to do did the dishes alone. She'd lied. She didn't like doing the dishes alone, at all.

Chapter 15

B rooke's eyes flew open, and she sat straight up. She'd had a dream that someone had offered to hire her as a private chef after she'd scrambled to post a description of her work on a popular seasonal job board for the island. She threw her shutters and curtains open, noting that it was another beautiful day on the island, and logged into the website. Nothing. It had just been wishful thinking. Her post was still desperately languishing, ignored, and she had no messages in her inbox. What was she going to do? Thank goodness for the house rental, but it wasn't enough. She circled back and checked on her disastrous attempt at a website. It looked so amateur. Well, it was better than nothing. She'd included pictures of a few of the dishes she had prepared in the past, and some positive upbeat messaging. She shouldn't be so hard on herself. She was just starting out. The problem was, she didn't have the luxury of starting slow. Even though she was sorely tempted to go back to bed and try to sleep the sadness away, she knew she had to maintain a regular, productive schedule. She threw on a light dressing gown and headed down to the kitchen.

Just as she was pouring herself a coffee, the phone rang. Again, she permitted her heart to do a little flip. Maybe this was someone calling her to offer her a job. But no such luck. Hunter's name was on the caller ID.

"Hey," she said half-heartedly. She really didn't want to speak to him, but she had sent him a text asking for at least something to survive on until a divorce settlement could be reached.

"So how much can you send me?" she asked without preamble.

"Nice to talk to you too. How are you?" said Hunter.

"Come on. I think we're past the pleasantries," she said. "How much?"

"That's the issue," said Hunter. "Honestly, right now I'm having a liquidity issue."

"Liquidity issue?"

"As in, I have zero cash, Brooke. I don't know how many times I have to say this to you, but there's nothing left."

Brooke froze, looking around her perfect house, fear of losing this, too, flooding her. How was it possible there was nothing left?

"Surely there's something. You can go look in one of the retirement accounts or something."

Hunter was silent on the other end of the line.

"What do I need to say so that you finally understand?" he asked.

"Well, then you're going to have to start liquidating some assets," said Brooke. "Didn't we have that wine collection in London? You could sell that."

"I sold that six months ago," said Hunter.

That was like a punch in the gut to Brooke. Six months ago, she had still thought they were getting along just fine. She thought back. Where was she six months ago? Oh, yeah. She'd been on that yoga retreat in Costa Rica, and she'd been working on the benefit at the library. There had been no hint that anything was amiss. Hunter had been acting relatively normal. They'd been getting along. True, she'd had a hunch that maybe he was doing something behind her back, but it hadn't been strong enough or compelling enough for her to act on it, and she had swept it under the rug. Now that she thought of it, she was a bit to blame for her situation. By not deciding to act, she had essentially decided on inaction, which had its own set of unsavory consequences.

"Well then, sell something," she told Hunter, her teeth gritted. She was growing a bit desperate. "Sell your watches."

"What about you, Brooke, why don't *you* sell something?" asked Hunter. Brooke stopped breathing for a moment. That wasn't fair. He couldn't ask her to do that, she thought. But then again, there was no way she could force him to do anything at all from where she was standing. She was now just starting to see the whole picture of how dire her situation really was. And being knocked down so hard, from such heights, made it all the harder to get herself back on her feet. No matter if there was money or not, if Hunter didn't want to put anything in her account, he wouldn't. Until she could afford a lawyer and a forensic accountant, her only solution lay in being civil and hoping that his situation changed enough to understand that he at least owed her something for these years of partnership. Yes, she could have been making money of her own, but this whole time, she'd been thinking that she was going to have kids and Hunter had been more than quite content with having her as a homemaker. And she'd been damn good at being a homemaker.

"Anyway," said Hunter, "I sold most of my watches already, and I don't know how to sell furniture or decor. I'm sure we'll lose money on it. If I'm forced to sell the apartment, I'm going to probably sell it furnished."

"Then do that," said Brooke.

"That's the last resort. Our main residence. And it's not like we have much equity in that house."

"Why the fuck didn't you tell me what was going on?" Brooke asked.

"Language," said Hunter.

"Fuck you, Hunter," Brooke seethed. "Why didn't you say something?"

"Because you wouldn't have understood."

"How dumb do you think I am?"

"I mean, you never cared about those things."

"Well, I care about fucking surviving," Brooke spat. "Listen, I've got to go."

She hung up and put her phone face down on the counter. She raised her coffee cup to her lips, and put that down, too. She couldn't even stomach the black coffee. It felt like her stomach was full of roiling acid. Bile rose in her throat. Just in time, she got herself over to the sink, and threw up into it. She stuck her head under the faucet and gulped at the lukewarm water. If she hadn't understood intellectually what was going on, her body had certainly figured it out. Now, her mind was racing, and tears built up in her eyes. What would she do? She literally had no money in her account. And she needed to get the house ready to rent it out. And she needed to keep promoting her services, but also, she needed to eat. She had some canned things and some frozen things left, but that wouldn't last her long. She couldn't survive by fishing and stealing fruit, could she? This was ridiculous. There were electrical bills to pay, water bills. And she was already at the end of her rope after only a couple days alone here. It was laughable how, just a few days ago, she had thought she would spend her month here reading and doing yoga. Funny how, seen from the outside, she was a rich bitch, but in reality, she was more destitute than anyone she'd ever met at this very moment. Sure, she could sell the house, but there was no way that she would let go of this piece of what her parents had built for her, and what represented the one thing she had achieved in ten years, the last shred of happiness she could hope for. She thought back to how happy her mom had looked when Brooke had told her about the property she had found on one of her trips, how her mom had convinced her father to give her most of the money from her trust earlier rather than later, and how proud she had been when her parents had visited. She saw her dad's face in her mind's eye, his exact expression as he nodded approvingly. They had expressed their dream of coming here for long visits to get to know the grandchildren they had hoped were coming soon. That visit to Sea Grapes had been the last time Brooke had seen her parents.

Feeling woozy, she hustled down the hall to the office. She'd told Hunter to sell his watches, and what was good for the goose was good for the gander. *Or vice versa, whatever.* She pawed through the contents of the safe. Thank goodness Hunter hadn't been so dishonest as to take anything from there. The jewelry she had here was all accounted for, but there wasn't much. Now she regretted leaving some of the good stuff she had in the safe in New York. She was afraid to ask Hunter if he'd pawned that off, too. If he hadn't yet, it might be better not to give him the idea. How differently she would have packed if she'd known that she was planning on staying here for the long term instead of just for a month of vacation.

As she went through the safe, her eyes went to what glinted at her wrist. Her gold Cartier Tank Française. Yes, she had considered pawning it off when she'd first found out about the financial situation. But she had then cast that idea aside, knowing that the watch meant much more to her sentimentally that what it would fetch at pawn. How ridiculously little it would mean when it came to surviving month to month. But now, she considered that it was also the most valuable commodity she had here. Now, she needed to survive. She wasn't going to wait until the last of the food disappeared from the freezer and the pantry to do this. The sooner she knew how much she could get for the watch, the sooner she could make herself a budget, and understand what else she was going to need to do. Even if she took a job as a receptionist at a hotel or at a restaurant, which by the way, she was sure was not available for this season, that wouldn't be enough to keep the house running. For now, her plan to live downstairs and become Nathalie for a time while renting out the house and cooking for house guests was her best bet. It was more money than working an hourly job, and it would hopefully allow her more time and freedom to explore a long-term career. But other than the Argentines, would anyone else rent her house so late in the season? She logged back into her computer and opened her email, hoping against hope that there would be some chef job listed. But there wasn't. And Ford hadn't gotten back to her. Just then, an email came in from Hunter. Funny, he was more the texting type. But he was forwarding a website. *Villa Azul rentals*, said the subject line. Below that, a terse message:

"Hey, just in case if you need to rent the house or something. This is a new rental agency for the island. I think they're aggressively looking for houses. And from what I hear, they're holding a few clients who tend to go on last minute vacations. H."

Weird. The name sounded familiar. Brooke clicked on the link for the website.

Duh. It was the site she'd already signed up on. What a coincidence. She wondered where Hunter had heard about it. Was it New York based? What would her New York friends think if they saw her house listing? Then again, what did she care about her so-called New York friends? She wasn't in any situation to be worrying about what others thought of her right now. She just needed to get back on her feet. It was the fastest way to make money, she thought. Might as well ping the owners of the site and remind them that she was actively looking for more renters. She'd often ascribed to the squeaky wheel theory, which had made her quite successful at fundraising- for others, at least. She navigated to the *contact us* section and sent off an email:

"*To whom it may concern: I set up my account a few days ago, and I'm pleased to find that I already have one week-long rental signed up. I know it's a bit late in the season to be thinking about this, but I really would love to accommodate any additional last-minute renters, even if it's shorter term. Also, can we add to my listing that I am a classically trained chef and can cook for renters or for any of the other houses in your Saint Barth portfolio? Thank you!*"

She knew the email reeked of desperation, but so what? She hit send.

Time to get dressed. She needed to go find a pawn shop.

A few minutes later, she was getting into the Mini Moke and starting to edge down the driveway when she noticed with a start that the gate was already open. Once she had gone through, she clicked the remote control to close it. Nothing happened. *Crap*. One more thing to deal with. Later. Driving down the road, she wondered whether she should rent out the Land Rover, as well. It was a gas guzzler. And it reminded her of Hunter, even if she'd paid for it. The Mini Moke would be more reasonable for her every day unless it was pouring down rain. But if she had guests at the house, she reasoned, she would need a vehicle that had a large capacity. And renting the Land Rover out might mean higher insurance premiums, which she hadn't even thought of. *Ugh*.

She drove down the streets of downtown Gustavia until she finally saw it- a small sign that she had ignored most of the times she had passed it, but which had remained in her subconscious. *Pawn shop*.

Tears in her eyes, she parked the car and slowly made her way towards the store. As she opened the door, a bell rang loudly, startling her. A man with thinning artificially black hair looked up from the counter. In the glass display case in front of him were gaudy jewels, diamond watches, thick gold chains, and even a crystal-encrusted gun. Brooke knew instinctively that this man wouldn't give her the fair value of the watch. "Can I help you?" asked the man in heavily accented English. Just the fact that he assumed Brooke was American at first glance struck a nerve. "I'm sorry," said Brooke. "I don't think I'm in the right place."

She escaped out the door, her mind racing. Maybe Cartier would take the watch. They, at least, might give her a fair price. She wavered. Might as well shop around. She went back into the pawn shop.

"Ah! Was this the right place, after all?" The man's tone was mocking.

"How much would you give me for this watch?" Brooke asked, reluctantly taking the watch off her wrist, and holding it up.

"Let me see."

The man took out a loupe and examined the watch, turning it and shining his light on it.

"It's authentic," said Brooke.

"Yes, sure. That's what they all say," said the man.

"How many of these watches do you see?" asked Brooke, dubious.

"You'd be surprised. Do you know how many women get left behind here? They come with these guys on yachts and then the guys dump them, and they need to get off the island somehow."

He smiled, and Brooke noticed his twisted, yellowed teeth. She shuddered. She'd become one of these women left behind on the island with no means, hadn't she? She'd always been so judgmental of the boat bitches. And now she wasn't much better.

"I'll give you 9000 for it," the man decreed.

"€9000?" Brooke sputtered. "That watch cost at least $25,000!"

The man shrugged. Brooke snatched the watch back from him.

"I'll let you know," she said. "I'll be back."

"Don't wait too long. The value might fluctuate. Not in your favor."

Brooke left the pawn shop, fuming and mortified all at once. Cartier was just a block across and around the corner, but it might as well have been a different world. Brooke composed herself, took a deep breath, and rang the doorbell, waiting for one of the saleswomen to push the heavy looking glass door open for her. Immediately, Brooke felt the air conditioning hit her in the face and send goosebumps down her sweaty back.

"Hi," she said. "I have a Cartier Tank Française with diamonds, and I was thinking of reselling it. How much could you give me for it?"

The woman, who had by now retreated behind the counter, scrunched her nose.

"We don't sell used things," she said. "Try the pawn shop."

She didn't come out and say it, but her expression clearly communicated that she believed Brooke to be one of the yacht girls. Shame burned on Brooke's cheeks. She stumbled out of the store, trying but failing to not bring up the memory of the time she and Hunter had come in to buy matching Love bracelets. How she'd felt that she deserved it. How she'd not stopped to think how much money they cost. Hunter hadn't worn his Love bracelet in years. It was probably sitting in the safe in New York, and hers was firmly bolted to her wrist, or else she would have pawned that, too. She walked slowly back to the pawn shop, feeling desperate and bereft. She pushed the door to the pawn shop again. The heavy, stale air a shocking contrast to the rarefied atmosphere inside the Cartier store.

"You're back," said the man. "*Quelle surprise.*"

His expression was predatory.

"Listen," Brooke said. "I know this watch is worth at least 25,000 for resale."

"Sure," said the pawnbroker. "But you're not doing resale, you're selling it to me. And it's worth however much I'm willing to pay for it. Nine thousand Euros."

Brooke thought for a moment. 9000 Euros. It wasn't a lot, but it would be enough, if she barely spent anything, to at least keep going for just a little bit, as long as there weren't any unforeseen expenses.

"Fine," she said, dangling the watch in front of him, reluctant to let it go. The man snatched it up and she noticed his yellowed fingernails.

"Just give me a moment."

He went back to a safe and counted out some bills.

"There you go. €9000. Have a great day. I'll see you soon."

Like hell, you will, thought Brooke. She hoped it was true that she wouldn't have to be back.

"Wait," she said, turning back around in front of the door. "Can I buy this back, if I get the funds before it sells?"

"Sure. For you, it'll be $12,000. But if I were you, I would hurry. These watches are awfully popular."

Brooke stumbled past the Mini Moke and headed to the bank on foot. She would deposit this money and make damn sure she spent as little of it as possible. All the utilities at the house were already linked to this account, though, so a significant portion would be evaporating. She had a stomachache coming out of the bank with just €200 for incidentals in her pocket. Feeling like she was going to cry, Brooke sat down in the car. And then, her phone pinged. It was an alert from Villa Azul rentals. *Thank you for contacting us. We indeed have other clients looking for a special house*, said the message. *The reason we didn't match you before is that their budget is slightly lower than what you were asking for. It's a French family, scheduled for just after your other rental.*

How much? Brooke wrote back.

The response came back quickly. Brooke considered the sum. It was lower than she'd hoped, but better than nothing.

I'll take it, she wrote. *Please let me know next steps.*

Check your account. It will all be on the website, came the reply.

Her phone pinged again. It was Antoine.

Thank you for dinner last night. I had a great time, he wrote.

I should thank you for dinner, Brooke responded. *After all, you provided most of it.*

Hey, this is a bit last minute, but a few of us are getting together for drinks at Bar de L'Oubli. Want to join?

Sure, Brooke wrote back. Despite her heartache, she now had a smile on her face.

She had never been to that bar. It had always struck her as a local's joint. Well, she was a local now, she reminded herself.

Chapter 16

B rooke finally found a parking spot and was happy that her Mini
Moke was so compact. Downtown Gustavia was chaos that
evening. She had hesitated to join Antoine after initially accepting
his invitation. But then, she'd decided that she couldn't be alone
forever. She had to become a local on this island and start getting to
know more people. Not the types of people they had known when
they were the wealthy New York visitors, *Americains*, as she knew the
Saint Barth locals called most people who had homes here but were
not French. There were other categories of people who had real lives,
and for whom this island was home, she had found out, thanks to
recent research. Not just the *Metros*, most of whom came from
France for six months or six decades but were never seen as true
locals. There were also the *Portuguese*, and the *Saint Barth*, who
considered themselves natives, because some had family roots going
back centuries. Brooke was technically a hybrid. She worried that any
of these groups would exclude her, but the fact that Antoine had
invited her was a good sign.

She grabbed her keys and stuffed them into her bag, straightened
up her skirt and top, which she had spent entirely too much time
choosing, trying to strike the right balance between casual and cute,
and headed down the street, to the bar on the corner. She had
noticed this bar quite a few times on previous trips, but Hunter had
never expressed any interest in trying it out, since it was so obviously
a local joint. There were none of the elegant decorative touches that
would attract the yachting and private jet crowd. As she looked
inside, sweeping the room with her eyes to locate Antoine, Brooke
noticed that the clientele seemed to skew younger, with a few old

salty dogs peppered in. Soon, she noticed Antoine, and they locked eyes. She tore her gaze away to notice that he was holding court with a group of people. She checked to see if the blonde was there. Thankfully, she was not. She hadn't dared ask yesterday, and he had not brought it up, but maybe, despite appearances, he wasn't dating her after all. Brooke noticed a friendly looking Creole man and a few artistic looking types. Most of them were drinking beer.

She made her way over to the group, anxiety in the pit of her stomach. What would these people think of her? Antoine stood up to greet her and gestured to a spot next to him.

"Everyone, this is Brooke- she's our newest resident."

"How long are you planning on staying?" asked a slim brunette who didn't bother to provide her name.

"Six months seems to be the maximum for most people," said a friendly-looking man with a grizzled beard. "And then there are the crazy ones like us, who are maybe lifers, but maybe not. I'm Georges by the way."

"Hi, Georges. Nice to meet you," said Brooke.

"Georges works at the harbor," said Antoine. "He's the one who decides where all the rich people get to park their yachts. A lot of them like to bribe him with champagne. So, if you want a good bottle, you know where to go."

"That's good to know," said Brooke, smiling.

"What do you want to drink?" Antoine asked as a waitress approached. She was young and pretty, and obviously knew the whole group.

"Patricia," said Antoine, "This is Brooke- she's a local, for now."

Brooke ordered a glass of white wine and sat there listening to the conversations playing out across the group as they discussed the latest gossip on the island. Which yachts had come in, who had moved away. Which houses were rented out, and which were not.

"Brooke has a house for rent," said Antoine. "It's very nice. I've delivered fish there."

Brooke noticed how he was stressing the professional nature of his visit and omitting the part where he had come over for dinner. *Fair enough.*

"In fact, I just got a second rental," said Brooke.

"You did?" asked Antoine, looking surprised. "That's lucky."

"Yeah. But if you know of anyone who's looking to rent a house..."

"Which house is it?" asked a short haired blonde woman who Brooke had not been introduced to yet.

"Sea Grapes."

A few people in the group tittered.

"What?" asked Brooke.

"You mean, if we know anyone who's got the budget to rent that kind of house," said Georges.

Brooke decided that she didn't like him as much as she initially thought she had.

"You never know," said Brooke. "I might be willing to go lower than you think on the budget."

"Don't tell that to Carlos. Seems like he's got his eye on it. You don't want to let him know you're desperate," said Georges, winking and taking a sip of his beer.

Brooke tried to make friendly conversation throughout the evening, but no one in the group, other than Antoine, really stood out to her as someone she would want to befriend, or someone that she had much in common with. But that was a feeling she was going to have to disabuse herself of. She was like these people now- she wasn't a visitor. Now, however, she was starting to truly sense the divide, and it worried her. The dream of spending time in St. Barth was already starting to crumble, replaced with the harsh realities.

She got up to go to the restroom, which, unlike the restrooms at Nikki Beach, or Gypsea, or any of the other places she was accustomed to, were filthy and utilitarian. As she came back, she caught one of Antoine's friends speaking to him in French. She was quite proficient at French, and she caught the tail end of what he was saying.

She's not your usual type, is she?

"She's just a friend," Antoine said, before noticing Brooke coming back to the table.

She smiled, despite the pinching sensation in her heart.

"So, are you going to cook for the people who rent the house? Antoine was telling us you're an amazing cook," said the slim brunette woman, who had eventually introduced herself as Helene. Helene was apparently an artist and a masseuse.

"Yes, I'm hoping to- it makes me more money if they choose to have meals at the house. I don't know what to expect in terms of whether they want to go out or have me cook for them. But I've been putting together some recipes that will be appropriate. And I happen to know the best meat and fish supplier on the island."

"Oh, definitely," said Helene. "We're all so proud of him. I think that no one really realized he would make it work."

Brooke looked around and saw several people nodding. This made her like them better, that they supported their friend.

"Not everybody is proud of what he's done, though," said Helene, her voice lowered so that only Brooke could hear her.

"What do you mean?" asked Brooke.

"Well..." Just then, Brooke caught Helene's boyfriend Emile giving her a warning look. "Oh nothing, it's just gossip," said Helene, as she leaned back and took a sip of her drink.

"I'm hungry," Antoine said abruptly, turning to Brooke. "Do you want to go grab a burger? I have to turn in early. I have an early morning tomorrow."

"So do I," said Brooke. "I think I'll just make something at home."

"All right," said Antoine. "I'll walk you out."

She couldn't tell in the darkness of the bar whether he was disappointed or not.

They said their goodbyes to the group and left the music and brouhaha of the bar behind. They walked down the streets, towards where Brooke had parked. Now, without all the noise, the light, and the energy from the others, which had built a wall between them at the bar, Brooke started to feel the same attraction she had noticed on the other occasions she had been with Antoine.

"I heard Georges telling you that he can help out with excursions for your visitors," said Antoine.

"Yeah, that would be great," said Brooke. "I need any competitive advantage I can get."

"It might take a little while to start up, but your house is beautiful, and you're an incredible cook. You should have no trouble finding cooking jobs eventually. Just keep trying."

"Well, for now, it was a lucky break that you gave me the link to that rental website," said Brooke. "And I pawned the watch my parents gave me, but hopefully I can get it back. I never thought I would have to do something like that."

"Oh...," said Antoine. To his credit, he looked appropriately sorry for her. But then, he seemed eager to change the subject.

"If you want to try out any more of your recipes, just to make sure they work for your visitors, I can make myself available."

"That could be arranged," said Brooke.

They were walking more slowly now, as if they both wanted to prolong the evening.

"Are you sure you don't want to have a bite with me?" asked Antoine.

He looked into her eyes, and she felt another jolt of attraction. She was embarrassed, though, because she realized that half of the intensity of that reaction was because of the fantasies that she'd had, and that he had no idea about. In fact, he seemed to have firmly friend-zoned her.

"I would love to take a raincheck, if that's okay with you."

As she said it, she suddenly felt a crushing exhaustion, and a sense of despair. She was so tired already. She'd been crazy thinking that she could make a go of this living alone thing. Especially with no support, especially being such an outsider on this island. In New York, she had thought she knew her place, and who she was, but now, without all the trappings of that, she felt disconnected.

"I really appreciate your inviting me to meet your friends," she said, "even if I don't think they liked me very much."

"Oh, you'll grow on them," said Antoine. "They'll see that you're not the spoiled brat that they probably think you are right now, and as they see you're serious about staying..."

"Why would they assume I'm a brat?"

"You just have to realize that there's a divide between the vacationers and the locals. And it's hard to bridge it. Some people do it, though, don't worry. It just takes time. If you stay around long enough."

"You keep alluding to your belief that I'll be leaving soon. This is where I'm going to be. I've chosen to make a go of it."

"You say that. But I've seen it happen too many times before. People say they're staying. And then they go running back to wherever they're from. The island does that to you. It's beautiful. But there's something about it that chews people up and spits them out."

"Well, I'm different," said Brooke.

They had arrived at her Mini Moke. She discreetly checked to make sure the tires were still intact, which reminded her.

"Hey, by the way, I see that the rumor about Carlos wanting to buy my house is officially all over the island."

Antoine's sensual lips formed a straight line, but then quickly went back to normal.

"Just steer clear of him. I'm sure he'll ease up, once he understands that you have no intention of selling."

"But you know him. You deliver things to him. You would tell me if you heard something, wouldn't you?"

"I supply most of the large houses on the island, including yours, now. I've learned not to gossip."

"That's a shame. What are you good for then?" asked Brooke in a teasing tone, even though she kind of meant it.

"He's just another rich guy," said Antoine.

"Okay," said Brooke. Her annoyance doused out the spark of attraction that had been forming during their walk.

"So, when do your first visitors come?" asked Antoine.

"Sunday afternoon."

"Tomorrow?"

"Oh. Yikes. Yeah."

"Okay, well, I'm sure you're going to be busy getting ready for them. But if you need anything, text me. You can let me know your menus when you have them."

"Yeah, I'm just working out the financials."

"Looks like you shouldn't have too much trouble with your finances," said Antoine. "Your husband seems to be pretty wealthy."

"I told you," said Brooke. "We're on a break. I pawned the watch my parents gave me, for God's sake. You think I did that for fun?"

"That's nice. But I've heard it before. I don't mess with married women. This evening out was just friendly," said Antoine, coldly, she thought.

"Why do you feel the need to keep telling me that?" asked Brooke.

She thought she had seen the way he looked at her; she'd been hoping that he reciprocated her attraction, at least even if it was just for her self-image.

"Because..." Antoine began.

She looked back up at him. No, she hadn't imagined that she saw his gaze lingering on her, moving down her body to where her shirt opened between her breasts.

"Listen, I'll be here for you- as a friend," said Antoine. "Nothing more. I don't want there to be any mixed messages."

"Got it," said Brooke. "No mixed messages. Good night."

She went up on her tiptoes and gave Antoine two friendly, almost barely lingering, kisses on the cheek. It wasn't her fault that her breasts brushed against his chest. It wasn't her fault that she looked into his eyes then and noticed him wanting her. Clearly, Antoine didn't know her. She was a girl who relished a challenge, and he had just declared open season, in her opinion. This would be fun. The one bright spot in her so far disastrous time on St Barth. She got into her car and turned the key in the ignition, then drove away, checking in the rear-view mirror to make sure that Antoine was watching her go. He was. *Good.*

Chapter 17

B rooke navigated the Mini Moke up the steep incline leading to her driveway, white knuckling it as the occasional car sped by, blinding her, and then leaving her in the dark. Now, she was more than a little annoyed with how the evening with Antoine had gone down. How dare he be so categorical and judgmental? Everyone was simply trying to do their best.

Brooke slowed down and pulled into the driveway, unhappy that the gate was still stuck in the open position. Hunter had only been away for a few days, and already, things were falling apart. How would she ever deal with all this stuff alone? Especially as she was painfully aware of the paltry amount of cash she had sitting in her bank account and in the safe. Sure, she had one or two more things she could sell, if it came to that, but her mother had always taught her to never sell the jewelry. *You think you're in dire straits*, her mother used to say, *but it can always get worse*. She peered at the Cartier love bracelet glinting at her wrist. It wasn't like she hadn't thought of selling it already, when she had started to suspect that Hunter was cheating on her. But she would have been able to get $4000 stateside. Probably barely half that here. Maybe she would call her old friend Grace, have her ask Hunter for access to the safe in their New York apartment, and have her sell some stuff for a commission. Grace was trustworthy, and always happy to make an extra buck. Brooke had always felt bad for Grace, when she was put on an allowance by her husband, but now, she realized that Grace probably felt sorry for her. *How the mighty have fallen*. She wished she had been a bit more gracious in the past, instead of thinking she was so untouchable.

She turned the car off and grabbed the keys, slipping them into her purse. Normally, she would have been able to leave the keys in the car, with the gate safely closed. But no more. While her bag was open, she rummaged through for her house keys. She had forgotten to turn the lights on in anticipation of her return, and now she felt stupid, feeling her way along the exterior wall to the front door. She listened for anything suspicious, any noise that might alert her to a trespasser, but the sound of the tree frogs drowned everything out. She had always loved that sound, had always found it romantic, until now, when she found herself alone and potentially unsafe. She finally made it to the door, feeling for the lock, hoping not to scratch the wood surface with the key. The moonlight was barely sufficient to see anything, but eventually she got the door open. A rush of air-conditioned air flooded out, chilling her to the bone in an instant. She made a mental note to turn off the AC until guests arrived. It was a needless expense. Feeling her way to the console table, she finally turned on a table lamp and breathed a sigh of relief as the yellow light illuminated the room. After looking around cautiously, to make sure she would not be locking an intruder in with her, she closed and locked the door.

There was something wrong, she realized, as she looked around the room. She couldn't put her finger on it. But something was amiss. She felt like someone had been here. Maybe someone who was still here. Her heart hammering in her chest, she rushed into the office and checked the cabinet with the safe in it. That, at least, seemed untouched. Just to be sure, she quickly tapped in the code, guarding the keypad with her body as if someone was behind her, and checked that the last of her jewelry and her cash were still there. They were. She finally let out a breath. She was just being paranoid. She went back through the living room, and her hackles raised again, despite all logic. By the time she got to the kitchen, she had calmed down again.

Stop it, she told herself. *You're safe. For now, at least.* She made herself a cup of chamomile tea to soothe her frazzled nerves, and made her way upstairs, tucking her handbag under her arm. Normally, she would have left the bag in the kitchen, but tonight, she fully intended on barricading herself inside her bedroom. She quickly inspected all the bedrooms, and again, the alarm bells went off. Why? What was wrong with her? Everything seemed normal. Was it a smell that had her on edge? Maybe the rooms were a little stuffy. She would do well to open the windows, but without Hunter there, she had no intention of giving up her perceived sense of security. She headed back to her room, checked the closets, terrace doors, and under the bed, pulled the curtains closed, and locked the door. Tonight was to be the last night in her own room, for now. The one advantage of Nathalie's suite downstairs was that, having smaller openings, it felt safer.

Brushing her teeth, Brooke went through all the tasks she still needed to complete the next day before she was due to pick up the Argentine clients in the early afternoon. She heard her phone ping and noticed a message from Antoine.

Hope you made it back home in one piece, his message said.

Brooke responded politely.

I did.

Succinct, but with a period at the end of it to show she was being a bit formal. She hoped he caught that.

Sorry the evening ended so abruptly; Antoine wrote back. *I was stressed about my clients tomorrow. Our shipment of eel is delayed.*

No worries. Brooke wrote. Followed by a period, of course.

I'd like to make it up to you, came Antoine's response.

No need, Brooke wrote. But she decided not to be a hard-ass and include a period this time.

Really. I do need. I'm sorry about earlier. I was rude.

If this is because you're afraid I'll buy my fish elsewhere, I'm pretty sure you're the only game in town.

Thank goodness, Antoine fired back.

Why couldn't he be fun and flirty like this when they were together in person? She was pretty sure he was as attracted to her as she was to him, so why make it so difficult? She decided to cut the exchange short before it could go downhill again. She wouldn't flirt with him by text like she planned to do in person, just so she could mess with someone the way the universe was messing with her.

Well, I've got an early morning, she wrote. *I'll ping you with my requests once I know what they expect, meal-wise.*

And we can plan to see each other for a re-do once you know your schedule, Antoine responded.

Brooke considered this. Tempting as it was to play hard to get, she didn't have the luxury. And how would that serve her flirtation campaign? No matter what, she would like to see Antoine. Still, no need to seem too desperate. She simply hearted the message and plugged her phone in, face down.

She got into bed and tried to sleep, but thoughts rushed around in her head. A sliver of tanned stomach. Her Cartier watch, gone forever. A Rolodex of recipes. The sad downstairs space she would be relegated to once the houseguests got there. The fact that Nathalie had not called her or texted her back. The articles of clothing and toiletries she had left in her closet, and which she would have to transfer to the downstairs suite in the morning. The long list of things she needed to do to get the house ready for the renters.

Chapter 18

B rooke must have eventually fallen asleep, as she woke up abruptly, her heart beating a panicked staccato. She looked towards the French doors leading to the balcony. She had overslept, hadn't she? Bright daylight was filtering through the curtains. *The curtains.* She had pulled the curtains closed last night before going to bed. But she was in the habit of leaving the bedroom curtains closed to keep the room cooler when she was away from the house. Sure, she'd had a lot on her mind lately, and there was a chance that she had deviated from her usual behavior. But considering that Hunter had always teased her about her OCD, it was hardly likely. Was she right? Had someone really been in the house? There was nothing missing, as far as she could tell. She took a deep breath and her pulse slowly returned to normal. She did not have time for this. She had so much to get done before her airport pickup.

She picked up her phone to check for messages. As expected, she had some falsely concerned missives; sent by frenemies who had heard the rumor that Hunter had returned to New York without his wife. She sent a thumbs up to each one. No added info. Screw them. She would make sure to create a few dreamy Instagram posts they could feast their eyes on, and which would fuel the gossip mill for a little while. Which reminded her, she really did need to start creating posts showing off her cooking if she wanted to survive.

Then, a text from Antoine.

You know, once your renters are settled in, maybe I can take you out tonight and we can discuss possible menus in person.

She hearted the message, a little shiver of pleasure going up her spine. No time to daydream and dilly-dally, though. She threw on the shorts and tee shirt she had set aside the day before, wound her long, curly hair into a bun, and shoved her feet into a trusty pair of espadrilles. She would shower and change before the airport run. Until then, she would probably be working up a sweat with her last-minute organization and cleaning. She had underestimated the work that Nathalie did to keep this place perfect, she realized. Dammit, where was Nathalie? Was she pissed at her? Maybe. Well, no time to worry about that at this juncture.

She made herself a quick iced coffee* from the concentrate she always made and stored in the refrigerator, pouring it over ice and adding a shot of coconut milk. *How decadent.* She posed the glass next to the flowers she had picked yesterday, which she had artfully arranged in a vase she had placed on the kitchen counter and went to get her phone. *Wait.* It still needed color. She whipped up an omelet and cut up some fruits at top speed, hoping the ice cubes wouldn't completely melt. *Fresh Mango and papaya for the win. There. Perfect.* Now, the glass was photogenically beaded with perspiration. The simple but delectable breakfast was set off by the gleaming marble countertops, the blue ocean beyond a perfect backdrop. Let the New York gossips chew on that.

Brooke barely had enough of an appetite to eat what she had made, but she forced herself. She needed the fuel.

As soon as she was done, she did a thorough sweep of the kitchen, emptied all the trash cans in the house, vacuumed all over, made all the beds, cut some greenery from the garden to arrange in vases large and small, and made sure there were fresh candles and towels everywhere. *Dammit.* She had forgotten that, when people rented a home, they probably expected the fridge and pantry to be impeccable. She opened the fridge first and tossed anything questionable. She picked up her phone and made a shopping list for herself.

-Mineral water, flat and sparkling

-Champagne 1 bottle

-Eggs 1 carton (for downstairs)

-Coffee

-Tea

-Salt

-Pepper

-Sugar

-Olive oil

-Vinegar

-Mustard

-Hand soap

-Crackers

-Potato chips

-Paper towels

-Toilet paper

-Bar of chocolate (downstairs)

She looked at her list and shuddered, imagining how these items would deplete her already paltry savings. But there was no choice. She undid her bun, ran her hand through her hair, and grabbed her bag. No time for even so much as lip gloss to make her presentable. She needed to hurry if she wanted to shop, do the last-minute straightening up, and shower, all before 1:20 pm. She hoped she didn't see anyone she knew, but then again, the odds were low, even on a small island like this one.

On the way back home, she saw Antoine's van going through an intersection ahead of her. *Meat my Fish*. At least there was something that could make her smile. She pulled into her driveway, still obsessing over the broken gate, and hustled the bags into the house. Everything looked great, but was it her imagination, or did the house smell a little stuffy? She threw the windows wide open and lit a candle, telling herself that she had to remember to blow out the candle and lock up before she went back out. This broken gate was a lot of trouble. Maybe she would get Antoine to look at it. It could be something as simple as a lizard stuck in the mechanism, she rationalized. Gross, but easy to fix. No time to think about it now, though. She was about to rush upstairs to shower when she realized that her shower was in the downstairs suite, for now. *Damn.* And she'd left some toiletries in the bathroom. She ran up, almost slipping on the landing and catching herself on the banister. She couldn't afford to hurt herself at this point. She grabbed the last of the toiletries, did one last inspection of the master suite, and headed down to what she still thought of as Nathalie's room.

The shower was nothing like the ones upstairs. Cramped, if she was completely honest. They should have made more of an effort with this space. Then again, she reminded herself, she had wanted to. She shouldn't have listened to Hunter. She shampooed her hair and caught herself thinking that she should get a haircut. Chop off the extra length that she could no longer afford to maintain. Hunter had always said he loved her long, dark hair. But then again, he liked any kind of hair, or whatever kind of hair the neighbor's nanny had. Blonde, probably. She caught herself wondering what kind of hair Antoine liked. She felt an unwelcome pinch in her heart as she recalled how his friends had pointed out that she wasn't his usual type. Maybe they meant rich New York bitch, though, to be fair. And also, Antoine wasn't exactly her normal type, either. Granted, fish and meat purveyors weren't a huge demographic in Manhattan. Maybe in Brooklyn...

As she emerged from the shower, she tried to figure out what to put on. Something pretty, professional, but that wasn't trying too hard. Something that made her look like the staff, but not. What had Nathalie worn? Nathalie had usually worn a white linen outfit that looked nurse-like. Well, Brooke didn't have one of those outfits, nor did she want to wear one. She flipped through her too-small closet and pulled out a pair of white jeans and a blue linen sleeveless top with white embroidery. She selected a pair of navy platform lace-up espadrilles and blue pom-pom earrings to complete the look. She noticed that the white line from her wedding band was fading, not quite gone, yet. How much longer would that take? She looked in the mirror. Something was missing from her look. *Maybe a bracelet*, she thought. The missing watch made her feel strangely naked. She threw on an armful of colorful bangles. All the real jewelry was in the safe and would not be appropriate anyway. She glanced at her phone for the time and grabbed her bag, double-checking that she had her keys. She rushed over to the garage, making sure that the Mini Moke was positioned so that she could navigate the Land Rover and whichever car the Argentines would rent around it. At least the gate being broken meant that the rental car agency could deliver without her needing to be there. At last, one good thing from the bad. Maybe it would start a trend.

She backed up the Land Rover and nosed out of the driveway, reminding herself to ask Antoine to look to see if there was a BBQed lizard in the gate. She smiled as she thought about him, but then grew serious as she replayed their last interaction in her mind. A do-over would be good. Driving downhill towards the airport, she made sure to keep her eyes dancing over the beautiful houses dotting the hillside, the sparkling sapphire sea beyond, the sailboats bobbing gently. Just because she was going to be serving these renters, just because she wasn't on vacation anymore, didn't mean that she should stop enjoying this place. She remembered what Georges had said the night before. The people who left the island soonest were the ones who started glossing over its magic- those who didn't appreciate that every day here was a gift. That the less convenient things were a small price to pay. She needed to keep reminding herself. Because she had nowhere else to go.

On the main road, the beach traffic was already building up. Mini Mokes, Mini Coopers, and electric Fiat 500's zoomed past, most of them rental cars, Brooke could tell. She wondered if she would catch a peek of Antoine's truck. She could use a smile. A plane was landing. She recognized the yellow and white of the St Barth Commuter plane. Just on time. It was probably the Argentines, coming in from St Martin. Brooke carefully pulled the car into the airport drive. She scanned the people standing around. The Argentines wouldn't be out yet, so she had time to park or double park somewhere to wait. As she waited for a hotel van to pull ahead, she suddenly noticed a familiar looking head of hair in a convertible Mercedes. *Hmmm.* If she didn't know better, she would assume it was Antoine. His light chestnut waves were certainly distinctive, especially when paired with such a golden tan. She thought about how his hair went lighter at the temples, and how the skin around his turquoise eyes crinkled when he smiled. Only then did she notice the other person in the car's passenger side. A blonde woman with long straight hair. Remarkably like the woman who had shared their flight in, just a short week ago. The Mercedes pulled over and the woman got out, leaning in, and kissing the man on the cheek, a teasing expression on her face. Then, the woman looked straight at Brooke through the windshield, at which point Brooke became acutely aware of two things. One, the woman was absolutely the same one from the plane. Two, the man was Antoine. And not that she even wanted to think of it, but there was a third thing. These two were definitely involved. Most probably romantically involved. Was that who Antoine's friends had been referring to when they talked about his type? Blonde, classical beauty? *How boring.*

Suddenly, there was a blur in her field of vision, and Brooke slammed on the brakes just in time to allow a child to run across the driveway. By the time she had caught her breath, Antoine and the Mercedes had disappeared. If he bothered to call her, she might have to bring it up. Now, she felt stupid even thinking twice about him. If she really thought about it, had anything he had said or done really been something that could be construed as romantic? Maybe he was just being friendly. Sure, maybe moderately flirty. But that was just the way men were.

As she was sitting there feeling like an idiot, Brooke was pleased to have her thoughts interrupted by the appearance of a group that was definitely her Argentine house guests. Three men, all deeply tanned, one of them a bit older than the other two, with silver hair, all of them clad in pastel linen shirts and white jeans. Two women in breezy dresses. One blonde, one brunette. Brooke fished out the silly sign she had made just in case, the one that said "Sea Grapes/Heguy." She held it up and waved. The man with the silver hair spotted her first and gestured to the others. Brooke opened the trunk of the Land Rover and greeted the group, trying to remember their names. She did pretty well, considering that it was not her forte. Armando, Ernesto, Jaime for the men. Ana and Lisa for the women. Lisa was apparently the American of the bunch. Brooke had not yet had the time to study the dynamic between all these people, so she couldn't tell yet how the couples paired up and whether Ana and Lisa were actually friends. Not that it was any of her business, she reminded herself.

Once all the bags were loaded in the car, the group settled in, in the two rows behind her, with the gray-haired man up front with her. He was the solo one, then. And seemed to be the friendliest one, the ringleader.

"Are we to expect good weather?" The man asked. He was Ernesto, Brooke remembered.

"Absolutely. It's the tropics, so we do have an occasional downpour, but this is the best season. You'll have a beautiful time. Is this your first visit?"

"Lisa has been here before. The rest of us have not."

"I used to stay at the Guanahani all the time," Lisa sniffed. "Before it became the Rosewood and was ruined."

Brooke nodded. Many of the old timers, or at least those who had been visiting the island for a while, were up in arms about the Rosewood's takeover of an island icon, especially as it seemed to constitute much too large an ecological footprint for that side of the island, which was known for its sea turtles.

"Have you made any reservations, or would you like me to help?"

"I have a list for you," said Lisa.

At least she was direct. Better than wishy washy.

"Fantastic. I'll get right on it once you're settled in."

"So how many staff do we have at the villa?" asked the other woman.

Brooke froze. Staff? She realized, then, that, even though she had never really given it any thought, they had technically had staff. Nathalie for pretty much everything. A girl who came in for more involved meals. Pierre to drive...where was Pierre, by the way? She wondered if Hunter had given him a heads-up as to their change of circumstances.

"It's actually pretty pared down, so you can enjoy your privacy," Brooke said, carefully. "The cleaner was there just this morning and will return as needed. The driver is off. So, anything you need, you can ask me. I'll be the liaison."

"Oh," said Lisa, looking confused.

"Also," said Brooke, "I am a classically trained chef, so I'll be taking care of all your breakfasts- that's included- you can let me know what time works for that and if you have any dietary restrictions, and if you would like a special meal or two, we can plan that. It would be a supplement."

Brooke held her breath. She'd been doing the math. Dinners were an opportunity to make more much-needed income.

"I don't know about dinner at the villa, there are so many restaurants we want to try," said Ana. Brooke's heart sank.

"I'm paying enough for this villa- from the photos, it looks like it has an amazing dining area by the pool. We should enjoy it," said one of the dark-haired men.

He was paying for the whole group? Or was it just a manner of speaking? None of Brooke's business, she decided, but she sure was curious.

"What would you make us if we had dinner at the villa?" asked Ernesto.

"We could do a local fish crudo. Local lobster or meat from the island. We have some fabulous micro-farms that produce vegetables...I made an amazing beet carpaccio the other day. There are fruits- maybe for a fruit galette for dessert, and to add to a salad, and we even have goat cheese produced on the island now."

"That does sound delicious," Lisa allowed. "Maybe in the middle of the week? What do you all think?"

The others nodded and went silent, taking in the surroundings. They were almost at the last intersection before the straightaway that led to the driveway, and Brooke saw a car pulling up on her right. A Mercedes convertible. The same one she had seen at the airport earlier. She focused on the driver. Even in profile, at a distance, she could see it was Antoine. She stopped at the stop sign and, as he turned towards her car, no doubt recognizing the Land Rover's unique shade, he met her eyes. Despite the windshield between them, she thought she could read the guilt in his expression.

That's right, fucker, try to explain that away, after giving me grief over my soon to be ex-husband, thought Brooke. The Mercedes pulled forward, and Brooke tailed it down the street, the German car picking up speed as it went. *Where was he going?* And then, she saw the Mercedes pull into Carlos' driveway.

Her mind was racing. When she'd seen his van there the other day, she'd chalked it up to a delivery. But now, at the wheel of a Mercedes? Her blood suddenly ran cold. The gossips on the yacht had been talking about Carlos having a child on the island. Was it possible? Was Antoine Carlos' son? Antoine with his off handed elegance, his wry sense of humor, his fancy French name? Crazier things had proven to be true before.

"Brooke? Brooke?"

Lisa's nasal voice tore her from her stupor.

"I'm sorry, what?"

"Do we get a clicker for the gate?"

"You will," said Brooke. "The gate has been broken though, so right now, you don't need it."

She heard Ana say something to the man behind her, and even though her Spanish was just a step above serviceable, she was pretty sure it translated to: *What else is broken in this shithole?* But once they turned the corner and the house came into view, she was pleased to hear the women behind her audibly gasp.

"Oh wow. Gorgeous," said Lisa. "I wonder who owns this-probably some gazillionaire."

Brooke smiled to herself and fought to keep a straight face. She would have to make up an exciting story to feed renters. She would make this fun. But then, her smile turned into a frown. What was Antoine playing at?

Chapter 19

B rooke stood in front of the bathroom mirror in her downstairs suite, dabbing at her face with a damp cloth. It had gotten hot that afternoon, and normally she would have had a swim, or would have gone to the beach. Not today. She had shown the group around the house and had confirmed that yes, Ernesto was something of a patriarch, though not particularly old, and he had come solo. Lisa and Jaime were an item, recently together and with her pushing for an engagement. They had met in Palm Beach. And Ana and Armando were married, together for a few years, and the parents of a toddler they had left with a grandmother on a polo estate outside of Buenos Aires. Apparently, they were looking forward to seeing one of their relatives, a polo champion named Diego, and his new bride, apparently an American. They had decided that they would plan a dinner at the villa to impress Diego, on Wednesday. Now, Brooke needed to call Antoine, but she didn't really want to. She settled on a text.

Hi. Argentines arrived. I will be needing a few things for breakfast. They are planning on a nice dinner at the villa on Wednesday. Hoping to score some fresh local fish for crudo and some lobster as well as a few standout local ingredients.

The response from Antoine came almost immediately.

Great. We can talk about it over dinner.

Brooke rolled her eyes. This morning, she had fully been intending on accepting Antoine's offer of dinner, if it came. But now, everything had changed.

Sorry, I think I need to plan the menu better and be there in case they need me. I need to get the gate repaired, too.

Hell if she asked him for help. And she was planning on doing some Googling of Antoine tonight, to see what she could find out.

I can come by and look at the gate now, he wrote.

Brooke hesitated. But yes, she really did need that gate repaired. *If it's not too much trouble.*

There in 10, I'm making a delivery nearby, Antoine wrote.

Bullshit, thought Brooke. He was probably hanging out at his dad's house, missing his pretty blonde girlfriend.

But what she wrote was, *Perfect.*

As Brooke walked around the house, heading towards the gate, she got intercepted by Ernesto, who was smoking a cigar by the pool.

"Hey, Brooke- we were thinking of going to dinner at Nikki Beach- and since you're being so helpful, we thought we would invite you along."

Brooke hesitated. Normally, she would have said yes, on principle. Because why not? Also, in her new impoverished state, a free dinner was nothing to sneeze at. But, considering these people probably viewed her as the help, she wondered how awkward the dynamic would be, and how she should even act. She had seen too many local boat captains or dive masters invited along on rich people's meals and had sensed the weirdness inherent in the situation. It was palpable. Then again, some people didn't care, and just went along with it. Was Ernesto trying to get a side bonus to his accommodations? She hoped not. He seemed sincere enough. Before her vacillation had a chance to grow awkward, she decided to throw caution to the wind.

"Sure, thank you. That's very kind. I would love to. I can drive us if that helps."

The Land Rover could easily accommodate six people, while their rental car could hold only five.

"I'll call for an Uber van," said Ernesto, and that was that. Ernesto's attention was diverted by something he saw beyond Brooke, at the entrance to the driveway. The Meat my Fish van.

"Are you expecting a delivery?" he asked.

"The delivery man moonlights as a handyman," said Brooke. "He's going to take a look at the gate."

"Huh. *Meat my Fish*," said Ernesto. "That's a bit cheeky."

Sure is, thought Brooke, as she headed towards the van, her sense of dread mounting as she debated on what, if anything, to say to Antoine.

Antoine emerged from the truck and tried to go in for a pair of cheek kisses, which she evaded, not that she really wanted to, but she was a woman of principle, and until she figured out what his story was, she was going to attempt to keep her distance. Damn, he was as hot as ever, though. Today, he was wearing a white linen shirt unbuttoned halfway down, which gave her a view of his exquisitely muscled chest and of the silver medallion hanging by a cord around his neck. She didn't usually like jewelry on men, but on Antoine, it somehow worked. As usual, he had on a pair of shorts, these in an indigo linen, and a pair of leather sandals. Brooke realized she was staring at Antoine, taking in all the details, and forced herself to focus back up at his face. But that was no good, either. She found it hard to look him in the eye without blushing furiously and then looking at his mouth, complete with white teeth, lips she decided would be perfectly kissable, and the perfect amount of facial hair to take him from beautiful to manly.

"How are your guests?" Antoine asked, lowering his voice.

"Fine. You probably saw them, though."

"What are you talking about?" Antoine asked, his eyebrows raised.

Wow. So, he was choosing subterfuge, was he?

"At the airport," said Brooke. "Weren't you there earlier? I thought I saw you, dropping off your girlfriend. I guess you were distracted. Funny, you never mentioned a girlfriend. Not that you needed to, of course, but..."

"She's not my girlfriend," said Antoine, still in a low voice.

"That's not what it looked like from where I was parked," said Brooke. "Nice car, by the way. Is it Daddy's?"

"What...?" Antoine started to say, and then he seemed to have a change of heart. "Listen, we can discuss this later, when your guests aren't within earshot. Let's have a look at this gate."

Brooke was only too happy to get that gate fixed, if possible. Everything else in her life was certainly broken.

"I was thinking that maybe a lizard got into the mechanism or something," she said.

"Yes, that happens sometimes," said Antoine. He opened a box in one of the columns. "Let me go grab my toolkit." Antoine jogged to the van and returned with a small duffel bag.

"You came prepared," Brooke observed.

"I was in this youth group in France. We are always prepared."

"You were a Boy Scout?" Brooke laughed.

Antoine hesitated.

"No. I was a Scout."

The way he said it sounded like *scoot* and made Brooke smile; despite being pissed off at him.

Antoine took out a screwdriver, undid another panel on the column, and shone a penlight into it.

"Hmmm. There's something in there."

"A lizard?"

"Doesn't look like it." Antoine reached into the column, wincing as he guided his hand to whatever it was that was blocking the mechanism. "Got it."

He pulled out his hand and showed her a strange object. Floppy. Blue.

'What is it?"

"Looks like one of those rags from the gas station. It was knotted around a lever."

Brooke stared at him.

"That doesn't seem like the sort of thing that happens by accident."

"No. It doesn't."

Brooke didn't like the sound of that.

"So, you think somebody did this on purpose?"

"That's what it looks like."

"Who would do that?"

"Good question. Let me see if it works now." He pushed a button, and the gate started to close. He pushed it again, to make it open again.

"Looks like it's fixed. Why don't you get your clicker, so we can make sure?"

Brooke nodded and jogged up to the Land Rover in the driveway. She had the keys in her pocket, and it seemed like a better option than going into the house, which essentially belonged to the Argentines this week. They would have to discuss how much privacy they expected, when she should come in and out to cook and clean. She grabbed the clicker out of the car and aimed it at the gate. Antoine took a step back as the gate closed. Brooke waited for a beat and then clicked again. The gate opened. She breathed a sigh of relief. Except the relief was short lived because this meant that someone had done this on purpose. *Who*?

Brooke walked back towards Antoine.

"Thank you so much."

"How are you going to thank me?" he asked.

Oh, so now he was playing the flirtation game. His eyes twinkled with a promise she was sorely tempted to make him keep. But then, she remembered the blonde, and the car, and she stayed silent.

"You sure I can't take you out tonight?" he asked.

"I agreed to go out with the renters. They invited me along, and I thought it would be rude to refuse."

Antoine frowned.

"That's not a good idea. That sort of thing never goes well. Believe me, many of my friends…"

He was interrupted by the arrival of Ernesto, who jovially cried out, "Looks like you fixed the gate, young man! Bravo!"

Ernesto extended a crisp 20 Euro bill towards Antoine.

"No thank you," said Antoine. "I was just doing a favor for my friend. Welcome to St Barth. I hope you have a wonderful time. You're certainly staying in the finest home."

"Looks that way," said Ernesto. "Except for that house over there- how much is that one to rent?"

He was pointing towards Carlos' mansion, which glowed in the afternoon light.

"It's not for rent," said Antoine, his lips set in a grim line. "I'll see you later, Brooke."

"Yeah, see you around. I'll send you my order soon," she said.

After Antoine got in his van and drove away, Brooke walked back towards the house with Ernesto.

"You might want to get ready for this evening," he said. "Our car service comes in an hour."

"All right," said Brooke. "Do you need anything before I go?"

"Everything is perfect," said Ernesto. She didn't know if she was imagining it, but it felt like he was giving her a lingering look. She didn't like it. Her girlfriend Grace would have said to welcome it, that maybe this was a way out of her current predicament, but she didn't want to think that way, at least not until desperation set in.

Chapter 20

B rooke pawed through the undersized closet in the downstairs suite. She had taken a quick rinse and again had thought about how much she missed her pool, and how annoying her hair was to her right now. She couldn't find anything to wear to Nikki Beach. She had locked most of her fun outfits into a storage closet in the garage, and she realized that she had chosen the items in this closet for practicality rather than style. She would have to go simple, she decided. She did have that black kaftan with neon embroidery that was slightly sheer, with high slits on either side, and she could wear it with a one-piece black swimsuit and big colorful earrings. For shoes, she would forgo the stilettos some ridiculous women wore even to beach bars and stick with her trusty black lace-up espadrilles. She would probably be underdressed, compared to the two women currently renting her house, but she knew deep down she would at least not look like she was trying so hard, which was a win in her book. She hadn't heard from Hunter all day, and she was almost tempted to call him and tell him how she'd had to pawn her watch, but then she worried he might ask her to send half the proceeds to him. Would he really lose their New York apartment? They didn't pay a mortgage on it, but there were the co-op fees and the utilities. Was he really in such dire straits? She realized she was in no mood to find out at this juncture. She shouldn't look a gift horse in the mouth. This was going to be a free dinner at Nikki Beach, and she would make it fun, dammit.

She checked the time on her phone and ventured out to the driveway. Hearing voices by the pool, she headed in that direction, and found the entire group nursing glasses of Champagne; probably the Champagne she had put in the fridge that very morning. She hoped they didn't expect her to restock. She should have included a paragraph about those logistics in the welcome packet she had adapted from one she had found on the internet. *Next time.*

"Oh," said Lisa. "There you are. Ernesto says he invited you to join us."

"He did. That's very sweet, thank you."

Brooke winced. Why was she thanking Lisa of all people, when it was obvious that, if it was up to Lisa, she would not be invited along?

A long honk emanated from behind the gate.

"Ah, that must be your ride," said Brooke. "They'll usually try to call on the speaker by the door, or you can have the gate open if you're expecting someone. There's a clicker in the kitchen in the drawer under the coffee machine, by the way. You don't have to take it with you as long as you remember the code to the gate. It's 1987."

"1987? That's the year I was born," said Lisa. "Do you think the owner was born in that year too? Pretty sweet to have a house like this at that age. Must be a trust fund baby. Do you know who the owner is?"

Brooke winced and remained silent. She hadn't yet made up her story. She reached into the Land Rover and clicked the gate open, making sure to lock her car just in case, and put the keys in her purse. She'd made sure to take a simple clutch, nothing with a label that might make the Argentines suspicious or, even worse, make them think it was a fake.

Five minutes later, Brooke sat in the van, listening in on the conversations around her, not really participating. She noticed that Lisa was annoyed whenever the language switched to Spanish. Lisa very much wanted to be the center of attention, it seemed. When they stopped in front of Nikki Beach, Brooke started to panic. She hoped that the hostess was not one that she was familiar with, who knew her as Hunter's wife. Just before they had left the house,

Hunter had sent her a message reminding her to not let anyone know that there was trouble in paradise. He was working on a business deal that hinged on his still being married and in a stable situation, he'd said, and now, she was wondering what the hell that meant. He wasn't trying to show that he had access to the St Barth house as equity, was he? Brooke had decided not to engage because she didn't want the argument. But how could he even think that she would protect him for long? For now, out of undeserved loyalty, she would. What could it hurt? Except for her chances of making out with Antoine, which, in any case, was now a moot point since he definitely had a girlfriend.

Brooke hid partially behind the group as they walked into the Nikki Beach foyer. Unfortunately, the girl at the podium was Melanie, a curvaceous redhead that Brooke knew rather well from her having worked there for the past two seasons. When she noticed Brooke with the group of Argentines and without Hunter, her eyes widened briefly. Brooke tried to give her a dissuasive look. Melanie obviously was good at interpreting looks, because she simply nodded at Brooke and then checked everyone in. Brooke breathed a sigh of relief. Crisis averted. For now. She followed the others to the table they had chosen. Someone had obviously called in a favor. They were at the pole position table, the one that was usually occupied by high end yacht parties. They were clearly connected. She started thinking about what she would order, and how she would strike the right balance between ordering the same as everyone else and not assuming that she would be paid for. She hoped she would be paid for- after all, she had barely any money left.

During the meal, they all peppered Brooke with questions about life on the island, and which hot spots were not on the lists that the usual people seemed to check. Brooke gave them a few tips on where to go and tried to figure out what their schedule would be, without seeming too nosy. She also gently tried to push for more meals that she could cook to make more money, but it seemed that Wednesday was going to be their only option. She would need to let Antoine know about this in the morning or in a message that evening. She was annoyed that he was judging her for going out with his group. After all, wasn't this a thing that people often did when they were hosting people or when they were working with them on the island? But yes, it felt strange to be treated as the staff, and she could tell there was a difference in how the women treated her, even though she was dressed to blend in with them.

Over the course of the meal, Ernesto started moving his chair closer to hers. A few times, as they had been speaking, she'd noticed him staring, trying to catch her eye. She was not a bonus amenity that came with the house, and she hoped he understood that. But then again, maybe he just thought she was cute. That wasn't completely out of the realm of possibility, was it? Even though she felt like she had been chewed up and spit out and was sure she looked like she had been trampled by life, Ernesto was quite a bit older- he probably thought she was easily in his league. As the evening wore on, his flirting became more insistent. At one point, he placed his hand on her thigh. Brooke found an excuse to swivel in her chair, dislodging his hand. She caught a disappointed look on Ernesto's face and realized that yes, he was flirting. She was not interested, handsome and obviously monied as he was. She was not going to jump right into an unequal relationship, right after finding out that her husband of 10 years had been cheating on her.

The rest of the meal went by uneventfully. Brooke tried to regale the group with some stories of Saint Barth lore and found the men laughing appreciatively, while the women gave each other looks. As soon as she noticed it, she piped down. She didn't want to give them any reason to give her a lower rating for the rental, or to be displeased with their experience. After all, word of mouth was the best way of getting more rentals. Not that she wanted to rent the house out all the time, but for now it was her only means of income. She found herself panicking that she didn't have confirmation of the French family rental yet and reminded herself to go check the website upon returning home that evening.

As the meal wrapped up, Ernesto texted the van driver; they came out of the restaurant to find the vehicle waiting for them. As they got back into the van, Brooke was unsurprised but displeased that Ernesto got in right next to her. *What a coincidence.* Within seconds, his leg started pressing against hers more insistently. Within minutes, it was his hand making its way back onto her thigh. She tried to pretend she didn't really notice. That seemed to be the best course of action, because accepting his advances was not going to happen, but rejecting them outright would also be awkward. She would just act discreet and quietly make her way to her room downstairs and everything would be fine, she decided. As she emerged from the van, Ernesto tried to take her by the hand. He whispered into her ear, "Fancy a nightcap?"

"Oh, no, sorry," she said. "I need to organize the menu for your dinner on Wednesday. And I also want to make sure I have everything for your breakfasts. Is there anything else I can do for you?"

The others were now out of earshot, so Ernesto boldly replied, "There are absolutely some things you can do for me."

Brooke pretended not to see the wolfish look in his eye.

"Well, definitely let me know," she said, in a curt manner.

She wasn't going to entertain this sort of tone or treatment from any of her renters. And now, her heart was beating hard, because she worried whether Ernesto would stand down or keep insisting. Suddenly, she realized how very exposed she was, sleeping in her downstairs bedroom. He could certainly try to break into it anytime if he felt so inclined.

"Well, I have to go," said Brooke cheerfully and loudly enough for the others to hear her. "I'll see you in the morning. What time should I come up to make your breakfasts?"

"You can come up anytime. Wake me up if you like. I'll be in the second room on the right upstairs."

Brooke pretended she didn't hear. All right. She would come up at 8:30, she decided. She stumbled down to her room, noticing now how the adrenaline coursed through her veins and made her feel jittery. Would all visitors be like this? She certainly hoped not. When she arrived in her room, she found a text from Antoine on her phone:

How did it go?

It was fine, she lied.

She wasn't about to let Antoine know that he had been right, that she should never have gone out with these people, that it wouldn't lead to anything good.

Sophie said she saw you at Nikki Beach, Antoine wrote back. *What will your husband think?*

I told you we're on a break, Brooke started tapping out, instinctively. Until she remembered that she owed Hunter marginally more allegiance than she did Antoine. She had already said too much. Was Sophie the blonde girlfriend? She deleted the text and instead wrote,

Ha! Small island. He'll be fine.

She wasn't going to discuss this with Antoine. They weren't anything, were they? If she couldn't get a response about his blonde girlfriend, she certainly wasn't going to gratify him with talk about her ex-husband, who was definitely more of an ex than this Sophie was.

I'm only going to need the dinner items for Wednesday, she wrote. *And breakfasts, of course.*

She tapped out a list of ingredients that she hoped for, and then breakfast stuff. She wracked her brain and wrote out those ingredients, too. She would make cinnamon buns one morning; that would be an easy, inexpensive recipe. And Antoine probably knew where to score some local fruit.

About that, Antoine wrote back. *Nathalie told me that you might have a problem with payment.*

Brooke held her breath, beads of sweat starting to form on her forehead. He had spoken to Nathalie, she thought. When Nathalie was not even speaking to her. And now, Nathalie was betraying her, talking about her finances? Where did that come from? She would have thought that they were close enough that Nathalie could bring up any concerns with her directly. Had Hunter said something to her?

Brooke was livid. Her fingers hovered over the phone's screen as she pondered how to express that she was on a restricted budget. She saw the animated ellipsis that told her that Antoine was typing again.

If you need to put things on credit, I completely understand, he wrote.

That's sweet, she responded. *Thank you. I'm on a tight budget but I'll be OK.*

We locals help each other, Antoine shot back.

Brooke smiled. This thought warmed her heart, and she was glad that Antoine was so understanding, but her relief was mitigated by the fresh knowledge that Nathalie had essentially tried to sabotage her. Why the sudden hostility towards her? Or had it always been there, but swept under the rug because Nathalie was in their employ? Brooke felt naïve for having considered Nathalie a friend, and started feeling sorry for herself, but then realized that she hadn't always treated Nathalie like an equal, either. She didn't worry about what her struggles were, what her life was like, or what she was going through. Brooke would suspend communications for months at a time when they were not on the island and expect things to resume where they left off. She could have treated Nathalie a bit better. Enquired after her son more. Sent gifts for birthdays and Christmas. She didn't have time to worry about this right now, but she realized that she would have to revisit it at some point soon, uncomfortable as it might be. Her ruminations were interrupted by another message from Antoine.

So... did any of them hit on you while you were out?

No, they were all perfect gentlemen and gentlewomen, Brooke lied.

Shocking, Antoine wrote back. *But just you wait.*

Brooke didn't like this certitude of his that things were bound to go south, even if he was correct.

It's late. I'll see you tomorrow morning? Brooke wrote.

Yes, I'll be there around 10:00 AM, Antoine wrote back. *Goodnight.*

Chapter 21

The next morning, Brooke woke up with a pounding headache. She hadn't realized how much she'd had to drink. Maybe she'd been tipsy, and she had just imagined that Ernesto was putting the moves on her. But when she started to wander upstairs, as she walked under the veranda, she overheard the two women having a conversation.

"Who does she think she is?" Lisa was asking. "I mean, we invited her out to be polite, or maybe because Ernesto wants to get in her pants. But I can't believe she accepted."

"It's fine," said Ana. "It's traditional to have the staff come out with us once. Now, we're on our own. We don't have to do anything with her again."

"Thank God. I hope she doesn't think that she's going to be included in the future," said Lisa.

"No, I'm sure she knows her place," said Ana.

Brooke started sweating, droplets running down her back and forming beads on her temples. She was mortified. Was this the sort of treatment she was to expect for the foreseeable future?

Now she heard Ernesto's voice.

"Don't worry. I won't invite her out again. She wouldn't even put out. Can you believe it?"

"Who does she think she is?" said Lisa.

Brooke had pretty much decided from first contact that she did not like this Lisa character, but this clinched it.

"Also, this house kind of smells," said Ana. "I don't think she did a really good job cleaning it."

Brooke's mouth fell open, and she almost audibly gasped. Didn't she do a good job cleaning it? The place was impeccable. But then, she remembered that stale smell she'd noticed. It had never been there before, even when they'd come back to the house after a long time away. She really needed to check that out.

"Yeah, it actually smells disgusting. It smelled bad last night, but this morning is even worse," Lisa confirmed.

Brooke cleared her throat and walked up the stairs to the veranda. She pasted on a falsely cheerful expression.

"Good morning, ladies. Gentleman. I hope you slept well. Did you have everything you needed for your first night at Sea Grapes?"

"Yes, thank you," said Ana politely, her face a mask of neutrality and detachment, as if it wasn't even worth mentioning the smell, as if this house was inherently rotten.

"Except there's a weird smell in the house," said Lisa.

"Thanks for letting me know," said Brooke. "I'll investigate. We've been having an issue with lizards getting into the house and dying," she lied. "Maybe that's it."

"It smells a lot worse than just one dead lizard," said Lisa. As if she was a dead lizard smell expert.

Ernesto just stood by with a slightly disgusted look on his face, refusing to make eye contact. *Charming.*

Brooke just nodded and headed inside, but when she walked into the kitchen, she detected something fishy in the air. It was even worse in the living room, the fumes hitting her full force as she approached the window. She decided she would have to investigate once they were all gone. In the meantime, she threw open all the French doors. She walked back outside, and now the other two men had joined as well.

"Your breakfast will be ready soon," Brooke said. "How do you all take your coffee? Or do you take tea? Also, I've noticed the smell in the house, too. I'm going to investigate after breakfast, once you are all out. Don't worry, I'll get to the bottom of this."

"You can inspect my room anytime, you don't have to wait for me to be gone," Ernesto said, smiling, probably for the benefit of his male audience. The others giggled. *Oh, so it was an in-joke amongst all of them now. How cute*, Brooke thought. Well, she would treat them politely, but nothing more. Brooke decided that a lack of reaction and general stiffness was the most appropriate reaction. She kept herself busy in the kitchen, preparing their coffees, putting together some omelets, toasting some bread, and arranging it in a basket, along with jam and butter, and depositing everything on a pretty tray. She brought everything out and placed the tray on the table on the veranda. She returned with some fresh squeezed orange-grapefruit juice. Everything looked perfect if she did say so herself.

"Oh, this looks wonderful," said Ana, looking pleased at last.

At least she'd made one person happy. Brooke retreated to the kitchen to make herself a coffee. She'd been wondering if she should go back down to her room to do so, but she decided she needed to be on call, should they need anything. Sure enough, she was soon called on for more toast and a refill of coffee. So, it looked like she was the maid as well as the chef. That was fine. You had to do what you had to do.

After breakfast, she took her time cleaning up while the others got themselves ready for their excursion. Apparently, they had rented a boat on one end of the island. Ernesto made one last attempt to ask her if she wanted to join, and she of course declined, while Lisa and Ana stared at her to see how she would respond. Just for kicks and giggles, she had hesitated for a moment and pretended to consider it, before politely retreating to the kitchen.

As she was scrubbing out a pan, her phone pinged.

Running late- I can come in about an hour if that works for you, Antoine had written.

Actually, I'm going to go to the other side of the island to go boating with them, Brooke wrote, to see how he would react. Toxic, but it amused her.

You what??? Antoine shot back.

Just kidding. I'll see you in an hour, Brooke responded. She wanted to keep him on his toes. And she was feeling a bit cruel after being so frustrated in the past 24 hours.

As soon as the group had departed, the women laughingly underdressed for a boating excursion, clad in risqué bathing suits with crazy cut-outs, Brooke started inspecting the house to determine the origin of the smell. She sniffed the air and got a whiff of something distinctly fishy. She headed upstairs. The stench was even worse up there. In fact, she was lucky that these people hadn't complained more than they had. It was positively repulsive. The bed in her room, which was Ana and Jaime's room this week, was completely disheveled. Clearly, they'd had a busy evening or morning or both. Brooke reminded herself that she was expected to make up the rooms in addition to getting rid of the disgusting smell. Funny how she really hadn't considered all the moving parts that went with renting out her house. All the things that Nathalie had done, she realized she had taken for granted. And Nathalie had been so good at doing these things in a way that was so discreet, so unobtrusive, that it almost seemed like things were happening on their own. Brooke reminded herself that she really needed to reach out to Nathalie and thank her. A bit belatedly, to be sure, but it was better than nothing. Even if she had the uncomfortable feeling that it was too late for that.

She checked every corner. How could it be that the smell was just as strong in every room? She went into the bathrooms. Was the odor coming from the plumbing? No. She decided it was not. If anything, it was stronger near the windows. All at once, she was reminded of a story she had heard recently in New York. A divorcing couple had been in a protracted legal battle. Finally, the wife had been awarded the apartment, where the husband had been staying with his much younger girlfriend. Before relinquishing the property, the new girlfriend decided to put raw shrimp inside the curtain rods. The wife's new boyfriend had been so disgusted at the smell that he had decamped within a week. *Shrimp in the curtain rods.* It was a possibility. Also, Brooke remembered how, when she had come into the house the other night and had decided that somebody had potentially been in there, it had been the curtains that had tipped her off. Yes, that must be it. She fetched a step ladder and started with the curtain rod in the bedroom, carefully lifting it off its bracket. She unscrewed the finial, and a rotten ammonia stench hit her straight in the nose. *Gotcha*, she thought. For the next half hour. Brooke went through the house, taking down curtain rods and disinfecting them on the inside using a small bottle brush soaked in dish soap and bleach. She hoped the mixture wouldn't prove poisonous, but it was not like she had much to live for at this point. By the time she was done, she was feeling both better, because she had taken care of the issue all by herself, and much, much worse, because after all, this proved that someone had done this on purpose. But who? Was it Hunter who had ordered it done to get revenge on her for staying in the house and not wanting to go back to New York with him? Who would have carried out this task for him? Pierre, the driver? Or was it someone else entirely? Nathalie? Or was it the same person who had blocked her gate and had put blood on it? For a moment, she suspected Antoine, because after all, he had access to shrimp...but that was ridiculous, wasn't it? Why, she wondered, was there someone who wanted to punish her so badly on this island? She thought back to the lunch on the yacht, the Russian people, saying that Carlos would stop at nothing to get whatever he wanted. Carlos had been sending all those letters wanting to buy the house, hadn't he? Was that what it was? Had Carlos sent some goon to break into the house and make it unlivable so that Brooke would get desperate? How would he have known that she was planning on renting out the house? He couldn't possibly know her financial situation. Not yet at least. It was a small island. Soon enough, everyone would know, just as Nathalie did. None of this made any sense.

Brooke checked the time on her phone and hurried up to make the beds and straighten up the bathrooms. Giving one last look to the upstairs, she decided it was as perfect as it would get. She headed downstairs just in time to hear a honk outside the gate. She clicked on the button at the door, and watched the gates open- how wonderful it was to have them working again- and the Meat my Fish van rolling up the driveway. Her heart leapt just a little bit in anticipation of Antoine's arrival, but then she remembered that she was mad at him.

Antoine emerged from the truck, wearing a light teal linen shirt that set off his eyes perfectly, paired with white shorts and a pair of canvas boat shoes. His hair was perfectly tousled as usual. She admired how his muscled forearms were set off by the rolled-up sleeves of the shirt. Well, even if she was mad at him, she could still objectify him, couldn't she? Of course, she could.

"Good morning," she cried out.

"Good morning," he responded, as he ambled up to her, his walk slow and feline. He leaned in to give her the kiss on each cheek she now expected from him. Feeling his face next to hers sent a flush of heat across her face and down her neck. She really needed to chill out. She was the one who was supposed to be playing at seducing him, not the other way around.

"They're gone?" he asked, gesturing at the house with his chin.

"Yep, they're going boating. I'm anticipating sun poisoning in their future. Seems to me like they have no idea what to expect."

"That's the fun part," said Antoine. "Just make sure you stay far enough away so you don't have to hear them bitch and moan about it. Nobody expects how strong the sun is in the Caribbean. They use that sunscreen Gwyneth Paltrow told them to buy for the Hamptons and get burned to a crisp."

Brooke giggled but then remembered she was mad at him.

"So, what have you brought?"

Antoine retreated to his van and brought out a large cooler bag.

"Do you want me to bring this to the kitchen? It's heavy," he said.

"Sure. I can make you a coffee if you'd like," Brooke said, leading the way.

"A glass of water would be great. It's already hot out there," Antoine responded, as he unpacked the bag.

"Where are the lobsters?"

"I was going to bring those to you on Wednesday so that they're fresh."

"Oh. I wasn't going to grill them. I was going to do a modified lobster roll."

"Nice," said Antoine, looking at her with a new appreciation. "I'll bring some tails by later today, then. Sorry, I hadn't considered how inventive you were. Your husband is a lucky man."

Brooke noticed how he had started the first sentence with a playful, even flirty tone, and had ended it looking less pleased. This couldn't go on. She was dependent on Antoine for his meat and fish, but also for his friendship. But she also couldn't flirt with him as well if he thought she was very much married. Too bad for Hunter. She needed to clear this up.

"I told you; Hunter and I are ..." She hesitated, then reconsidered. Saying something could hurt her finances, too, in the long run.

"On a break. Sure. None of my business," Antoine shrugged.

Really? None of his business? She wished he felt that it was, but what could she do?

"Well, here is some local goat cheese. I have some dried local fruits. And some of our local tomatoes."

"I didn't ask for these," Brooke said, puzzled.

"I know, but unfortunately, I didn't have some of your ingredients, so I bought you whatever I had. You know how it is. You can always go to the Super U. But they're not local."

No, she realized. She didn't know. But it made sense. She couldn't just get anything she wanted regardless of season if she wanted to support local growers. Here, there would be challenges tied to the supply and demand, as weather and whichever billionaire wanted something dictated everything. She would have to roll with the punches. It would be a good creative exercise.

"OK, I might need you to keep scavenging to see what else you can get before Wednesday. I'll try to create a menu from these things," she said.

"Welcome to life on an island," said Antoine.

Brooke smiled. Antoine smiled back, his eyes sparkling, making something stir in her heart and in her nether regions, as they just stared at each other. Antoine cleared his throat gently, breaking the spell.

"I'd better go. Lots of clients wanting to Meat my Fish," he grinned.

"Of course," Brooke said, leading him towards the door, already sad that he was leaving her so soon, not that she knew what she expected.

But Antoine paused just as he was walking out the door and turned around, giving her one of those looks she was starting to crave.

"So ...they're not eating here tonight?" he asked. "Did I hear that correctly?"

"Yes, unfortunately, they just want one dinner, but it's going to be a good one," said Brooke, focused on the blow to her finances.

"Well, that means you're free... to see me," Antoine specified.

Brooke hesitated. She was still upset about the blonde, but then again, she didn't have much of a leg to stand on. Maybe she could find a way to clarify what was going on with Hunter in a way that didn't go against her ex-husband's wishes. And, she was bored, and lonely, and needed to clear her mind a little bit.

"You know, I would love that," said Brooke.

"You would?" Antoine grinned at her, looking surprised and pleased. Brooke decided she would say anything it took to see that smile again.

"I can pick you up," Antoine said, quickly, as if he was afraid she would change her mind. "I can take you on my scooter, if you like, for a real local experience."

"That would be fun," said Brooke.

"I'll pick you up at 6:30, and we'll figure it out from there?"

"All right," said Brooke, pleasant anticipation inflating her heart as she watched Antoine retreat and get into his truck. *Look at that ass*, she thought. She waved as the ridiculous van pulled away and went back into the kitchen. What in the world was she going to make with these paltry ingredients? She could also go forage for some things on the island. She had seen that there were some sea beans in the swamp down by the beach, which could make an interesting salad ingredient.

But as fun and challenging as planning this menu would be, the sad reality was that she needed to make more money, and that meant renting the house again. She grabbed her laptop and logged on to the rental site and was pleased and excited to see that she had managed to secure the French family's rental for the next week. Reading the renter profile, she learned that the renters in question were from Paris. Brooke was thrilled that there wouldn't be too much of a language barrier. After all, Brooke's half Tunisian mother had been fluent in French and had taught Brooke as much as she could. Studying at the Cordon Bleu and learning *sur l'oreiller*, or on the pillow, as a few French boyfriends had called it, had ensured that Brooke's French, while not perfect, was competent enough to order at Club 55 or live and work on an island like this one without embarrassment. Brooke started wondering what French people would expect in terms of service, compared to the Argentines. She was dreading the day that she would get a booking from a New York family that she might know or know of. No sense in worrying about that now.

The rest of the day, she spent daydreaming about her upcoming outing with Antoine and looking through her phone for food photos she could post on her Instagram and putting them in a special album. Far from making her feel confident, it made her worry. The photos were pretty, but they weren't unique enough to attract the kind of attention that would get her the kind of traction she would need to go viral and support a private chef's career.

Her head started hurting, as did her shoulders. Normally, she would have gone for a swim in the pool, but she was worried that the renters might come back early and find her there. It was too late for the beach, too. But she needed a break, and encouragement. She would call Grace, she decided.

Grace picked up on the first ring.

"Tell me you've changed your mind and are coming home," Grace said.

Brooke's heart flew into her throat. Who had told Grace she was staying behind?

"Has Hunter been talking to you?"

"What are you talking about?" asked Grace. "Isn't he there with you? You know a month is way too long to leave me, right?"

Oh. Grace didn't know anything, Brooke realized.

"How about you leave your boys and come visit instead?" Brooke countered.

"That does sound tempting."

"I could show you a good time," said Brooke, wincing as she said it because she could tell her voice sounded a bit pathetic.

"I have no doubt you could," said Grace, wistfully. "But wait. What is up with your voice? What's wrong?"

"Nothing," said Brooke. Tears started flowing from her eyes, but she stemmed their flow with a hastily retrieved paper towel and took a deep breath to compose herself.

"Honey, are you OK?"

"I'll be fine," said Brooke.

"What's going on? Why don't you tell me? I'm your friend, remember?"

"I know," said Brooke. "And I appreciate you so much."

Brooke thought about how Hunter had told her not to tell anyone about their issues. But Grace wasn't really friends with all the toxic gossips, was she? She was far too busy with her children. She wouldn't have time to spread any rumors... and she was a real friend, wasn't she? They'd always been there for each other. Surely Brooke could tell just one person? But then, she remembered that sometimes, someone might make a simple, innocent statement to the wrong person, not knowing that it could change everything. Brooke hesitated some more. It would really help to have someone on her side, someone who knew what was going on in her life. Maybe she could tell Grace just part of it.

"Is Hunter home?" asked Grace.

Brooke froze. So she *did* know something.

"Why do you ask?" she said, warily, her motivation to spill the beans to Grace evaporating.

"Because you should talk to him after you hang up the phone, honey. Maybe he can make you feel better," said Grace, innocently.

"Oh. He's not here."

"Wait, what do you mean? Your tone of voice makes it sound like he's gone, gone...did you and Hunter break up?" asked Grace. "What happened? Where is he now?"

"No, nothing that dramatic. He just went back home early," said Brooke, now remembering that Grace had not been that present for her that entire autumn, when Brooke needed her most. To be fair, it wasn't like Brooke had expressed what was going on with her, but still, she didn't owe her a truth that might return to bite her on the butt.

"Oh. And you're staying there? What are you doing? A yoga retreat or something?"

"No," said Brooke. "I'm planning to explore the creative possibilities of living here more of the year."

"What? Why would you do that? You've got everything in New York!"

"Yeah. I thought it would be good to try to step out of my comfort zone," said Brooke.

As she said it, she realized that she in fact didn't have anything in New York at all.

"Man, I wish I could run away," said Grace, "I hate Ed right now, but I need that fucker to help me with the kids. Having twin toddlers is not for the weak."

Brooke smiled wistfully. She imagined that was so, but she wouldn't know.

"But it's all worth it, right?" asked Brooke.

"Yeah, I guess I'm happy," said Grace, "but let's go back to you. So... you're serious about staying in Saint Barth? And Hunter's supporting you in this?"

"Well, that's it," Brooke lied smoothly. "It's not fair to have him paying for my extended vacation. I'm trying to figure out how to make money. I rented out the house this week, to a family from Argentina..."

"I would hate to have someone sleeping in my bed," said Grace.

Coming from someone else, that could have been casual cruelty, but she knew that Grace was just being sincere.

"Yeah, I think it will take some getting used to... and anyway, I'm hoping I'm going to get some more rentals and I'm trying to do some cooking or something, but I have no idea how to promote my businesses at all. I'm embarrassed that I did nothing with my career for the past few years."

"Yeah, you need an Instagram account," said Grace.

Brooke smiled. Of course, Grace would say that. She was the queen of social media. Even though Grace hadn't worked in almost as long as Brooke hadn't, she had an active Instagram account with pictures of her kids and funny quotes. Brooke also knew that Grace was addicted to something called Pinterest, which was another thing she hadn't had time to explore very much.

"I suck at that," said Brooke.

"I could help you."

"Well, I posted a couple pictures of food, but I'm not getting any traction..."

"No, of course not. You need an angle," said Grace.

"What does that mean?" asked Brooke.

"I don't know. Brainstorm something. I wish I could come over there and be with you. I could help you brainstorm." "I wish you could too."

"OK, here's a thought: is there anything that you're in a unique position to observe that nobody else is?" "Other than the *nouveau pauvre* life in St Barth, not really," said Brooke.

"That's a start," said Grace, sounding unconvinced. "But you're hardly *pauvre*."

Little did she know.

Suddenly. Brooke heard a piercing scream in the background.

"Oh crap," said Grace. "I'm so sorry. Sounds like I'm needed. Talk later?"

Brooke heard the click on the other end of the line before she had a chance to say anything further.

At least the flow of tears had ebbed a tiny bit, but objectively, she didn't really feel much better at all. She needed to figure out the social media thing. It wasn't an instinctive skill that she knew she would be good at. That *nouveau pauvre* thing was funny, but only in theory. In practice, it would be humiliating. Maybe she should experiment with different angles. She spent the rest of the afternoon taking photos of fruit and going through Instagram and looking at other accounts from chefs. Nothing really made any sense. There was nothing that she could borrow and transform for her own uses. Somehow, she was going to have to get her share of the attention and harness the magic of word of mouth. She was going to have to exploit the pride of place that people from Saint Barth had, and the fact that everybody wanted to come here. She had to sell the dream somehow, but in a different way. There were a million people doing glamorous travel shots...and she didn't have the money to be glamorous anyway. She looked around to see what else needed to be done in the house. Nothing. She'd done a good job that morning. She was relieved that she didn't have to serve these people until tomorrow. She needed to get out of the house before they came back or retreat to her room, which was not a pleasant place to spend the day. Perhaps she would be able to go to the beach, after all. That would be nice. And then afterwards, she would take a nice shower and wait for Antoine to come pick her up. Her heart beat faster as she wondered what they would do and where they would go. What would she wear on their excursion? She would have time to think about it at the beach. She went down to her room to change into a bathing suit and a cover up, grabbed the keys to her Mini Moke and tossed them in her straw beach bag along with a novel to read. She closed and locked her apartment door, made her way to the driveway, and jumped into the Mini Moke, heading towards the gate. She pressed the clicker, and the gate opened smoothly. Thank goodness it was still working. Which beach would she go to? She was always so used to going to the beaches by the airport. But maybe she should just go to the local one down the hill. The one that she had seen Antoine at that first morning alone, when she'd first started thinking of herself as a local. She drove down towards the beach and decided to make a short detour to see if she could find some sea beans in the swamp. Sure enough, there seemed to be plenty growing on the edges. She stepped closer to the mud and broke off a green stalk. She took a nibble. Yes, delightfully crisp. And salty. These would make a great salad ingredient, but she would go pick them fresh on Wednesday, instead of keeping them in the refrigerator. She got back into the Mini Moke and headed to the beach. There weren't many people there today, and the water seemed choppier than usual. Maybe a storm was coming in. She hoped that if so, it was far away and wouldn't reach the island. That would negatively impact her rentals. Which made her panic anew. How would she survive this summer and the low season? She would have to think about some more ways to monetize the house.

She chose a spot on the beach and sat there, watching an influencer type do a yoga routine.

Cooking retreats, she thought. That would be amazing. She could have people come and visit and do yoga and cook and find out about local ingredients. She could get Antoine involved and all the fishermen and the farmers and give farm tours. People would pay a lot for that, even in the low season, wouldn't they? She tapped a note into her phone so she wouldn't forget. She used to think that if the idea was good enough, it would be unforgettable. But she had realized with age that this was simply not true. And anyway, ideas were a dime a dozen. It was what you did with them, if anything, that mattered. The yoga girl left the beach. Brooke sat there for a while more, looking at the waves. Did she want to go for a swim? Or had she just come here to meditate? Either one was fine. Now that she lived here, she didn't need to make the most of every second of sunshine. Though perhaps it was a good lesson to live as though you had but limited moments. She decided to walk to the edge of the water, but the wave break was right by the shore, and she remembered there was a big drop after that. Brooke knew this would make it difficult to get in and come out today. She hesitated for a moment, not seeing anyone else in the water. As she swept the beach with her eyes, she noticed a blonde head. A familiar one. Was it the girl she had seen Antoine with? She'd been hoping that she was out of town. But now, it looked like she was here. Would Antoine dare to take Brooke out in public with his girlfriend around? Brooke hoped that the blonde girl did not recognize her. That would be awkward. She decided that she wasn't going to let herself miss out on a friendly evening with Antoine just because she thought he had a girlfriend. The girl seemed not to notice her at all, staring out to the water and then looking up to the house on the cliff above them. Carlos's house. At one point, the girl waved towards the house. Who was she waving at? Was Antoine there? Brooke felt uneasy being on the beach at the same time as this woman, and so, while the girl had her back turned, she packed up her things and headed back towards the parking area, disappearing down the sandy path lined with sea grapes before the girl could see her. Thankfully, this time, no one had messed with her tires or with anything else. As she drove back up the hill, she looked through Carlos's gates and down his driveway. She had the unpleasant surprise of noticing that the Meat my Fish van was indeed parked in front of the house- again. So maybe Antoine *was* who the blonde had been waving at. She would have to get to the bottom of this. She couldn't expect to flirt with someone if she thought he had a girlfriend, one who cared enough to wave to him from the beach.

But maybe she was stalking him. How would she know he was there unless he had texted her to tell him? It was weird. Antoine really was involved with Carlos somehow, wasn't he? She would have thought that Antoine would have said something when she straight out asked him about Carlos, but then again, everyone said St. Barth was such a small island. Maybe people tried to hide who they were, and not talk about the details of their lives, more than in other places. She didn't like this feeling of wondering what Antoine was up to, and she got a bad feeling from the blonde, as well. Why did she have to have the friendly hots for a guy who was so problematic, especially after being betrayed by Hunter? She deserved something nice, simple, and fun. Something to ease her into dating. Even if it wasn't something that would last. Was that too much to ask? No matter, she would try to get to the bottom of it when they saw each other. She came back to her house, pleased to notice that the Argentines were not yet home, and headed to her downstairs suite.

After a brief shower, Brooke went to her small closet to find something appropriate to wear. Going out with a local, she could go a lot more casual than one would go with New York types or Argentines. She eventually settled on a pair of cropped blue jeans and a sheer printed voile shirt with a contrast-colored bralette under it, paired with lace-up espadrilles with a low heel. That would probably look appropriate for wherever Antoine was choosing to take her. She didn't know what to expect. After a moment of reflection, she decided to swap out the jeans for a pair of jean shorts. That was more casual, and it showed off the tan she was finally starting to acquire. The top was pretty enough to dress the whole look up, and the platform espadrilles would lengthen her legs. She packed a sheer, long sweater into her bag to warm her up, especially if they were going to be riding the Vespa. Evenings could get a little bit cool, she reasoned. She shivered, thinking of the night air, but also thinking of sitting on the back of a Vespa, with her thighs straddling

Antoine's back. *Control yourself.* She really did deserve a fun fling, but it was growing increasingly clear that Antoine was probably not a good choice after all. He seemed to be intent on remaining friends, and she was counting on him for food, which was kind of a big deal. She now realized that going on a date, even a supposedly friendly one, with Antoine was probably the worst thing they could do. The smartest thing would be to remain friends with him- at a distance- and use him to get to know more people on the island. After all, if they had a falling out, it could be a disaster. For her, at least. With new resolve, she checked herself out in the mirror and decided that she looked cute enough for a platonic evening. What did she care if he had a girlfriend if they were just friends? *Forget the flirting,* she decided. She would be on her best behavior from here on in. Funny how making that decision made her feel a lot better, too. However, she did deserve to have a fun fling with *someone*, but maybe a tourist- someone who would go back home, to their real life, and she wouldn't have to deal with it impacting *her* real life- on the island.

She checked her phone, remembering that she missed her watch terribly already. The Argentines still weren't back, and she had half an hour before Antoine arrived. She remembered that she had taken the paperwork from Hunter's drawer downstairs, so she could look at it when she had more time. This was as good a time as any. She would see what those letters said.

She leafed through them, putting them in chronological order based on the date in the upper right-hand corner of each sheet. Though they bore Carlos' house address, they weren't from Carlos after all, but from someone she decided may be an assistant or a lawyer or family office employee. As she'd suspected, the letters requested to buy the house, the person making various offers that got higher and higher as the letters progressed. When she saw the final number, in the most recent letter, Brooke's eyes grew wide. *Seven and a half million dollars.* When they had purchased the land and built the house, it hadn't been nearly that much. That sum would solve all her problems, wouldn't it? It would put some money in her pocket. She could start a new life somewhere in the States or in Europe. She could even help Hunter out- not that he deserved it. But then, she shook her head. Her house was probably worth even more than that if this person was offering it off market. She should find out from a realtor how much she could get- just in case, just to have that information in her back pocket for a rainy day. But then, a pinching in her heart at the very thought of it told her that she realized that she had no intention of selling this house. She'd worked too hard for it, made it her own. It was all she had left. And those last happy memories of her parents, that was worth everything. Sea Grapes had been her dream, and it still was. She just needed to make sure that she secured her future here. Surely, she was capable of supporting herself. She wasn't that pathetic, was she? But of course, being on an island might have limited what she could do. She thought back again to her idea of the retreats. And the cooking school. How could she do something that paid for her life here, and promoted the real businesses on the island, not just the Nikki Beaches, the Eden Rocs, and the shiny yachts in the harbor? What about the people who had lived here for generations? Who fished here, who grew vegetables in the sandy earth? People like her ancestors, who were buried in the cemetery. She needed to be a voice for the real inhabitants of the island, but did she dare? The true locals probably considered her an interloper, but over time, maybe she would gain their trust. Taking aspirational pictures from her villa was one angle, but the other angle was the small cottages, the places where people swept the sand out into the street.

She wondered where Antoine lived. She knew a lot of the seasonal people rented small apartments in town or on the outskirts, but Antoine had been here for a while, and had been intent on settling in. Maybe she would find out more today, especially if they were going to be actual friends, after all. She checked the time on her phone again and realized that it was 6:30. Right on cue, the phone pinged.

I'm at the gate, Antoine had written.

Chapter 22

Brooke's heart beat out a little pitter patter. *Just friends*, she reminded herself. She picked up her bag, double made sure her door was locked, and stepped outside. As she walked below the verandah towards the driveway, she heard voices. Lisa and Ana. So what if they were home? It was not her problem. She didn't need to serve them 24/7. That wasn't part of the offer. She decided it was time to start putting up some boundaries.

She hoped she wouldn't bump into Ernesto, but of course, she did. As she stepped into the driveway, and before she had a chance to open the gate, she heard a shout from the pool area. Ernesto was standing on the pool patio. Even from a distance, she could see how his eyes were running up and down her body, focusing on her bare legs.

"Where are you off to?" he called out. "I was going to go for a swim. You want to join me?"

"Enjoy your swim," said Brooke politely. "I'm going out with a friend."

"Ohh. A girlfriend? Invite her, too."

His eyes twinkled.

Brooke ignored him as she clicked the gate open, hoping Ernesto wasn't looking after her, but knowing that he probably was. She smiled when she spotted Antoine on a turquoise Vespa.

"I like the color," she said as she got closer. "It matches my Land Rover."

"I noticed," said Antoine. "Is yours a custom paint job?"

"It is. Hunter wanted a Land Rover, but I got to decide on the color," said Brooke.

"That's nice of him," Antoine responded.

"Not really," said Brooke. "I paid for it."

Antoine's eyes widened, but he was discreet enough not to ask any further questions.

"OK, get on. I have a great idea for where to take you," he said.

Brooke straddled the bike and there she was, her thighs on either side of Antoine, feeling his hard muscles between her legs. She hesitated on whether she should hold on to him or hold on to the metal bar behind her. She settled for the safer option. Safer for their friendship, that was. She didn't want him to get any ideas.

"It would be less dangerous if you wrap your arms around me," said Antoine.

"I'm fine," said Brooke, as they started to make their way down the hill.

She hadn't been on a Vespa in years, not since she'd been a teenager, and she was realizing now that it was a little scary as they whizzed past all the cars on the windy roads. But on principle, she wasn't going to hold on to him. However, her thighs did clench him on either side a few times. He felt hot under the fabric of the white jeans that made his legs look so muscular and strong. She forced herself to look away.

"So where are we going?"

"It's a surprise," he said.

They made their way to the far end of the island, past the Rosewood hotel. The sun was just starting to set.

"I haven't been here in several years," Brooke mentioned. "It's funny- when we're here on vacation, we tend to stick to the same old spots."

"I know," said Antoine. "That's usually the way. When we want to be without the visitors, we know we have a few corners of the island that are still ours."

"Good point," said Brooke.

Antoine nosed the Vespa down a narrow ribbon of road that cut through a scrubby forest. When they hit the first series of bumps, Brooke yelped and grabbed for Antoine's waist.

"I told you," he said.

"Oh, what's this?" asked Brooke as they headed down the bumpy road, trying not to breathe in Antoine's after-shave now that she was leaning into his back, feeling self-conscious about her breasts pressing against him. "You're taking me here to murder me, aren't you?"

She always reverted to humor when she was emotionally overwhelmed.

"It's a guerilla pop-up restaurant," said Antoine. "One of my friends runs it, and sometimes has to move it, depending on whether he gets caught."

"You're friends with gorillas?" asked Brooke as they pulled up to a structure that looked like a treehouse. Well, a treehouse on the ground with planks laid out as a floor. There were a few folding tables. Everything was sheltered by a large tree. Tarps stretched out from the branches of the tree and attached to surrounding trees to provide a cover from the frequent rain showers.

"This is so cute," said Brooke, regretfully letting go of Antoine's waist.

"It's as farm to table as you can get on this island," said Antoine.

"So fun," said Brooke. "I can't believe I didn't know about it."

"Don't tell any of the tourists," said Antoine, getting off the Vespa and engaging the kickstand. He held the vehicle steady so Brooke could get off. Her legs were trembling a bit- from the ride and from the adrenaline of being so close to him, she had to admit. *Just friends*, she whispered to herself.

"What did you say?"

"Nothing," said Brooke. "Thank you again for picking me up. This is really a treat."

"Just wait till you taste the food," said Antoine.

They walked to the structure. A petite woman emerged.

"Beatrice," said Antoine. "This is my friend Brooke. I wanted her to check out the most exclusive restaurant in Saint Barth."

"Glad to see you," said Beatrice. "Welcome, Brooke. Well, Antoine, I think you know what's on the menu, since you delivered most of it, but we did collect a few surprise ingredients. Come in. Come say hi to Roger."

"Roger is Beatrice's husband," said Antoine to Brooke. "He's the chef here."

They headed to a sort of lean-to outfitted with camping stoves and what Brooke decided were containers of water.

"How long will you stay in this location?" Brooke asked.

"It depends," said Beatrice. "Usually, the police look the other way. The trouble comes when an outsider tries to complain, or when we find out that the land we're on was purchased by a New Yorker or something."

"Careful," said Antoine, smiling. "Brooke is from New York."

"Oh," said Beatrice, her eyes shining in a less friendly manner now.

"...But she's one of us now," said Antoine, quickly correcting course. This pleased Brooke, especially when she noticed that Beatrice was back to smiling warmly.

A barrel-chested man came back from behind the lean-to.

"Antoine!" he exclaimed, a pleased expression on his strong-featured face. He looked a bit sunburnt, but the kind of color that came from repeated exposure to the elements. Maybe he was a bit windburned too.

"Roger is not only an exceptional chef. He's also a wonderful fisherman."

"And don't forget I have my goats," said Roger.

"Yes, who could forget that," said Antoine. "That goat cheese I brought you," he said to Brooke, "that was from Roger's farm. His goats are wonderful. They all have quite distinct personalities."

"I'd love to see them sometime," said Brooke, wondering how she could share this on her Instagram account, without betraying local secrets. She realized that it might be more challenging than she'd thought, to strike the right balance between promoting local products and keeping the good stuff for the locals. She would have to pick Antoine's brain about that.

"Well, you guys go sit down. I'll get you a cocktail. And I'll start getting some food for you."

"Are you expecting anyone else tonight?" asked Antoine.

"Maybe one more table?" said Roger. "Looks like there are a few events on the island tonight. Seems to be all hands on deck. I think Carlos is having a party."

"He is," Antoine confirmed.

So that was why Brooke had seen him at the house. He was just making an innocent delivery. She was probably way off base, imagining that Carlos was Antoine's father. Granted, both men were blond, though Antoine skewed darker gold, and they had similar builds, but that wasn't exactly damning evidence. And interestingly, the way Roger had mentioned Carlos didn't betray any relationship on their part, but who knew? Maybe it was a secret, or an open secret, and maybe they still saw her as an outsider who was not to be told what was going on. She would get to the bottom of this, she swore to herself.

"Well, you can get whichever table you like," Beatrice smiled. "I'll be back."

Brooke loved this kind of restaurant; the sort of place where you got what you got, and it was the best of the best. There was always a sense of surprise and delight. Beatrice came back with two glasses filled with a sunset-hued liquid.

"My famous punch," she said, smiling.

"What's in it?" Brooke whispered once Beatrice was out of earshot. She could smell the alcohol off-gassing even without picking up the glass.

"The Saint Barth equivalent of Moonshine," Antoine smiled. "And whichever fruits Beatrice managed to find on any given day."

Brooke took a sip. It didn't matter what was in it- it was strong, but it was also delightful and fresh and sweet- tropical, all at the same time. Now that they were sitting at the table, facing each other, and that Beatrice had retreated to the kitchen to help Roger, Brooke and Antoine looked at each other a bit awkwardly.

"So how was your day?" Brooke asked, making small talk.

"The same as usual," Antoine said. "Food deliveries. Dealing with some fish stuff. People who think I'm charging too much."

"They think you're charging too much? You gave me a very fair price!" Brooke exclaimed.

"Well, I gave you the friends and family discount," said Antoine.

Brooke started to blush. She was pleased to score the friends and family discount, but she also didn't want to take advantage.

"Antoine, when I have a better budget, I would like to start paying you your normal rate. Something that can help you to make a bigger profit. Everybody has to live," she said.

"I know," he replied. "But I feel that right now, you're in more dire straits than I am."

Brooke considered this. So, he was finally believing her that she was not the spoiled little rich girl simply playing poor. She couldn't blame him- it was hard to process the fact that her husband had left her high and dry.

"Well, I appreciate it," she said.

They spent the rest of the meal taking about how the island had changed in the past years. Which locals had passed away or moved away. Which new restaurants were good and which ones were held by outsiders.

"About that," said Brooke. "I've been thinking of my Instagram feed..."

"That's all anyone can think of these days," said Antoine.

"Actually, I didn't really have one until now," said Brooke. "And I think I need one to advertise my cooking. I'm a little worried, because even though I have a rental for next week, there's nothing else lined up. I set this all up a little bit late. And really, rather than rent out my house, I would rather be cooking for people or doing cooking retreats."

"I get it- It must be hard to have people in your space," said Antoine. "It would kill me to have people sleeping in my bed. I mean, unless I invited them in."

He winked.

Brooke barely even blushed at this because she was far too busy considering it. Grace had mentioned the same thought to her as well on their phone call, and until now, Brooke hadn't really allowed herself to realize how much she resented strangers being in her bed. But she didn't have the luxury to think about it too much. It was just necessary.

"I think that, when you don't have a choice, it changes things a lot, don't you?" Said Brooke.

"You have a point," said Antoine. "Wow, you're really not kidding about being on a strict budget, are you?"

"As if I would joke about something like that," said Brooke.

"So, it's not just a break, is it? It's over between you and your husband," Antoine said. It wasn't really a question, so Brooke was sorely tempted to agree. But still, what did it matter to Antoine either way? He just wanted to be friends. And Hunter had expressly told her not to tell anyone. It wasn't out of loyalty to him; it was out of self-preservation. If one of his deals went through...

"It is just a break, but even if it wasn't..."

"Well, if I had someone like you, I would do everything in my power to make you happy. Are you the one who asked for the break?" he asked. "Don't answer if it's an indiscreet question."

Brooke looked at him. His aqua eyes staring back at her, inquisitive, not teasing, sincere. It made her feel marginally better that he thought she was the kind of person that no one should leave. *Just friends, stupid*, she reminded herself.

"It's a long story."

Now, Brooke was dying to change the subject, and happily, she noticed that Antoine seemed just as thrilled to do that.

"Tell me more about you," Brooke said. "Before you moved here, how long had you been coming to the island?"

"Just a few years," Antoine replied.

Brooke nodded her head. How many years had Carlos been on the island? She tried to remember. A couple ...several.

"I started coming maybe a decade ago," said Antoine. "Time seems to stop on this island. I'm sorry if I'm being a bit vague about the details."

"I'm not trying to be nosy, by the way. I mostly want to know how long it took you to be considered a local. I'll be happy when that happens."

"I don't think it's that cut and dried," Antoine smiled. "Like you, I had some family links to the island through some relatives. And I guess I didn't give anyone a choice- I started selling fish and fishing. And then I tried to build my company and believe me, they were resentful at first."

"You don't say," Brooke laughed. "Did they get the name Meat my Fish?"

"I don't know- I didn't care, as long as I thought it was funny," said Antoine. "I wanted to have a sense of humor about things, in a less than ideal situation."

"Do you think you would ever go back to working in wine? Weren't you at a winery?"

"Yeah. My mom's. And I doubt it- it's frustrating because I went to business school, wine school, everything...and still, after all of that, when my mom passes away, my uncles will take over- I mean, they pretty much have already."

"How is that possible?" Brooke asked.

"Long story," Antoine sighed. "And I don't think I have the fight in me."

"I'm so sorry," said Brooke, seeing the hurt on his face, wishing she hadn't asked.

"I'll be fine," said Antoine. "It was really my life's purpose, or so I thought but.... I feel like I'm making headway here too, I'm finding things to love. That's why I thought, let's have a sense of humor about things. Life isn't always so serious, especially when it is."

Brooke smiled.

"You're quite a philosopher," she said.

She didn't complete her sentence with what she was thinking, which was, *a hot one*. Beatrice deposited a plate of cod fritters on the table.

"My favorite," Antoine said.

"Says the guy who has the island fish and meat monopoly," Beatrice laughed.

"You're flattering me," said Antoine. "But it's true you can't beat my meat."

Brooke burst into a fit of giggles.

"I guess we are definitely lucky you didn't put that on your van- I'm starting to realize how tempted you must have been."

Antoine erupted into laughter, too, now.

Beatrice, who had been hovering over the table to see what they thought of their first bites, considered them both.

"I imagine I'm lucky my English isn't good enough to fully grasp that."

Grasp that. Brooke looked at Antoine, and they laughed even harder. Beatrice merely rolled her eyes.

"I don't want to know. So where did you two meet? Antoine doesn't usually bring any new people around. Especially new pretty people."

"I'm a client," said Brooke. "I saw the van. Noticed the name. I thought it was brilliant. How could I not order my fish from this one?"

"Agreed," said Beatrice. "But how did you find him? I've told him a million times he doesn't have a good enough website."

"And I've told you it's Instagram and word of mouth," said Antoine.

"My... friend...Nathalie gave me his card," Brooke said, both to show Beatrice that she agreed with her that maybe Antoine needed to optimize his website, and, to see if she would get a reaction from Nathalie's name.

"Are you talking about Nathalie Mainart? The one who used to work at Sea Grapes?" said Beatrice.

Antoine flashed a funny look, as if worried that Beatrice was about to say something horrible.

"Yes. That's my house," Brooke said.

Might as well lance the abscess before it festered.

"Oh," said Beatrice, standing up, her posture projecting formality.

"It's not like that," said Antoine.

"Alright," said Beatrice. "Anyway, let me go check on your food."

Once Beatrice was gone, Brooke looked at Antoine a bit desperately.

"Is this the reaction I'm going to get every time I mention Sea Grapes?" she asked.

"Beatrice and Nathalie are friends," said Antoine. "Nathalie has a bee in her bonnet."

"No shit. But about what? Does she think we mistreated her?" Brooke asked.

"I don't want to be a gossip," said Antoine.

"I think that ship has sailed, Antoine. Now tell me what you know."

"You'll have to ask her. All I know is that I think she thought you were friends at first, but then I think that your husband made it clear what her position was, and she had to take a step back."

"Surely, she knows I had nothing to do with that. I've been dying to find a way to make enough money to get her to come back to work with me, as teammates."

"Too late for that. Someone else offered her more money. A lot more money."

"Who?" asked Brooke.

"I'm not at liberty to say," said Antoine.

Brooke froze. So, he was on Nathalie's side, was he?

"Let me ask you something," said Brooke, narrowing her eyes. "Why did you invite me out? Because you wanted to be my friend? Or because you wanted to feed the gossip mill?"

Antoine reached across the table, putting his hand on hers. She pulled away.

"I invited you out because I like you," said Antoine. "Nothing sinister about it."

"And I only said yes because I needed a friend," said Brooke. "So why is it that I can't trust that you want to be a friend to me?"

She felt vulnerable saying this, and kind of stupid. She was so alone here on this rock in the middle of the Caribbean Sea.

"I promise I'll be a true friend to you," said Antoine.

Brooke looked at him. Those gorgeous lips over those white teeth. The aqua eyes, the tousled mane. The golden hairs glistening on his tan forearms in the candlelight. Every time she looked at him, he just got hotter. She reluctantly put her hands back on the table. Antoine reached back across. His skin felt hot against hers. Did friends hold hands across the table here in St Barth? She really shouldn't be entertaining any of these thoughts, but she couldn't help the fantasies that started running through her head. Thankfully, Beatrice interrupted her coursing thoughts as she approached the table again.

"I'm sorry if I was rude," said Beatrice. "This is an island where everyone gossips. And I need to give everyone an equal chance, don't I? So welcome to St Barth. What are you planning on doing here?"

Brooke pretended not to hear the *if you stay* that was inherent in the question.

"I'm renting out my house, and acting as property manager and chef, so if you know anyone who needs a rental..."

"You are? But why?" asked Beatrice.

"She's wanting to make her own way in the world, just like we all are," said Antoine, and Brooke gave him a thankful look.

Chapter 23

They were heading down the road, a rainforest blur on either side of them. The cry of the tree frogs was primal in her ears. She allowed her hips to rock forward a bit and squeezed Antoine's legs between her thighs. As she gripped him tighter, she knew he could feel her breasts against his back, just as she could certainly feel his muscles rippling under his linen shirt. She was trying to be subtle about rubbing against him, but finally, she couldn't control it anymore, and she ran one hand from where it was placed on his waist to between his thighs. She started stroking the bulge in his jeans, undoing the zipper, and finding him already rock hard. She gripped him in her fist, squeezing gently.

"We're going to have an accident," he observed. "But don't stop."

Antoine pulled the Vespa over onto the side of the road. Brooke noticed now that the road was in fact more of a path, with no one around. In fact, they hadn't seen any cars in a while. Antoine dismounted from the bike and set the kickstand. With one hand, he pulled her skirt up, and her bikini bottoms aside, then squatted down, and put his head between her legs. She was shocked, and deliciously surprised- they were supposed to be just friends, weren't they? But she held her breath, waiting to see what would happen next. When she felt his tongue make the first exploratory lick, she shivered in pleasure. Antoine's tongue probed further and deeper, eliciting a moan from her. She put her hands on the back of the motor scooter, briefly worrying that it would topple over from her weight, but far too excited to care. Now, Antoine's head was buried between her legs as he spread her thighs further apart, gripping them with his hands, massaging them, and then using one finger to plunge inside her, then two. Now, she arched her back, and moaned more loudly. She couldn't take it. It was too delicious. She wasn't the kind of girl who did this with near strangers. But at that moment, she wanted to be. It felt illicit and dangerous that they could get caught at any moment. *Screw just friends.* This was exactly what she'd been craving ever since she had seen Antoine that first day at the airport. She squirmed, trying to position herself on the motorbike so that she wouldn't fall off, but so she could offer herself to him more completely. What would he do next, she wondered, as he gently moved his fingers in and out, hitting just the right spots, his tongue working its magic on her. She could already feel the first waves of her orgasm. Her body was shaking, vibrating. But still, she wanted more. She hadn't come this fast or this hard in so long. But then, just as she was abandoning herself to her own pleasure, she heard a noise. At first, she thought it must just be her heart beating in her temples. Her eyes were screwed shut, and she returned her focus to feeling every last delicious shudder of her orgasm. But then, that noise again. Where was it coming from? Was somebody around? It sounded like a banging. It was getting louder. She opened her eyes in panic and found herself in her room- in the downstairs apartment. In the narrow bed. Then, she remembered how the rest of the evening before had *actually* gone down.

It had ended with her and Antoine arguing about why she would never be a true local, about whether she could be a true friend to him, about whether she had ever been a real friend to Nathalie. To be fair, Brooke had been the instigator. The dream version of that evening would have been so much better. Now, she realized, with great mortification, that the reason she'd been so combative was that she had allowed herself to drink way too much. That fruit punch was lethal. She owed Antoine an apology, that was for sure. She was pretty sure she'd also said a few other things that she didn't want to remember right now.

Then, she noticed that the banging was continuing. It wasn't from her dream, after all. Someone was knocking at her door. Her heart beat a tattoo. Who was trying to come in? She was terrified. She jumped up from bed and came closer to the door.

"Who is it?" she yelled through the wood door.

"Lisa can't sleep. There's a light shining directly into our window."

She recognized the voice. Jaime.

"What time is it? Can't you just close the curtains for now and we'll figure it out in the morning?"

"It's like a flood light," said Jaime. "And there's a weird clanging noise. First, we had the smell, and then we have this. It's very disturbing. This is something that you need to take care of."

Subtext: if you want us to stay and give you a good review. Brooke rolled her eyes. *Yes.* She needed them to stay, and she needed a good review, even though she was pretty sure none of them would even bother to give her one.

"OK, I'll be right there," she said.

She checked her phone for the time. It was 11:30 PM. Well, at least she could get some sleep after she had dealt with this. She was surprised that she'd already fallen so deeply asleep so early in the night, but then she remembered. It was more like she had been in an alcohol coma. At least she was reasonably sober now. She threw on some leggings and a T-shirt and scraped her hair back into a ponytail to look presentable. She wiped some makeup remover under her eyes and opened the door. Jaime was gone. He probably expected her to come to the main part of the house, which she did. She found him on the veranda.

"Look at that," he said, pointing. "See? Somebody's literally shining a light into the house."

Brooke squinted. Yes, it looked like someone was on the boat that was often parked in front of Carlos' house. And indeed, it seemed like a Klieg Lite was aimed directly at the upper windows of Sea Grapes. That was strange.

"Listen," said Brooke. "I'm so sorry, but it's 11:30 at night. We can't go out there, and we aren't going to call the police for this. I'll find out who it belongs to in the morning, and I'll make sure it doesn't happen again. Or I'll buy some blackout curtains for you."

Brooke wasn't about to reveal that she was pretty sure the boat belonged to Carlos, lest Jaime demand she call his house at 11:30 at night.

"You mean we have to spend all night with that light on?" asked Jaime, indignant.

"Well, who knows if it's going to last all night?" said Brooke. "You know what? I have a screen in the living room. I can help you to bring it upstairs. It will help to block the light more."

"Fine," Jaime sniffed. "Yes, do that. I don't think I should have to help. Isn't this your job?"

Wow.

"Absolutely," said Brooke with a big smile. "I'll bring it up right now. Is that OK?"

"Yes, the sooner the better," said Jaime impatiently.

Brooke followed him into the house, with the uncomfortable feeling that Sea Grapes was no longer hers. She was tiptoeing around, as if disturbing these people, who were on *her* turf. It just didn't feel good or natural to her. But she was going to need to deal with those feelings because this was survival. She went to the office and folded up the screen in the corner. It was upholstered with grass cloth and a beautiful fabric trim in the house's signature colors. It was heavier than she remembered, and she struggled to bring it up the stairs, cursing the fact that some people thought they were too good to help a woman carry a heavy object. Jaime merely looked at her, arms by his sides, as she slowly made her way up. *This reflects worse on him than it does on me*, thought Brooke. They got to the master bedroom. Remembering the disheveled state of the bed each morning, Brooke blushed, hoping the cheap mattress protector she'd bought was doing its job. She'd carefully selected the perfect mattress for herself back when they had constructed the house and would hate to see it defiled. Eventually she would have to buy a better mattress cover. People tended to lose all self-control when they rented a house or went to a hotel. It was filthy, what humans would do when they stayed somewhere other than their home. As Brooke was focusing on struggling to make sure to bring in the screen without damaging the door or the fabric, it was only once she had gotten the screen near the window that she saw that Lisa lay on the bed, on top of the sheets, naked and unperturbed, as if Brooke didn't even exist. She didn't try to cover herself up, or anything. Something in the back of Brooke's mind sent off a little signal of alarm. She hoped these people weren't expecting other services in addition to the rental and the cooking, just like Ernesto seemed to. Some people could be like that, she'd heard. She decided to focus exclusively on the screen, which she positioned in front of the window, checking to make sure that it was blocking all the light.

"There," she said. "I'll get to the bottom of this tomorrow, but for now, you should be able to sleep just fine."

"Great," said Jaime.

Lisa didn't bother to say anything at all.

Great is not a synonym for thank you, thought Brooke, but she simply bade them good night and headed back to her downstairs apartment, her cheeks burning in shame at this latest humiliating situation she had somehow found herself in. She would be glad when these people were finished with their week. She was dreading the dinner the next evening- that evening, now, and she was also dreading Antoine's food delivery, knowing that he would be unhappy with her, and rightfully so.

Back in her room, She lay there, trying to fall back to sleep, wishing she had a delicious dream to look forward to, instead of the fretting about how she was going to survive the next few days, and how she was going to survive the next few weeks and months. She was so relieved to have another rental lined up, but she needed to look them up to see who she was going to be dealing with, so she would be prepared. She also was not looking forward to calling Carlos's house in the morning to see why a Klieg light had been aimed at her house. That was unacceptable. Eventually, she drifted off, much too late, absolutely not in time for her to get the sleep she needed to be fresh in the morning.

Chapter 24

B rooke woke up to her phone's rude alarm clock sounds, already panicked, already dreading the breakfast she was going to have to make for these people. Today, she needed comfort food, so she decided to make cinnamon buns*. That made the best of local ingredients and reminded her of her grandmother. She made sure to make a few extra for herself. The Argentines wouldn't give a crap, so she would save the story of her upbringing in the Caribbean and how they sourced cinnamon when she was a child for her Instagram. That might resonate and be interesting for people. Might as well start getting people to know her and her story. That, at least, felt more meaningful than simply trying to be an influencer, especially when she certainly did not feel like she could influence anything, let alone her own life.

Once in the kitchen, she squeezed some of the fruits Antoine had brought her to make some fresh fruit juice and watered it down to extend it. The fruits in the Caribbean were so concentrated that she didn't feel bad doing this to save resources. Then, she went about making the cinnamon buns. She would add a little banana to them, she decided, to make the dish a little bit richer, and perhaps serve some soft-boiled eggs with soldiers as an option. It was an economical breakfast, but a luxurious looking one, especially when combined with the fresh foliage and flowers she cut from the plumeria on the edge of the property. She was getting the hang of this thing, expertly timing the coffee and the tea, remembering what each person had requested on the days before.

When she brought the tray onto the veranda, all the Argentines were already assembled.

"Did you call the person who owns the boat?" asked Lisa in lieu of a greeting.

"Not yet," Brooke said. "It's a bit early, so I focused on making your breakfast."

This being polite and taking the high road thing was a bit exhausting, but she'd had so much practice in her charity career that it was second nature. She noticed that Ernesto was now looking everywhere but at her. Possibly, seeing Antoine picking her up had cemented the idea in his mind that he wouldn't get anywhere with her. At least he wouldn't harass her anymore, or at least she hoped.

"I'm looking forward to creating a very special dinner for you all this evening," said Brooke. "I just need one last confirmation of how many of you will be there, as well as which time you would like to get started."

No one spoke, so finally Ernesto piped up.

"It will be all of us. Plus, Diego and Ashley. Let's start at 7:00."

"Sounds good," said Brooke. "I'm going to make it special for all of you. I'll see you later. What is your plan for the day?"

Ana gave her a look, as if it was an inappropriate question, but it was fair enough to ask. She needed to get their rooms cleaned and the rest of the house done and start cooking without being obtrusive. She was learning that Nathalie's main quality had been being almost invisible, until she was needed. This was now a goal of Brooke's, too.

"We are going to go shopping and go to lunch," Ana finally said, her mouth set into a straight line. "We all have sunburns."

Brooke challenged herself not to smile. Of course, they had sunburns. She'd seen their stupid getups when they'd set off for their boating trip the day before. Her first reaction was to want to text Antoine and say *We were right. They have horrible sunburns.* But then, she remembered that he was probably mad at her. She hoped he would do the professional thing and still deliver the food on time.

"Great," she said. "I'll make up the rooms once you're gone. And please let me know if there's anything you need?"

"Just for you to get to the bottom of that stupid light thing," said Lisa, as if she was still being impacted once Brooke had brought in the screen.

"Of course," said Brooke, smiling.

She kept busy cleaning up the kitchen, and discreetly stuffed her face with two of the cinnamon buns. It almost brought tears to her eyes, remembering her grandmother making these for her.

It was exactly what the doctor ordered, because somehow it brought her back to who she really was. She wasn't defined by the comfortable life that Hunter had afforded her back when things were going well. She wasn't defined by how much money she had. She wasn't defined by the things she owned. She wasn't even the same person who had originally built Sea Grapes. She could make a beautiful life for herself without any of these trappings if she survived. She was going to be OK, she decided. She was going to do whatever she needed to do. And one of the things she needed to do was probably to stop being so weird with Antoine. Now, she remembered what had set her off. He'd been asking too many questions about her marriage. And she hadn't been able to tell him, because of a stupid promise she'd made to Hunter. This was her life, she decided. What would Antoine have to do with anything in Hunter's life, or in his business? She was going to set things straight. And yes, she was still going to be just friends, but at least Antoine wouldn't think that she was the on-the-brink-of-cheating spouse he seemed to think she was right now. It was kind of ridiculous that he was so judgmental when it was obvious that he had a girlfriend. *Whatever.* She tried to breathe deeply and slowly until that fact didn't bother her so much. It wasn't working. Eventually, she heard the others leave. She hoped they didn't come back too soon.

Brooke raced her way through her chores, straightening up the bedrooms, throwing the sheets in the wash and swapping them out for other ones, intermittently checking her phone to see if she had any messages from Antoine. Normally, he should be here at any minute. But with her egregious behavior, who knew anymore?

Finally, just as she was starting to fear that he had decided to leave her high and dry, she heard a buzzing at the intercom. *Thank goodness.*

She ran downstairs and hit the button, waiting for Antoine to show up. She needed to talk to him, clear the air, make him understand that her behavior the night before had been caused not only by alcohol, but by the fact that she'd been having to hide the truth from him. Did he even care about that? She wasn't sure. Again, she remembered that he was hardly single himself. *He* wasn't being honest.

She leaned against the door for a moment, collecting her thoughts, and then opened it. There he stood. That disheveled hair, those turquoise eyes. She let her eyes trace down his body. He was wearing a thin T-shirt that highlighted every muscle. She shuddered as she remembered the dream from the night before.

"I'm sorry, but I have to apologize," she started to say.

"No. I'm the one who should apologize," said Antoine. "You made it very clear that you just want to be friends, and I kept harassing you about your husband, and about your long-term plans here."

"No, I'm the one... I was sending mixed signals and..."

Now, they were both talking over each other, babbling.

"Listen, Brooke," said Antoine, putting his hand on her arm to quiet her. "I'm sorry. But I don't think I can be your friend."

Brooke's mouth fell open. Tears sprang to her eyes. She thought she might be sick. Much as she couldn't stop herself from lusting after Antoine, she also felt strangely close to him. She had already come to value his presence. And now, he was going to take that away?

"Why not?" Brooke asked, feeling stupid and desperate.

"Because I'm just so fucking attracted to you," Antoine said, closing his eyes and shaking his head, as if in shame. "I'm sorry if I have a hard time keeping my thoughts in check, and maybe it influences how I talk to you... and I snap at you because I'm frustrated at myself."

"Wait- what?" Brooke asked.

After the day before, she had convinced herself that she'd been misreading his looks, misreading the attraction between them.

"But...You...you have a girlfriend," she stammered.

Antoine looked at her, astonished.

"Girlfriend? No, I don't. What are you talking about?"

Brooke closed her mouth and considered him. She'd thought he was going to be honest with her, and now he was lying again. Smoothly, expertly. If she hadn't known better, she would have completely believed him.

"Listen, it doesn't even matter. You can do whatever you want. I just wanted to tell you that my husband and I are in fact completely broken up. We're not on a break. We're not getting back together. He cheated on me, and he told me not to tell anyone that we were splitting up, because he thought it might be bad for business. And now that I'm telling you that, I think you could at least be honest with me too. I've seen you with that girl."

"Which girl?" Antoine asked. His surprise seemed authentic. "If I had a girlfriend, I would tell you. And if I had a girlfriend, believe me, I would send someone else to do my deliveries to you. Because you're way too dangerous for me."

Much as hearing that warmed her heart and made her knees feel weak, Brooke was not to be distracted.

"Come on, Antoine. Then who's the blonde girl? I've seen you taking her to the airport," Brooke said accusingly. "Does that ring a bell?"

Antoine's face slacked, comprehension dawning.

"Oh! You mean Sophie? Sophie's not my girlfriend. Well, we had a brief thing, ages ago. But believe me when I say that we are absolutely, positively not together," said Antoine.

"Doesn't look like she's an ex from where I was parked," said Brooke.

"Yeah, sometimes Sophie comes on a little strong," said Antoine. "But I swear to you there's no mixed messages on my part. She's very much an ex, and believe me, if that was not the case, I would be up front with you. But I still help her out sometimes. I feel a bit sorry for her."

"You feel sorry for her. She seems like she's got a pretty good life... She looks like she's rich. Travels all the time. Gorgeous, well dressed."

"I know what it looks like," said Antoine. "But believe me, she's got her own issues, none of which have anything to do with me."

"Why do you feel the need to help her out?" asked Brooke.

"That's something that I think is best discussed at a later date," said Antoine.

Brooke groaned. Now she felt stupid for telling him the truth about Hunter and her. "Listen," she said, frustrated. "What I said about my husband and me being broken up- you can't repeat it to anyone."

"Who would I tell it to?" asked Antoine. "I don't know anyone you know. And I don't spread that type of gossip. But... since you're really separated... do I have a chance?"

Brooke looked at him, considering it. He was so gorgeous. And she did enjoy talking to him. She felt that he had some strange things in common with her. His business goals, his determination. He was admirable. As long as he was telling the truth about the blonde.

"I wouldn't be opposed," said Brooke, cautiously. "We could try to...maybe see how it goes?" she said shyly.

Suddenly, the possibility of her fantasies coming true froze her in her tracks. She smiled.

"We take it really, really slow, though, right?"

"I would certainly try... no promises," said Antoine, giving her a devastating look that made her knees almost buckle and wetness form between her legs.

"So... let's start over without this whole *just friends* thing in the way, shall we? Can I take you on a date? A real one?"

"I would like that," said Brooke. "Not tonight, as you know, we've got that big dinner..."

"Thursday, then?"

"Thursday," said Brooke.

Antoine leaned in and gave her a gentle kiss on the cheek. And then, on the lips. She parted her lips and returned the kiss more forcefully. Now, all the pent-up fantasies she'd had about him flooded her mind, making her want him to throw her onto the kitchen floor there and then. Antoine ran his hands down her body. He cupped her ass in his hands and lifted her up onto the island. He stood between her legs, kissing her deeply now, his hands running over her body, over her breasts. It was astounding, the way she reacted so immediately to his touch.

Suddenly, she heard the crunch of gravel.

"Crap," she said, her mouth still against his. "I think the renters are back."

"Talk about bad timing," Antoine groaned, stepping back, and readjusting himself. "I can't be seen in this condition," he said, smiling.

Brooke smiled back, awkwardly, trying to smooth down her hair.

"Sneak out the veranda. I'll see you soon," she said.

"I'll be looking forward to it," Antoine replied, winking at her. He scooped up his cooler bags and slipped out onto the veranda, just before Ernesto opened the front door. Thank goodness Ernesto hadn't caught them making out in the kitchen. Just a few seconds more, and he might have been greeted by a scandalous sight. Brooke smiled to herself. She wondered what they would say to that. What that would do to her ratings.

"Hello," she cried out, friendly. "I was just starting to work on your food. You're back already?"

"Yes, Lisa stepped on some kind of a jellyfish or something, or maybe an urchin," said Ernesto. "We had to bring her back. The rest of us will be going back out."

"All right," said Brooke. "Well. If she needs anything, I'll be in the kitchen."

"Do you have to be in the house while I'm in the house?" Lisa whined.

"Only if you want dinner tonight," said Brooke.

What the hell did this girl think she could do? Be in two places at once, or be invisible? Is that what she wanted from her? She realized then that that's what most people wanted from their staff: for them to be invisible until they needed them. Lisa rolled her eyes and let the others deposit her onto a pool chair in the shade.

"Can you bring me a book?" Lisa whined.

"Of course, baby," said Jaime.

He came back with a romance novel that Brooke knew to be absolutely filthy. The girls on the charity circuit had talked about it and joked about presenting it in their book club, but ultimately it had been shot down because it was too bawdy for that. *Happy reading*, thought Brooke.

She focused her attention on her ingredients again. She had the lobster now, and she'd be able to create these wonderful lobster rolls.

Antoine had brought her some brioche buns, and all the fresh herbs she needed. She considered the delightful local goat cheese* that she would bake with walnuts, herbs, and olives, which would yield a delicious creamy dip to spread onto some crostini. She would make a simple salad. Ah, she needed to grab the sea beans, she reminded herself. She jumped up and grabbed her bag. After double checking all the other ingredients, she had realized she needed some seltzer water. She would have to go to the store and then she'd go pick up the sea beans. She had plenty of time. Driving her Mini Moke towards town, she smiled to herself. She had everything under control. As she drove past Carlos's gate, she noticed the Mercedes convertible edging out, and a blonde head behind the wheel. She did a double take to see if Antoine was in the car too. He was not. *Good*, she thought to herself. That reminded her- she needed to see what was going on with the light on the boat. She picked up her phone and dialed the number she had for Carlos White, knowing his secretary or assistant would pick up.

"Hello," said a young woman's voice.

"Hi, this is Brooke from next door. I just wanted to talk to somebody and ask about what's going on with the boat you guys have anchored out front. Last night it was shining a powerful light at my house. And it would be great if you could keep that from happening again. It's not very comfortable for my guests."

"I'm sorry- I didn't see any lights on the boat," said the voice.

"Well, were you guys on the boat having a party or doing something like that? There was definitely a very powerful light that seemed to be coming from your boat."

"I'll ask the captain," said the voice. "As far as I know, there was no one there last night."

Brooke sighed. It hadn't been her imagination. It had been light enough with the full moon for her to see that it was Carlos's boat out there. She had seen the dinghy attached to the boat, and the light on deck.

"All right. Well, can you just double make sure that no one shines a light at my house in the future, please?"

"Absolutely," said the voice.

"OK, thank you," said Brooke, hanging up and feeling frustrated that she hadn't really achieved anything with this phone call at all.

Not wanting to drive all the way into town, she stopped by the local market near the Hotel Manapany to buy her sparkling water. Through the open shelves in the potato chip section, she thought she noticed a precise strawberry blonde bob and an aquiline nose. No question. It was Ilaria, one of her acquaintances from New York. She quickly ducked behind a tower of cases of Carib Beer, not wanting to be seen. Not because she had anything to be ashamed of, she rationalized. She was, after all, making a life for herself, but she just didn't want to have to answer any questions about the situation with Hunter in case anyone had seen him in the city and was wondering why she was still here in Saint Barth. Still, she waited for a few moments, steeling herself, and then stepped out, faux casual, making her way to the cash register. Ilaria was gone, thank goodness. Brooke lugged the packs of water back into the Moke, trying to resist giving a nasty look to the group of able-bodied men who seemed to convene regularly in front of the market, and headed to the marsh near Saline to gather some Salicornia, commonly known as sea beans. She pulled over to the side of the road, found a good spot and started cutting the succulents and placing them in a paper bag. These would add a delicious, salty crunch to her salad. She was thinking of the other ingredients as she went. Yes, she had everything she needed. She checked the time on her phone. She still had time to go to the beach, didn't she? Saline beach was right next to the swamp. Yes, she decided. She should do it. One of the great things about living on an island is that one tended to wear one's bathing suit most of the time, and she could just take a quick dip. Not that a bathing suit was required on Saline. Living on Saint Barth had to have some advantages other than sheer survival, didn't it?

Brooke drove down to the beach parking lot, made sure her paper bag full of sea beans and her sparkling water were secured in the Mini Moke's lockable trunk, and headed to the beach with the Turkish towel she always kept in the car. There was no one on the beach, as far as the eye could see, and the water lay in front of her, turquoise, sparkling. She stripped off her clothing and dove in.

She swam out, intent on evacuating the nervous energy that threatened to subsume her. She was already in the zone where the water had turned a dark navy when she felt herself being carried out to sea. But she was a strong swimmer, and she welcomed the effort it took to get her back to more shallow waters. Now, feeling calmer, she could enjoy a more relaxed swim, floating on the surface of the water, then looking down and enjoying the play of the sunlight on the sand. Giving in to the undulation of the sea. Now, she looked up at the sky and took a deep breath. Everything was going to be OK. She was going to make a great dinner. She was going to go on a fabulous date with Antoine the next day. She was going to start living her best life. She would figure this out. It was all going to work out. It wasn't that hard. What had she been afraid of before? Yes, some people were difficult. The ones who were renting now were not optimal, but they weren't the absolute worst. And the next ones would be better, she reasoned with herself. Just as she was heading back to land, a sea turtle crossed her path, an auspicious omen, she decided. This was the turning point. From here on in, things were going to be good. Not just good. They were going to be great.

She got back to the beach, toweled off, and headed back to her car. As she got behind the wheel, she reminded herself that she needed to plug it in when she got back. She had noticed it was running a bit low on charge, but at least no one had let the air out of the tires this time. She smiled to herself. Whoever had decided to target her at the beginning of her stay had probably given up. But then she thought of the light on the boat. Was that just a warning shot? No, it was probably an accident, she decided. Somebody had forgotten to turn off a light and it had shone in the wrong direction and Lisa was just being overly sensitive. But now, Brooke realized that a powerful Klieg light, to point in exactly that direction, with the boat turning around at anchor, had to be manned by someone. Well, she wouldn't worry about this, until she absolutely needed to, she decided.

She got back home without further incident, happy, peaceful, and salty, and started working on her food prep. She'd learned about *mise en place* at the Cordon Bleu. It made everything go that much more smoothly and gave one a sense of control and organization. Brooke cut up all the onion and the herbs and placed them into little bowls, keeping them ready for when she would create the food closer to dinnertime. She went through all the steps in her mind, and decided she could poach the lobster now and create the lobster salad. She had always excelled at making mayonnaise. She had a few secret ingredients under her belt. Lemon zest, of course. Dill, which gave it a delicious edge. And garlic, to make it almost more like an aioli than a simple mayonnaise. She also liked to add a few little cut up cornichons. It was what made all the difference. She would lightly toast the brioche just before serving, baste it in butter and lightly toast it again. It was decadent, but always a hit. She wondered about these guests that the Argentines were having over. She hoped that they at least would be kind.

Once she had all the ingredients ready, Brooke looked at her phone again. There was a message from Antoine.

Looking forward to tomorrow, he had written. *Good luck tonight.*

Brooke smiled, and tapped out, *Thank you,* but this also reminded her that she still hadn't heard from Nathalie. She tapped out a message.

Hope Ziggy is feeling better. Hope you're good. Hope to see you soon.

There was a lot of hope there, which she had a bad feeling would not result in much. She kept checking her phone as she put the finishing touches on the *mise en place* for dessert. She was going to make lemon ice cream*. In fact, she could make it now. It wouldn't freeze too badly, and it would be one less thing to have to put together at the last second. She started putting the ingredients together, taking out her ice cream machine. She could have made it without an ice cream machine as well, but having the tools she needed was one of the few luxuries she had left, for now. Other than the gorgeous house, of course. Checking her phone again, to of course find exactly zero messages from Nathalie, she thought of the one luxury she truly missed. Her gold Cartier watch, sitting in the pawn shop. Would she be able to get it back before it was sold? Also, why was she so obsessed with reaching Nathalie? Was she simply trying to reach out to her out of guilt? Had she really been unfair with Nathalie? Did they even have a real friendship? Or was it just that she thought that she owed her some kind of sympathy, or that Nathalie was the only other full-time person she knew on the island other than Antoine? In any case, she couldn't worry about this right now. She had some more immediate problems to deal with. She checked on the progress of the lemon ice cream. The sugar, cream and lemons had been perfectly incorporated. She knew that this would be a special treat that would satisfy her diners without overstuffing them, especially after the rich lobster rolls and the rest of what she had prepared. She tasted the goat cheese concoction. It was perfect. Brooke reminded herself that she could prepare this for herself sometime, too. It would make a great sandwich spread for a beach day. She wondered how many free days she would have in the future. She would eventually find a work life balance, she decided, as she started to focus on what she was going to wear to serve these people. She wanted to strike the right balance between professional, chic, utilitarian, and not subservient. After all, she was the owner here, not that they knew it. Why should she even hide that? People came into tough situations, and they did what they needed to do. She thought that was more honorable than being a spoiled brat who didn't want to face reality. She settled on a pair of white trousers, and a tunic with deep slits on the sides and white piping. She would add some great pink earrings, for a fun detail, as well as flat Moroccan slippers in the same hot pink tone as the earrings. Time to concentrate. She surveyed everything in the kitchen. All right, everything seemed to be set. Except for the playlist, which she had on her phone. She ran out into the garden to snip some branches. It would be a delightful evening for all. She had a special cocktail in mind that they would all enjoy, which she could make on the fly.

Phew. She just had time for a shower, and a bit of makeup. She decided she would try to make herself look as gorgeous as possible tonight. None of this faux servitude stuff anymore. Too bad for Lisa's and Ana's egos. She worked on lining her eyes in that way that highlighted the green flecks in them. She chose her favorite lipstick, the one that stayed on, but made her lips look more luscious than she thought they were in real life. She twisted her hair into an elegant knot, to keep it out of her way as she cooked, double checked her outfit, and went back upstairs.

Chapter 25

Ana looked surprised when she saw her.

"You're just now coming up?" she asked. "We have dinner at seven."

"Everything is under control," said Brooke. "Why don't you relax? I can bring you a cocktail- I have a special one planned for tonight."

"You do?" asked Ana, as if she was surprised.

"Of course, that's what I do," said Brooke.

"How did you learn?" asked Ana, now genuinely curious.

"I attended the Cordon Bleu," Brooke replied, noting Ana's surprised expression. Who did she think she was?

"You have to know," Brooke said, "here in Saint Barth, most of the people who are here choose to be here. Some of the Metros, as we call them, have been here most of their lives, but they are highly educated. They all have excellent training. Our level of service is so high because we take pride in what we do. Service is a choice."

Brooke stopped short of telling Ana that she was the owner of the house. She wanted to give her the opportunity to turn it around without that knowledge.

"Oh," said Ana, with what Brooke decided was new respect shining in her eyes. Just as she'd hoped. Lisa was probably a hopeless case, but Ana was fundamentally not a terrible person.

"How is Lisa feeling? How is her foot?" asked Brooke, as she mixed a cocktail for Ana in the kitchen.

"Oh, she always complains about everything. I don't even know that she even stepped on anything. She just wanted attention," said Ana.

Wow, how quickly she betrayed her friend. Brooke decided that it was none of her business, though it did amuse her.

"Alright, you go enjoy the veranda; just shout if you need me."

"Thank you very much. You've done such a great job here. I'm sorry I was difficult at the beginning. And I'm sorry if Ernesto was inappropriate," said Ana.

Brooke simply smiled and returned to her tasks in the kitchen, feeling marginally better. But she realized that she couldn't force anyone to respect her. She thought, again, back to how she had treated Nathalie. She'd thought she'd always treated her exceptionally well, but was it enough? Had Nathalie developed some kind of resentment that would never evaporate? It was quite possible. Well, time would heal all wounds, hopefully- and otherwise, Brooke would make new friends. Maybe some of Antoine's friends, even, at least those who had not made snide comments about how she wasn't his type. From his behavior in the kitchen earlier, and from what she had felt rubbing against her, it seemed like she very much was his type. She smiled to herself. This cheeky attitude was not one she had usually had. But it was kind of fun to think this way occasionally. Maybe she could write a dirty book like the one Lisa was reading.

For the next hour, she worked, completely in the zone, putting together all the remaining parts of a grand feast. It was going to be quite spectacular if she did say so herself. Finally, with just the last-minute things to do, she ran off to set the table. After she'd put out the plates, the napkins, the cutlery, and filled the vases with tropical foliage, she stood back and admired the effect. It looked great. She lit a few candles and placed them in hurricane glass and allowed herself to breathe a sigh of relief. This evening would be beautiful.

As if on cue, she heard the buzzer at the front door. It must have been their guests arriving. She buzzed the gate open and waited patiently for the doorbell to ring. She swung open the door to reveal a couple. Both were ridiculously attractive, with the added sheen of love. The woman was blonde, with a slight build and porcelain blue eyes. The man was an olive-skinned god with a devastating smile and a sparkling green gaze.

"Hi," said the man. "I'm Diego. This is Ashley. I trust we're in the right place?"

"Yes," said Brooke. "Welcome. I think everyone is on the veranda waiting for you. I'm Brooke. I'm the house manager and the chef. I've created a fabulous meal for you. Welcome to Sea Grapes."

"Thank you so much. You have a stunning place here," said Ashley.

Brooke smiled.

"Thank you."

She liked how this Ashley character gave her the same respect as she would anyone else.

"It is stunning," said Diego. "It's probably hard work, but it must be lovely working here."

"Yes, it is, said Brooke.

She led them out onto the veranda. Everyone except for Lisa crowded around the newcomers, asking them about their honeymoon, peppering them with questions. Lisa was hanging back. Not just because of her fake foot injury. But also, Brooke realized, because she probably didn't know these people as well as the others did, and she didn't like being out of the limelight. Well, good. Served her right, Brooke thought.

"Can I take everyone's drink order?" Brooke asked. "I'm going to be putting the finishing touches on your appetizers and give you a little cocktail time. And then we'll eat."

"Sounds wonderful." Said Diego.

"Thank you so much, Brooke," said Ana. "Brooke made us a special cocktail for tonight. I highly recommend it."

The evening flew by. Brooke was dashing back and forth, bringing various dishes to the group. She couldn't help but notice how Diego looked at Ashley and how she returned his smiles. They were clearly deeply in love, and it made her happy to see that that was even a possibility. She thought back to when she and Hunter were first together. Yes, they had gotten along, and they had a lot of things and people in common. But really, their marriage had boiled down to a smart business decision. Nothing much more. There had been attraction, and a certain type of understanding and friendship, but not the deep type of connection that she saw here. Was it just wishful thinking when she thought that maybe there could be an attraction like that with Antoine? Was she being ridiculous and desperate? This was very much a rebound situation, wasn't it? After all, she'd literally just landed from a very bumpy ride. That had been the moment of realization that things would not work out with her husband, the plane ride in. And then the first man she saw, quite literally, was Antoine. But maybe it was a sign. Maybe it was a gift. She deserved that, now.

As Brooke brought yet another dish out, the compliments kept coming. Now Lisa was silent, as was Ernesto. And she thought she caught a look between them. How strange. Were they united in disliking her now? It was funny that all of a sudden, they seemed to be allies. Well, she didn't really care. There were only a few more days of this, and then she would have a new group visiting. She allowed herself to worry for a second- she'd been pleased to see that the new family would be a French one. She had looked them up. The husband was an executive in one of the big French banks. The wife wasn't on the internet. The reservation stated that they had two small children. That was a bit more problematic. Brooke was going to have to get a cot somewhere. She had hastily checked the box on the website saying that a cot could be provided, but she had assumed that it would never come up, and now she worried also about the swimming pool and any other dangers for a small child. Hopefully these people would be responsible enough. She needed to make sure that she had the correct insurance for liability. She made a mental note to check on it in the morning.

Finally, she brought out the lemon dessert*.

"Bravo, Chef!" Diego exclaimed, standing up and clapping. A few of the others stood as well. Ana, and Armando, who up until now had been so discreet as to be almost invisible. If only she could have people like Ashley and Diego as guests instead of the others. That would be a treat, she realized. She really did enjoy the cooking part and cooking for a crowd. This was something that she was meant to do. And, she reasoned with herself, soon she would once she had managed to make a name for herself. This was just a transition, this renting out the house. She had to have faith in that. All it would take was hard work, persistence, and focus.

The meal was finished. The final nightcaps had been had. Ashley and Diego had returned to the Manapany, and everyone else had retreated to their bedrooms. Brooke hurried to do the cleaning up so she could get to bed. She was exhausted, but in a good way.

Her phone pinged. It was a message from Antoine.

I hope it was a triumph, he had written.

She smiled.

It was, she wrote back. *Thank you, exhausted. See you tomorrow.*

Looking forward to it, Antoine responded.

Brooke retreated to her little guest apartment downstairs. Little by little, over the week, she had personalized it, had made it more hers, moved some objects around, had brought in a few decorative touches. And really, she could make this into something nice for herself. It wasn't an obligation for her to have a certain view or certain square footage, as long as it was all hers. She went to sleep with a smile on her face, hoping for good dreams.

Chapter 26

The alarm rang and her eyes flew open. She'd had no dreams that she could remember. Oh, well. Tonight was her date with Antoine, and maybe reality would be as good as any dream.

She prepared breakfast, the ritual of it becoming more familiar to her now. She was putting less thought into the preparations, and just getting into the flow. She smiled kindly as she brought out the food. Things were looking up. She cleaned up, and Ana popped her head into the kitchen.

"We're going to the beach for the day," Ana said. "See you later. I wish we could have you cook for us again, but Ernesto is insisting on a dinner out."

"You'll have a great time," said Brooke, smiling. "I'll be out as well, but I'll see you either in the afternoon, or in the morning."

"I think Lisa is still in pain from whatever she stepped on, allegedly," said Ana, winking. "And Ernesto went back to sleep. Apparently, he had too much to drink last night. Maybe they'll join us later."

Brooke nodded. She was a bit disappointed. She's been looking forward to having the house to herself, thinking that maybe she could even have a swim in the pool. Well, there was always the beach, if she had time. First, though, she needed to check on that insurance.

She went back downstairs and sat at the little cafe table she had set up for herself in front of the downstairs apartment. She opened her laptop and logged in to her insurance policy. Sure enough, it looked like she needed more coverage. She shuddered as she realized that the premium would go up. Still, it was worth it. She called up the company and spoke to an agent to make sure that she had comprehensive coverage in case of any accident around the pool or anywhere else on the property. She was proud of herself for figuring that out before anything terrible happened. She logged onto the rental website and was pleased to notice that she had another rental directly after the French family. This one, a group from New York. She scowled as she saw the name. It was a family name she recognized, not friends of hers, but friends of friends, and acquaintances she had seen around before. That was uncomfortably close to home. But she would make the best of it. She was all in now, no worrying about petty stuff.

She was happily working on her Instagram posts and coming up with new recipes when her phone pinged. She smiled ahead of time, expecting it to be Antoine or Grace. She had sent Grace a text the night before and was looking forward to hearing back from her. Grace always made sure to send her funny memes to make her smile throughout the day. But it was a number she did not recognize.

I like those white jean shorts, said the message. *They really show off your body.*

Brooke froze. *What the...?* She looked down, to make sure that she was indeed wearing white shorts. Yes, she was. She looked at the camera of her computer, as if it was somehow filming her, and then looked around her. What in the world was that supposed to mean? Maybe it was just Lisa or Ernesto playing a sick game with her. After all, they were still in the house, and probably regretting that they had decided to stay behind. She decided to ignore it. That was the best policy. She deleted the message. After a while, she decided to go back to the house to create some bouquets, to decorate the coffee table and the dining table inside. As she was arranging the flowers, another text came in.

Don't you think you should add more greenery?

Now, she looked around her, panicked. Was there somebody inside the house? She didn't hear any sound. She froze, listening intently to see if she heard anyone upstairs. Silence. Lisa and Ernesto were possibly sleeping. She was getting a bad feeling from this. She decided she needed to get out of the house, to clear her mind. She was going to wait until the afternoon to clean, to make sure that Ernesto and Lisa had left the house. She didn't want to be upstairs cleaning up. If they were up there, they might view it as an imposition. If Ana came back before the room was clean, Brooke could explain it to her. Hopefully she would understand and explain it to the others.

Brooke decided to head down to the bay where the Rosewood Guanahani hotel was located, as it was one of her favorite spots for sea turtles. She remembered the sea turtle she'd seen the day before. It had been a good omen, and maybe she would see some more. A good omen, and a good swim, were exactly what she needed. And then after her swim, she would come back up to the house, clean up a bit more, and get ready for her date with Antoine. She parked along the road and walked down to the beach, the sand rustling pleasantly under her bare feet. She was becoming an island girl now, scarcely bothering with shoes. She put down her beach towel, stripped off her shorts and T-shirt, and made her way to the water. Just a little bit down the beach, she noticed two familiar figures. Ana, Armando, and Jaime. *Crap.* Keeping her head down, Brooke plunged into the water. They wouldn't notice her if they weren't looking for her, and besides, she had every right to be at the same beach. There was no rule against this. She swam until she felt exhausted, diving under the water and feeling the ocean washing away any leftover anxiety from those strange texts. Maybe it was just someone trying to unnerve her. And they didn't know anything at all. They had just seen her in her white shorts at some other point. And maybe it was Lisa and Ernesto. That was the best theory for it. Lisa seemed like a twisted one. Well, Brooke only had to put up with Lisa for a couple more days, she reminded herself as she swam back towards shore. She dove

under one more time, and just as she bobbed back up, she spotted
a sea turtle near one of the white boats that was moored between
her and the shore. She smiled. There. There was her good omen.
Everything would be OK.

When she got back to shore, the Argentine renters were gone.
Maybe they were going to pick up their friends and head into town.
Brooke would be able to clean up the house in peace. She sat in the
sun for a moment, drying off, and then threw on her T-shirt and
headed back to the Mini Moke, not bothering with her shorts. She
was thirsty. She couldn't wait to get home. Get a shower, a cold glass
of water, and then do her work. Really, if she thought about it, this
house rental thing, while it had a learning curve, was not too bad.
However, having done her budget that morning, she realized that,
though it seemed like a lot of money up front, she would have to
save a lot, because one never knew what would happen during the
offseason. That's when the cooking would come in. If it came in.
Again, she wondered, would she have to pawn off another piece of
jewelry? Her phone pinged as she drove. When she arrived a stop
light, she took the opportunity to glance at it. It was a meme from
Grace. Good. Nothing stressful. The rest of today would be great, she
decided.

She got home, cleaned the house, using it as an opportunity to
do some exercise, and then showered again, this time taking her time
and washing her hair. She couldn't wait to make an appointment to
get the haircut she had been dreaming of getting for a while now as
soon as the money from the French family was in the bank. Hunter
had always been against the idea of her chopping off her long, thick
dark locks, but he didn't have a choice in the matter any longer. This
would be a symbolic change for Brooke.

For now, she hesitated over what to wear for her date with
Antoine. She thought back to her dream, and what she'd been
wearing. She didn't often wear short skirts. But when she thought

back to her vision of them on his scooter, she smiled and selected a short shift dress made of linen, in light pink with white piping, and pom-poms on the hem. She decided to wear a bikini bottom in hot pink in case her skirt blew up. She had no idea what they were going to do, but with flat sandals and this outfit and a jacket thrown over her shoulders, she would be ready for anything. She wondered if Antoine would come on the scooter or in the van. She smiled to herself. Would it be embarrassing to ride around in a van that said Meat my Fish on it? Well, she was past that now.

At 6:30, she checked her phone to see if there were any updates from Antoine. As if on cue, the phone pinged.

I'll be there in five, said the message.

She decided to head out to the gate to meet him out front, to minimize the chances of running into Ernesto, who still made her feel a little creeped out. She didn't see anyone on her way out, which was great. She was standing by the side of the road when she saw Antoine approach in the van. She smiled as she got in, though she was a little disappointed that there were to be no Vespa antics. Antoine leaned over to kiss her on both cheeks more slowly, lingering more than one would do with a simple friend. Brooke smiled as she recalled their earlier conversation about the tagline he had planned for his company.

"What are you smiling so big about?" asked Antoine. "You look positively naughty."

"Still laughing about your would-be tagline."

"You mean, you can't beat our meat?"

"But what if some people could?" Brooke asked.

"Could what?"

"Beat your meat, I mean, if you let them?"

Antoine laughed, a sincerely shocked expression on his face.

"I didn't know you had a filthy sense of humor!"

"Oh, try me," said Brooke.

"I plan to," Antoine replied, lifting an eyebrow.

Now it was Brooke's turn to be shocked.

"You're way worse than I am! You promised to take it slow."

"I will. But I didn't say anything about being a gentleman."

"So where are we going?" asked Brooke, blushing furiously.

"I thought we might head over to the far side of the island. Have you been there? There's a hotel there called Le Toiny. It's one of the older hotels. It has a beautiful 250-degree view of the ocean."

"I did go there, eons ago. On my honeymoon, in fact," said Brooke.

Antoine blanched.

"Oh, I had no idea- would you rather not?"

"No, I haven't been there in years," said Brooke. "Don't worry, my separation from Hunter is very civilized, I'll have you know."

"It is?" asked Antoine. "Didn't you say he cheated?"

"He did, but I think I had a feeling about it for so long that I had time to process it, and frankly, I feel like we're more civilized and adult together now than we ever were."

Brooke looked out the van's window. It was going to be a beautiful sunset. As if reading her mind, Antoine said, "I think we'll make it just in time for sunset. I've called ahead, and they're making a wonderful cocktail for us."

"You did?" asked Brooke.

That was the sweetest thing anyone had ever done for her. At least, in recent memory.

"So... tell me more about yourself," said Antoine. "What did you do in New York?"

"To tell you the truth," said Brooke. "Not too terribly much. I mean, I worked for charities. I used to have a career, but for some reason, Hunter didn't really want me to work. I think there was an assumption that we would have children."

"And why didn't you?" asked Antoine.

It was a bit of an intimate question, but she was OK with it, coming from him. So, she responded.

"I don't know, it just didn't happen... and then, after a while, when things started going south, I guess I was glad it didn't."

"Well, do you want children?" asked Antoine.

"Eventually," said Brooke. "I mean, I feel like I've just lived a million lives and like I'm 1000 years old, but I guess there's still time," she said. "How about you?"

"Yes, I've always wanted children," said Antoine. "Eventually. For now, it makes me happy to deliver food to people and to champion my friends who create things on the island."

"About that," said Brooke, "I was thinking about how I could kind of ... become more of a local?"

She told him about her idea of promoting local businesses and locations. Out of everyone, he would probably have the best idea on how to keep the balance, so that this initiative benefited locals more than simply exploiting them further for tourism. She knew that tourism was the main industry on Saint Barth. But surely the locals had the right to have their own special things for themselves as well. They spent the next few minutes discussing the nuances of helping locals while not ruining what made their businesses special.

And then, they arrived at Le Toiny. The whole property was bathed in the dying light of the day. So beautiful. The sea below them was turning a purple tone. Contrasted with the orange sky, it was absolutely striking.

"Let's hurry," said Antoine, jumping out of the van and going around to open the door for Brooke before she had a chance to. They walked towards the bar, hand in hand. She liked this. She wondered if they made as striking a couple as Diego and Ashley did.

"How was your dinner last night, by the way?" Antoine asked. "You said it was good, but...details?"

"It was wonderful," Brooke said. "The friends they invited were a couple on their honeymoon. Honestly, seeing them gave me renewed hope. They were so cute together."

"I like to hear that," said Antoine.

He looked at her with a smile that warmed her heart. A few minutes later, they were standing on a patio, looking out to the ocean, watching the sun kiss the horizon.

Antoine leaned over and nuzzled Brooke's neck, resulting in delicious shivers coursing down her back.

"I'm glad you changed your mind about the just friends thing," he said. "Have you changed your mind about taking it slowly?"

"I never said what I meant by taking it slowly," said Brooke, raising an eyebrow.

"Oh, is that so?" Said Antoine. He turned to face her and gave her a slow kiss, exploring her mouth with his tongue. He ran his fingers along her jaw, and down her neck. Just with that small gesture, she was already aching for him. It didn't help that her dreams and fantasies were full of him already. But she did want to take it slow, she realized.

"I do actually want to take it slow," she said. "In every way. But you can keep kissing me, for sure."

The build-up was always the best part, she decided. "I don't want to jump into anything. I don't know why... I have a feeling that..." she hesitated. She felt stupid saying it. She barely knew Antoine.

"I have a good feeling too," he said. "A feeling that we'll have all the time in the world." He squeezed her hand. They were silent for the next few minutes, watching the sun disappear.

"Are you hungry?" He asked.

She nodded. Yes, yes, she was.

Chapter 27

B rooke woke up to the sound of the birds singing in the tree next to the window of her room. She was in a great mood. The date with Antoine had gone great. She hadn't seen or heard from him in two days, because they'd both been busy. She knew he was providing supplies for a big catered party on a yacht, but he was coming by at ten o'clock, right after the Argentines were due to leave, to bring supplies for the next guests, the French family. She only had one more breakfast to deal with for the Argentines, who had ended up being quite satisfied with their trip. Well, except for Lisa, but no one could satisfy someone like Lisa. And Brooke was getting the hang of this hosting thing. She had reason to hope that the French family would want more meals at home. After all, they had two young children. She had purchased a cot from a local family who no longer needed theirs and had fixed it up, so it looked brand new. And she felt that everything was under control. She was looking forward to some one-on-one time with Antoine, to catch up. He had likened these past 48 hours to the perfect storm: three different yachts wanting food, each one fancier than the next.

"Don't any of these people need private chefs?" Brooke had asked.

"They travel with private chefs," Antoine had replied. "We're going to have to think about more ways to create events for you, when things calm down."

That statement alone had made Brooke very positive about the future. She'd been trying new things on Instagram and had been using this time to explore the island and take photographs of local farms and local creatives. She'd noticed that the French were a bit more cautious about becoming friends, but she was confident that in time, she would build a network.

She hadn't heard anything from Hunter. She should give him a call or a text one of these days to see if there was any progress on his business deal. It was strange that he was so silent, especially if he was as poor as he claimed. Maybe he too had been selling his jewelry, but she hoped he wouldn't be selling hers. Not until she could get Grace into the apartment, to grab things from the safe. In fact, that was exactly what she was going to do, she resolved. She would speak to Hunter and organize a time when Grace could pick up her things. She hoped it wouldn't set him off, but he'd been very reasonable up until now. It shouldn't be a problem.

She quickly showered and got ready in what was now feeling like a good working uniform: white jeans, a linen tunic, and flat shoes. She started to head up to the kitchen in the main part of the house. She could hear a few of the Argentines already talking amongst themselves on the veranda.

"What do you mean, delayed?" Lisa was whining.

Oh crap, thought Brooke. Just when she thought she had everything under control. Well, that was fine. She had a few days' buffer until the French people got there. It would all work out. A few more hours with the Argentines wouldn't hurt. She would plan to be generous with them and not hold them to their departure time. But it did mean that she wouldn't have unmitigated alone time with Antoine, which was something she had been looking forward to.

"Hello," she said cheerfully, as she walked up the stairs.

"Oh, good morning," said Ana.

Brooke noticed that Ernesto was not up yet, which was just as well.

"Everyone ready for a delicious breakfast?" she asked cheerfully. "I'm thinking of making you some crêpes, with some local goat cheese and tropical fruits. Everyone want the same coffee orders?"

Everyone nodded.

Brooke proceeded to the kitchen, happily in the zone as she prepared. Once the skillet was hot, she started flipping the crèpes perfectly, congratulating herself for her expert wrist movement and for her batter, which she'd learned at her mother's knee, and which had the perfect consistency. Even the Cordon Bleu couldn't improve on that. Soon enough, she had a complete portion of crepes in a serving dish, and brought them out on the tray, along with the coffees and teas. She also had some soft-boiled eggs and soldiers with butter, for those who wanted something savory.

"You're spoiling us," said Ana. "It'll be hard to leave this place. I didn't expect the food to be quite so good. We will definitely recommend this home to others."

After breakfast, Brooke was cleaning up when Jaime came into the kitchen to talk to her.

"Our plane has been delayed," he said apologetically. "I think we'll be leaving closer to 2:00 PM, if that's alright. I know that it said we should be out by 10."

"Don't worry about it," said Brooke. "Please enjoy the house, enjoy the pool until you leave. I'll be getting a delivery of food, but don't let that disturb you. The house is yours until your flight time. Do you need a ride to the airport?"

"Oh," said Jaime. "Yes, that would be really helpful."

"I'll organize for the rental car company to come pick your car up right here," said Brooke.

"Thank you. That's very kind," said Jaime.

Brooke nodded and picked up the phone to call the car company, which she by this point had on speed dial. Once she'd organized for a car pick up around 1:00 o'clock, she settled back into her cleaning and checked her watch. Antoine should be there any minute. In fact, he was already late, which was not what she expected from him.

Are you on your way? She texted.

Yes, was the response.

Was he being curt or just in a hurry? Brooke wondered. Maybe he was driving.

She heard splashing and glanced out to see that a trio of Argentines were sitting by the edge of the pool. She was glad they were enjoying themselves and enjoying the house. It would hopefully mean a good review. Just as she heard the buzzer from the gate and hit the button to open it, all hell broke loose. She heard screaming and growling, and some kind of frenzied barking. It didn't make any sense.

What in the world was going on? She rushed outside, forgetting all about Antoine. It took her a moment to process what was happening. There were two massive dogs. Rottweilers, from what she could tell. Lisa and Jaime were beating at one of the dogs, while the other one was biting at Jaime's ankles. What the hell? How had they gotten in here? Where did they come from? Panicking, Brooke tried to think. What to do? Able to think of nothing else, she ran to the kitchen and grabbed a pot of water, and threw the water at the dogs, of course dousing Lisa in the process. Lisa started shrieking even more loudly. This was a disaster. Brooke could see bite marks on Lisa's legs already. Of course, the biggest complainer now had even more reason to complain. Now, Jaime was screaming bloody murder as he beat one of the dogs over the head with a magazine. Brooke had little experience with animals like these. She'd discussed getting a dog with Hunter, but it didn't make any sense in their New York apartment. She'd grown up with dogs, but these vicious creatures bore no resemblance to the friendly Labradors of her youth. Suddenly, she saw a blur, as Antoine rushed towards the chaos. Thank God. Maybe he knew what to do. He yelled something, and as soon as the dogs saw him, they stopped cold. Antoine yelled what sounded like a few more orders. Brooke couldn't even tell which language he was speaking. Was it French? German? Before she knew it, Antoine had both dogs by the collar.

"Let me get these guys into my truck," said Antoine, over his shoulder. "I'm sorry. I'll be back later this evening for the delivery."

Brooke watched him go, still completely in shock. How had he calmed these dogs down? How had he controlled them? How was he going to get them into his truck, and where was he taking them? She didn't have time to worry about that. She had to deal with her injured guests. She rushed over to assess the damage. Thankfully, the bite marks didn't look too terribly deep, but still, she could tell that her guests were in shock.

"Do you need a doctor?" asked Brooke. "I'm going to get something to disinfect these bites."

"No, no, we'll be fine, I think," said Ana.

"No, we won't," Lisa shrieked. "Look at this! This will leave a scar! I could have been killed!"

"But do you need a doctor?" Brooke asked, losing patience.

Lisa simply pouted in lieu of response.

Brooke rushed back into the house. *Dammit.* She realized her medical supplies were in the master bedroom. She ran back outside.

"Excuse me. Is it OK if I go into the master bedroom to grab the medical supplies? I don't want to intrude, but..."

"No, it's not OK," said Lisa.

Jaime caught Brooke's eye over Lisa's head and nodded. That was all the permission Brooke needed. She rushed up to the bedroom, almost bumping into Ernesto as he walked down the stairs.

"Well, hello," he started to say.

"There's been an accident," Brooke said as she kept running up the stairs. In the master bath, she grabbed her medical supplies. Hydrogen peroxide. Bandages. Mercurochrome. That wonderful product from her childhood that dyed everything red brown but seemed to make everything better. She also had Neosporin and cotton gauze. For once, she was happy that Hunter was so paranoid about injuries. He'd stepped on an urchin once and had wanted to make sure that they always had everything they needed on hand. They could outfit a complete sick ward. And at the Cordon Bleu, funnily enough, Brooke had always been the one they called on when another student would inevitably mutilate themselves with a mandolin. She had this under control, she decided.

After a bit of time and effort and dealing with Lisa's ever-increasing rudeness, Brooke had everyone bandaged up and calmed down.

"Let me get everyone a glass of water," she said. "Everyone OK? Are we sure we don't need a doctor?"

"I'll need a rabies shot," said Lisa.

Jaime and Ana both shot her a look that said *Oh, come on.* But it was fair enough. Brooke didn't want anyone to be able to say that she had withheld care.

"All right, let me find a doctor for you," said Brooke.

She texted Antoine.

Do you know a Doctor who can come give a rabies shot?

Antoine texted back.

They don't have rabies. They are trained attack dogs.

How did the hell did he know this?

How do you know? she shot back.

Trust me, was Antoine's infuriating response.

As if, thought Brooke. Well, that wasn't going to be good enough. Even if Antoine was somehow certain that these dogs were trained for this, which worried her, how the hell did he know? And by the way, whose dogs were they? She was going to need to find a doctor to put Lisa's mind at ease. Who else could she reach out to? In desperation, she texted Nathalie.

Nathalie, I know you're ignoring me, but I really need the name of a doctor. There was an accident at the house- dog attack- and I need someone who can administer rabies shots.

To her surprise, Nathalie wrote back right away.

Rabies? Dog attack? Are they Carlos's dogs? How did they get out?

Brooke shuddered. Carlos's dogs. Of damn course. How *had* they gotten out? And was it on purpose? Was it another harassment technique? She didn't have time to worry about this, but it was indeed very worrisome. She saw three dots blinking on her message app. Nathalie was still typing.

Call doctor Gerard. He'll come to your house.

Brooke copied the number and shot back a message.

Thank you so much. Please let me know when we can talk.

Nathalie did not respond; Brooke didn't have time to dwell on that. She dialed the number. A man with a kindly voice responded. Brooke explained the situation and gave him the address. She decided to open the gate preemptively, so she didn't have to listen for the doctor. She headed back outside to check on her patients.

"All right, the doctor is coming," said Brooke. "I'm so sorry this happened. I have no idea how..."

Lisa interrupted her.

"This was very irresponsible. I had no idea this house was so unsafe. I think I should let people know," said Lisa. "You can be sure I'll mention it in my review."

Brooke groaned. That was it. She was losing the positive feedback she'd been hoping for. She'd convinced herself that Lisa wouldn't bother to write any kind of feedback, and that maybe Ana would write something positive. And now she was pretty sure she was going to be getting a single, horrible, review. That would pretty much put her at an abysmal level straight out of the gate. Well, there was nothing she could do now.

"Is there anything else I can do for you until the doctor gets there?" she asked.

"You've already done quite enough," Lisa sniffed.

This morning has started off so well, but now, Brooke was back to worse than when she'd started. She decided that this was probably not the right day to call Hunter, because considering how things were going so far, he was probably going to tell her that he'd already sold all her jewelry. She hoped that she could trust that he would be honest enough not to do that, but who knew what desperation pushed people to do? Well, tomorrow was another day. She still had to get herself psychologically prepared to take the Argentines back to the airport, but it would be a relief to get rid of them, and she was looking forward to the couple days of respite until the French family arrived. She was going to need a good swim.

The next few hours flew by with the doctor's visit, helping the rental car company check the car out, and getting everyone into the Land Rover. They headed to the airport. Everyone was silent. Brooke was almost holding her breath, afraid that something else disastrous was going to happen, like an accident or a flat tire.

You've got to stop thinking that way, she told herself. Bad energy brought about bad things. She pulled into the airport driveway and breathed a sigh of relief. *So far so good.* She stepped out of the car. Everyone got their bags, and then Brooke stood there like an idiot, waving goodbye until they were safely in the tiny terminal. She got back in the Land Rover and took a deep breath. Now, she needed a rest and maybe a swim, and everything would be alright. She would talk to Antoine, and he would tell her why he was so strangely familiar with those dogs. Because, if she was honest with herself, it seemed very much *not* accidental that they had happened to show up. But why did Antoine know them if he wasn't a frequent guest at Carlos's house? She'd seen his van there multiple times. Was he the child that everyone was talking about? Was he Carlos's son? If that was the case, it was a severe omission on his part. She'd mentioned her worry about Carlos wanting to buy the house out from under her. And he'd been bizarrely evasive, hadn't he? She gripped the wheel and put the car in drive, taking another deep breath and trying to focus so she didn't have an accident because of her distraction. And then, just because nothing else could possibly get worse that day, it did.

Chapter 28

The Mercedes pulled up a few cars in front of her, with Antoine at the wheel and the blonde next to him. *Sophie.* Sophie leaned over and gave Antoine a mocking look and a lingering kiss on the cheek and walked into the airport. Hands clenching the steering wheel, Brooke prayed that Antoine wouldn't look in the rearview mirror and notice her. He'd told her there was nothing between him and Sophie, but clearly, that was not the case, was it? And that car? She'd seen it at Carlos's house, hadn't she? Antoine was lying to her. She couldn't trust anyone on this island. Shaking, she drove herself home. She didn't even have the strength to think about swimming or going to the beach. Instead, she paced around the house. What was she going to do?

A text came in from a random number.

I like your hair when it's up, it looks pretty.

Brooke looked around. Who had seen her? Was it Sophie trying to freak her out? She'd been out and about, so somebody could have seen her out. Or was it somebody who could see her inside her house? She felt chilled to the bone.

And then, because there was literally nothing useful she could think of doing in reaction to this, she decided that the text was a sign: maybe she would go get that haircut after all, even though she'd sworn to herself that she would wait until she had a little more money in the bank. She'd noticed a small hair salon in Gustavia that had a friendly looking woman inside. In fact, she'd had a nice chat with her on the sidewalk, about the crêperie up the street. Barbara, she thought she remembered the woman's name was. How much could she possibly charge for locals? Brooke would go and investigate. Screw this. Screw everything else, she was going to go get her hair chopped off, and maybe it would be the beginning of a new chapter. Isn't that what people did after a breakup? After a change of life? She'd certainly earned it. Taking another deep, shuddering breath, she gathered her bag and keys, got into her Mini Moke, and headed into town. Luckily, she found a parking spot across from the hair salon. She timidly tapped at the glass door of the salon and stepped into the space, which was pleasingly air conditioned, with bright turquoise walls.

"Bonjour," she said. "Barbara, right?"

"Hello," said the woman. "Yes. I remember you. Brooke?"

"Yes, that's me," said Brooke, pleased. "I was wondering if you had time for a haircut?"

"You're in luck. I just had a cancellation. Why don't you sit down?"

Finally, something was going Brooke's way. She sat down in the chair and explained to Barbara that she was ready for a change. A big one. Barbara considered her. Looking at the hairdresser, Brooke had a moment of worry. Barbara's style was far from what she aspired to, all red hair and thick bangs, with riotous curls that were probably the result of a perm, quite retro, if you asked her.

"I envision you as a silent film star, very gamine. Very French influencer. What do you think?" asked Barbara.

Brooke smiled. That was exactly what she had been thinking.

"You mean a bob with bangs?" she asked, making sure they were on the same page.

"Yes, I know your hair is wavy, and normally people wouldn't recommend that, but if I cut your bangs a little longer, you can slick them to the side or tie them up if you want."

"I have nothing left to lose," Brooke told her.

"Oh, dear," said Barbara, "let me wash your hair. You'll feel better already. And you can tell me everything. I know this island is full of gossips, but as your hairdresser, I'm the one person who will keep your secrets."

Brooke smiled. For some reason, she believed her. She allowed Barbara to lead her back to the shampoo station and leaned back in the chair, angling her head so the back of her neck rested against the porcelain of the sink. Brooke closed her eyes, and as Barbara massaged her head and rinsed the suds in and out, she fell into a deep sleep. Barbara kindly shook her awake.

"I can tell you really need the rest," she said. "But we also need to get your haircut done," she smiled.

"Yes, absolutely," said Brooke, disoriented. "I'm sorry. I've just had a tough day."

As Barbara combed and snipped and considered every angle, Brooke talked about her recent misfortunes.

"Wow," said Barbara. "You're so strong."

"No, I'm not," said Brooke. "I'm not handling this well at all."

"If I tell you you're strong, you are, my dear," said Barbara. "We all have our own crap to deal with. But believe me when I say you're doing very well. Don't worry. Things will get easier. Or maybe they won't, but you'll figure it out."

Somehow, this fatalistic attitude made Brooke feel better.

"Thank you," she said. "I think I needed to hear that."

"So, you've let your husband go back to New York on his own," said Barbara. "Do you have any suitors on the island yet?"

"I thought I did," said Brooke. "But I don't think he's for me."

"Do tell," said Barbara. "One of the local billionaires? A captain of a yacht, perhaps?"

Brooke blushed. "Much more low-key than that."

"Really," said Barbara. "I'm surprised. A girl like you..."

"Well, what I was doing before wasn't working for me, so I thought I'd try something different, but now I guess that didn't work out either. So, if you know anyone to set me up with, I'm taking suggestions."

"Well, there is one young man," said Barbara. "I don't know, seeing you... I just have a feeling that it would be a good match."

"Oh really?" asked Brooke.

"You might be taken aback at first when I say this, because, well," said Barbara, "he's a fishmonger."

Brooke groaned.

"Don't say Antoine," she said.

Barbara looked surprised.

"Yes! You know him?"

"He's not for me," said Brooke.

"Ohh. Why not?" asked Barbara. "It's funny- I'm something of a witch and I had a strong feeling."

"He has a girlfriend," said Brooke.

"Really?" asked Barbara. "I think I would have heard that if he did. But all right, maybe I missed some crucial gossip. I'm going to have to catch up, I think."

"His father might be someone who doesn't have my best interests at heart," said Brooke.

"His father?" asked Barbara.

"Yes," said Brooke.

She started to open her mouth to say the name Carlos, but then the bell on the door rang and a 6-foot-tall blonde walked in.

"I'm late," said the woman in a Russian accent.

"Darling, you're not late," said Barbara. "I'm just finishing up here. Have a seat over there."

The blonde woman stalked into the corner, crossing her impossibly long legs, and starting to leaf through a magazine.

"All right, darling, let's finish this up. I would dry it for you, but unfortunately, I think we were gossiping too much and ran out of time."

"No worries," said Brooke. "I don't dry my hair on the island. I just let it be."

"Smart girl," said Barbara. "Here. I'll just give you this cream. My gift. Controls the *frisottis*."

Brooke thought that was a much more glamorous word for frizz. She smiled.

"Thank you so much. How much do I owe you?" she asked.

"Since you're such a chef," said Barbara. "Why don't you just invite me over one day, cook me a meal and we'll call it even? That's what we do on the island. We locals work on trade."

Brooke felt like her heart was a bubble that was about to burst. This was the most kindness someone had shown her in a long time.

"Thank you so much. That's ...that's incredibly kind. Well, here's my phone number," she said. "We'll make a plan."

"Absolutely," said Barbara. "It's a small island. I know I'll see you again. You can't hide from me."

"Nor would I want to," said Brooke. "It was a pleasure, best part of my day, I promise."

"Nooo! You go out and seduce some gorgeous young man with that hair of yours," said Barbara.

Brooke got back into her Mini Moke, feeling infinitely lighter. But still, she wondered about Antoine again. What the hell was the story? Was he, in fact, Carlos's son? Having Barbara over would be helpful. She could perhaps get a few more details. But she was going to have a hard time waiting until that time, whenever it may be.

She went back home, made herself a simple meal, and stared at her phone, willing it to ping, and as if on cue, it did. A message from Antoine.

I'm so sorry, he had written. *My day turned to hell right after I saw you at yours. Big storm coming and I need to organize around it. I know your people aren't coming until day after tomorrow. Is it OK if I deliver tomorrow morning, and we can spend part of the day together?*

Fine, Brooke wrote back. She didn't want to jeopardize her food delivery, and she wanted to have it out with Antoine, but she was sick of his lies. Maybe he would finally start telling her the truth. She finished her meal, put everything away, and debated on whether she would sleep in her own bedroom, which didn't feel like hers anymore, or downstairs. She decided on downstairs. She didn't have the energy to bring her things up and down. And besides, she should just get used to her new condition in life. The minute her head hit the pillow; she fell into a deep sleep.

Chapter 29

Brooke was in the kitchen, organizing the refrigerator, dreaming up new recipes that wouldn't cost too much money, but would impress her guests and all of Instagram, doing research on which local farms and resources she could explore on her day off before the French family got there, and wondering when Antoine was going to bother to come deliver the stuff to her. Was he avoiding her because he didn't want to tell her the truth? Did he know that she had seen him with the blonde? He had sworn he wasn't dating. When was he going to explain what was going on? Sure, he didn't expect to know all the messy details of her life, and she supposed he didn't owe her a full explanation on who he was, and who his father was. But still, she thought they had been on their way to building a relationship. And this wasn't the way you did that. Her phone rang at the very moment that she was starting to stew in a way that was completely useless to her productivity, and she jumped on it. Maybe it was Antoine or Grace. But no, it was Hunter's number. She inwardly groaned, but she did have to talk to him.

"Hey," she said, answering the phone. "How's it going?"

"Not good," said Hunter.

"What's going on?"

"Well, none of the stuff with Quentin panned out. I'm getting the feeling that he's not so honest when it comes to business. I thought this was going to be my way out, but it looks like he's opened a whole can of worms. This might be problematic. You're going to have to be a little bit more patient with me. How's it going with you?"

"Fine, I guess," said Brooke. "I had renters all last week. And now I'm going to have another family coming in. But on the flip side, there's apparently a big storm coming in, which is rare for this season. Everyone is worried about it."

"Sounds like you're doing great," said Hunter, his voice a little surprised, and ignoring the part about the storm. "Maybe you could send me a little portion of your earnings to help me out. The electricity bill is coming due and our co-op fee."

"Are you kidding me?" said Brooke. "I'm barely making ends meet here. Do you know how much it costs to start up an operation like this? I can't believe you let it get to this. I even had to pawn off my watch!"

"As if you're the only one," said Hunter.

Brooke froze.

"I hope you haven't touched any of my jewelry."

Hunter was quiet for a moment.

"Did you touch any of my jewelry?" Brooke asked, livid. "That's mine, you know. In fact, I was going to ask Grace to come pick it up if she could."

"I gifted you most of that stuff," said Hunter. "You have more than I do."

"Those pieces were gifts, Hunter. Do you know what that means? And you're the one who fucked up here, remember? Most of that jewelry is not even from you, anyway. It's from my parents. So don't even think about it. When can Grace come by?"

Brooke was shaking. Thank goodness she'd spoken about this now, before things started disappearing.

"Listen," Hunter said. "Don't you think we can fix this? Don't you want to come back home and try to work on this? If we sold Sea Grapes..."

"Hunter, how many times do I need to say this to you? I'm not selling Sea Grapes. I spent all my money on this house, and I worked my ass off trying to build a life together."

"Ha! You never worked," said Hunter.

"You didn't want me to," said Brooke, thinking that if only she had worked, she would be in a much better situation. "Listen, this conversation is over. I'm sorry you're not doing well, and I'm keeping my end of the deal- I'm not saying anything about our relationship..." *Except for saying it to Antoine, but that didn't count, right?* "Anyway, at this point I don't know what function that is possibly going to serve in your business dealings."

"Just give me another week or two," said Hunter.

"Well, I'm going to talk to Grace and see when she can come over. When are you home?"

"Well, pretty much all the time," said Hunter bitterly. "Until this is not my home anymore. Do you want me to have it auctioned out from under me?"

"Not my problem," said Brooke. "Except that it should have been both of ours, and you leveraged it to the hilt. Mortgaged it to the hilt. So, there's nothing left, right?"

"Pretty much," said Hunter.

"Well, thanks for nothing," said Brooke. "This whole time I thought we were building something together and it turns out that you were just stealing from our dreams."

She slammed the phone down and texted Grace.

-Hey Hun, I know you're busy with the kids, but I really need you to head over to my apartment ASAP to pick up my jewelry.

-What's going on? Is something up between you and Hunter? Grace responded almost immediately

Brooke froze. She could trust Grace, couldn't she? But you never knew. Even an innocent comment could change everything. Much as she was frustrated at Hunter, she didn't want him to starve to death or anything.

-*No, there's just some stuff I'd like to wear in Saint Barth.*

Brooke watched the moving dots on her phone screen. That told her that Grace was considering how to respond to this. Finally, Grace just wrote back,

- *I can go over this afternoon. Does that work?*

- *Yes,* Brooke wrote back. *Hunter will be home. Just grab anything that is mine and we'll discuss how you can send it to me. I can Venmo you the shipping amount or whatever.*

- *You want me to just put that stuff in the mail???* Grace wrote.

-*Unless you want to hand deliver it,* Brooke wrote. Grace was right, it was risky to mail it. But she had no choice.

- *OK,* Grace wrote back.

Brooke quickly tapped out a message to Hunter.

-*Grace will be over this afternoon. Make sure she gets everything.*

-*OK. But we still need to talk.* Hunter wrote.

Brooke ignored this and went back to her tasks. She couldn't believe that she had nothing to show for 10 years of marriage. It was like she was literally starting from zero. But she was one of the lucky ones. After all, she had this house, which was quite a significant asset, but she couldn't afford to lose it. She would do whatever it took. Now, where the hell was Antoine? She decided to give up her pride and text him first.

-*Hey Antoine, I really would love to know when you're coming by with the food,* she wrote.

-*I'm so sorry. I'm super busy,* Antoine wrote back. *Is it alright if I come early evening, like at six, and we can have a glass of wine?*

-*OK. But you're going to come for sure, right?* Brooke wrote back. She didn't want to say anything that would make Antoine think that she was revving up for a fight with him. He certainly didn't seem very interested in seeing her, but the glass of wine was something...

even though, did *she* want to see him, considering he was still lying to her? Well, she couldn't waste her time thinking of this. She spent the rest of the day cleaning up, organizing some more, strategizing, trying to write out a business plan for an event company that would probably never come to fruition, and picking out the perfect outfit to wear when Antoine arrived, without making it look like she'd tried. She settled on a bikini with an open white linen shirt over it, white linen pants, and colorful sandals. She checked her hair in the mirror. What would Antoine think of the new haircut? It did set off her cheekbones and highlight her neck, a part of herself that she'd always liked. She tried to stop herself from imagining Antoine kissing her neck. The continuation of their relationship, if she could even call it that, hinged on what he had to say for himself when she saw him.

She poured herself a lemonade and decided to check her email. And wished she hadn't.

Chapter 30

Brooke stared at the computer screen, uncomprehending. Where had the French family's reservation gone? It was as if it had never existed. She went into her account page on the website and noticed that there was no deposit from the French family there at all, nor was there yet a deposit for the New York group who was, thankfully, still listed as coming next week. She had thought that the deposits landed in the account at the time of reservation. Had something changed in the policies? She was supposed to at least have half of the amount to work with if anyone canceled at the last minute. Then, of course, she assumed that people could contest that, but that was up to her discretion, wasn't it? She thought those were the conditions that she had read initially. *Stupid.* She was meant to be making this a business, but she wasn't staying on top of it. In the future, she would have to run a much tighter ship. But what about now? She was seriously running out of money. After spending a chunk of her budget on the cot and on preparations, she was afraid to go look into her bank account, but she knew she had to. She logged on to the bank's website and shuddered. Her funds were rapidly dwindling. Could she ask Antoine to redistribute some of the things she was going to receive from him for the next few days? She pinged him.

-*Hey, I just got a last-minute cancellation*, she wrote. *I don't think I'll be needing the food after all, but I understand if I have to eat that expense. Literally. Ha.*

-*We'll figure it out*, Antoine wrote back. *Be there at 6:00.*

Brooke sat there, as if frozen. What was she going to do? Hopefully Antoine would be understanding, but at the same time, she had to understand that he ran a business as well. She couldn't imagine his margins were that huge. He couldn't be expected to compensate for her mistakes.

Her phone pinged again. It was Grace.

-*Hey girl, so I was looking at some dates. If only you didn't have people coming this week, the cheapest plane ticket is literally one that arrives tomorrow*, Grace had written. *I'm dying to get out of here. The kids are driving me nuts and the weather sucks in New York.*

-*Amazing timing*, Brooke wrote back. *Really, you would pick up and leave tomorrow?*

-*Well, tonight, actually.* Grace wrote. *But yes.*

-*Well, listen, the renters just canceled, so I've got five days. If you want to come now.*

She sat and waited for Grace to respond, hoping she wouldn't change her mind or find that the tickets were no longer available. What would Brooke do for the next week otherwise? She had been stupid to think her plan to stay on St Barth would ever work. She'd also been stupid to put all her eggs in one basket, income wise, but then she reassured herself that she had not done it, it had been determined for her.

-*Awesome*, wrote Grace.

-*Don't forget the jewelry*, Brooke wrote back.

They spent the next 5 minutes going back and forth, with Brooke pretending to be interested in what Grace was going to pack and wear for her vacation. This would not be a vacation for Brooke, but she owed it to Grace to make it fun for her. She was still sitting there, catatonic, when the gate buzzer went off. She opened the door for Antoine. As always, he looked like he had stolen an unfair share of the sunshine. His eyes got a shocked expression when he saw her. And she remembered that she'd chopped off all her hair.

"What did you do?" He asked, his hand going out to her neck, but she evaded it. He needed to explain this latest Sophie sighting.

"I know. Do you hate it?" she asked. "I know that I'm already not your type, so..."

"Stop it," he said. "You shouldn't listen to things like that. You look gorgeous," he said. "You look like a real French girl now."

"Oh, thanks, I think," said Brooke. "So... I'm so sorry about your delivery."

"Don't worry," said Antoine, looking distracted. "Listen, I'll just give you some eggs and bread and a few other things. You need something to eat. And don't worry, I'll redistribute the rest."

"I don't expect you to compensate for my idiocy," said Brooke.

"No, I'll manage to pawn it off as specialty items," said Antoine. "It's the least I can do."

"You don't owe me anything," said Brooke.

And she meant it, especially now that she was mad at him, and that he probably wouldn't ever be her boyfriend, after all.

"About that," said Antoine.

"What?" asked Brooke, looking at him suspiciously.

Was he going to admit that he wasn't emotionally available? Antoine certainly looked a little guilty now that she thought of it. What was he going to try to tell her?

He sighed.

"Listen. I don't even know how to say this, and I don't even think I have it in me to go into detail right now, and I'm sorry- you just have to trust me, but there's something... I'm trying to fix everything."

He looked absolutely tortured now. Brooke felt sick to her stomach.

"What do you mean?" asked Brooke, her voice trembling. Now she didn't even know if she really wanted to hear what he had to say.

"I'm just saying that...God, there's no easy way to say this...there's something going on that I'm trying to...trying to look into something and fix something that I messed up," said Antoine. Now, he looked as sick as Brooke felt. "Please," he begged, and her heart went out

to him, even though she was mad and suspicious and didn't know
what he was begging her for. Her mind was reeling. She'd just been
building up to trying to trust him. And now she didn't know what to
think, what to do.

"One thing you can never doubt, Brooke, is that I'm serious.
About you." Antoine reached out to her again, stroking her neck
gently, almost regretfully. This time, she let him. Why did this feel
like a goodbye?

"Then why does it feel like you're ending things? They've barely
begun," Brooke began.

"No! I'm still very much moving forward with you- if you'll have
me. I just... It's just a long story... please."

Tears came to his eyes, and of course, this made Brooke start to
cry, too. She couldn't take another disappointment today. This whole
St. Barth adventure, this supposed time in Paradise- it had really
gone to hell.

"I promise," Antoine whispered. "A few days and we'll have this
settled," he said. He took her into his arms. She stiffened. What
wasn't he telling her? But it felt too good to be held. She needed a
hug after today. She let him kiss her gently. On the forehead, on the
nose. And then lightly on the lips. And then, as if regretfully, he let
go of her, and said, "I'll see you soon, I promise. Please don't hesitate
to reach out. If there's anything, anything at all."

He picked up the small cooler bag he had walked in with and
placed it on the kitchen island.

"Eggs and bread," he said. "And a few other things... on me."

"No," said Brooke.

"On me," said Antoine firmly.

And then he walked out of the house.

Brooke stood there, feeling empty, oddly bereft. Looking out to
the pool, and to the ocean beyond. There were a few sailboats out
there, but they weren't moving. She felt like the air had been taken

out of her sails, too. What was she going to do until Grace arrived? She was used to being on task. And now she was alone with nothing immediate she could occupy herself with. She was not motivated to do anything with her Instagram or anything else.

Her phone pinged again. Maybe it was something fun. Maybe it was Barbara suggesting they grab wine that very evening, but no, it was another mysterious number.

Alone again? said the message. Brooke groaned. Again, this nightmare, this was the last thing she needed. She looked around the room. She had forgotten to tell Antoine about these messages. But what if he was the one sending them, for some twisted reason? No. She couldn't be that bad a judge of character. There had to be somebody watching her from somewhere. She went through the house, looking to see if she could find anything that looked like a recording device or a camera, but not knowing what she was looking for. She absolutely couldn't see anything at all, especially not through the tears that filled her eyes.

Exhausted, hoping that no one could see her there, she went and sat outside on the overstuffed outdoor sofa, and tucked herself into a ball. She didn't know how long she sat there. Crying, rocking herself. Grasping onto her knees. When she heard the tree frogs and felt the hunger pangs, she got up and reheated some chicken orzo soup* she had made on a whim a few days earlier and poured herself a full glass of rum from the bottle Antoine had gifted her on that first day. As soon as she'd forced down both the soup and the rum, she went up to bed, in her old bedroom, and cried herself to sleep.

Chapter 31

B rooke pulled up to the airport, looking around to make sure she didn't see Antoine dropping off or picking up any blondes. She didn't know if she could stand any more bad surprises. She'd taken a little bit of care in looking cute, throwing on one of her flattering pairs of linen palazzo pants, a one-piece bathing suit, and a beautiful little linen shirt thrown over it. She noticed with some satisfaction that her tan had gotten to an ideal level without her even trying, and that she was a bit more toned than she'd been before she arrived, even though she had done daily Pilates in the city. She supposed the swimming, the housework, and the stress had been more helpful than artificial forms of exercise.

She saw a plane cresting the hill. It must be Grace, she decided. It was funny how she'd always felt vaguely sorry for Grace, starting when Grace had had the babies, and had started spending most of her time knee-deep in diapers, and then most of her money on nursery school for her twins, while Brooke and Hunter were footloose and fancy free. Grace and Ridley hadn't gone on as many vacations as Brooke and Hunter had. They lived in a more chaotic, smaller apartment in a less desirable location, but now Grace seemed to have it made. The boys had been accepted in the kindergarten of Grace's choice. She'd gotten a new apartment not far from theirs, and she'd gained a whole new group of friends, through school, who were socially more desirable than the previous ones. Brooke hoped that they hadn't grown apart too much, as they hadn't seen each other as much as usual that fall. Grace had apparently taken on some roles with the Parents Committee at school. And of course, Brooke had had her charity work, which she now felt stupid about doing. If only she'd been focusing on making money that whole time, she wouldn't be in this situation. But she looked forward to a few days with Grace. She would have to make sure they didn't spend any money. And she didn't want Grace to know how far she had fallen, even though they were meant to be good friends. She of course wondered whether she would break down and break the news to her friend that she was splitting up from Hunter, despite her protests on the phone leading up to this trip. Brooke looked around at the people being dropped off and picked up from the airport. She remembered that first day, when she'd been wondering about whether people were feeling the same way she was. She noticed that she saw some familiar faces, employees of hotels and restaurants who were casual friends of Antoine's and who she'd spotted around town. A few even waved at her. She was starting to get her bearings, and that felt good. She wondered if she should go into the airport to find Grace. But she didn't want to leave her car illegally double-parked. A few minutes later, she saw Grace emerging from the airport terminal, all skinny limbs and bouncy hair.

She was wearing dark Chanel sunglasses and black city clothes. Brooke smiled to herself, knowing that her friend would soon regret having packed such formal outfits. No matter, they would find something that she could either borrow or cobble together, and besides, Grace was only here for a few days. Brooke was relieved that Grace hadn't expected her to pay for the trip. Then again, she was putting her up in her place. It would be strange to be back in her old master bedroom for a few days. She reminded herself not to get too used to it. Grace spotted her and hurried to the car. She threw her arms around her.

"Oh my God, look at you. You chopped all your hair off. I can't believe it. You look so cute," she said, all in one breath.

"It's so good to see you," said Brooke. "I can't believe we don't see each other in the city and then it takes me going to Saint Barth for us to make a plan."

"I know," said Grace. "Those damn kids, they take up all my time. Oh, we've got so much to catch up on."

"I know- I can't wait. I've got a plan for us, but if there's anything else you want to do, you tell me," said Brooke.

"Oh, I totally leave it all up to you. I trust you that you've planned the best stuff for us," said Grace. "I just need a drink and a swim, not necessarily in that order. Or maybe at the same time."

"Well, that sounds doable," said Brooke. "Listen, we'll go drop off your stuff at home, you can get freshened up, change into your swimsuit, and I'll take you to Gypsea."

Brooke had decided to bite the bullet on a more expensive venue that first day, before tightening her belt again. She owed that much to Grace.

"Gypsea?"

"Yeah, it's a beach club. It's like Nikki Beach, but a little bit more fun and bohemian."

"Sounds like a dream," said Grace. "I can't wait. New York has been freezing. What a nightmare. It's been slushy. The salt's been destroying all my shoes. And here you are in flip flops."

"Yeah, I am," said Brooke, smiling but feeling a little guilty that she hadn't told Grace exactly what was going on. Why have an allegiance towards Hunter, who had lied to her, and cheated on her?

"I can't believe Hunter is OK with letting you hang out here and have fun while he's laboring away," said Grace, pointedly.

Brooke stiffened. Grace knew something, didn't she?

"I used to see him before the holidays all the time," Grace mused, as if absently, but Brooke could tell that this comment was strategic. She didn't want to, but she took the bait.

"What do you mean, used to see him before the holidays?" Brooke asked, glancing at Grace briefly as she navigated the car onto the main road.

"Well, you know, my boys are friends with your neighbor's kids, so I would see him at their place sometimes, when I picked them up."

Brooke froze. So, she'd been correct. Hunter *had* been screwing the nanny. At this point, she might as well stop playing stupid and ask Grace for the details she was no doubt dying to spill.

"Do you think something was going on with their nanny?" Brooke asked. No use beating around the bush.

"God, not the nanny, but..." Grace suddenly quieted, as if suddenly reluctant to divulge the rest.

"Spill it," said Brooke sternly.

"I mean, I don't know if I should tell you this, but now I feel I have to- after all, this is the reason why I kind of was avoiding you a little bit this fall, but..."

Brooke rolled her eyes. This was getting tiresome. She knew Grace was dying to say it.

"Go ahead. Tell me. I know Hunter was cheating on me. If it wasn't the nanny, who could it possibly be? Not Allegra, I hope?"

Allegra Carmichael was insufferable. A corporate Barbie who ruled her kids, husband, household, and office with an iron fist.

"God no! The Carmichaels had a personal assistant. She was some kind of...event planner and travel planner for them. I don't know what exactly she was doing. I had a feeling she was sleeping with Tim, at first. And honestly, I wouldn't put it past Allegra to contract that out, so she didn't have to do it..."

Brooke smiled at this despite the bad feeling in the pit of her stomach. She wouldn't put something like that past Allegra, either.

"But then, I started seeing Hunter showing up more and more," said Grace. "I think at first Tim had him come over to help their nanny with her résumé, because they were gonna reduce her hours, now that the kids were in school. But then, like, every time I went to pick up the twins, he was there. At first, I thought that he and Tim were awfully friendly, and then I realized that Hunter was coming over mostly when the Carmichaels weren't home."

"And it's definitely not the nanny?"

Grace shook her head vehemently.

"No. She was taking care of the kids. It was that assistant person for sure."

Brooke froze.

"Can you describe her to me?"

"Yeah, she's pretty. Blonde. Looks like an Upper East Side socialite. Young, you know, maybe 30...well, not much younger than us. And she seemed like she was completely implicated in their business."

"And this is still going on?" Brooke asked.

"Seems that she suddenly decided to quit, like a month ago at most. I haven't seen her since, and of course haven't seen Hunter around since then either."

How like Hunter to be truthful when he'd said it was over, but to gloss over everything else. Lying by omission was his specialty. But now, Brooke shuddered. The blonde from the plane... the blonde in the car with Antoine... Was it possible that this was the same person, the mysterious assistant? *No way.* That simply seemed like too huge a coincidence. However, in Brooke's experience, this meant that it might not be a coincidence at all.

"Did you get this girl's name?" Brooke asked.

Grace thought for a moment.

"Sylvie, maybe? Or Sophie...something French like that," said Grace.

Brooke gripped the steering wheel, trying to ground herself in the present moment and not let her distraction get them killed on the road. This *could* mean that Sophie was involved with everything.

Was Antoine part of the plan, too, then? Brooke's head was spinning. Grace was saying something, but she couldn't hear her through the blood rushing in her ears.

"Sorry, Grace, what did you say?"

"I was saying, I'm sorry if I upset you. Are you sure that you knew? I had a feeling you knew. I thought maybe that's why you asked for all your jewelry."

"Yeah, I did. This just confirms it," said Brooke.

She was relieved that she didn't have to lie to Grace anymore about everything being hunky dory with Hunter. But how to explain everything that was going on with her now?

"Isn't Hunter sending you money while you guys figure things out?"

"No. Hence, the jewelry. I already pawned off my watch."

"What? It's not fair for you to have to sell your jewelry," Grace opined.

"Hunter has no money left, apparently."

"Really? Wasn't he always doing business deals? I mean, he was always entrepreneurial, wasn't he?"

"Yes, he was," said Brooke, her mind still spinning. This all had something to do with Sophie, didn't it? But why? Was Sophie trying to ruin her life because she wanted Hunter? No. If that was the case, why would she damage his financial prospects, if indeed that was her doing. It was all very strange. Did it have something to do with the house? Was she the one behind the harassment campaign, and all the bizarre, disturbing things that had happened, and not in fact Carlos? But why? And what did all of this have to do with Antoine?

"Forget Hunter. He sucks. So, have you met anyone on the island?" asked Grace. "Now that you're footloose and fancy free?"

"I thought I had," said Brooke truthfully, "but it's complicated and messy and it's probably not going to go anywhere."

"Shit. Must be hard avoiding someone in a place like this- the joys of living on a small island, right? That used to be the story of my life on Nantucket. What's it like, living here, you know, as a full timer?"

"Believe me, it's not the same as vacationing here," said Brooke. "It's not all glamor and yacht parties. I mean, I'm renting the house out, so I'm basically in a service profession, you know what I mean? It can be hard to swallow."

"I remember when my mom decided to be an interior designer," Grace said, nodding her head in understanding. "She went into it thinking that she would, you know, be the superior of her clients. And she learned the hard way that she was just providing a service. It was ugly. I remember her quitting pretty quickly after that."

"Yeah, I sometimes feel that we weren't really equipped for the real world," said Brooke. "I mean, my parents hated that I went to the Cordon Bleu. They wanted me to go work at Sotheby's as soon as possible."

"Where we got paid $21,000 a year. I mean, thank God we got married. I don't have any skills other than picking up a phone and calling rich clients. And barely any of those are still rich, or still alive, or both," Grace laughed.

"It's been a learning curve, but it's been an ego adjustment too. That's the hardest part," said Brooke wistfully.

"I admire you," said Grace. "Listen, I'm here for now. Let's have fun. On me. Let's get your jewelry to a safe place," she said, patting her carry-on bag. "You can't imagine how stressed I was carrying all this shit around."

"You're an angel. Thank you so much for doing this. Was it all there?" asked Brooke.

"I hope so," said Grace. "I mean, I took everything he would give me."

Brooke nodded. She would put everything in the safe in the office. She hoped there were no cameras there, if indeed that was what was happening- but it was the only explanation for the creepy text messages she had been receiving. But she would block the safe with her body to make sure nobody looked at her. Would she ask for Antoine's help to locate any other cameras? Maybe, unless he had something to do with it.

"This is so beautiful," said Grace, looking around. "I always forget how green things can be."

Brooke remembered what it was like for her a few weeks ago. How she'd thought how lucky she was, how green, how blue, how vivid everything was. It was good to have visitors to remind her of the good side of being in this place, despite all the difficulty.

"I can't believe you've had this place for almost 10 years, and this is the first time I'm coming," said Grace.

"I hope it's not the last," said Brooke. "Come back whenever you want, as long as I'm not, you know, renting it out, or out on the street."

"Is it really that bad with Hunter?" asked Grace.

"Oh yeah," said Brooke. "I don't know how he let himself get to this point."

"Probably thinking with his other head," said Grace.

She and Brooke started laughing. They had always loved making immature jokes together. At least they still had that in common.

"All right, we're almost there," said Brooke, pulling up to the gate and hitting the clicker.

The gate slid open, and her heart swelled with pride, knowing that Grace would be blown away when she saw the villa. Grace sighed appreciatively.

"It's lovely. This is all yours?"

"For now," said Brooke glumly. "Let's enjoy it while I have it. I don't want to ever get rid of it but...you know how it is."

"Well, we're going to enjoy the heck out of it while I'm here," said Grace. "We're going to live like queens. Remember, everything's on me."

"You don't have to do that," said Brooke.

"Well tough shit, 'cause I am," said Grace.

Brooke parked the car, helped Grace with her bags, and let them into the house.

"Why don't you take the upstairs bedroom next to mine?" Brooke suggested. "It's got the nicest view. And a great shower. You can get freshened up, and we'll leave as soon as you're ready."

"Sounds great," said Grace. "I don't want to bother you, but I'm starving- do you have anything I can snack on, so I don't get drunk immediately when we go out?"

Brooke smiled. Grace had always been a snacker. She remembered her sneaking pretzels to her office at Sotheby's, and how they had ended up with a huge vermin problem, to which Grace had never fessed up to creating.

"I got you, girl. I made you a watermelon and feta salad* to tide you over. With local feta, I'll have you know."

Chapter 32

After Grace had freshened up and Brooke had locked all her jewelry in the safe, Brooke and Grace got back into the Mini Moke. Brooke, ever the tour guide, gave Grace the lay of the land as they started down the driveway. As they pulled into the main road, she pointed back in the direction of Carlos's house.

"My neighbor, Carlos White, lives back there," she said.

"Carlos White the billionaire?"

"The very same," said Brooke. "There's a rumor that he wants to buy my house and it's been a little bit chaotic."

"What do you mean, chaotic?" Grace looked concerned, and rightfully so.

"There have been way too many accidents around here to chalk them up to coincidence," said Brooke.

"Like what?"

Brooke told Grace about everything that had happened- about the gate, the slashed tires. The shrimp in the curtain rods. The vicious dogs. The light. The creepy text messages, and the possibility of video cameras in the house.

"Holy shit," said Grace. "This sounds like a soap opera. I can't believe all this stuff has happened to you and you're still standing. You are one tough cookie."

"That's what Barbara says," said Brooke.

"Barbara?"

"Oh, she's my hairdresser here."

"Well, you should be nice to her, she did a great job on your hair. And it's always good to have a hairdresser on your side- they know all the local gossip."

Brooke nodded in agreement. She thought back to what Barbara had said about thinking that she and Antoine would make a good match. She shook her head to clear the thought. It didn't help to think this way.

"Maybe your hairdresser can find you a nice guy," Grace suggested, right on cue.

"Funny. She thinks me and the guy I'm in that complicated situationship with would be perfect together."

"So maybe it's true."

"Doubt it," said Brooke.

As if Grace could detect that Brooke did not want to talk about Antoine any further, she changed the subject.

"So where are you taking us?"

"Still the Gypsea."

"Sounds good to me," said Grace. "I'm easy. All I want is some eye candy and a great cocktail. Oh, and I'm starving."

"Then we're headed to the right place," said Brooke. They pulled up to the Gypsea and Brooke was delighted to find a parking spot not far from the beach club, an absolute rarity in high season. These days, she took every little piece of good luck as a miracle. She was certainly not taking anything for granted anymore.

They walked into the Gypsea and snagged a table in the front row, closest to the beach. Another stroke of good luck.

"We can ask for beach chairs if you want, but I feel like it's a little late in the day to bother," said Brooke. "I brought some towels, just in case."

"Let's get some rosé in me and then we'll figure it out," said Grace, peering at the menu.

"Tell me more about renting the house."

"It's been absolute shit," Brooke admitted. She told Grace all about the Argentines, and the French people canceling, and how she did not have high hopes for the New Yorkers.

"Sounds like a pain in the ass," Grace agreed. "At least the boys here are cute," she observed. "I mean, they're a little young for us, but...in terms of eye candy."

Brooke nodded. Compared to American guys, French guys had that wiry, athletic thing going for them.

"American men look like bulls when you really think about it, don't you think?" Brooke laughed.

"You have a point," Grace agreed. "Americans do seem a bit overfed compared to these sleek Europeans. Which I know is an aesthetic you respond to, historically. Remember that hot Eurotrash guy from Au Bar? Where was he from again?" Grace asked.

Brooke simply laughed it off. She was far too busy concentrating on the image of Antoine that was popping into her mind. Antoine was the perfect combination of wiry and comforting. A little taller than the average Frenchman. And with slightly lighter coloring.

"Oh my God, you're getting this dreamy look in your eyes," said Grace. "Who are you thinking about?"

"Guilty as charged," said Brooke.

"I'm willing to bet that it's Mr. It's Complicated," said Grace.

"Well, it's really complicated, and probably not worth discussing. I'll let you know when there's anything to talk about."

A bit of movement, in the corner, near the kitchen, caught Brooke's eye. She saw a tanned leg and a ratty espadrille. She thought she recognized those espadrilles, but it was probably just wishful thinking. Or worst-case scenario thinking, depending on what Antoine was really up to. Then, the owner of the espadrilles and the tanned legs backed up, and she confirmed that it was Antoine, talking animatedly to the chef. They were laughing, as if Antoine was telling a joke or a really great story. The chef made eye contact with Brooke. She recognized him. She'd met him that one time she'd gone out with Antoine and his friends. Obviously, the chef immediately nudged Antoine, saying something to him that made him turn around. Antoine and Brooke locked eyes, as always.

"What are you staring at?" Grace started saying. She turned around to follow Brooke's gaze. "Wow. Will you look at that one. Dibs," she said.

"You're married," said Brooke, without taking her eyes from Antoine's.

"So are you... legally, at least."

"I still win. Besides, that's my Mr. It's Complicated."

As she said it, Brooke scowled, remembering everything she had learned from Grace, which now made her even more suspicious of Antoine. Sophie was the lynchpin of all of this. What part did Antoine play? She needed to get to the bottom of it.

"It wouldn't be complicated for me, if I were you," said Grace. "He is an absolute smoke show."

"That, he is," said Brooke.

Antoine came towards the table. The irresistible smile on his face was making Brooke's private parts ache already. Her memories flashed back to all the fantasies she'd had of them together, and of their interrupted time in the kitchen. Their sweet kisses at sunset, taking it slow. But also, her mistrust of him. The damning evidence, stacking up ever higher.

"Hey," she said.

Antoine leaned in, presumably to give her the traditional French greeting, two pecks on the cheeks. But instead, he took her face in his hands and gave her a slow, delicious kiss, which she didn't want to return at first, because she was mad, and because he owed her major explanations, but her damn body betrayed her. Wasn't he worried about carrying on this way in a public place? She hadn't told him that she wanted to keep her separation from Hunter quiet, so she couldn't blame him for exposing their relationship. But still. In front of Grace?

"Get a room," said Grace jokingly.

"Grace, I presume," said Antoine.

"In the flesh," said Grace. "Nice to meet you. Your name is...Sorry, I only know you as Mr. It's complicated."

Antoine raised his eyebrows and looked at Brooke. Brooke was busy giving Grace a furious look.

"Is it that complicated?"

"That's an understatement," said Brooke. "And you know it."

"I promise you. I'm untangling the knots," said Antoine.

Grace lightly kicked Brooke under the table.

"Can I borrow Brooke for a second?" Antoine asked Grace.

"If that's all the time you need, I guess," Grace said with a wink.

Brooke groaned and obediently followed Antoine to an isolated corner of the restaurant.

He bent down and whispered into her ear.

"All the bad luck with your house. It's not all coincidences. I just wanted to warn you. Be careful."

"Oh, stop it," Brooke hissed at him. "I know you're involved. Grace just told me some things about your girlfriend Sophie. Very interesting things."

Antoine sighed.

"Brooke, come on. What do I need to do to make you believe me? Why would I warn you if I was involved?"

"I'm not sure," Brooke admitted. "So...what? Are you going to help me to deal with this? Or am I on my own?"

"Of course, I'm going to help. But we need to be strategic. Trust me, OK?"

"This is probably where you tell me that you can't explain it right now, right?"

Antoine gave her a tight smile.

"Listen, I have to go. See you in the next day or two?"

Brooke simply nodded. Antoine looked into her eyes. She wondered if he would try to kiss her again, but he seemed to reconsider. He sighed and led her back to the table.

"Take care of her for me, Grace. I'll see you around."

As Antoine walked away, Grace opened her mouth wide mouthing to Brooke. *Oh my God, he's so hot.*

Brooke simply shrugged. She didn't have the strength for anything more.

"I don't even understand why you would stay away from him for even a microsecond," said Grace.

"I told you- it's complicated," said Brooke. "I've gone through enough humiliation with Hunter already. I don't need to pile on some more."

"Well, keep me posted. How is he in bed?" asked Grace. "Or is that an indiscreet question?"

"Stop acting like you have a problem with indiscreet questions," said Brooke, "And I hate to disappoint, but I've only had him in bed in my dreams," she admitted. *And on a scooter*, she thought, starting to blush at the thought of it.

"Hope you don't get jealous if I have a few dreams of my own starring him," said Grace. "I am officially jealous."

Brooke smiled. Grace had always been so sincere about her wishes and her dreams. She'd never been competitive. Not really. She'd always been a refreshing breath of fresh air. Brooke hoped that socializing with the moms from her twins' school wouldn't change her in the long run. Grace really was the one bright spot of Brooke's New York life.

"I really hope you'll come back often. I need you here," said Brooke.

"Twist my arm."

They had a few more drinks. A delicious tuna tartar. And of course, the requisite cod fritters. Then, Brooke drove them back home.

Chapter 33

The next few days sped by, a blur of fun, normal activities of the sort that Brooke had been expecting to do during her vacation. Grace had insisted on treating her, and it had been a welcome respite from reality. Brooke had done her best to enjoy it, and not to worry too much about what would happen next. She hadn't heard from Antoine since the restaurant sighting and had started worrying that he had reconsidered whose side he was on.

After dropping Grace off at the airport on her last day, Brooke returned to the house. Now that her friend was gone, the harsh reality of what she would have to sell next to stay afloat started settling in. She decided that one of the good side effects of the French renters having fallen through and the New Yorkers not arriving until the day after next was that she could at last go for a swim in her own pool. The storm they had announced was due to hit later that afternoon, but other than a few clouds on the horizon and whitecaps out at sea, everything seemed fine. She walked out to the terrace and noticed something amiss.

What the hell?

The water level in the pool was significantly lower than she remembered. In fact, it dipped below the filter, and she noticed an alarming cloudiness that had never been there before in the water. Why hadn't she noticed this? Granted, she'd been so busy with Grace and with everything else. She probably hadn't been skimming the pool every morning, as she used to. And even that was not something she was accustomed to doing, as they had always had help with the pool. Someone who just appeared and took care of it, so it remained perfect and sparkling, its infinity edge melding in with the horizon. It felt limitless, just like her life had, just a few short weeks ago. *Where did the water go?* She wondered. She hoped she didn't have an underground leak. That would be devastating. Before calling the pool company, which would cost her another fortune she didn't have, she decided to try to investigate on her own.

Or maybe Antoine could help; put his money where his mouth was. She texted him and waited for a response but received none. Time to put on her big girl pants. She headed to the small machine room down the hill. Sure enough, upon opening the door, she noticed water pouring out. A spigot had been loosened. It was meant as a safety valve to avoid overflow, but instead, water was spilling into the machine room, threatening to damage all the equipment as it went. *What the hell?* Brooke exclaimed to herself, as she worked to tighten the spigot. Fortunately, the flow of water stopped immediately. How had this happened? Had it been loosened on its own, or had somebody done this? Hard to tell. She was paranoid after all the so-called coincidences, which all seemed to work together to evacuate her from Sea Grapes.

She ran into the house and fetched a mop and spent the next half hour getting all the water out of the machine room. There. It now seemed that everything was fine. Nothing was short circuiting, as far as she could tell. But she was no expert. She searched in the machine room for the capsules and the chemicals that the pool boy used to add to the pool, no questions asked. She didn't know the proportions she would need to take the pool from cloudy to clear. Nor did she know how best to add water. Should she just do it from the tap in the garden, or would that be exceedingly expensive? She needed to do something, though. She went back up to the pool deck, connected the hose, and shaking her head, started running water into the pool. She consulted Google to see what kind of proportions of chemicals would best clear up the situation, but unfortunately, theirs was a saltwater pool. She couldn't just dump in chlorine, could she? And she didn't know whether she would do more harm than good. Maybe putting in the wrong thing would corrode the pipes or make the pool unusable in the short or even long term. That was it. She needed to suck it up and call the professionals in. While she was at it, she would cut off the water for now, to make sure that she didn't cost herself any extra money. Maybe the pool company had a source for water that was less expensive.

She went through the directory she kept in the kitchen drawer of all the local work people but couldn't get an answer from the pool company. The number had been disconnected. That was typical. Many companies in Saint Barth didn't last beyond a few years. But surely there would be several more to choose from. After all, swimming pools were a major feature of Saint Barth villas. But each time she called and gave the name of the property, she was told that they had no time for her, or the person on the other end of the line simply hung up on her. What in the world was happening? Was there a conspiracy against her? Again, she tried to ping Antoine. Maybe he had a friend who worked for a pool company. But it was to no avail. The New York people were coming in two days. That was barely enough time to get this situation resolved. She was desperate. Her livelihood and her survival on this island depended on it.

She decided to hop in the Mini Moke and go visit the pool companies in person, but that was no better. There was no one available who could help her. To make matters worse, the news reports were now confirming that the storm that had been brewing out at sea all week was due to make landfall that evening, with high winds and lashings of rain. Brooke decided to put that out of her mind. Winter storms were usually overhyped. And she had more immediate fish to fry. Speaking of fish, where the hell was Antoine? In the past, he'd always been around when something bad happened, which she now found suspicious, though granted, in his defense, he'd always been there to fix whichever disaster had befallen her. Maybe he was simply sick of taking care of this accident or coincidence prone American girl.

Sick of running around in circles looking for a pool company that would help her, Brooke decided to go back home, log on to her computer, double check the details for the New York renters, and look into her accounts. Was there any way she could get back that Cartier watch? Nope. According to her bank account, she needed to bring something else to the pawn shop, stat. What she really needed was a big cash infusion. It was exhausting being desperate like this.

She opened the safe to look through all the jewelry Grace had brought her. Feeling a bit paranoid, she was careful to hide the code. She separated all her jewelry out into piles, according to what was most sellable. The stash included the gold screwdriver that had come with her Cartier Love bracelet. She lay her arm on the desk and slotted the beveled tip of the screwdriver into the first screw. She struggled to turn it. She hadn't taken that bracelet off in 10 years, ever since Hunter had gifted it to her. She had loved it, once. But now, it just felt like shackles that needed to come off. So what if she would only get a fraction of its worth at the pawn shop? She didn't want this tying her down anymore, and it could do her some good. It wouldn't be enough to get her watch back. But it could be exactly what she needed to make the house ready for future customers, including bribing a pool company employee to come after hours, and perhaps eventually even pay for a social media manager to increase her Instagram reach. Once the bracelet was off, she considered her wrist, now completely bare, without the watch. Without the bracelet she had worn all this time. She took a deep breath and put everything else back into the safe, closing it carefully and checking that it was locked. She took a deep sigh and put the bracelet in her handbag. Time to go to town again.

Just then, her phone pinged.

Antoine? No. Of course, it was another unknown number. She was getting good and tired of these.

Are you going to sell anything good?

Brooke gasped but tried not to react too visibly. She wouldn't give this creep the satisfaction. There had to be a camera somewhere. Had to be. She looked around and backtracked into the office. Was it in the office? That was the only explanation because, unless a camera was positioned to see her putting the bracelet into her bag and looking depressed, there had to be a camera trained on the safe. But try as she might, she couldn't see anything out of the ordinary. She would have to revisit this. But for now, the pawn shop was going to close if she didn't hurry. Her heart in her throat, she drove the Mini Moke down to town, cursing at the snarl of traffic and the impossible parking situation. She finally nudged into a microscopic spot between two luxury cars and stepped out, twisting her ankle on the uneven sidewalk. Tears formed in her eyes. Why did it have to be so hard? She walked up to the pawn shop, feeling nauseous, but when she tried the door, it was locked. She peered inside. All was dark. *What the hell?* Why wasn't it open? There wasn't even a note on the door explaining when it might open again. She was horrified. She was running out of options so fast; it wasn't even funny. She needed a pick me up. She headed to the Creperie and bought herself a crepe and a coffee. On second thought, she ordered a second coffee, and ventured over to the hair salon just down the block. She had no friends. Barbara was more of an acquaintance, but she needed her right now. She walked up to the salon and found the door wide open, which was a good sign. Barbara was inside sweeping the floor, her red hair curling on her shoulders.

"Knock, Knock," said Brooke.

Barbara turned around.

"Ohh, my dear. Glad to see you again. Please tell me one of those is for me," Barbara said, eyeing the coffees.

"Yes, and you can even have half a crepe," said Brooke.

"You're the best," said Barbara. "How have you been doing? I thought we were going to go for a glass of wine, one of these days."

"Sorry, I had a friend in town," said Brooke. "And now I'm just trying to reevaluate everything. I've been urgently trying to find a pool guy. I have a problem with my pool, and no one seems to have time for me."

Barbara's lips formed into a straight line.

"Is that so? Well...my daughter's brother-in-law has a pool company. Do you want me to call him?"

"Please," said Brooke. "I'm desperate, in case you couldn't tell."

"All right, let me see what I can do," said Barbara, picking up the phone and taking a sip of her coffee at the same time. "Thank you for this, by the way. It's been a long day."

As she searched for the phone number in her phone, Barbara innocently asked, "Did you ask Antoine if he knew a pool company? I think he's got a few friends..."

"Antoine's not answering my texts," Brooke shot back.

"Oh," said Barbara. "Well, I'm sure he'll turn up. Ah, here's the number," she said. She put her phone to her ear.

"Yes, Remy. Bonjour, this is Barbara. Yes, all is well. Thank you. I have a dear friend here who has an emergency with her pool, and she's not been having much luck...Yes, yes, that's the one."

Brooke's eyes opened wide, and she froze, listening in to see what she could hear. This was not promising. Remi must have been one of the ones she had called already.

"Listen, darling, that's ridiculous, isn't it?" said Barbara. "Do it for me? Well, yes, I'll ask her if she can pay cash... Of course, she won't tell anyone. Neither will I. You know I'm a tomb."

Brooke froze. What did this mean? Had someone told all the pool people on the island that they were not to help Brooke at Sea Grapes? She narrowed her eyes.

"All right, yes. Thank you. How much do you think it will be?" asked Barbara.

"It's going to be €500 for the consult," said Barbara, turning to Brooke. "Can you get that in cash?"

"I can try," said Brooke, gulping.

Barbara hung up.

"3:00 o'clock. He'll be there if he knows what's good for him."

"Am I right to understand that they don't want to work at Sea Grapes for some reason? Did Hunter not pay them or something?"

"It's not that," said Barbara. "It seems that someone has compelled them not to work for you for some reason, and they're running scared."

"That's crazy," said Brooke, the gears in her mind spinning. Again, this was part of the campaign to destroy her. But who could be behind it? Carlos? Antoine? Sophie? Probably Carlos. Because the light was coming from Carlos' boat, and the dogs were his, but Antoine certainly seemed to be at his house more often than would be expected for fish deliveries.

After they'd finished their coffees, Brooke gave Barbara a hug and promised a coffee or a wine in the future.

"Thank you so much for your help. I have to go to the bank and make sure I can take out that money."

Brooke went to the bank machine and crossed her fingers. 500 Euro was the maximum, and thankfully, she was able to withdraw it- not that it didn't mean she wasn't overdrawing the account, but she would deal with that later. All of this absolutely meant selling something else sometime soon. The closed pawn shop- that wasn't also part of the plot to make her life hell, was it?

Maybe Hunter had a little something he could give her, to tide her over, Brooke thought, as she drove back. Yes, they'd had that little argument before Grace came, but maybe things had changed for him in the past few days. Maybe one of his deals had panned out. Maybe he'd been exaggerating. He was prone to doing that.

As soon as she parked in front of the garage at Sea Grapes, she dialed Hunter's number. He picked up on the first ring.

"How's it going?" she asked, nudging the gravel of the driveway with her toe, trying to infuse her voice with a lightness and positivity she did not feel.

"Same, same," said Hunter. "Nothing new. What's up?"

"Well, I was calling because..."

"I'm glad you called," said Hunter, interrupting her.

"You are?"

"Yeah. I really, really need you to reconsider this whole stupid plan of yours, Brooke. You need to sell Sea Grapes. We can't stay afloat if you don't."

"Hunter, there is no way," said Brooke, ice forming in her veins. There was no *we*. How convenient of him to try to invoke that, after everything he had done.

"If you're not going to sell the house, what are you calling me for?" asked Hunter coldly.

Brooke gasped. She hadn't expected him to be lovey-dovey, of course not...but she hadn't expected this cruelty either.

"Well..." now, the question she'd been meaning to ask felt like it was not worth even asking, but she let it spill out of her mouth anyway. "I was hoping you could spot me a little bit of money."

"You were *what*?" Hunter scoffed.

"There's a problem with the pool... and I had a cancellation with some guests," Brooke started to say.

"Explain to me how that's my problem," Hunter said.

"Since we're explaining shit, explain to me how you think you would benefit from me selling Sea Grapes," said Brooke. "I wouldn't give you a penny, not after everything you've done, and especially now that you're not even lending me something to tide me over."

"Are you dumb? Brooke, I don't have anything left," Hunter hissed. "If you sold Sea Grapes, at least I could..."

"At least you could what? I told you- I'm not going to give you any of the money."

"Yeah, but..." Hunter hesitated for a minute.

"But what?" Brooke snapped, struggling to understand. "I can't see any benefit to you. I mean, worst case scenario, if you're out on the street, you can come work for me. Which is a generous offer, one I'm disinclined to extend at this juncture. Why would you want me to sell the place?"

"Just consider it," said Hunter, "Please."

Brooke hung up, feeling confused and conflicted. Was she really being selfish by holding onto this house? No, of course she wasn't. It was all she had left. Hunter had not done anything to deserve her charity. And besides, what could it possibly change for him if she were to sell it? As she'd said, she would not give him any of the money, not even for old times' sake. Their past few years together had all been a lie.

Her phone pinged again. She looked at it, hoping it would be Antoine, which it wasn't. It was Hunter.

Please just consider it. You don't understand the pressure I'm under.

Pressure?? Brooke wrote back. *This is all your own doing,* she started to type. *I'm under pressure too. The damn planet is conspiring against me. So, I guess we're even.*

But then, she decided she was being pathetic, and just deleted the message.

How had it come to this? Cheating was one thing. It happened to lots of people. In fact, there had been an epidemic of it in their social circle recently. But the money issues were a mystery. Hunter had normally been successful before, not in any spectacular fashion, but he'd at least not lost money. It was strange that he was having such a streak of bad luck, right when Brooke was struggling, too. But she didn't have time to worry about that. She needed to consider how to turn this around. She checked the phone for the time. It was 3:00 PM. She could see the top of a white van at the gate. Brooke grabbed her key fob and opened the gate.

The van parked next to the Mini Moke.

"Thank you so much for coming," Brooke said to the man who had gotten out of the van. He was a boy, really, with dark hair and eyes and a slight build. He gave her a worried look.

"You're not going to tell anyone I came, are you?" he asked.

"No, I promise," said Brooke. "I really appreciate what you're doing for me."

"Well, show me the pool," he said, without further preamble.

Brooke guided him up to the pool area.

"I'm Brooke," by the way," she said.

"I know," replied the man.

She noticed he didn't supply a name. Fair enough.

"Your pool level is low," he observed.

Duh, thought Brooke. For 500 Euro, she expected more.

"Yeah, somebody opened a drain. I've gotten it stopped; I think. But now it's cloudy for some reason, and I need to add water to it."

"You can do that from the garden hose," said the man. "Same price. Let me check the chemicals."

He took a kit from his bag, gathered pool water into a tube, and dipped a paper strip into it. He removed the paper and frowned at the results.

"All right, you're going to need to fix this. And well, I'm guessing that you don't have the budget to have me come weekly, do you?"

"Not right now," Brooke admitted. "In the future, I would definitely use you if you..."

"I'll give you my card, but in the meantime, I can sell you some chemicals. I'll tell you how much to put in there and how often."

"Thank you so much," said Brooke, relieved. "How much is this all going to be?"

The man sighed.

"Barbara told me you were having difficulties," he said.

That's the understatement of the year, Brooke thought, but she simply nodded.

"All right, just €150 for the visit. But it will go up when you can afford it," said the boy.

Brooke thought her heart might explode.

"Thank you so much," she started to say.

"Plus 125 for the chemicals," said the man.

It was still less than the 500 he'd quoted, but considering she'd still have to use a huge amount of water to refill the pool, she'd still spent a fortune today.

The pool man then showed her how to do everything to keep the pool clear, as she took notes on her phone.

Once he was gone, she went back into the house.

She logged back onto her computer to make sure that the New York group was still coming. Yes, they were. It would be good to get that money in the account. She made a calculation. How many meals would she have to cook to make the kind of money she needed to get the watch back and even to stay afloat? There was no way she could get ahead unless she rented out the house for two months solid, cooking at least a meal or two per week. And then, the off-season... She shook her head. And her friend Ford hadn't gotten back to her at all about any rentals. So, this Villa Azul site seemed to be her only option, not that it had a great track record. So far, it had yielded a horrible Argentine group, a no-show French group, and then this New York group- who knew what to expect from them? Brooke felt like she was suffocating inside the house. Breathing deeply to stave off the vastly overdue panic attack she was sure was waiting for the most inopportune moment to manifest itself, she rushed outside and took big, greedy gulps of sea air into her lungs.

Once she had calmed down a bit, she collapsed onto her outdoor sofa and sat there, staring at the horizon. Great. Big, dark clouds were rolling in at an alarming speed. Still, she sat there, wondering what in the world she was going to do. She was completely alone. She had no support, no money, no prospects. And a nemesis who wanted to hurt her.

She looked out to sea again, noticing that Carlos's boat was gone. Which, come to think of it, it had been for the past day. Maybe he was finally cruising somewhere else in the Caribbean. Maybe he had taken his boat to a safer harbor in anticipation of the storm. Did this mean that he would temporarily let up on the attacks? Which, now that she thought about it, were specifically designed to make her want to sell the house. All this so-called bad luck, it was all happening to make her financially desperate and emotionally destabilized, wasn't it? Was this being done to her so that Brooke would feel that her only option was to get rid of Sea Grapes?

Selling it would have been the easy option, granted. But whoever was doing this to her had underestimated what a stubborn person she was, and how much she wanted to protect what she had done with her family's financial legacy. Tears started running down her face. God, she was so pathetic. She'd been pushing and pushing and trying to do the right thing and trying to be good, and look what it had resulted in. Nothing, nothing good. She sat there by the pool, hugging herself, crying. She'd fucked everything up. She let her face crumple into a bitter smile for a second, thinking how much Hunter would hate her thinking in those vulgar terms. Funny how she might have had a mouth on her, but he was the one who was fucking someone outside of the marriage. He had undermined her to such a degree that she hadn't even had a chance to succeed.

Rain started falling. *Of course, it did.* She almost laughed then. This was ridiculous. This was such a cliché scene- the desperate woman crying in the rain. The wind began howling around her, all at once, frightening in its intensity, scaring her a bit. Would the house get damaged? Who in the world would help her if something happened to it? Not Antoine. Was it stupid that she was doubting Antoine when he kept proving to her that he was helpful, and that he wanted to be with her, just because Hunter was someone that she couldn't trust? Why couldn't she trust Antoine? She'd asked him once if he had a relationship with Carlos. She'd asked him if he was still with Sophie. And she thought that she had read his body language clearly enough, even though he had been avoiding her in the past few days. But if he had been willing to believe her, when she'd said that she and Hunter were broken up, why couldn't she take him at his word too?

Because everything was conspiring against her, that was why.

It had gotten pitch dark, and the rain was torrential, the wind whipping around her, and still Brooke was sitting outside, tears still running down her face. This was just ridiculous. Pathetic. She was not equipped to survive on her own. Grace was right. They had no life skills. Should she give up? Should she just sell the damn house, and try to start over somewhere else with at least a little bit of money in her pocket? She'd failed, if that's what she was going to do. But at the same time, she saw very little choice. It would make Hunter happy, at least, and it would shut everyone up, and she could just pocket the money and rent an apartment somewhere. Get a job like a normal person and see what she wanted to do. She wasn't stupid enough to believe that even 7.5 million dollars would sustain her for long, especially if she stayed alone for the rest of her life. A palm frond smacked her in the face, dealing a stinging blow that was no match for her bruised ego, and she sobbed harder.

The worst part was that what she wanted to do was to cook for people, and entertain, and start a new life on this island that she had fallen in love with, with the guy that she thought she'd fallen for, if only everything hadn't fallen apart. But she could start over here, with a bit of money, to boot, couldn't she? If she sold the house? $7,500,000. It was a huge amount. She could just admit that she'd lost. Wasn't that much money a win? This old, stupid pride of hers was self-destructive. Yes, she would have lost everything she had used her parents' money on, but really, at the end of the day, she had probably made a wise business decision with it. She could build something else one day. Something special. Would she be as in love with it as she was with this house? No. Would a new place have memories of her mother and father visiting right before their deaths, looking at her approvingly, pleased for her, that she would have this to remember them by? No, but maybe she shouldn't be holding on to these things. At the very least, she could get her watch back, if it hadn't been sold, which, considering her luck, it probably had been.

That does it. She was going to sell the house. She was going to call Carlos, right now. She had a feeling that she was giving in to the drama of the situation, being impulsive and self-destructive, but there was absolutely no one to talk her out of it.

She got up and, still sniffling, tears and snot mixing in with the rain that had soaked her to the bone and headed towards the house to find her phone.

Suddenly, the lights flickered and went out.

Seriously? Fuck you, Universe! Brooke screamed into the wind. She stumbled towards the house. There was barely enough light to see by, but somehow, she found her way into the kitchen. She would find some candles somewhere. But for now, she was on a mission. She picked up the phone. Looked at it. Tried to dial Carlos's number. But the phone wouldn't work.

What the hell?

How pathetic was she, that she couldn't get her phone to work? Seriously, had someone put a hex on her, or what? Was it the network that wasn't working, with the electricity out? Not likely. Suddenly, she realized. Hunter had been paying for the phone, and he probably hadn't paid the bill. *Ugh.* Was there any limit to the crap that could hit the fan on a single day? She would have to go get a new wireless plan tomorrow, if the storm ever stopped, and if she could even afford it. Antoine would have to earn the right to get her new number. Would the New Yorkers even be able to fly in? Anyway, she was positive they would be total assholes. She had a lot to do tomorrow if this damn storm blew over. But the second she had a moment, she would call Carlos and tell him he'd won. The house would be his. For the right price, that was.

OK, she was being too crazy, maybe, she decided, as she finally located a candle and lit it, illuminating her beautiful kitchen in dancing light and shadows. Maybe she should talk to a real estate agent tomorrow first, see how much the house was truly worth. After all, it would feel better to sell to someone who hadn't tried to ruin her life, she decided. And then, she would sell. And leave the island, for the time being. As much as she loved it, it just hurt too much to stay, having failed like this. And nobody gave a crap about her. If Antoine cared so much, wouldn't he have checked on her, with this storm? There were other islands, if island life was what she wanted. Once she had the cash in her account, the world would be her oyster. Even if she had the devastating certitude that it would be a long time before she was able to build up to anything remotely pearl-like.

She dabbed at her eyes with a paper towel and blew her nose. She was sore. And hungry. But she didn't have the heart to make herself anything. Besides, there was no electricity, and so little food left. She needed everything she had for the guests. Tomorrow, she would go to the big modern supermarket, the Super U. That would devastate Antoine and would serve him right. If he even cared anymore. She would have taken a shower, to warm up and rinse the sadness from her body, but the water pump was electric. They should have gotten that generator, like she had wanted to. She had made the mistake of listening to Hunter when he had said that they would only be there in the nice season. She toweled herself off, changed into dry pajamas, and got into bed. At one point, she thought she heard a honking down by the gate. But then, she decided it was either her imagination, or yet another disaster that she couldn't deal with right then. This was, she decided, officially the worst day of her life.

Chapter 34

B rooke woke up late, gasping when she saw the time on her phone through bleary eyes. *Dammit*. She had less than an hour to get ready and go pick the New Yorkers up at the airport. The day before, she had checked her account and had been pleased to see that half of the rental fee had made it into her account at last. She had gotten herself a new local phone number, and, since she had not heard from Antoine when she had needed him most, she decided he wouldn't earn her phone number until he'd done some explaining. She had gone shopping at the new Super U supermarket for the essentials with which she would be able to create some good breakfasts. She had been thrilled, in fact, to find frozen blintzes with which to create her aunt's famous blintz soufflé*, which was easy to prepare, but a decadent crowd pleaser. Like a big girl, she had gone to visit some of the local farms she had discovered earlier and had picked up a few fruits and vegetables. She had even visited a real estate office, where the agent had been elegant enough not to mention the rumor that everyone had heard already: that Carlos wanted to buy the place. The agent had told her they would be running comps and would circle back in a few days.

She took the quickest of showers in the downstairs apartment, not even caring that she was being displaced from her room, and thankful that her newly short hair made it that much easier to look polished. She threw on a navy linen shirtdress and pom-pom sandals.

Checking the time on her phone, she rushed up to the driveway, got in the Land Rover, and headed to the airport. The New Yorkers would be here any minute.

Pulling into the crowded airport driveway, she had the unhappy surprise of seeing the now-familiar Mercedes convertible parked in the taxi lane. There was no Sophie in sight, but sure enough, Antoine was leaning against the car, as if expecting someone.

Brooke didn't even care to pussy-foot around it anymore. She parked right behind the Mercedes and hopped out of the Land Rover.

"Waiting for your girlfriend?" Brooke asked, a cruel smirk on her face.

"I am," said Antoine.

Before she knew what was happening, he had swept her into his arms.

It felt ridiculously good to be touched by him. Some magical alchemy that happened each time they were close to one another. She felt herself melting into his embrace, despite worrying what the New Yorkers would think if they saw her in such a compromising situation. Still, she wouldn't give in completely.

"I'm mad at you," she whispered into his neck.

"I'm mad at you right back," he said, pulling away from her a moment to look into her eyes before leaning back in and giving her a slow, delicious kiss.

"You're avoiding me," he said when they came up for air. "Did you change your number? And why wouldn't you open the gate for me the other night? I was so worried about you. Half my damn roof blew off in the storm, but as soon as I was able, I took some supplies and candles and a little generator to you..."

"You did?" Brooke asked, her heart bursting. But no. He wouldn't get off so easy. "You should be worried. It's been hell. But I'm selling the house, and I'm going..."

"No, you're not. Trust me, Brooke. We're about to solve all your problems."

"How?"

"I just put Sophie on a plane- with her dad."

"Her father?" Brooke looked at Antoine, perplexed. Antoine ignored her question.

"Listen, they'll be gone for a few days. And we need to get to the bottom of this once and for all. I think there are some cameras or recording devices in your house."

Brooke gasped.

"I was going to tell you..."

She was reassured that she wasn't just being paranoid, but this opened up a lot of more terrifying possibilities. Why was this happening?

"How..." Brooke started to ask. But Antoine turned his head away, towards the airport.

"Shit. I think your New Yorkers are here." Perfect timing, as usual. Brooke turned to look. Two couples, and two spotty teenagers, were making their way out of the airport, blinking in the bright sun.

"Ugh." Brooke pulled out the little Sea Grapes sign she had made and brandished it.

Antoine gave her hand one last squeeze and looked deep into her eyes.

"Give me your number, please."

Brooke sighed and did as she was told. Antoine wrote the number onto a scrap of paper.

"As soon as your guests go for a beach day, we're going to find those devices. I'll call you."

Brooke nodded and watched him get into the Mercedes and drive away. Sure enough, the group was coming towards her. They were pretty much exactly as she imagined and or remembered. The men were interchangeable. Tall, beefy, balding master of the universe types with big designer watches and leather satchels. They had obviously changed out of their finance bro Patagonia vests and into their resort wear in the St Maarten airport, so as to be in vacation mode the moment they arrived. The wives were prettier than the men merited, which told Brooke all she needed to know about the financial situation. There was one slim brunette with long curtains of straight, glossy hair. Brooke thought she might have recognized her from the pages of Vogue, or from seeing her at a few parties. The woman seemed to be the mother of the two teens. There was a spotty, gangly boy with auburn hair who would eventually grow into his looks until they headed south, and he turned out exactly like his father. The girl, also a redhead, was like a Xerox copy of her mother- if the printer had run out of toner, minus the studied elegance. Her posture and the set of her mouth communicated her boredom and embarrassment at being on vacation with her loser parents and their friends. The other woman was a stylish blonde with perfect features, definitely surgically enhanced. Her "bohemian" outfit, which included a pair of Golden Goose sneakers, was something Brooke had seen before. She was pretty sure this woman managed her own art gallery and fashion line and spent her time attending industry cocktails and taking lunch meetings. Maybe a month ago, Brooke would have been a little envious of this lifestyle, but now it just made her a little sad.

"Welcome to Saint Barth," she said, trying to generate enough enthusiasm to be convincing.

"Who was that guy you were making out with?" the teenage boy asked without preamble.

"Asher, that's not an appropriate question," the girl snapped, elbowing the boy in the ribs.

Brooke decided to just ignore it. They did the obligatory round of introductions. The parents, Chris and Rebecca, and Sebastian and Katrina. At least, she thought that was how they paired up. It was hard to tell. And the kids, Asher, and Esme, who belonged to Katrina. Brooke got everyone into the Land Rover without further incident and drove them back to the house, delivering her monologue on the island and on the house as she went.

"We're familiar with the island," said the blonde woman. *Rebecca.* "I actually lived here."

"You did?" asked Brooke.

Too bad this Rebecca character gave off an air of insufferableness. It would have been interesting to hear about her experience.

"You did?" asked Chris, scorn writ large on his face.

"Yeah, when I was 19. I told you before..."

"You were here for a month. That's not living somewhere, that's vacation," said the man. "It makes you sound pretentious and stupid when you say that."

Brooke decided that, as much as she disliked the woman, she might dislike the man more. This Chris character was without question the husband. Only husbands could be capable of such contempt.

As they arrived at the house, Brooke was annoyed to learn that the group expected a welcome dinner at the villa, which they had not reserved.

"We made a note in our booking," the brunette said boldly.

Lies.

Brooke would figure it out. She now had some things in the refrigerator and in the pantry. She was sorely tempted to call Antoine to the rescue, but he had told her that he would call her, not the other way around. Also, she still needed some explanations from him. Also *also*, she didn't want to spoil these people with superlative ingredients. They seemed like the type who would think that the dinner was included, and she didn't have the strength to argue about it. She decided on her mother's favorite in-a-pinch recipe, Weeknight Coq au Vin*. She was missing a few ingredients, such as the mushrooms, but she did locate some dried porcini in the pantry, which she started re-hydrating in warm broth as she chopped the onion. She would make a cheese wonton* recipe she knew the teenagers would enjoy as an appetizer from things she had in the freezer.

She had just barely started cooking when her phone rang. It was Antoine.

"What happened to texting?" she started to ask.

"Shhh. Don't say anything. Can I take you out tonight?" he asked without preamble.

Brooke froze. Was he worried about the recording devices in the house?

"I wish," she said cautiously. "I have to cook dinner."

"OK. Listen to me. Don't text me anything important. I don't know if my messages are being hacked. And don't say anything sensitive in the house. Don't type in any passwords... don't even open a safe if you have one. Are these people going to the beach tomorrow? Just say yes, no, or not sure."

"Yes...probably," said Brooke, her mind racing.

"OK, when they leave, just text me something about whether I can deliver some tuna... don't mention your name or address. I'll write you back that I'm waiting on a shipment, and I'll be there as soon as I can."

"OK," said Brooke, a bit shaken. "Good night."

"Good night," said Antoine. "I can't wait to untangle this. I've missed you so much."

Brooke was silent. Responding would count as something sensitive, wouldn't it? And she still needed to hear his side of the story.

Chapter 35

When Antoine arrived at Sea Grapes the next day, in the late morning, he gestured for Brooke to come outside with him. Once they were far enough from the house, on the other side of the pool, she could contain herself no longer.

"Are you finally going to tell me what's going on?"

"I think there's some kind of video camera or surveillance device in the house- maybe more than one."

"And I presume you know who did this?"

Antoine nodded, his teeth clenched, leaving Brooke to wonder: was it Carlos or someone who worked for him who had done this to try to harass her into relinquishing her home? And what did this Sophie character have to do with anything? Was she Carlos' daughter? And was she indeed the one Hunter had been cheating with? That would be a crazy coincidence. Brooke was relieved that Antoine was maybe on her side for this, but also livid that he may have had an idea of what was going on and that he hadn't told her until now. Who was he protecting?

"I don't know anything for sure," Antoine said. "I just have a strong suspicion."

"What are we going to do? I've looked for cameras- I haven't seen anything."

"They can be tiny. And well hidden. Remote operated. With higher resolution than you would think. Some are hidden in picture frames, Alarm clocks. Remote controls. Electrical outlets..."

"How do you know so much about these?" Brooke asked.

"The same way everybody else here does. There was a scandal on the island. Some people were making extra money by selling X-rated footage of renters in their villas."

"No way," said Brooke. "They did that? Do you think that's what someone's doing to me? Or do you think someone's doing it to intimidate me?"

"Let's discuss all of that if and when we find something," said Antoine. "We'd better hurry. Your renters may be out for now, but who knows when they might turn up?"

"Yeah- and they've been impossible about me cleaning up the house when they're in residence," said Brooke. "So far, they're very unreasonable about wanting me to be invisible and super serviceable and responsive, all at once. It's exhausting. I've got this horrible feeling that they're just waiting for any excuse to ask for a refund, and I'm not going to give it to them."

"Damn right," said Antoine. "Unfortunately, if I understand properly, with these rental sites, the money is held in escrow until the guests check out... so you're kind of screwed if they contest a payment."

Brooke blanched. Antoine was correct. And she couldn't afford for that to happen. She still needed to have a series of rentals to finally break even and have a little bit of a cushion, something where she didn't need to worry about liquidating the jewelry or other objects she had left.

"OK. Well, let's look in the back bedroom first," said Antoine. "And work our way to the front of the house."

"Good, and, that one is unoccupied, so if they went on a short errand instead of to the beach, we could better justify being in there. In terms of the kitchen, I have some excuse for being in there. They expect me to cook occasionally, after all."

"OK, let's go upstairs."

Brooke hesitated for a moment. It would be complete nightmare if the New Yorkers came back while she and Antoine were upstairs. Granted, the renters were probably enjoying lunch at the beach, so chances were that they safely had at least a couple of hours in front of them. But considering her luck of late, who knew? But she didn't have much of a choice, especially now that she knew she was not just being paranoid. They needed to be thorough in their search for whatever they were looking for.

They headed upstairs. Brooke was still so torn between trusting Antoine and not trusting him, being attracted to him and resentful of him. She needed a concrete expression of his sincerity. Actions spoke louder than words. She was glad she had told him that Hunter had cheated on her and that it was completely over between them, rather than leaving him dangling, thinking she was just a cheating wife like all the others, which he'd no doubt encountered on the island in the past. But still, not trusting him one hundred percent, she worried that maybe he would do something harmful with that information, especially if he was on Carlos and Sophie's side- though she still didn't understand how they all possibly fit together.

They walked up the stairs, she acutely aware of the fact that Antoine was just behind her and might be staring at her ass at that very moment. She was wearing a short tunic with a bikini underneath. Maybe too short. She forced herself to focus on the task at hand.

"OK, so divide and conquer?" she asked once they got to the back bedroom. "Should I start looking in the closet? And you look in the rest of the bedroom and the bathroom?"

She knew all the nooks and crannies of the closets, having designed them carefully for optimal storage. It was probably the most effective way to conduct their search.

"Great idea," said Antoine.

They split up upon entering the room, and Brooke headed into the closet. Without clothing in it, it was much easier to see what she was dealing with. Still, there were shelves, and some cabinets and drawers that had a door detail that could potentially hide a small camera. Even the louvered doors of the closet could potentially hide a tiny recording device. In the Caribbean, you had louvered doors everywhere. Brooke had insisted on solid doors on the bedrooms, for privacy, but in the closet, of course, no one wanted the humidity getting to the clothes. Brooke was running her hand along all the shelves, when suddenly Antoine rushed into the closet, breathing hard.

"What's going on?" Brooke asked. "Did you find something?"

"No," he whispered, pulling the door shut. "I think I heard someone coming up the stairs."

"What?" Brooke whispered back, "that's impossible. We didn't hear a car driving up."

"Who knows? Maybe someone walked back. Fuck."

"We would have been better off rushing onto the landing and acting like we were cleaning."

"Too late. Anyway, no one is using this room, so we'll be able to sneak out if whoever it is closes their room door."

But then, Brooke heard a step in the hallway by the bedroom door, and giggling, and hushed voices. What the hell was going on? She and Antoine huddled in the closet. At the last moment, she remembered to switch off the light, and then, she heard the bedroom door open. *What the hell?* Brooke could feel her heart beating wildly in her chest. She reached back to Antoine, who stood close behind her, for support. He wrapped his arms around her. She was about to throw up or pass out, she wasn't sure which.

"I thought you said this room is unused." Antoine whispered into her ear. Brooke shuddered despite the panic of the situation. It felt so good to feel his lips brushing her delicate skin. She tilted her head to better peer through the slats of the louvered door. All she could see was a pair of legs. She leaned back and whispered softly into Antoine's ear, as he put his head over her shoulder.

"It's two of them. This is very suspicious. I don't think these two are married to each other."

"Oh oh, so you mean they're getting it on in the empty bedroom out of some misplaced loyalty. Perfect." Antoine whispered into her ear, accidentally hitting against one of the hangers. Brooke flinched, then relaxed. Thank goodness for hangers that were the felt kind, which didn't make any noise.

She whispered in Antoine's ear, "If they open this closet, we're absolutely screwed."

She tried to look out the door again.

"What are they doing?" Antoine whispered into her ear.

Brooke stood on her tip toes to see more of what was happening. All she could see was the couple embracing, pawing at each other. Now, the man's hands were going for the woman's swimsuit top.

Brooke whispered into Antoine's ear, "They're making out. He's fondling her breasts, and now he's taking off her bathing suit top."

She repressed a gasp as Antoine put his hands over her breasts as well. He whispered into her ear.

"Tell me more. What is he doing now?"

Brooke looked through the slats.

"He's running his hands down her stomach, and further down, now," she whispered, craning her neck to reach Antoine's ear with her lips.

Antoine's hands ran down her sides and hiked up her tunic. When he encountered her bathing suit bottom, she concentrated hard on not groaning as a hand snaked between her bikini bottoms and her skin, his fingers making their way dangerously close to between her legs.

"What about now?" Antoine's whispers were soft, but hoarser, now. She could hear his excitement, and feel it, poking into her behind her.

"He's teasing her. With his fingers."

She bit her lip to stifle the intake of breath as Antoine did what she had just described.

"Shhhh.... We're going to get caught," she whispered.

But she didn't want him to stop. Her knees were growing weak, as his fingers expertly teased her, one finding her clitoris and the other moving inside of her. She writhed against him, fighting to control herself so she wouldn't move and make any noise that might alert the other couple to their presence.

"What now?" asked Antoine.

She couldn't take any more of this, but she obediently described the scene she could partially see playing out in the bedroom.

"He's squatting down in front of her. Licking her, and reaching up to play with her breasts," Brooke whispered. Now she could confirm that the man was Chris. Rebecca's husband. She couldn't imagine Rebecca being quite so enthusiastic about a midday tryst with her husband.

Antoine kept one hand between Brooke's legs and snaked the other one up her belly to her breast, and gently pinched one of her nipples between his fingers as he cupped it. Brooke held her breath. She was terrified, but more excited than she'd ever been.

"What now?" Antoine whispered. "Tell me."

Brooke held her breath, arching her back as Antoine moved to her other breast, teasing that nipple, biting her neck deliciously, tickling it with his tongue, while still working his fingers between her legs.

"I'm not going to tell you. There's no way you can do it quietly."

"Tell me," Antoine whispered.

"He's got her bent over the bed. She's got her hands on the mattress. He's spreading her. He just entered her. He's thrusting."

Sure enough, on cue, Antoine started thrusting his fingers more deeply inside of her. She couldn't help but moan then, but thankfully, it was covered by the sound of the woman in the bedroom, moaning more loudly as the man pumped into her. Brooke could now see that it was Katrina.

Oh no. Brooke could feel something inevitable bubbling up inside of her. The unmistakable tension building between her legs, and in her whole body. *No.* She couldn't come right now. She couldn't. She would make a sound, wouldn't she? They would get caught. Of course, at the same time as she thought this, she thought of how much she wanted Antoine inside of her, too, how she wished that they were in the bedroom, with him behind her. How would it feel to have him inside of her at last? Would it be everything she'd imagined? Just thinking about him thrusting into her sent her over the edge. She clenched her teeth as she came, waves of pleasure coursing through her body. Antoine squeezed her against him as he felt her body react. Feeling the erection in his shorts sent another shock of pleasure through her. When she finally regained control of her body, she whispered in his ear.

"I owe you."

"I'll hold you to that," he whispered, kissing her neck.

The other couple was finally finished, too. Chris had come on Katrina's back, and he went to the bathroom, returning with a washcloth to wipe her off.

He'd better rinse that before he puts it in the laundry, thought Brooke. She'd heard all the horror stories about hotel maids and what they dealt with. Well, this was to be expected, wasn't it? Katrina pulled her bikini bottoms back up and retrieved her top.

"You'd better take a shower," she said to Chris. "You stink."

"You smell delicious," he retorted.

"Whatever. This isn't happening again," she said. "I know your wife doesn't give a shit, but Sebastian is gonna get wise to it, and he makes way more money than you do."

Charming, thought Brooke. *Come on. Just leave the room.* Brooke didn't know how much more stress she could take. She couldn't believe what she and Antoine had done while in the closet, and while that had been exciting, she now realized the very real danger in which they found themselves. If they were perceived to be spying on guests, that would be something that her business could never recover from. *Please leave,* she begged in her mind. *Please.* Finally, the couple left the room. She and Antoine both heaved a sigh of relief. But how would they know when it was safe to come out? Chris, at least, was probably going to obediently take a shower. Was Katrina? Brooke assumed she would if she didn't want to make Sebastian suspicious.

"Do you think it's safe to come out?" Antoine whispered.

Brooke held her breath and listened.

"I think I hear the water running through the pipes..."

"OK, it's now or never," said Antoine.

Brooke was frustrated that, after all of that, they hadn't found what they were looking for. But then, as Antoine opened the closet door slowly, carefully, something glinted on one of the shelves.

"Strange," said Brooke.

"What?"

"I didn't remember putting a charger in the closet. Maybe someone forgot it."

"Here, give it to me."

Antoine took the charger, and they started tiptoeing out. They slowly opened the bedroom door.

"All clear," Antoine whispered.

Brooke followed him out, and they rushed to the stairs. They hurried down, through to the kitchen, and then outside. Once they were at the café table outside of the basement apartment, Antoine shone his phone flashlight at the charger, a black model Brooke didn't remember purchasing, let alone leaving on a shelf in the closet. Sure enough, something glinted incongruously on the surface. It was something that looked like a tiny lens concealed behind black plastic.

"Is that what I think it is?" Brooke asked.

Antoine's mouth set into a grim straight line.

"I've got to go," he said.

"Wait, what do you mean?" asked Brooke. "I thought we..."

"Yeah, I'm so sorry," said Antoine. "I really need to go. I'll talk to you later."

"Can you at least explain to me what's going on?" Brooke hissed, incensed.

"Later," he said. He gave her a quick peck on the cheek and left.

Brooke's mouth fell open. After what they've just done, he was going to leave her like this? She just shook her head. This was ridiculous. But there was nothing she could do now. She headed back up to the kitchen, where she got busy cleaning. She was just sponging off the counters, when she heard a voice behind her that made her jump. It was the brunette. Katrina.

"Hey, I thought I just heard someone in the driveway," Katrina said.

Guilty conscience? The woman was probably on high alert, waiting for her husband and kids to come home.

"Yeah, I had a food delivery," said Brooke.

"That's funny. Seemed like it was parked there for an awfully long time- what did they deliver? I thought we said we weren't having anymore meals here," said Katrina.

"Well, you're having breakfast, aren't you? And... a funny fact about me is, I eat sometimes," said Brooke. She found it hard to be polite to this woman who not only was rude, but who, despite her superior airs, had a dirty little secret. Not that Brooke was going to judge, because Katrina's husband was probably doing the same thing.

"Were you upstairs just a little bit earlier?" the brunette asked, her eyes narrowing in suspicion.

"Not yet," said Brooke. "I do need to go upstairs to clean the rooms, but you can let me know when it's a good time."

Katrina considered her for a moment.

"Right," she said. "I'll let you know."

"I thought you were at the beach," said Brooke.

"Oh, I had a headache," said the woman. "I came home, and Chris had some work to do, so he came too."

He sure did, thought Brooke. *All over your back.*

"Oh, I see," Brooke said. "OK, well, let me know when it's a good time to clean up upstairs and I'll do that. Let me know if you need anything."

"I will," said the woman.

She kept staring at Brooke, as if trying to make up her mind to say something. Brooke wished she would either say it now, or forget it, because the stress was killing her.

"I know you were there," said Katrina. "Spying on me."

Brooke summoned up her most indignant expression.

"What are you talking about?" she asked. "How dare you accuse me of spying on anyone? When did this supposedly happen? What would I have seen?"

"You'd better keep your mouth shut, if you know what's good for you," said Katrina.

Wow. Katrina had dropped her pedigree papers, as Brooke's mom used to say. Brooke looked at her, making sure to keep her face completely neutral.

"OK, what is it that I'm not supposed to say?" she asked innocently.

But then she realized that, in the very possible case that these people tried to screw her over, she did have something valuable over this woman. She didn't want to become a blackmailer, but self-defense was a different story.

"I mean, *if* I saw something..." she added.

Before Katrina could react, Brooke went back to cleaning the kitchen, turning her back to the woman, waiting for her to leave. She didn't want to turn around to check if she was gone, because that would take away from her small victory.

The day progressed, and Brooke was still waiting for Antoine to call or text her back. Why the hell couldn't she have a normal relationship with someone who was nice and consistent? Was this even worth it? Good as he made her feel, attracted as she was, as bonded as she felt to him sometimes, she felt so conflicted. This wasn't what she needed right now. She decided that she'd done enough waiting. She picked up her phone and texted Antoine a series of three question marks. How was that for no sensitive information?

Out on deliveries. I should get to yours by day's end.

Great, she wrote back. She didn't have anywhere else to be, which was frustrating. Well, now she had a whole afternoon ahead of her, with not much to do. She should think about her Instagram. But her mental health was more urgent. She was already wearing her swimsuit. She grabbed her beach supplies and pawed through the fridge for something she could snack on. She settled on leftover mango-quinoa tabbouleh*, a surprisingly delicious and refreshing dish she had whipped together from disparate ingredients she hadn't known what to do with. She made sure not to forget a water bottle. Which beach would she go to? Certainly, nowhere where she would run into any tourists, that was for sure. She would go to her local beach, she decided.

She hated to do it, because going there took her past Carlos's house. But she wasn't going to be intimidated, not here in her own neighborhood. She realized that she hadn't thought of calling Carlos to offer him her house in a couple days. She drove past, refusing to look down the driveway to see whether Antoine's truck was there. She didn't want to know, she decided.

Chapter 36

When Brooke arrived at the beach, she was shocked to find Judy, her favorite neighbor, sitting under a festive pink and white striped parasol.

"Hey, you," Brooke called out. "I didn't know you were still here."

"You inspired me," said Judy. "Rick went back to work a week ago, and I told him that I'd be like you, and I would stay on the island for a bit. I thought I would run into you on the beach, and then I was going to call you, but so far, it's been great. I've been getting so much reading done. Massages every day. I think tonight I'm going to take myself out to dinner at the Rosewood or the Eden Roc- want to join?"

Brooke considered this. She might have loved that, just for a taste of normalcy, an echo of her previous life. But she decided she had to be honest.

"Truthfully, Judy, there's nothing aspirational or fun about what I've been doing. Hunter and I...we're splitting up."

"Oh! So, you're doing your *Eat Pray Love* thing on the island, huh?"

Brooke noticed that Judy did not look in the least bit shocked at the news of her breakup.

"Barely," said Brooke. "There's no money. I'm having to try to build a new life here. I'm the staff now. You probably don't want to be seen talking to me."

Judy looked at her, incredulous.

"What are you talking about? Do you know how many people I know who actually try to support themselves? Like, zero. I mean, if you thought you were my role model before, it's like times ten now.

303

I don't think I'd know how to start my life again if Rick left me high and dry."

Brooke scoffed.

"You'd do better than me, I'm sure."

"No way. Listen, why don't I take you out?" Judy asked. "We'll have fun. It's on me. You've cooked for me so many times. We never had a chance to reciprocate."

"That sounds good," Brooke said, a bit hesitant. Would anything she said to Judy get back to people she knew? Would she get in trouble? Would she be judged? Was Judy just trying to get more information out of her? Frankly, she kind of didn't care anymore. She was trying to learn to stand on her own two feet, and Hunter had to do that, too, so any gossip about their imminent divorce shouldn't impact him that much. And besides, why were all his businesses falling apart so completely, when in the past he had always been relatively successful? He'd been so hopeless at making deals in the past few months, it was as if someone was thwarting him every step of the way. And if Brooke really thought about it, the same went for what she was doing. Had anyone ever had as many weird problems and coincidences as she had when simply trying to rent out a house? If only Antoine would call her back. He likely had at least some of the answers. But what was his role in this? She knew that Antoine had said he would come by at the end of the workday, but she didn't know what to expect- it wasn't even like he'd said he would take her out. Besides, she might need a drink after whatever Antoine had to say.

"How about I pick you up, at 8?" asked Judy.

"Perfect," said Brooke.

"Wear something slutty. We're going to go out and have fun. Let's go pick up some Russians or something," Judy laughed as she gathered up her belongings.

"You're funny," said Brooke. I'll be looking forward to it."

"Well, time for my massage," said Judy. "I'll see you in a bit."

"Can't wait," Brooke smiled.

She sat on the beach, letting the sun caress her skin, and replayed what had happened in the closet with Antoine in her mind. Had she ever done anything so naughty in her whole life? Frankly, the stress had almost been worth it. But now what? Where did they go from here? She watched the turquoise water, the gentle waves. She wondered to herself what came next. She didn't have another rental lined up yet, which was something she'd been forcing herself not to think about too much. There had to be a way to make money that did not subject her to these situations. She still wanted to figure out how to celebrate the things she'd learned and discovered on the island, and to create a business she could be proud of. She thought of that farm where a woman was making artisanal fabric with natural dyes. That artist with the cool treehouse in the center of the island. The other local artisans and artists that Barbara had introduced her to, the pop-up restaurant. All the farmers and fishermen Antoine knew. There had to be some way of putting all these things together, into something special that people would pay for, without taking advantage of locals. As she was sitting there thinking, Antoine texted her.

-*I can come by quickly now if you want.*

-*No can do, I'm at the beach at the end of the road*, Brooke typed back.

She was sick of being at everyone's beck and call. She needed to take time for herself when she could get it. Brooke kept sitting on the beach, trying to meditate and stay calm, even though she *did* want to see Antoine. He owed her an explanation, and he knew that. She wondered if he might try to come to the beach to find her. Sure enough, as she turned her head to glance in the direction of the parking area, she noticed Antoine, walking out to the beach. She watched him, considering how attractive she found him. It really was kind of ridiculous.

"Hey," she said, once he was within earshot, feeling awkward after what they'd done, and about the fact that he had left so quickly, after.

"Hey," he said, dropping onto the sand next to her. He took a deep breath and took her into his arms. Instinctively, she leaned against him and breathed in his scent. *This.* This was exactly what she'd been needing. They stayed there for a moment, and he gave her a gentle kiss on the temple.

"Listen," he said. "I know I was weird, earlier, and I understand how hard you're finding it to trust me."

"That's an understatement."

"I just had to check on something and see if what I thought was true, and unfortunately it is ...so now we have to figure out how to move forward with that information."

Brooke's heart started to beat faster. She pulled away from Antoine's embrace to look at him, to read his expression.

"What did you find out?"

"Sophie set up those cameras," said Antoine.

"Sophie, your girlfriend?" Brooke stammered.

"Brooke, I'm telling you, she's not my girlfriend. I've been... I've been in a terrible situation."

"What? Carlos is your father?"

Antoine's eyes grew wide.

"What? Why would you think that?"

"Everything adds up. You're always over there at his house, and every time something happens, you happen to be close by..."

Antoine laughed.

"Oh my God. I can't believe you thought that..." When he noticed the look on Brooke's face, he stopped laughing, and took her hands in his. "No wonder you were so suspicious. No, I'm always over there because Carlos expects me to help him with Sophie. Sophie is his daughter. I'm at his beck and call, and at hers, by extension."

Ohhhh. It was all starting to make sense, now. But there was one piece Brooke still didn't understand.

"But why are you involved?"

"I owe him," said Antoine quietly.

"Why?"

"Because he...he financed my business. And helped me to buy my house."

"What? But why would he help you like that if you aren't his relative? Because you were dating Sophie?" asked Brooke.

"No...When I was younger, I had an... altercation with someone at my mother's winery. That's the reason I had to leave. I was defending a girl who worked there, whose husband was beating her. I caught him being violent with her, and let's just say that I lost my temper. I shouldn't have done it, but I punched the guy..."

"That sounds reasonable," said Brooke. "So what's the big deal?"

"That should have been the end of it, but he fell back onto a bucket, and ended up almost dead."

"But that's an accident," said Brooke.

'The guy had connections, and I ended up having to do some time in jail."

"Oh no." Brooke looked into his eyes, registering the hurt in them. How devastating it must have been for him. "For how long?" She asked.

"Six months. And when I got out, I learned my mother was under pressure from her brothers and had no choice but to throw me out."

"What did you do?"

"I couldn't find anything else to do, so I started working as a seasonal worker in restaurants in resorts, and that's how I met Carlos. Carlos makes it a policy to help guys like me."

"Probably because he's a criminal himself," Brooke scoffed. "Sorry, I didn't mean that you're..."

"You're partially right. Carlos did do a stint in juvenile detention, and this is how he gives back. He had faith in me. He hired me to do odd jobs. And eventually, he brought me here, to the island."

"Why here?"

"Because Sophie wanted to live here. And he can never just have a vacation house, he needs to get involved, start a business..."

"I'm still processing that Sophie is his daughter. She sounds like an utter sociopath. Looks like the apple doesn't fall far from the tree."

"No, everything you hear about Carlos...OK, most of it, at least, that's Sophie. He's not completely innocent, nobody who is that rich is, but she has always been a huge problem for him."

"But you dated her..."

"Dating is a big word for what it was, and it was a huge mistake, but considering everything that Carlos has done for me, I have felt a responsibility to help him to keep her in check. That includes some babysitting and chauffeuring duties."

"If Carlos is such a baby angel, why couldn't he just accept the fact that I didn't want to sell him my house?"

"It wasn't him who was so focused on it. Yes, he mentioned that it would be nice to have the whole peninsula, and your house, or one of your neighbors' houses, as a guest house. You can't fault a guy for trying. He sent the first letter to your husband and was rejected, and he moved on. But Sophie wanted to prove herself to him, prove that she could get him something he wanted."

"So, she decided that she was going to ruin my life because her daddy wanted my house for a second and he couldn't get it?"

"She's always looking for his approval, and to be honest, she doesn't often get it. Carlos always thought she was soft and spoiled, and yes, crazy, and he gave his protégés, including me, preferential treatment, and more respect."

"Let me get this straight. This absolute sociopath went to the trouble of moving to New York and getting a job as an assistant with our neighbors so she could screw my stupid husband and mess up his business deals, just so she could ruin my life? She somehow single-handedly created all our financial issues. Is she really that conniving?"

"Ha. You have no idea," said Antoine, bitterly.

Brooke started to laugh.

"I'm glad you find it funny," Antoine said, looking concerned for Brooke's mental health. "But I doubt you'll be able to get any of your money back. Despite everything, Carlos will defend her."

"Honestly, I'm just relieved. I was thinking that the universe was conspiring against me. Knowing it was a single psycho bitch makes it so much easier to swallow."

Antoine cracked a smile.

"I love your attitude."

"Ha!" said Brooke. Before she could say anything else, Antoine kissed her, making her forget whichever wise-ass thing was about to come out of her mouth.

"And I love your tenacity," said Antoine, before going in for another kiss. "And I love your strength." A deeper kiss, now, his fingers tickling her jaw. "And I love your cooking." His hand came around the back of her neck as he kissed her more deeply. "And I love the way you feel. And the way you smell."

It wasn't fair. Brooke still had so many questions, but that damn man had a way of making her forget absolutely everything. She returned his kisses, wanting more, as she always did when she was close to him. Before she knew it, she was in his lap, straddling him. He was cupping her ass, starting to grind her against him, driving her crazy.

Suddenly, a cough behind them. They sprang apart like guilty teenagers. Brooke looked up and recognized the teenage boy,

Katrina's son, dressed in running shorts and sneakers. Getting a bit of sun and relaxing a little had erased some of the awkwardness from him.

"Don't stop on account of me," he said, "but there are innocent children here." He gestured down the beach, where a family Brooke hadn't noticed before was busily constructing sandcastles and trying not to look in their direction.

"See you at the house," said the boy, turning around and starting to jog back down the beach. He stopped after a few steps and turned back around, catching Brooke and Antoine in mid-kiss.

"By the way, thanks for those chocolate chip cookies* you left on our pillows. They were the bomb. My sister swears there's some awesome secret ingredient, but we can't figure it out."

Brooke grinned.

"Maybe I'll tell you, if you promise to start putting your wet towels in the hamper instead of on the bed."

"Oh. Oops. Sorry. OK. Deal," said the boy, resuming his jog.

"Will you tell me the secret ingredient?" asked Antoine.

"Maybe when you finish telling me everything I need to know," said Brooke. "How many cameras did Sophie plant in the house?"

Antoine started to laugh, shaking his head.

"What could possibly be funny?" Brooke asked, annoyed.

"Oh, it's not funny, except apparently, she got quite an eyeful with the closet cam the other day. She was livid."

Brooke blushed, but Antoine was right. It *was* a little funny. And the fact that he found it amusing proved to her that he had no lingering feelings for Sophie.

"Why doesn't her father just shut her down?"

"He thinks she's a loser and incapable, and that he can just distract her with shopping trips to Miami and more new clothes, but she's much smarter than he gives her credit for. I told Carlos about her surveillance equipment, by the way. Turns out she wasn't tapping our phones, at least," he said.

"Small consolation. Wait a second," said Brooke, horrified. "Did Sophie... was Sophie also the one who created the villa rental agency?"

Antoine blanched and groaned.

"At the time I gave you that number, I genuinely thought that she was trying to make something of herself. I hadn't realized what she was up to. I thought that it would help you, and that Carlos would be pleased that I was supporting her business. You've got to believe me. That's why I was so panicked when I realized..."

Brooke looked him in the eye. Those gorgeous turquoise eyes. She could tell he was sincere and sensed that he had indeed done everything he could.

Antoine looked back at her, distraught, guilt etched into his features.

"Listen, I know that we're going to have to start over. On a more solid foundation, something built on absolute transparency... but will you give me a chance?" he asked.

"Of course," said Brooke. "But only because you're the only meat and fish purveyor on the island. I'm a little desperate."

She smiled, but then her smile faded. Yes, it was good to know that the universe was not conspiring against her, but the reality remained that she was still running out of money and needed to figure something out. Desperately. Even if Villa Azul had been a fake company, it had yielded two rentals that had kept her afloat.

"What? What's wrong?" asked Antoine, brushing her hair back from her forehead and looking into her eyes.

"I still need to make money, and I don't have any more renters lined up."

"Forget the tourists for now- why don't you rent your downstairs bedroom to somebody local?"

Brooke looked at him.

"How much would someone possibly pay?"

"Brooke, you don't understand rentals in Saint Barth. Prices are astronomically high. Your downstairs apartment isn't huge, but it's cute, and it has outdoor space. Somebody would think they're extremely lucky to have it, and it would be money you could make with your eyes closed. There are visiting doctors, traveling nurses, restaurant managers, teachers...your space and location are high-end."

"How much are we talking?" asked Brooke.

"Maybe 3500 a month?"

Brooke did a quick calculation. Well, there was no property tax. But she still had to pay for utilities, and food. Saint Barth was expensive. That wasn't enough to cover everything. But it was something.

"You know," said Antoine, "I think Barbara said she was looking for a place."

"Barbara, the hairdresser in town?" asked Brooke.

"The very same. I don't know her well, but people seem to like her, and I heard it through the grapevine."

"She's a superfan of yours," said Brooke.

"Oh, is she?" Antoine winked, but Brooke grew serious.

"OK. But then what? I don't want to just be a boarding house..."

"What about renting out plots of land you can't see from the house for farmers?"

Brooke looked at Antoine.

"That's genius. There's a lot of land. I could charge vastly below market in exchange for produce...not to cut you out of course..."

Antoine smiled.

"You're not cutting me out. I don't deliver produce. Just meat and fish."

Brooke stared at him.

"What the hell are you talking about? You've always...wait..."
Antoine shrugged.

"Yeah, I just got that stuff for you because I thought you were hot, and I wanted to make myself indispensable."

"You *are* indispensable."

"I hope so," said Antoine. "And now that you've started to build a little community here, what about the events we talked about? Why not do some wonderful farm to table meals? Even locals would pay to do that. People would come from islands all around. Influencers would attend and be thrilled to do so. They're sick of all the slick same old, same old."

"I know," said Brooke. "But I've been trying to build my Instagram following and I haven't really gotten very much traction."

"Well, you know who's got a huge Instagram following?" asked Antoine.

"Who? Sophie, probably," said Brooke, bitterly.

"Well, yes. But also, Meat my Fish."

"You're on Instagram?" Brooke asked. She hadn't even thought to look it up.

"Sophie forced me to be on Instagram, back when she thought we were an item, and she made it her project to post things. She wanted to prove to her dad that she could have a job as a social media manager. I think she didn't want to be seen with a simple fishmonger, so she was heavily invested in making me look as successful as possible. The funny thing is, I started growing more when she shifted her energies to ruining your life. I guess people like my stupid sense of humor."

"How many followers are we talking?" asked Brooke, narrowing her eyes. She grabbed her phone and logged onto Instagram, searching for Meat my Fish. "Holy crap. You have over 200k followers?" She scrolled through the images. "Come on, be real- they don't like your sense of humor so much as the shots of you doing hot fishmonger shit."

"You've got to know your market," Antoine shrugged.

"This is how you get your business?" Brooke asked.

"Hardly. That's just vanity metrics. I get most of my customers through word of mouth, like you will, and through my stupid van. But those influencers that follow me did help to create a buzz and get me local magazine articles."

Brooke's head was spinning.

"So, I could partner with you for events..."

"Yes, we could start with an event for influencers."

"That would kill Sophie, for us to use the account she so carefully created for you to help me. But she'll be pissed at you. What do you get out of it?"

"I mean, I'm not a saint," said Antoine. "I would want a share of any profits. But also, what you don't understand is, you've made me see the possibilities of my ingredients more than ever before. I was busy trying to source the best meat and fish, but I didn't have the imagination to see what could be done with them, and that was limiting me. You've taught me so much about how I can package and promote my stuff, and how much I can charge."

"When I think you charged me 250 euros for all the stuff you brought me that first week..."

"That was my lust talking," Antoine admitted. "But also, I didn't even understand how much I was undercharging at the time."

"If we're meant to be working together, I want to help you, too," said Brooke. "I've been doing nothing but event planning for the past decade, and I'm good at it. I can see it now. Meat my Fish in Miami.... Meat my Fish in New York... Meat my Fish in the City, in the Country...in the Field... farm to table events that include and promote all the different artisans in an area. It could even be a cookbook. With hot pictures of you in it, I'm sorry to say, because that certainly seems to help."

Brooke's imagination was racing ahead with the possibilities. She had also spearheaded the creation of a charity cookbook for the Junior League. She knew how to do this!

"See? You have a vision that I do not. But I'm good at math despite undercharging... How much do you think that people would pay for tickets to an event like what you're describing?"

"An event like the one I'm visualizing for us, Outstanding in the Field, charges over $350 per person," said Brooke. "I would charge that for tourists. Influencers with over 100k followers get a 50-dollar discount. Locals go for $100."

"100 for locals? That's high," said Antoine.

"We'll get large local businesses to sponsor so we can reduce the actual price," said Brooke.

"I have access to folding tables to accommodate 40 people," said Antoine. "That means..." he did a quick calculation in his head. "We would make 14 k for a tourist event, 12 k for an influencer one, or maybe 10 k because some will whine about not wanting to pay, and 4k for a local event. If we mix and match guests, which is best, we will probably get about 10k."

"Food and alcohol costs would probably be 1500. Décor and other supplies and maybe a helper or two, another 500," Brooke interjected.

"That's 8k."

"Way more than I make for two weeks' rent, at the end of the day," said Brooke.

"So, if we do two a month..."

"Two? Let's say 4 in high season, I'll get bored otherwise...."

"All right. That's 36k plus your 3k rental, plus the farmland, which could be another 3 k...at least. That's a massive amount."

"You get some of that," Brooke pointed out.

"Obviously. But you get more. I'm the muscle. You're the brains."

"Sorry, no, half and half. You're a genius."

"It was mostly your idea," Antoine shrugged.

"So...partners?" asked Brooke.

"Partners," said Antoine.

"The first event is going to be crucial. It must be perfect. They say desperation is good for creativity, and I am the very definition of desperate. But we need to make sure no one sabotages us."

"Consider that my job," said Antoine. "Shall we discuss it over dinner?"

Brooke was about to accept, but then she remembered.

"Crap. I promised my neighbor she could take me out. She's picking me up at 8. She wants to go try to pick up Russians at the Rosewood."

"I think I should meet you there, you know, to chaperone you," said Antoine.

"Wait- what? It's a girls' thing, Antoine..."

Antoine winked at her.

"I look fetching in a dress..."

"I don't think so," Brooke laughed.

Antoine checked his watch.

"I have three hours to wax my legs."

Brooke burst out laughing.

"Please don't!"

"Try me," said Antoine. He leaned in and gave her a delicious kiss. "I have a few more deliveries. Maybe I'll see you later?"

"I'll text you when Judy's sick of Russians."

Antoine gave her a devastating smile and one last kiss, and Brooke watched him leave, missing him already.

Chapter 37

B rooke and Judy sat on the blue slipper chairs in the dimly lit Bar Mélange at the Rosewood Guanahani. When Brooke and Hunter had vacationed on the island, they tended not to think of coming here, favoring spots along St Jean or in town. But it was a fun change, and the people watching was superb. In general, the crowd was more sophisticated and less showy than in some spots in Gustavia. They had ordered some mezze, which had already been brought to their low café tables, and Brooke was savoring a Fizz Me I'm Famous, a drink with truffle gin and citrus flavors. Judy was playing it safe with Champagne, but she had certainly not played it safe with her outfit. Her pink backless dress dipped dangerously low, barely containing her assets. Brooke had never seen her wear such risqué ensembles.

"You certainly are a hottie tonight," said Brooke.

"Look who's talking," Judy responded.

Brooke looked down at her outfit, a red slip dress worn with beaded sandals. It was positively demure by comparison. She'd considered wearing a jumpsuit, but had decided that, if Antoine did follow through on his threat, she might want something more easy access. She blushed at the way she was thinking. But anyway, Antoine wasn't there. In fact, there were few single men there, save a trio in the corner, who she had caught looking over at them.

"Sorry I didn't choose the right spot," said Judy. "I was hoping to help you to find a boyfriend, but other than those three, who are not exactly our type, this place has slim pickings."

"Don't worry about me," said Brooke. "But it's a good thing you're happily married and were just kidding about picking up Russians, or I would have felt disappointed for you, too."

"Ha," said Judy, downing the rest of the contents of her wine glass.

"Ha, what?" asked Brooke, finally noticing that not only was Judy dressed in a much more revealing fashion than usual, but her ring finger was bare. "Oh crap. Are you...?"

"I'll have another," Judy barked at a cocktail waiter. "Yeah. Trouble in paradise. Honestly, I thought you and Hunter had way more chemistry than my husband and I did...so when I heard that you broke up..."

"Wait- when did you hear that we'd broken up? How?"

"Our housekeeper told us. She's friends with Nathalie."

Ugh. Nathalie. Brooke hadn't worried about her in a day or two, and now the bad feeling was back. But at some point, she just needed to face facts. Nathalie was not interested in being her friend. And now, she had proof that Nathalie had gossiped about her. No use worrying about that now. She had spent all this time feeling sorry for herself, and now, Judy needed a shoulder to cry on.

"I'm sorry. It doesn't even matter how you heard. So, what's going on?" asked Brooke.

"Thank you for giving me the strength to be truthful, through your honesty. Rick and I...It's over. Honestly, it's been over for a while. There's no drama. That would almost be better if there was. It's like, there was nothing holding us together, and, well...I figured, why not try to go it alone?"

"Are you going to be OK?" asked Brooke. "Financially, I mean?"

"I'll be totally fine. Rick's being fair. We're going to sell the house. That's why I'm here- I'm getting all our personal affairs packed up. The other crap will stay- I'll sell it furnished. Hey, if you know anyone who wants a house on St Barth, I'll give you a commission. Double bonus: you get to pick who your new neighbors are."

"I actually might have someone in mind," said Brooke. "Someone looking for a rather luxurious guest house. Hey look. I think there may be a Russian over there."

"Really?" asked Judy. She turned to see where Brooke was looking. Sure enough, a tall, dark-haired man with Slavic features, dressed head-to-toe in Ralph Lauren, a Rolex Yachtmaster glinting at his wrist, stood by the bar, ordering a drink.

"What are you waiting for?" said Brooke. "Go work your magic."

"Will you be OK sitting alone for a minute? I need to test my flirting skills," said Judy.

"I'll be just fine," said Brooke, waving Judy away with a wink. Brooke had other quarry to pursue. She had just noticed another man entering the bar. A very good looking one. She locked eyes with him as he approached.

"Is this seat taken?" the man asked in a thick Russian accent, gesturing to where Judy had been seated moments before.

"No- be my guest," said Brooke.

"I'm Andrei," said the man, extending his hand to shake Brooke's.

"Brooke."

"Do you come here often?" Andrei asked.

"Barely ever," said Brooke.

"Me neither," said the man. He looked at Brooke's glass. "Let me get you a drink."

"No need. I don't accept drinks from strangers. Even handsome ones."

"I insist. Besides, I introduced myself. So, we are no longer strangers."

The man gestured to the waiter. "The lady will have another...what is that?"

"Fizz Me I'm Famous," said Brooke.

"Are you?" asked Andrei, as the waiter walked away.

"In some circles," said Brooke, deciding to have fun with it.

They continued to make small talk until the drinks arrived.

At that point, the man moved over to the seat next to hers, and she had the chance to admire him from close up. He smelled good. Fresh, with a little musk. His white linen shirt brought out his tanned skin, and his blue trousers highlighted muscular thighs.

"So...Are you single?" he asked.

"It's complicated."

"I don't mind a little complication," he said. "I suppose it really depends on whether both parties have the best intentions."

"In this case, I believe they do," Brooke said.

"And... you would say you're serious about this...man?"

"Yes, it's a man," Brooke smiled. "And yes, I believe I am."

"I guess it's fair to assume, then, that you aren't looking for anyone else tonight."

"Yes. That's fair," said Brooke.

"But be honest," said Andrei, looking her square in the eye, so she couldn't look away. "You want me as much as I want you."

Brooke considered him for a moment.

Yes. Yes, she did want him.

"Shall we go?"

Andrei stood and extended his hand to Brooke. She could feel excitement coursing through her veins. She took his hand and stood.

"I'd better tell my friend that she doesn't need to drive me home. I mean, I'm assuming you'll drive me home?"

"Of course."

They headed over to the bar. Judy was so busy breathily bantering with her new Russian friend that she didn't even see them come up.

"Judy...Um...I'm going to go home, if that's OK," said Brooke.

Judy finally turned her attention to Brooke, her head swiveling from her to Andrei, and back.

"With him? Are you sure that's safe?"

"Perfectly safe," said Andrei.

Judy narrowed her eyes at him.

"I asked my friend. Not you. What's your name, anyway?"

"Andrei," he said, shaking her hand. He also extended his hand to the man Judy had been conversing with. "And you are?"

"Ivan," said the man. "Where are you from, Andrei?"

"Saint Petersburg."

Ivan scowled.

"I don't think so. My mother is from Saint Petersburg, and you don't sound like..."

Brooke grabbed Andrei by the arm.

"Come on, Andrei, let's leave these two to their conversation."

They hightailed it out of the bar and soon made their way outside. Andrei steered them down a dark path.

"I think we're going the wrong way. Valet parking is over there," said Brooke, her heart beating faster.

"I self-parked," said Andrei.

He stopped walking then and pulled Brooke closer to him. She gasped. Before she could react, he was kissing her neck, pressing against her.

"How was that?" he growled into her ear.

"Your Russian accent is laughable. I can't believe you decided to try to keep up the act with that guy Judy was talking to!"

Brooke doubled over, the laughter overcoming her.

"You knew I had a stupid sense of humor from the first moment you met me," said Antoine.

"True," said Brooke, composing herself at last. "I have only myself to blame."

Antoine pulled her towards him and kissed her again, deeply.

"Now can I take you home? To my home? It's closer, and there are no New York teenagers there."

"Yes," said Brooke. "Drive as fast as you can."

"The scooter is right over here."

"Hmmm. I didn't know that suave Russian guys drove scooters."

Chapter 38

Antoine held the door open for Brooke, and she took in the space. The exterior was limestone, the building a boxy two-story structure, built in the 1800's by Swedish settlers, as Antoine had explained. The ground floor was a big open-concept space with high ceilings and a decidedly minimal décor. Very elevated bachelor chic. There was a serviceable, slightly industrial kitchen in the corner, and what looked like large barn doors across from where they stood.

"You could do events in here- it's really cool!" Said Brooke.

"You should see it in the daytime, with the doors open- I'm right on Shellona Beach. I thought of events, but I hadn't met an event planner I liked enough- until now."

Brooke nodded sagely.

"And what's upstairs?"

"I'll give you a tour."

Antoine led Brooke by the hand, up a set of wooden stairs. When they arrived at the landing, she saw that the space was divided into a large bedroom, a small office, and a bathroom with a clawfoot tub and rain shower.

"Nice bathroom," said Brooke.

"What can I say? I like my baths and showers," said Antoine.

"But Saint Barth has water shortages- that's not very responsible," Brooke chided.

"From now on, I pledge to save water by never bathing alone."

"You have a deal," said Brooke, letting Antoine lead her into the bedroom. The space was romantic, as far as bachelor pads went, with a large bed draped in mosquito netting, two antique nightstands, and a linen bench at the foot of the bed. Antoine took Brooke over to the large set of French door windows, through which she could see the lights of Gustavia twinkling, as well as the yachts in the harbor.

"This place is amazing," Brooke marveled. "How come no one mentioned that your house is party central?"

"I don't like to advertise it. I would have every expat on the island beating down my door. Better to have them laugh at my van and think I'm a nice, dorky guy."

"Dorky. Right," said Brooke. "Enough about your crash pad, I think you mentioned that I owed you something for your selfless performance the other day?"

Antoine traced along her cheek with his finger, allowing it to run down her neck, across her collarbone, and then over to the strap of her slip dress.

"Why yes, now that you mention it, I believe that I made you feel rather good," he said, tugging gently at the strap so it dropped over her shoulder, then reaching for the other one and doing the same. "And I believe you were saying that you wanted to reciprocate?"

He pulled her dress down, the slippery fabric sliding over her breasts, and then down, so the garment pooled around her waist. He reached down and cupped her breasts in his hands, ducking down to tease a nipple with his tongue. Running his hands down her sides, he shimmied the dress over Brooke's hips, until it was in a puddle around her feet, and she stood there, naked in front of him.

"No underwear, naughty woman?"

"Well, I was going to this girl's night, and I was expecting a third girl...she's kind of masculine, to be honest, but she said she would wax her legs just for me, and I thought she might be interested in seeing how I wax my bikini line. You know, girls talk about those things."

"You do?" asked Antoine.

"Not really," Brooke smiled.

"You hoped I would come?" Antoine asked, leading her to the bed, where he sat her down, so she had front row seats as he started unbuttoning his shirt.

"Yes. I was hoping. And I thought that if you didn't, I would beg you to come see me after."

"I couldn't wait for a text."

"Frankly, I was about to leave when I saw you."

Now, Antoine's shirt was off, and Brooke let herself take in his gorgeous build, backlit by the golden hued light of the streetlamps. She felt terribly exposed, sitting there in front of him in nothing but her jewelry.

"You're still awfully dressed," she remarked.

"Apologies, I'll correct that right away," Antoine said, unbuckling his leather belt and unbuttoning and unzipping his pants. The trousers fell and he stepped out of them, revealing himself in all his splendor.

"Ah. I see I'm not the only one who went commando tonight," Brooke remarked, beckoning him, and stroking the spot where his muscles formed a V pointing down towards something she had been fantasizing about for almost a month, now. She peppered Antoine's torso with butterfly kisses, teasing him as her mouth came closer to his member. His skin felt smooth, hot, under her lips. She couldn't believe that she was here with him at last, and that this time, it wasn't just a dream. Antoine gently pushed Brooke back onto the bed, lowering himself over her and kissing her again, tugging at her lips with his teeth, discovering her body with his hands. She, too, was stroking him, learning him by heart. She was hungry for more. She arched her back, yearning for him. Antoine moved down, kissing her breasts, circling each nipple with his tongue, before moving down her stomach and kissing down, down, until he spread her thighs with his hands. She gasped as his tongue made first contact, gently finding its way to her most sensitive parts, and then becoming bolder as he teased her and pleased her, his fingers coming in to help with the excellent job he was already doing, his beard tickling her in the most delicious way. She writhed in pleasure, her hands on his shoulders. But she wanted even more than this.

"Wait, I owe you, not the other way around," she panted.

She beckoned to him to come up to her level, kissed him deeply, tasting herself on his lips, and on his tongue, and pushed him over so he was on his back. She didn't waste much time with the teasing. She headed straight down and settled in between his legs, taking him into her mouth. Now, it was his turn to moan as she used her tongue to tease the head of his penis, then took in more of the shaft, using one hand to stroke the base.

"Slow down," Antoine groaned, his voice gruff. "You don't know how long I've been dreaming of this. I'm far too excited. You promised we'd take it slow, remember? Come up here."

He reached down and pulled Brooke up, so she straddled him as he kissed her. From this position, she could feel him against her, hard and hot, as if begging to come inside, and she wanted it. Wanted it so badly.

"Shhh...," said Antoine. "I don't want you to hold up your end of the deal too quickly."

He pushed her back onto the bed and propped himself up onto one elbow, trailing the other hand down her body.

"You're so beautiful," he whispered, as he kissed her again. His fingers found the magic spot between her legs, and he teased her again, expertly. She groaned and tried to angle herself so she could grind herself against his hand.

"Please," she begged. "I can't wait any longer."

"Neither can I," Antoine admitted, kissing her one last time before getting up on his knees, giving her an eyeful of his perfect form.

"A second more, though," he said, as he reached over to the nightstand, opening the drawer and retrieving a condom.

"Always prepared, huh?" Brooke asked, smiling as she remembered their conversation about Antoine being a boy scout. A *scoot*. She was glad someone was responsible, here. She would have been just as likely to give in to the heat of the moment.

"When I went to the pharmacy for the leg wax," said Antoine, as he fumbled with the wrapper, "I thought that these would be a better purchase."

He unrolled the condom onto his shaft.

"I agree. Now you're all wrapped up, like a present."

Antoine didn't answer. He lowered himself back down, between Brooke's thighs. Never mind what was coming, it felt so good just to feel his skin against hers. After another kiss that left her breathless, he moved onto her nipples again, sucking on one as he teased the other with his hand. Delicious as it felt, it was not needed. She'd never been so wet in her whole life. She felt throbbing and tingling between her legs, a deep want that could only be satisfied in one way.

"I need you inside me," she whispered.

Before she knew it, Antoine had plunged inside of her, making her gasp in pleasure. She wrapped her legs around him, her hands grabbing his muscular ass as he thrust slowly, deliciously, in and out. It was too much. She had dreamed of this, and the dreams paled by comparison. There was good sex, and then there was this. Finding someone who surprisingly fit so perfectly against her, and inside of her. Someone whose every touch felt amazing. It was next level.

"You feel so good," she whispered into Antoine's ear.

"Stop it...I'm busy thinking about taxes," said Antoine. "You're too sexy, and I want to make you come."

Brooke wasn't even worried about that. Every stroke threatened to take her over the edge. As much as she wanted it to last as long as possible, she also knew that they would have other opportunities to take their time, to get to know each other.

"Do you want to change position? To something less...exciting?" Brooke asked.

"Yes. Get on your knees," Antoine ordered.

Brooke obeyed, feeling exposed, kneeling there with her ass up in the air, balancing on her elbows to give Antoine deeper access, her nipples brushing the bedsheets. When he entered her from behind, she gasped, waves of pleasure running over her. He called this less exciting? Now, it was her turn to ask for it slow, so she could feel every ridge of his shaft as it filled her. She looked forward to when she could have him skin-on-skin, but for now, this was perfect. Antoine's hands held her hips as he ground into her, thrusting himself deep inside of her, eliciting a moan, now, from each stroke, as the pressure and the pleasure built up. She could feel her insides now, squeezing his cock, which now felt even bigger, as if it was even more engorged than before.

"I'm so close," she whispered.

"I can feel it," Antoine groaned, taking his hands from her hips, and cupping her breasts. That did it. The waves of pleasure hit Brooke and she cried out, feeling him coming too, fucking her harder as he allowed his orgasm to finally erupt.

When it was all over, they lay together, Brooke's body tingling all over as Antoine gently traced the outlines of her face with his fingers, looking deep into her eyes.

"Was that good for you?" he asked, kissing her gently.

"What do you think?" she smiled, kissing him back. She felt warm, safe, happy, for the first time in months. Before she knew it, she was drifting off to sleep.

Chapter 39

They had just pulled up to Sea Grapes. Brooke gave Antoine one last full-body squeeze, made possible by her position on the back of the scooter.

"I need to tell you," Brooke said, "about the dream I had about you, and me, and this very scooter, back when we were still just friends."

"If I'm not mistaken, I'd rather you act it out for me," said Antoine.

"I'm actually not sure it's physically possible," Brooke laughed. "But we could try."

She dismounted from the back of the scooter and came around to give Antoine a kiss.

"I'd better go," she said regretfully. "I don't want their last breakfast to be late."

"I'll see you as soon as they're gone. And we'll celebrate the beginning of the next chapter."

"Nowhere too expensive- I'm going to be on a strict budget for now," Brooke reminded him.

"Not that strict a budget," said Antoine.

"What do you mean?"

"You mentioned your neighbor was offering you a finder's fee if you found a buyer for her house. I happened to know that Carlos would be ever so interested in that house. Not as much as yours, but..."

"That is making a lot of assumptions, but you're right, that would be amazing," Brooke said, allowing herself to dream for a moment.

How much would such a finder's fee be? Would it be enough to get her watch back, provided it hadn't been sold yet?"

"I permitted myself to make a call to Carlos while you were in the shower this morning," said Antoine. "It's a done deal."

"It is?" Brooke was reeling, this time with happiness and relief.

"And he's paying you an additional finders' fee, for your patience and understanding."

"That's very generous, but..." Brooke couldn't possibly accept that.

"It's 50K."

Brooke gulped. Or maybe she could.

"But I'm sorry, you're only getting 41K of it," said Antoine.

"OK. I'm guessing you're taking a cut," said Brooke. "That's more than fair, after all..."

Antoine smiled.

"It's not a cut. It's reimbursement."

Brooke was confused.

"Wait- for what? Surely that food discount you gave me didn't add up to that?"

"No, silly. Close your eyes," said Antoine.

Brooke did as she was told. She felt Antoine take her left hand and slip something over it. The thing encircled her wrist, and she heard a click. *What*? Her eyes flew open. Tears sprang to her eyes as she saw her old Cartier Tank Française, back in its rightful spot.

"What? My watch? How did you..."

"I bought it back for you- eons ago, back when we were just friends. I knew how you felt about it, and I couldn't bear to see you lose it. Don't worry, I only gave the guy what he paid you for it. The pawn shop is another one of Carlos's businesses. Which is how Sophie was able to shut it down in your darkest hour. I guess she didn't count on you being as tough as you are."

"You're incredible," said Brooke. "How can I ever thank you?"

"I have a few ideas, to be implemented starting this evening" said Antoine, smiling. He gave her one more kiss, full of promise, and Brooke ran up to the house, a smile playing on her lips.

Acknowledgements

First and foremost, I wish to thank my sweet and patient husband, who agreed to travel with me to revisit St Barth "for research" and put up with me as chose to publish Stick and Ball while we were supposedly on vacation. His only demand: that I not laugh too hard when he claims to be the cover model for my books. Much love and appreciation to my children, who cautiously refuse to read my books, but haven't disowned me completely yet. Thank you to advance readers and supporters in Santa Barbara and further afield, with a special nod to the ever-fabulous, ever-encouraging Linda. Thanks for nothing to my furry so-called writing buddy, Fiona, who thinks that it's easy to write a book while balancing an extremely demanding small dog on one's lap. Thank you to all the fabulous people in the TikTok community who have supported and encouraged me. And thank you to those who submitted recipes for this book! When Auntie Kiki was coming up with the world of this delicious story, she decided she needed some recipe inspiration; and where better to get it than through her fabulous readers? The recipes that follow are for the dishes marked with an asterisk* in the book.

Sandra Stingle's Eggplant Trick

According to Sandra, "eggplants are sexy. Just look at their rich colors. Did you know there are male and female eggplants? How do you tell them apart? I'll let you find out." But she is correct when she warns that, in order to use eggplant in a recipe, one traditionally fries it in oil, which is messy, time consuming, and makes it highly caloric.

But there's a hack for that:

"-Wash the eggplant and coat it with a little bit of oil. Use a fork to pierce it many times so it doesn't explode! Put it on the dish you wish to serve it in. Microwave for four minutes. You will see the eggplant has exuded oil and reduced in size. Test to see if it's done to your liking depending on how you want to use it.

-If you wish to make slices and use it for eggplant Parmesan or dice it into a salad probably you want to take it out when the eggplant is about 1/3 smaller. But if you want to make baba ghanouj or you like your eggplant soft and mushy, or oilier, add two minutes at a time, and keep going until it's done the way you want. For baba ghanouj, keep it in until it gets really flat!

-The eggplant paradoxical. Fried, it absorbs so much oil. However, when you microwave it, it exudes so much oil and tastes almost the same! You can season and salt the eggplant, you can slice it, top it with cheese and tomatoes, add herbs, and put it back in the microwave for a quick eggplant Parmesan. Or cook it until it's flat and soft, mash it, add seasoning, serve it as a dip, baba ghanouj.

-This is a recipe for people who have an interesting life, love to eat and entertain, and don't want to spend too much time in the kitchen. As a chef, the product is what counts not the amount of time put in. The less time spent cooking and cleaning up, the more time you can spend with interesting people and things!"

Natasha Lajeira's Weeknight Coq au Vin

"Coq Au Vin is a French recipe that translates to 'rooster cooked in wine'. The original purpose of the recipe was to soften tough chicken meat. The birds used for it were typically old hens and the older the bird, the more tough the meat/muscle is, especially the thighs, which is what is used in the recipe.

I've created an easier recipe for weeknight cooking.

Weeknight Coq Au Vin served over Mini Roasted Potatoes

Important Kitchenware:

Dutch oven or deep pan with a lid. I'll be referring to it as just a "pan"

Sheet pan or Casserole pan

Ingredients:

Salt, Pepper, Extra Virgin Olive Oil, Butter, Flour

Sweet Red Wine, Chicken broth/stock

Boneless Skinless Chicken Thighs

6 Strips of Bacon

2 tablespoons Tomato Paste

1 Red Onion

Pack of Mushrooms

2-4 Carrots

2-3 Bay Leaves

5-6 Fresh sprigs of Thyme and any other fresh herbs that you like, like rosemary

Fresh Garlic

Chopped parsley for garnish

Small potatoes or fingerling potatoes (any kind)

Dried herbs of choice for roasted mini potatoes. I like garlic powder, salt, pepper, rosemary, and thyme.

Prep:

Chop Carrots, and Mushroom into big chunks, set aside.

Chop Onion into big chunks, set aside from carrots and shrooms.

Cut Bacon up into big chunks.

Finely chop a bulb of garlic

Chop handful of parsley (garnish)

Heavily salt & Pepper the chicken and coat them in flour, set aside

Half chopped mini potatoes

Instructions:

Pre-heat oven to 365 (for mini potatoes, which will come in later)

Oil &/or butter in pan, saute bacon. Once cooked, scoop bacon out, set aside, and leave bacon grease in pan.

Saute onion til translucent, add garlic in the mix, saute for an additional 3 minutes or so. Don't burn the garlic. Set aside with everything else.

Add more butter & garlic to pan and brown the chicken thighs.

Once all chicken thighs are browned and in the pan, add equal amounts of wine and chicken stock until all the chicken is covered.

Mix in the 2 tablespoons of tomato paste.

Mix in onion, garlic, carrots, mushrooms, half of the cooked bacon, 2-3 bay leaves, and sprigs of fresh herbs.

Bring to a boil and then simmer covered up for a good 35+ minutes. It will be done when the carrots soften.

While it's being cooked, get started on the mini potatoes.

Put them on a sheet pan or casserole dish, drizzle/coat with olive oil, sprinkle dried herbs of choice. Pop them in the oven until cooked, which should be around 20-30 minutes.

Once the coq au vin is done, get the sprigs and bay leaves out of the pot, start plating the mini roasted potatoes and serve with coq au vin over it using a ladle to get plenty of sauce and veggies on the plate. Garnish with parsley and leftover bacon.

Voila!

It should look very rustic and the taste should be herbaceous and full bodied."

BigPinkHair's Lemon ice cream:

"Unbelievably easy. I send this when I send my lemons to far-flung friends. The joy of this recipe is that it is not precise.

I zested about seven lemons (mine were quite small Meyer lemons). Throw about 2 tablespoons of the zest into a food processor with two cups of Blend it with 2 cups of sugar. Add four cups of half & half (or milk).

Blend until the sugar is dissolved (when you stick a spoon to the bottom of the mixture it doesn't sound sandy).

Add a cup (and a quarter - if you like it tart) of lemon juice. Blend. Pour it in a loaf pan or individual cups or whatever and freeze.

You don't need an ice cream maker! The magic of chemistry!"

Joanna's Blintz Soufflé

Joanna writes:

"This is one of my mom, Brenda's, signature recipes. She often made it for holidays and special occasions. It's easy and relatively budget friendly but looks fancy and elegant.

Once, she chose a pan that wasn't deep enough. The ingredients overflowed, causing a small fire. Mom wasn't too upset since she's always loved a man in uniform. :) Nobody was hurt. The soufflé, on the other hand, didn't make an appearance at our holiday that year. Mom made noodle kugel for our next holiday and now cautions friends making her famous blintz soufflé to use a pan that has enough room for the soufflé to rise (which it does gloriously).

This recipe is light, airy, and beautiful and just sweet enough to eat for brunch or dessert.

———◉———

Ingredients:
   2 pkgs blintzes (I use a combo of Cherry and Cheese)
   1/4 lb butter
   4 eggs well beaten
   1 1/2 c. sour cream
   1/4 c. sugar
   1/2 teaspoon salt
   1 teaspoon vanilla
   1 tablespoon orange juice (optional)
   Directions

   1. Preheat oven to 350
   2. Melt butter in 2 quart casserole
   3. Place blintzes over butter in one layer
   4. Beat eggs well
   5. Blend other ingredients with well beaten eggs and pour

over blintzes

6. Bake 45 minutes at 350 degrees.

Serve with powdered sugar, ice cream or sour cream on the side.

I have used several different types of blintzes in the soufflé (i.e. cheese, cherry, blueberry) and it's delicious and beautiful that way. Works fine no matter what kind of blintzes you use."

Porche Gardener's Miso Glaze

"This recipe is very adaptable.

-Miso/soy bean paste, the darker the better

-Chinese 5 spice blend

-Edible oil

-Red onion

-If using with meat, then some type of acid. I have used vinegar, shaoxing wine, orange juice + zest would be good as well.

For 2lbs of mea,t I use 2 heaping wooden spoons of miso paste. To that I add several tablespoons of the spice blend (more is better).

For the acid it varies based on type, it can be skipped if you're not cooking meat.

Vinegar = 3 tablespoons, should not be able to taste in finished dish.

Shaoxing wine = 1/3 cup, other wines could be used but I don't think red wine would be pleasant.

Orange juice = a couple cups

Enough oil is added to form a paste. If using juice then an adjustment of sequence will be needed.

To make the marinade mix the miso, spices, acid, and oil into a paste. Coat the meat and leave for at least 2 hours.

When you cook it 1-2 cups of water will be added to the pan unless juice is the acid, then use that instead. Simmer until thickened. 5 minutes before serving mix in sliced red onions.

If 5 spice blend is not available, then the whole spices can be simmered until fragrant in the oil to flavour it instead."

Fabienne Payet's Watermelon and Feta Salad

"Dear Auntie Kiki,

I am truly delighted at the idea of sharing a recipe for your next book.

I had mulled it over and a a lovely Watermelon and Feta salad came to mind. Not too frou frou nor too expensive.

You'll need:

500 grams cubed watermelon

150 grams crumbled feta

1 small red onion

120 grams of diced cucumber

15 grams of coarsely chopped mint

2 tablespoons of red wine vinegar

1/2 teaspoon salt

A dash of flaky sea salt

60 ml extra- virgin olive oil

Make a vinaigrette by whisking together the olive oil, vinegar and salt

Combine the other ingredients, drizzle with the vinaigrette and finish off with the mint and flaky sea salt.

Alternatively: replace the red wine vinegar with raspberry vinegar. Of just drizzle balsamic vinegar instead. I could also recommend a Marc de Champagne vinegar (on its' own)

Finish off by adding some black crushed pepper and a teaspoon of honey.

If so inclined one can add a large handful off arugula to the mix. Fresh blueberries and raspberries also make a nice mix.

So you see, you can fully create something unique within the bounds of the original recipe.

It can remain fairly easy and low cost or for just a little bit more you can fancy it up quite a bit!"

Kerri McComb's Chicken Orzo Soup and Super Secret Ingredient Chocolate Chip Cookies

1. Chicken Orzo Soup

"Less than 10 ingredients, and delicious!" Kerri writes.
-Olive oil, salt, & pepper
-1 Onion
-Garlic (measure with your heart)
-60 ish oz of Chicken stock (reserve one cup)
-Half a box of orzo
-3-4 oz of baby spinach (optional)
-One rotisserie chicken
-Half a lemon of juice
Chop up one onion and sauté in medium heat in a little bit if olive oil. Add salt and pepper to onion.

When the onion is translucent all garlic and cook for about 2ish minutes.

Add stock (except for reserved cup) bring to a simmer and then add half a box of orzo and cook to box instructions.

When orzo is done, add spinach and chicken.

Turn off heat and add reserved cup of stock and the juice of half a lemon.

———————●———————

1. Chocolate chip cookies

2 sticks of Unsalted butter (one softened one browned)
   1 C of AP flour
   1 C of Self-rising flour
   2 teaspoons of salt
   1 teaspoon of baking soda

3/4 cup of DARK brown sugar

3/4 cup of granulated sugar

2 eggs

Vanilla extract (measure with your heart)

5-6 oz of semi-sweet OR dark chocolate

5-6 oz of milk chocolate

The smallest dash of ground clove (SUPER SECRET INGREDIENT!)

Brown on of the stick is butter and let sit until room temperature. Mix with softened stick then add sugars.

Mix flour, salt, baking soda and ground clove in a separate bowl.

Slowly add flour tot he sugar/butter mixture about 1/4 cup at a time.

Then add eggs and vanilla.

Cut up chocolate (note: I prefer using Hershey bars and chopping them)

Mix chocolate in well.

Use a 1/4 scoop to divide out 2 cookies (1/4 cup = 2 cookies)

FREEZE COOKIE DOUGH FOR AT LEAST 2 HOURS OR OVERNIGHT!

(Due to the large amount of butter, baking the cookies immediately result in one large cookie pancake.)

Preheat oven to 350 and bake for 17-19 min.

Katarina Aubrecht Cheese Wontons with Guacamole

"Definitely a crowd pleaser," writes Katarina, who also had the superlative idea of adding butterfly pea/violet syrup to lemonade, of this recipe.

———————◉———————

"This recipe comes from a small wood fire restaurant that has long since gone out of business in Delaware, Ohio.

You take wonton wrappers and sliced hot pepper cheese. Cut the cheese into triangles. Make a paste of flour and water. Tuck the cheese triangle into the wonton wrapper and use the flour paste to seal the cheese in the wonton wrapper.

Fry in a flavor neutral oil, like avocado or canola. Use tongs or a spoon or something to flip the wontons to fry both sides.

Serve immediately with fresh guacamole made to your taste. I like lime juice so it won't brown and lots of cilantro a bit of jalapeño pepper, some tomato possibly a little mayo or sour cream for added creaminess.

If you can't do heat Gouda or Jack cheese can be substituted"

Lisa B Wolf's Baked Goat cheese

But first, Lisa inspired Brooke's iced coffee:

"I keep a pitcher of my Iced Coffee Concentrate in the fridge all summer long. Grabbing a travel mug on my way out the door is way quicker than going through a drive-through. I get my coffee exactly the way I want it every single time with no hassles, and it doesn't hurt the pocketbook, either.

They grow coffee on St Barths, but Brooke might also choose to acquire it from Haiti, Jamaica, the Dominican Republic, or Puerto Rico.

Iced Coffee Concentrate:

- Good quality coffee, roasted to your pleasure and ground as finely as possible (Turkish or Espresso grind).

- Put 1¼ cups coffee in a filter in a drip coffee-maker's brew basket.*

- Fill the coffee-maker's water receptacle to the 10-cup line.

- Brew coffee.

- Chill and store this highly concentrated brew in a lidded pitcher in the fridge.

To serve:

- Fill a large mug almost half full with iced coffee concentrate.

- Add 4 ice cubes.

- Add a good dollop of heavy cream.

- Fill to the top with water and stir.

- Adjust strength to taste by adding either more coffee concentrate, water, or cream.

- Sweeten to taste.

*Pour-over works well but takes too much attention and I'm easily bored.

I wouldn't be averse to using a percolator (I really don't find perked coffee egregious), but I don't have one.

I never found a French-press large enough that making ahead made sense.

I did try the Macedonian method once—mix the coffee and cold water together in a pot, put it on the hob on high, and just as it begins to foam, take it off the heat. From there, they pour it and drink it, grounds and all. I am not made of such stern stuff. Instead, I attempted to filter this sludge. Do-able, but so messy and time consuming as to not be worth the effort.

Not terribly chic, but I'll just stick with my Mr. Coffee. Form follows function, after all."

Now, for the baked goat cheese...

Baked Goat Cheese:

"Recreated from Stephane Bezzina's restaurant, Gigi's, in Youngsville, NC (with my own alterations). Sadly, Stephane closed shop and went home to France. Gigi's is no more, but I do keep in contact with Stephane via social media. By the way, Walnuts are grown in the Caribbean, and a very nice goat cheese is being made on Barbados.

Quantities of ingredients to your own taste:
- Slice **goat cheese** into rounds about 1/2" thick.
- Lay rounds in an oven-safe dish so that they touch.
- Sprinkle with fresh or dried **rosemary, thyme,** and **black pepper** (coarsely ground is best, but not essential).
- Scatter **walnut** or **pecan** halves.
- Drizzle with a good **olive oil.**
- Bake at 325°F until melty—about 10-15 minutes (or 300° for longer time—this stuff is forgiving).

Serve with:

Crostini, focaccia, or some kind of **warm crusty bread,** and **Niçoise, Sicilian,** or **Kalamata olives.** (The cheese likes the salt)."

Ila Z's Mango Tabbouleh

"Tropical, colourful, citric and surprisingly budget friendly. It brings together all the cultures that make the Caribbean a melting pot of traditions," writes Ila.

Quinoa/Mango Tabbouleh:

Ingredients:

For Salad:

2 cups of "riping-not-yet-ripe" mango, diced

1 cup of fresh coriander: chopped

1 cup of fresh italian parsley: chopped (or flat parsley as some call it)

1/2 of fresh mint: chopped

1 cup of cherry or grape tomatoes in many colours: diced

1/2 cup of spring onion: diced

1 cup of pomegranate seeds

1/2 cup of multicolour quinoa

optional: 1 cup of persian cucumbers: chopped

For Vinaigrette:

60 ml of lemon juice freshly squeezed

20 ml of olive oil

10 gr of fresh garlic: minced

Salt and pepper to taste

Method:

1. Make the quinoa. Rinse it in cold water. Bring one cup of water to a boil in a pot. Reduce to a simmer. Pour the quinoa in the pot with the simmering water. Cover the pot. Let the water dry. Be vigilant. When the vein of the quinoa grain is visible and the water dries, the quinoa is ready.

2. Move the freshly made quinoa to a plate. Put the plate in the freezer.

3. Toss the remaining salad ingredients together in a bowl. Combine well.

4. Combine the Vinaigrette ingredients. Shake/mix vigorously

5. Is the quinoa cold to the touch? If so, remove it from the freezer and combine with the salad ingredients.

Salad can be dressed all at once if serving for a group. If keeping for a few days, it's best to only add the vinaigrette when serving.

Taya Taya's cinnamon buns

"Here is a great cinnamon buns recipe. The cinnamon aroma would charm anyone.

Cinnamon is a spice that is not originally native to the Caribbean but is an essential part of Caribbean cuisine and is cultivated and highly popular in the region. This recipe is vegan-friendly but some ingredients could be substituted with regular ones like dairy milk and butter."

Ingredients for buns dough:

500 grams of coconut milk 150 grams of coconut oil

50 grams of fresh yeast (or 25 grams of dry yeast)

100 grams of sugar

1 kg of wheat flour (1000 grams)

10 grams of salt

Ingredients for buns filling:

200 grams of cane sugar

100 grams of grinded cinnamon

200 grams of coconut oil

Ingredients for buns glaze:

250 grams of cane sugar 150 grams of water

Preparing the dough: Combine coconut milk and coconut oil in a bowl. Add fresh yeast or dry one and stir it well with a whisk. Add flour, sugar and salt to the bowl. Knead the dough with your hands or with dough hooks using a mixer. Let the dough rest: return it to the bowl, cover the bowl with a damp, clean tea towel or food film and let it rest in a warm place for half an hour. The dough will be twice bigger. Take the dough out of the bowl, place it on a clean, lightly floured surface, and knead a bit for a few minutes to make it even more elastic. Cut the dough in half, cover one half with food film and leave it for now. Take the second part and roll it with a rolling pin into a rectangle with an approximate size of 40x30 cm.

Preparing the filling: Combine cane sugar, grinder cinnamon, and coconut oil in a bowl. Stir until completely smooth.

Shaping buns: Spread half of the filling on the rolled dough and fold the dough in two. Make cuts with a 1.5 cm width along the dough. Alternate two short cuts with one full-height cut till the end of the dough rectangle. Twist each piece of dough into a braid. Line a baking sheet with non-stick baking paper and carefully place the buns onto this, spaced well apart to allow room for them to rise. Cover buns with food film and let them rest for half an hour to increase their size. Preheat the oven to 160 degrees Celsius (320 Fahrenheit). Remove the food film and place the baking tray on the middle shelf of the oven. Bake the buns till golden.

Preparing the glaze: Using a saucepan bring water and cane sugar to a boil and turn off the hob.

Coating the buns: When the buns are fully baked, take them out of the oven and carefully coat hot buns with glaze and brush. Do the same actions with the second half of the dough.

Enjoy!

Don't miss out!

Visit the website below and you can sign up to receive emails whenever Kiki Astor publishes a new book. There's no charge and no obligation.

https://books2read.com/r/B-A-LWPBB-SCARC

BOOKS 2 READ

Connecting independent readers to independent writers.